ACCOLADES FOR
AT FIRST LIGHT

An exciting read you won't want to put down.
—Amber Hellmann

Surprising twists behind every page.
—Kristy Jonet

Man, what a ride. Never saw the end coming, but I wanted to keep flying with this book.
—Trevor Pedersen

Interspersed with original adventure and emotion, coupled with characters you care about, and clever dialogue, 'At First Light' makes for a fun read.
—Nancy Putman

How glorious a greeting
the sun gives the mountains!

–John Muir

A NOVEL

AT FIRST LIGHT

SPIKE PEDERSEN

AT FIRST LIGHT

Published by Spike Pedersen

ISBN 978-0-9856050-1-8

eBook ISBN 978-0-9856050-0-1

UPC

Book design by the eBook Artisans

Cover design by Damonza

Editing by: Editing for Authors, Jon VanZile

Visit my website at: spikepedersen.com

Email; spikepedersen57@gmail.com

Spike Pedersen resides in Madison, Wisconsin. He worked as a columnist with the *Green Bay Press-Gazette*, writing for the Sunday Home & Garden section. As a professional project manager, he travels across the Midwest, always in search of a story or character.

ACKNOWLEDGMENTS

To my writing group, Tuesdays with Story, especially Jerry Peterson, thank you for the education my schoolroom could not duplicate.

To Jeff Franz & Chris Lacey, thank you for the continual effort you put into shaping this book into a work of fiction to be proud of. Both of you were essential to the success of this book.

To Nancy Putman, the love of my life, thank you for encouraging me to sit in a dark hole and dig like a badger until I came out with a book.

To my first readers, Nan, Amber, Kristy, Misty and Trevor, thank you for your advice and direction in throwing dirt over the dreadful writing and pointing out where to dig to uncover the omitted holes.

To Chris, thank you for teaching me courage in the canyon.

To Jon VanZile, my editor, thank you for removing the marbles from my mouth. AT FIRST LIGHT is superior in every way with your wisdom gifted upon it.

Do not go where the path may lead,
go instead where there is no path
and leave a trail.

–*Ralph Waldo Emerson*

*This one is for
Landen, Cooper, Larkin, and Harper.*

CHAPTER ONE

Sunday, first light, Jesse Nickols awoke with the pink rays of daybreak in his eyes and the endless turmoil of sleep and dreamscape repeating in his head. Pulling on jeans, T-shirt, and boots, he was glad to be conscious again. The doorknob felt cool in his palm, the sensation brightening his mood.

Outside, his red Ducati motorcycle glowed orange in the new light. He raised his hip over the kick-starter and smoothly rode it down. It lit, and Jesse rode into the morning air.

It had been a hot night in his room. The cool wind flowing past him kept the events of last week from him. He was too old to be orphaned, yet that is how he felt.

Tall, as raw as his youth presented him, his intellect had defined him at the university in Madison. They tried hard to get him into grad school. He preferred the first light.

He eased off the throttle, letting the bike roll quietly. The awakening air was full-bodied and had an aroma reserved for the best summer mornings. Swallows darted after their meals, spinning skyward and then belly rolling toward their prey, snatching their feast out of the air before a man's eye could catch it. The last songs of the crickets wafted in, and the bullfrogs were still calling for mates as the morning haze mingled with brilliant orange hues, unfolding and blending with the rising sun.

The first rays broke over the horizon, rushing into his pupils, capturing his thoughts and reaching his troubles, locking them away for the entire day. First light was the best part of the day.

Jesse throttled up, racing into the long, sweeping turn leading up onto the shelf. Sculpted by ancient waves when the bay waters were much deeper, the shelf ran all seventy-five miles of the peninsula of Door County, swiftly rising from the city of Green Bay on the south shore.

He had traveled this road in his car many times. It led to his boyhood, his past. Unfiltered by windshields, the ride was never more vivid than when the dew held the aromas up to the wind, sweeping it from the fields to be captured by his senses.

Today, the aroma of fresh-cut hay seized Jesse. He had hated baling when he lived at home. He felt imprisoned, stuck on the hayrack while his friends chased sweet little vixens through the bay waters. He never realized it then, but it was the labor his father had imposed on him at that young age that forced him to develop his mind. To think deeply, closing out the mindless labor. He did know, however, that it was to blame for his hard-body ruggedness that made those same sweet little vixens turn their heads.

Up on the shelf, he could see the distant aqua-blue waters of the bay. Perfect little farmsteads dotted the corners of the green fields, each squared off by borders of stone fences and some still with the stump fences of cedar that refused to rot back to the soil. Catholic steeples stood above the oaks and the elms, shading the headstones of Belgian immigrants. The ones who shaped the land. The same ones who built a tavern adjacent to every steeple.

Places like Euren, Namur, Rosiere, and Frog Station… where they say in the spring that the roads were liquid with the leaping frogs lost from the marsh.

Each no more than a graveyard, church, and tavern. At night, the churches stood dark save for the reflection of a Pabst Blue Ribbon sign shining onto the road.

The shelf road would turn away from the bay soon. However, this road was not Jesse's road. The road that swept beneath him now would lead to his road. Jesse had a place he returned to, maybe always. That road lured him like a maiden calling him to Valhalla. He never thought it, never heard it, but it was inside him.

The first drop of adrenaline plunged into his bloodstream when the lower road, his road, dropped steeply away to the left. Braking hard, he dived into the turn. Listening intently for the sizzle of the tires against the grainy pavement, Jesse strained for the tone that would tell him the front tire had just begun to slip.

Instantly, he called on the big twin motor to load the rear tire with power. He twisted the throttle, his wrist seeming tied to the whole length of the frame, and the bike began to turn. The adrenaline had delivered its entire dose, and now there was no trace of fear.

Both engine and tire were under full load, dancing from the turn. Momentum forcing him upright, Jesse slashed through the gearbox. The top gear and the motor became one entity.

He flew at 136 mph, running downhill toward the fog, a wall that removed his first sense. What lay behind that wall was unknown, yet the need for more adrenaline kept Jesse speeding toward the fog. Jesse was coming at it hard, but the seconds just stopped. He kept the bike railing, engine wailing, throttle wide open. He willed the fog to come to him, to engulf him. His entire mind ached as if it would kill him before he reached that barrier.

Jesse burst through the edge and his eyes could help him no more. Musk and vapor, sharp and tacky, enhanced the juice that still fired his every muscle. He became alert to everything. His senses bursting, his mind accelerating to the velocity of the speed.

Only his instincts could reach him now, reason and thought had been left behind. The endorphins mixed with the adrenaline, the elixir of thrill-seekers and danger addicts. Beyond the highs of a distance runner lay a utopia deep in the intellect that all coveted—but only the ones daring enough to vanquish their fear would, could, ever know.

The suspension bucked against ruts carved in the road from years of trucks trying to scrub enough speed to make it. The turn was coming up in the soup ahead…just how far?

His time to brake was coming, but he had to wait, wait while the bike raced. Inside his mind, a trigger went off, and he grabbed handfuls of brake. Jesse threw the bike left till his knee dragged on the pavement.

The tires began to sizzle. But the tone he listened for was not for the tire to slip. The turn was wet and banked downhill; he knew the tires would hold at a hundred miles per hour. At least they always had.

The tone he waited for was of rubber and pavement and space. The pavement at the ragged edge, where rips and tears made the tires rumble. It would be death if he heard it. But Jesse had chosen well: the trigger in his brain closed, and he stood the bike upright.

The stuff in his bloodstream told him to go now, the oceans of the living world thundered inside his head. He resisted with all his will. He waited for it. The trigger fired, and the adrenaline screamed out from his subconscious. Jesse responded. He dropped the bike over all the way right. It felt like the pavement would come up and slap him, but the bike stopped its fall and rounded the turn.

It was sweet sizzle, no rumble…but he was ready for either. He welcomed either sound right here, right now.

The trigger closed a second time, and he lifted the bike upright and exited the fog, the road dropping even further toward the water. He was shaking hard—adrenaline, the morning caffeine of danger addicts, would take awhile to settle in.

A few twisty turns and the road dropped Jesse along the edge of the bay shore. Two hundred miles north of Chicago, the Cape Cod of the city…thick with summer homes, the places people could see in their minds when they weren't on the water.

As distinct as the fields upon the shelf, the shore was a mariner's culture. Before first light, the nets were deployed, and at the late dawn, the water was smooth as glass.

This was the moment when trawler captain and crew alike sat with their coffee and enjoyed the benefit of their employ. The gulls crossed the sun, the aroma was musty and full and somehow soothing, the clink of the diesel and the creak of the wooden trawler so satisfying. The gurgle of water, where the hull cut through the liquid, held, and then returned to the hollow void behind.

The chill was being replaced by the warm summer, that moment between when it is just right and you wonder why you would ever do anything else. Endless serenity and timeless pleasure along the shores of Door County.

Jesse came for the opposite reason. The roads were a biker's paradise. Nothing was straight, and they could be run hard just after first light. Before the shore people got out of bed, he could ride all the way to the top of the Door.

Eventually, the road turned to dirt and stone and ran out at water's edge, as far north as the bike could take him. Jesse stepped off his ride and stood at the road's end, basking in the reflection of the sun off the water.

A hundred paces down the beach stood an aging house with a hand-dug cove whose proportions and craftsmanship attracted attention from tourist and townie alike. It sheltered a trawler that had not been to sea since Jesse had found it.

"Jesse! Bring your cute ass up here."

Jesse hurried across the beach and up the steps, his boots clicking against the wood, gritty from the sand. He took her outstretched hands in his and bent at the waist to kiss her cheek. She smelled of rosewood perfume, sweet and tangy. She was clad in an oversized and crisp white shirt, with the shirttail worn free, just as her lover had worn it. Blue jeans were rolled up to her knees.

"Good morning, Emma."

Emma Johannsen motioned Jesse into a rocker next to her own with a leathery hand. Emma had almost all of her years behind her. Age had taken her beauty, but her eyes were wonderful—they told of the youth still in her.

"I knew you would be here today, that's why I am out on the porch. Saw the dew before sunset, did you?"

"Yeah, the fog was right where you said...God, Emma it was just beautiful out there this morning. I felt...I can't tell you how..."

"Jiminy Jesus boy!"

"What?"

"I hope to God you are still growing that brain. I will tell the story for you. First light is as a woman in your embrace, bare-breasted against your chest."

Jesse emitted a grin. "You want this story?"

"With all my heart."

Jesse moved to the railing. He could not sit still. He paced across the open porch; excitement leapt from his blue eyes as he swung his arms, leading Emma through the morning.

It seemed to put a joy in her, and that was all he wanted.

An old Coke machine sat on the porch. It was the type where the bottles hung from their necks in icy cold water. After he had finished, Emma put a dime in the machine and lifted the lid. She pulled out two Coronas.

"It's noon somewhere." She always said that.

Emma opened each with the bottle opener built into the front and swigged from both bottles.

"This one's yours, it tastes like it's stolen."

"I got a dime for you right here," he retorted, but she waved him off.

"Jesse, your uncle still blistering your ass?"

Jesse lost his smile. "Screw him, I don't need that job."

"Jesse, baby, your daddy—"

Jesse interrupted with a pointed finger. "My dad didn't kill himself. He fell. Everybody knows it was a year to the day Mom died in the accident. He was just not good that day, not careful...he should not have been working that day...that day..."

He faded, silent for a time, his gaze on the water. "He was strong though...always was so strong...stayed alive, hanging on for weeks. Don't know what he was waiting for...I think it was for his brother to come and see him..." Jesse turned back to Emma. "Dad loved that land. When his brother sold the farm...hell, he took it...and to save his own ass too. Got himself too deep in a damn venture. It was Dad's home. It was his!"

Jesse flopped back onto the porch swing. "They were born there for Christ's sake...he should never have gone to work that day."

"Jesse, you told me your daddy was no fool." She paused, then she said, "You need to tell me. You know, it would stop a lot of anger."

They sat quietly, the rocker and the porch swing playing their tune, Emma waiting for him, for when the time was right. Jesse held his bottle to the sun, the color streaming through, creating a golden shadow. "Tell me about Johan?" he asked.

"Don't you change the subject." Emma steeled herself as his aqua blue, puppy dog eyes met hers, but it was no contest. Jesse could melt her will, something not easily achieved or allowed.

Emma sighed. "Let's walk down the beach. Bring your bottle, it's a long tale, and I will fill it with lies."

Jesse kicked his boots off and leapt from the porch to hold out his hand as his princess descended the steps.

"Smartass."

Emma took his arm in hers, and they strolled along the edge of the surf. The waves washed over their feet. Soothing and liquid cool. The wind blew inland like it always seemed to, bringing the water's aroma to them.

"I wish it were salt air," Emma sighed. "I used to have the salt air coming through my window at night, before we got too damn old."

The summer air was warm, and they moved leisurely past the sand and shells. She began. "I fell in love with a Swede when I was sixteen. He was twenty-four. And handsome, more than you," she teased. "He had forty acres and two Belgians. They were matched roans. He even built a fancy buggy before he would call on me. What a sight he was when he would pull up to the porch. I was madly in love. He made me shiver all over when he kissed me, you know."

Emma gestured with her fist, like her father had. "My father said, 'You not going to be marryin' no Swede!' So he put me on a train to Chicago."

"You were sixteen, by yourself on a train...to Chicago?" Jesse asked.

Emma looked away and then down. She kicked at a bright stone. "Yes, and I was terrified, not of Chicago, but because I had disappointed my father."

"And your handsome Swede? Did he come for you?"

"A man's pride demands he respect the wishes of the elders,

even if they wouldn't even speak to him in the street." Emma chuckled. "I didn't know Chicago would make me forget him so soon.

"Within a week, I had found my way down to the docks. Fish houses lined the docks, full of fish by day and sailors all night. And it was a different ship every night. I took a job in one of them, and it wasn't long before I was running the place. The boss made money from the fish, and I made money selling whiskey at night, which made them want to sell their fish to us. Even if it was for a lower price…after all, whiskey and women are what bring a man home from the sea. We danced and fought and passed the pipe. Never slept…least not the first night a ship was in.

"After a while, I realized I felt left behind when the ships pulled out and it was back to the fish. So I signed on an ore ship. I'd had enough fish by then, and besides, the ore ships went all the way to the top of the lakes, and I had never been there."

"Wait a minute. They let a woman on a ship?" Jesse looked at her, cocking his head, which is where Emma was aiming her bottle. He caught her hand and wrestled the bottle from her grip. "Whoa! I guess that answered that."

"I could always hold my own."

Jesse kept the bottle in case the fire hadn't gone out yet.

In a second, Emma's smile was back. "Some time, a few crews, and a few boats later, I had some adventures to tell, but that, as they say, is a different story.

"It was an August day, just north of the Door, the deck was blazing from the sun, the whole crew full of tension that comes with the sticky heat. The mate, now he was a hell of a boss, he knew we needed something to do. He put to shore to cut some firewood for the cook stove, so the crew could burn some tension in the shade of the trees. I was third mate, and as it was, my watch was over. So I rode to shore with the crew. I was going to enjoy a bath.

"There was a small river on my charts 'bout a mile up, so I went to find it. When I got there, the river had reduced itself to a brook thanks to the summer heat. It was ankle deep, and you could easily walk on the gravel bottom. I heard splashing from the water falling over some large rocks into a pool. It was just a wonderful place. I remember the water was ice cold, and standing below the rocks, it was refreshingly decadent.

"I didn't hear him right away. I stood upright and listened, and a voice from overhead came down to me. It was a deep voice singing with a sweet lonesomeness."

Jesse stopped walking. "Emma. You didn't look, did you?"

"I moved up the rocks and peered over the edge, and there he was." Her eyes twinkled. "He was the man of my dreams, and I didn't even know I had one."

"You could tell all that with one look?"

"He was only in ankle deep water."

Jesse snorted and fell down on the sand. "Emma, you are so bad."

"You want this story?"

"With all my heart."

Emma sat next to him. She brushed her hair behind her ear and began.

"Johan had an extraordinary voice. In our years together, he only ever sang to me. Johan knew how to make me special. I watched for a good while…"

"A good while! You little voyeur!" Jesse teased, rolling out of her reach. But he wanted to hear more and came back to take his punishment.

"After a good while, I thought I would embarrass him, so I climbed up and stood on the rocks. But without missing a beat he changed the lyrics, and sang of a maiden who appeared from the sea to steal a man's heart with her beauty…I left with him that day."

"Did you tell the crew you weren't coming back?"

"I waved my shirt at them as we sailed past."

Jesse laughed. "What a tease. I bet the whole crew didn't sleep that night."

"Uh hum," Emma said with a smile.

"Johan moved diamonds from Antwerp to Chicago. He took a steamer across the Atlantic. Then he sailed a sloop from New York to Chicago. 'Could have taken the train, but what fun is that?' he would always say." Emma took pleasure in repeating his words out loud.

"My God, how did he get a gig like that?"

"Johan could make anything happen. He was born in Norway and grew up in the North Sea. Herring fishermen, his family were. I found him after he had already made his fortune. We saw the world, lived with the sea, but the Pacific coast of Mexico is where I was happiest."

"That explains your obsession with Corona. Come on, Emma, we both need one, let's head back."

Emma looked in his eyes. "Jesse, baby, talk to me. There is something you have not told me."

"I came today because you can make it go away Emma."

"Not forever."

"For today." Jesse stood up and brushed off his butt. "For today. Okay?"

Emma held out both her hands to him. He took them and pulled her up. When Emma was upright, she let Jesse's hands slip. He fell back on his butt.

"That is where you are in your life. On your ass. When you going to fix it?" Emma said.

"Tomorrow. How about tomorrow?"

She frowned and held out her hand; Jesse pulled himself to his feet. "You're a good friend, Emma."

He wrapped her arm in his own. Quietly, they strolled in the sand, enjoying the pleasures and sounds where the waters meet the shore.

Emma talked about her life until the sun was in the west and it was time to go. Jesse headed south, reliving the stories he had heard. He was jealous of Emma, wishing he were she— or maybe wishing he was Johan.

Emma was right. He had to fix his life, and that meant confronting his uncle.

Tomorrow.

CHAPTER TWO

Jesse slipped past the paper mills that lined the north edge of the city of Green Bay. Trucks and dense, soiled aromas held their ground against the aromas pushed ashore by the waves dead-ending on the rocks.

He would have to pass the lower road today. It was Monday, and he had commitments. Still, the air streamed by and the bike purred—a good start to the day.

He swung west and throttled up. A shadow engulfed him, blocking out the sun for a second. It moved past him and sped down the pavement, disappearing into the distance. "Big ol' jet airliner," he sang out, "goin' all the way to the coast." Jesse had never been past the Twin Cities—he did not have a reason why. But that single shadow put a dark spot on his mind, the same way anything that left him behind always did.

He downshifted into the driveway at the job site and, in

a full-throttled slide, spit gravel at the white Jag parked just outside the gate like a trophy on display.

Jesse put the kickstand down, stepped off the Ducati, and pocketed the key as he strutted to the guard shack and thumped on the rear window.

Jojo turned with a smirk, his face coming alive when he saw it was Jesse. "Hey hey, Jesse. Where's it at, man?"

"It's good. It's all good 'cept I'm here with your ugly."

Jojo let out a good-hearted laugh. "That's right. An' this ugly's gonna pound your

skinny white ass next time you fly by my gate without stoppin'." Jojo put his fists up and pranced like Ali. "Lay you out, man."

Jesse grabbed a hardhat through the open window. "It'd be the only lay you ever got."

Jojo leaned out the guard shack door and yelled to Jesse as he was walking away. "Hell, no. But it might be the prettiest. An I ain't runnin' no storage locker here. You keep hold of your own hardhat from here on…hear me!"

Jesse waved a good-bye, swinging his hand behind his head without turning around. He hurried to catch an I-beam that was just starting the ride to the top.

Terra firma rolled away, speeding outward as the beam carried him up. The horizon expanded and floors slipped away, each presenting its own scene. A sledgehammer banged home, the sharp clang soaring away, and the burly operator recocked before the scene cut short. The next floor glowed with the sparks sprayed from a cut saw.

Smoke stacks rose to the south, then steeples followed by sprawl, and finally the city gave way to the fresh fields readied for corn, beans, and oats.

"Jesse!" Elton Nickols boomed. "Get off that beam and bring your ass over here. Now!"

Jesse's uncle stood on the twelfth floor with all the foremen, who trailed him like dogs who had been beat too much.

Jesse saluted with his middle finger and stayed on the beam.

The beam climbed another four floors before it swung over the top. Jesse made eye contact with the crane operator, giving a small nod as he put on his cowhide gloves.

Forty feet of steel separated the ends of the beam. Jesse gripped the sling with one hand and leaned out, pushing out with his legs to swing the far end toward its final home. The steel wobbled. He strained backward, letting his fingers straighten out so just the last joint contacted the sling, his heels on the edge of the beam. The beam creaked, wobbled, and the far end finally began to turn.

Signaling the crane operator, Jesse pulled himself back on top of the beam and stepped away from the center of the beam. The far end teetered upward as the crane let out cable, lowering the entire beam. As the far end swung over the intended position, where it would form the next horizontal piece, Jesse leaped toward the center of the beam so the change in balance allowed the far end to come down. An ironworker sat straddling the previous beam. He took a bolt from a coffee can and slid the bolt home, then spun a nut onto the bolt.

Jesse called out, "Tom, throw me a set."

Tom reached in the can, pulled out a bolt, and spun a nut onto the threads. He arched it high in the air. Jesse stepped forward and to the left. He brought his right leg out for balance. Jesse cupped his hand behind his back, watching the bolt fly. The bolt landed in his hand behind his back.

"You crazy bastard," Tom called out, his laugh punctuated with forty years of smoke.

Jesse twisted his finger in a circle pointing down. The crane operator nodded and the beam moved down. Jesse took four giant, hurried steps toward the swinging end of the beam. It hovered just above the spot where two more beams sat on top of a support, spaced just far enough apart to accept the new one. The crane operator lowered the beam slowly.

At the last second, Jesse pushed on the beam. It caught along the edge instead of landing where it belonged. Jesse moved quickly back to the center and released the sling. He pointed upward and spun his finger. The crane swung away. Returning to the cocked end of the beam, Jesse stepped on the bottom edge of the I-beam along one side, then cupped his hands over the top edge on the far side and leaned back as far as he could.

He didn't pull on the beam but waited. Elton appeared on the stairway. Jesse shook the beam to get it to settle the last foot. It gave way and fell with a great metallic clang. Jesse absorbed the force with his legs and rode the ensuing wobble.

The building swayed, and Elton and the whole entourage on the stairwell grabbed onto each other to keep their balance. Jesse let out a quiet laugh. The bolt went in and secured the beam.

"Damn you, boy, I said come here." Elton, Jesse's uncle, stood panting at the top of the stairs.

Jesse climbed down the structure of beams, jumping the last couple of feet to the floor. He stood, cocked his chin, and smiled.

Elton scurried over to him. The foremen crowded around him. More men scrambled up the stairs to watch the spectacle.

Elton stuck a finger in Jesse's face. "I don't know how many times I cussed your ass about riding a beam on the jobsite. OSHA is ridin' my ass anyhow, without you giving them cause. And you dropped that beam on purpose, you little son of a bitch.

"George!" Elton snapped his fingers. "Write him up for not havin' his safety glasses on."

Jesse spit between his uncle's shoes.

"You little son of a bitch, I can fire your ass right here and now."

Jesse spit on his shoe this time.

Elton stomped on the metal plate. His entourage jumped.

"You miserable punk, what in Sam's hell you doin' here any-way? I told you to work the estimate for the P&G job. I want it not tomorrow...oh no, I want it today!"

"What happened, Uncle Elton, you get a paper cut? You shouldn't use new bills when you wipe your ass."

"Goddamn it!" Elton slammed his fist into Jesse's nose and drew blood. "Hold him!" Elton boomed. Men grabbed Jesse and struggled with him. "Hold him still." Elton put a boot into Jesse's gut.

Pain rolled over Jesse. The men held his arms but not his legs. Elton tried to deliver another kick, but Jesse blocked the blow with his boot.

Braced against his holders, Jesse's other leg spiked Elton's knee.

Elton went down in a heap. Holding onto his knee, wheez-ing and moaning, Elton hissed from the floor, "You do what I tell you. What I say...do what I tell you, you little bastard."

Jesse muscled clear of his handlers and staggered past them. He wiped
the blood from his face and snapped it to the floor.

"You spray rocks against my car," Elton gasped, "with that bike again and I will have your paycheck!"

"You can count on that, dickhead. I quit!"

Elton spit toward Jesse, then threw his hardhat at Jesse.

Jesse strutted toward the edge and leaped onto a load of lumber going down. Cheers erupted from the job site.

Jesse acknowledged his audience, waving as he descended. When he hit the ground, he tossed his hardhat into a dumpster.

Jojo stood next to the Ducati. "Lord, son, what you done now?"

"You'll hear about it in a few minutes. Me and him. It wasn't pretty."

"I can guess that. That's an awful lot of money to give up."

"I still own half the company. It and he can go to hell for all I care."

"What you goin' to do now?"

Jesse started the bike. "I'm following that shadow."

"Follow what?"

"West. I'm going west."

CHAPTER THREE

The Amazon

Evenel pleaded with those eyes and that goofy little grin, stretching her arms behind her back with her fingers locked together. It was the same look she used on her father to get her way.

Gathering aguaje fruit in the jungle had no appeal to her, but a whole day with her Daddy did. Evenel's seasons were few—so young she was of no help—yet she knew who was Daddy's favorite.

"How will you help?"

"I will dance of course, Daddy."

He was tall as the trees to her and the strongest thing in all the Amazon. The warrior smiled, placed his brown hand upon her head. He had been charmed.

"You can come along if you dance."

He sometimes sang to her when they were alone in the

canoe on the great brown river of her home. She sat in front, facing him with her little straw dolly beside her.

Copper-skinned and rail thin, with ebony hair that glistened in the sun, cut so that it flowed and fairly danced upon her shoulders, Evenel could run fast and climb with the best of them. And in the entire village, everyone knew her as the little joker who would lark about, always seen and certainly always heard, who could charm even the crankiest gecko or villager.

They took turns telling their stories while the canoe slid through the water, each stroke of the paddle pushing their craft forward, a tiny ebb left behind when the paddle rose from the water.

She made up her stories, trying to make him laugh. It was an easy thing when it was just the two of them. His stories were true, about the old ones and tales of great hunts and amusing stories of Evenel's mother when she was just a little girl, growing up with Daddy in the village.

The river turned ahead and behind them, and they were but two in a world of water, scented with earth and plant, green and sky.

The canoe came to shore, and it was time for the work. Daddy would find the aguaje palms, climb up, tear the fruit from its base, and bring the harvest to the river's edge where Evenel stripped off what fruits she could.

Most of the day she spent laying waste to the bugs she found, or sometimes she danced about when Daddy returned with a tangle of green.

Now he came into view a few yards away, pulling the long branches with his arms stretched out behind him. Evenel danced her own little dance, looking for his approval, when she heard the arrows stinging the air.

Her father crumbled to his knees and slumped to the ground. An arrow stuck through his outstretched forearm and into his back, pinning his arm behind him.

He got to his knees and onto his feet, shouting to her. "Eve-nel...Run, baby... run!"

She turned to the river to run, straight into the legs of a man, the collision knocking her backward to the ground. She rolled to her stomach and tried to get up.

The man stepped on her head, pinning her to the ground. The rest of her little body flailed about.

Evenel sucked in dirt, expelling it with a cry of terror. She could see Daddy being held by two men, who beat him with clubs until he fell flat on his chest to the ground. She saw blood ooze from his body.

The man who stood on her head lifted his foot. She got to her knees to run to her daddy, but the man swung his foot and kicked her, sending her flying.

She landed on her back. Her breath forced from her, unable to move.

He picked her up by the hair and punted her toward her father. She landed in front of him. Close enough that she could hear his labored breath.

Why didn't her daddy help her? He always helped her when she was hurt, when she needed him.

Her lungs began to work again. She cried out, "Help me! Daddy!"

The man again held her head down with his foot, her cheek smashed, conforming to the dirt. She could see Daddy's eyes. They spoke of despair.

The man thrust a spear toward her father. "I am Tohanna. Today your child will float on the river. When the crocodiles find her, they will drag her to the bottom and pin her under a log until she rots. They will eat her flesh. She will die in terror."

The man twisted her head into the dirt, then released her.

Evenel got up, sobs coming from her little form, and ran toward her father.

As she made the steps that separated them, he held his head

up, looked at her, and the sadness in his eyes struck her in her bowels.

One more stride and she would be with him.

A jagged club fell onto her daddy's head, driving his face into the ground, spraying his blood into her face, into her mouth. The heat of it gagged her, and she was ashamed.

Evenel stopped. She stood over her daddy. She knew he could not get up, that even now he was trying with all his heart to help her. Still she cried out, "Daddy, help me, why won't you help me?"

The man dragged her to the shore. He picked her up and threw her toward the canoe.

CHAPTER FOUR

Canada

Jesse had been out a full week when he hit the edge of British Columbia. He'd turned north in Minnesota, then spun west on the Canadian flats, past the wheat fields that seemed to go on forever. He was ready for the change the Canadian Rockies promised in the distance.

The road ran uphill for a long time before the foothills became mountains. It cut through the canyons and twisted around the snowy peaks. The pavement was not black but brown, its coarse and grainy surface singing under the tires.

Each approaching turn was a beck and call, its mantra pulling on the soul to come and see. A great smoky gray peak salted with white rose overhead. Then wildflowers, ablaze in purple and yellow, strained to be seen, while the waving grass grains entered stage left as the bike leaned across the turn and the wall of stone gave up its long secret of color and scent, rock and towering sky. Sparkling streams unfolded from the next turn and lifted their own cry across the boulders.

One more turn and snowmelt ran across the rocky lips and fell between the crags in spectacular waterfalls until it found the stone again, the fluid bursting into spray from the violent meeting. Condensing back to water, it slid along the rock until it fell again, always seeking the ocean, the brilliant liquid carving the Rockies, erasing one pebble at a time.

Jesse passed by a little cutback of a road that ran north. It took some time for it to bear fruit in his mind, then he let off the throttle and coasted to a stop. Something in him kept telling him to try that road. He turned back and watched for the road to come into view.

He stopped at its base, urging his thoughts along. *Tell me*, he thought, waiting for his mind to clear and the lesson to seep in.

Emma said, "Lessons sit on a shelf inside your mind waiting for when you needed them. The trick is to pull them off the shelf and spill them across your mind."

Jesse thought back to his parent's farm and calling to his mother in the barn. Pigeons cooed from the silo, cats slept in the stone windowsills, and the cool breeze floated down from the ladder to the haymow. He climbed, and the aroma of a hundred crops filled the bountiful structure. Giant wood beams had been pegged and shaped by hard hands that built not only for themselves, but for their legacy. "Mom?"

Sunshine striped the floor, bales lay askew, she lay so still...

He slapped the door shut. He trembled, gripped his chest—there were places in his head he never wanted to go to.

Jesse closed his eyes. Emma rocked on the porch, pointing at him with her bottle. "Let the lesson seep in. Spill it!"

"Tell me, Emma, I can't do it."

"Jimmanee Jesus! You have to be strong in your head, sort the bad thoughts out and face them. Fix them one at a time."

"Emma, tomorrow, I will tomorrow."

"Alright, alright then, here you go."

The road ran steeply uphill and turned from sight, losing itself among the towering spruces. There was still a clamoring in his thoughts. An allure to fill a void. It made him uncomfortable in his own self, much as one feels when someone too beautiful to approach walks away and is lost forever.

The road continued upward. The light reflected jade green from the evergreens. It was impossible to tell whether the road turned left or right until you were right there, the trees twisted the sunlight so.

Sometime later, Jesse found a little diner stuffed between the trees. The siding was made of tar paper and faux stone to look like bricks before it had been tattered by the years. A sugar pine held a sign that just said "Eat."

Jesse pulled up to the side of the diner. The asphalt parking lot cracked and split where it wasn't covered with pine needles. The front door sang with bells when he opened it. A few diners waved at the door, expecting to know whoever had come in. The floor had been worn into a basin from decades of high-top lacer boots grazing over it, followed by the straw broom at every close. It was the kind of place that kept its soul on display.

Jesse threw a leg over a stool at the counter. He leaned back, shook out his hair, and sat his sunglasses on the counter next to him. He wore blue jeans and a black T-shirt.

A chalkboard hung on the wall announcing meatloaf and mashed potatoes as today's special, the sprawling handwriting nearly in code.

The cook behind the counter walked past Jesse, stopped, and chin-pointed toward him. Jesse caught the scent of salt and oil. "You lost, tourist?" The cook didn't wait for an answer, just moved to the kitchen through the French doors. "Hey Za, you got one."

Za sat down his tub, poured some water into a glass from

the ancient spigot that hung from the wall. He put the glass in front of Jesse and came around the counter, taking the stool next to him. Jesse guzzled the water, sweet and cold from the mountain itself.

"The cook rips on everybody, that's why they keep 'im in the back," Za said.

"What did the cook call you?"

"Za, because I'm always last, but it's really Danny, Danny Cocoza. So, you lost?"

"I don't know where I am, but I ain't lost."

Cocoza broke into an infectious smile; he used his whole face when he smiled, especially his eyes. "If you're here, man, and you're not a bear, rabbit, or logger, then you're lost. We don't get anything else."

"I'll take the special," Jesse replied.

"Za, order up!" the cook boomed an order.

Cocoza stood up. "Tips are calling my name, I better tend to them. I'll get you one special on the way."

"Two."

"Got a horse outside or just a big appetite?"

"The first one."

Za smiled. "One for you and one for Trigger. You got to pay for both of you, though."

"Za! Order up!" The cook slapped the counter with the spatula.

Jesse felt the eyes walking over him from around the room, like he knifed their mothers. There was conversation from men who held their forks with their thumbs jutting out, their tattered flannel sleeves rolled to the elbow. They spoke in veiled and incoherent sounds, yet to Jesse, they were threatening.

When Jesse finished eating, he dropped some bills on the counter and headed for the door. The cook smirked as Jesse walked past the grill. Jesse didn't know why, but the cook hated him too.

He headed north up the road, the afternoon fading away as he stopped to take in the view. The range ran west, with each peak higher than the last until they glinted with snow God knows how many miles in the distance.

Jesse saw a plateau off in the haze. He rolled to a stop. Maybe he could hike to it before dark, he thought, if he left right now. Jesse pulled the bike into the woods and shouldered his pack. After taking his bearings, he jumped the rail protecting the curve. He slid downhill for a hundred feet before the landscape changed directions and began to climb. The pines were spares because of the rocky soil that wouldn't allow a root to run too deep. Strong winds tipped them over before their time, and they began the slow return to the soil from where they had come. The downed trees hardly slowed his climb.

The plateau was about a hundred yards across at the top, but ten times that size at the bottom, and flat as a table. The sides of the plateau rose straight up nearly ninety feet and were adorned with black rock and granite. Jesse found a finger hold and pulled his frame toward the top. Zigzagging across the face, gaining elevation with every step, he reached over the top edge just as the setting sun touched the far side of the plateau.

He pulled himself upright, then he sat down, mesmerized and panting. It was as if the sun was setting right at his feet. When the yellow orb gave way and the stone sat in shadow, Jesse moved to the far edge of the plateau to watch the sun set all over again.

After the colors in the sky turned to black, he put out his sleeping bag and crawled in with his eyes to the sky. The endless stars kept him from sleep for many hours.

CHAPTER FIVE

A silent wind rushed over Jesse, bringing him to consciousness. It was just light enough to see. He rolled to his back, trying to connect with his brain, blinking his eyes, and trying to focus.

Instantly, a scream split his ears; his vision filled with motion and shape. Jesse flew out of the sleeping bag and scanned the sky, but he had no idea for what. He was fully awake, and the sting of surprise and foreboding sat in his throat. Jesse held in the silence, trying to figure out what had happened.

He moved toward the edge of the plateau just a few feet away; whatever it was, a vulture maybe, was below the lip. Just as his eyes caught the horizon, it cleared the lip and swept over him. Jesse instinctively leaped for it, trying to tear it from the sky.

His hand caught and lifted him off the ground; Jesse twisted around to look up and see…Cocoza! Jesse let go and thumped the clay like a stone.

Danny Cocoza flared his hang glider to a stop and stood with a Cheshire cat grin on his lips. He was laughing.

Jesse lay flat on the ground, letting his feet and intestines find their way back home.

"Wooo, that was good, man. Watching you trying to get out of that sleeping bag was the funniest thing I ever seen," Cocoza said, still snickering.

Jesse grunted.

"I need a favor, man, there's a white van up the mountain a ways," Za motioned with his hand, "past your bike a few miles. Can I get you to bring it to the Flats and pick us up?"

"Least I can do," Jesse mumbled.

"Thanks, man." Cocoza took a few steps and dropped off the lip. Belly laughs followed him as he yelled while diving, "COCOZA!"

Jesse got up and watched the glider soar into the clouds. He saw another glider in the distance, below the clouds and moving west. "Must be the damn cook."

Jesse packed his sleeping bag and swung his pack onto his back. He worked his way down the edge and hiked back to the bike. After starting the Ducati, Jesse rode uphill toward the top of the mountain, where he found the white van parked in a small clearing.

The keys were in the ignition, with a note taped to the mirror that said, "If you find this van, please bring it to the Flats and pick up its owner." Jesse climbed inside and pumped the gas till the old bucket snorted to life. He loaded his bike inside, tied it down, and closed the rear doors.

A semi-tractor bellowed just up the road as he walked around the passenger side of the van. Then he noticed old tire marks rubbed into the side.

❧

Johnny crawled out of the rack at 4:00 a.m. He poured straight coffee, tomato juice, and a hit of Wild Turkey into a cup and slurped on it, wincing from the sting. Redhead Joe they called it, because it made you sharp-eyed and ready to fly.

He filled his thermos and made for the truck. After swinging north, he started the long climb to the top of the mountain. The stereo was full of Toby Keith, and he was filling himself with Redhead Joe and Copenhagen. It was a hell of a day.

Johnny Huntoon had spent all of his twenty-five years right there on the mountain. Long in the leg and square-shouldered, his kind were bred for the job, and he stayed true to the family tradition when he dropped out of school to get a job peeling logs for pulp. Then he ran the saws and the skidders, did everything it took to get the wood out of the hills.

For Johnny, though, his dream was driving the logging trucks. It was good money, but more than that, it was the ride. There are two ways down the mountain. Put the gearbox in third and let the motor hold the load; it was safe and damn boring. The other way was the ride. It used guts, brakes, banking, and guardrails sometimes.

When Johnny reached the top of the mountain, he swung his rig around and dropped the empty trailer. The next loaded trailer sat waiting for him; he backed his Mack up to the trailer, giving it some throttle as the fifth wheel slipped under the trailer and into place. He opened the passenger door and pulled out a three-foot pipe from among the extra chain binders that sat on the floorboard next to the coffee can where he spit his chew. He jumped to the ground and walked along the load. The pipe clanged on the handle of each chain binder as he moved past, inspecting each one. The tone of the pipe measured the strain on the chain holding down the logs. He liked the tang that echoed through the woods. It seemed to wobble through the air forever. By six o'clock, he was pulling out with twenty tons of logs, topped with another ten of overload. It wasn't just the extra money, it was the extra push.

Huntoon knew the road would be empty the first ride of the day. It was always empty at first light, the best one of the day. His anticipation grew as the gravity pushed him down the road. He spun the wheel over the top and rounded the turn.

When he looked ahead, the old white van was there again. Only this time somebody was standing beside it. "Kite boys," he thought. The coffee can clanged from the chew Johnny spit expertly across the cab. He rolled his lip to sop up the excess and gathered it back in with the upper one. "Out playing instead of workin'." He slowed and downshifted.

The brakes squealed as he stopped beside the van. The air released, clamping the brakes on. Huntoon rolled down the window. "That your van, flyboy?"

Jesse didn't respond, looking at the big black wheel marks on the side of the van.

"I said flyboy! You dumb, boy?"

Jesse turned around cautiously.

"That your van, boy?" Johnny said again.

Jesse looked up at Huntoon. "No, that not my van, boy."

"Then what you doin' with it?"

"I'm taking it to the guy who owns it."

"Dat right?"

"Yeah...dat right."

"Then you go on now, I don't want to hold you up, ya hear?"

Jesse said, "Thanks, I appreciate that. You happen to know where the flats are?"

"Nope."

"Nope you don't know, or nope you ain't telling me?"

"Nope."

"Yeah." Jesse got in the van and pulled away down the road.

❧

Jesse watched his mirrors; the truck still sat idling when he rounded the corner.

Jesse shook his head. He hated men like that, a redneck punk looking for a fight, testing him. Plenty of them where he came from, and Jesse suffered for it. They pissed him off.

Jesse rounded a few turns, trying to enjoy the morning, when the van lurched forward with a crack. Jesse looked in the mirror and saw the logging truck was tight to his rear bumper. The van spun around and slid to a stop beside the road. The truck horn sounded as it went down the road.

When the road flattened out, the trees gave way to a large grassy plain. A glint of sunlight off a pole alerted Jesse, and he caught sight of the gliders already on the ground maybe a hundred yards down an old two-track.

Jesse pulled up beside the pilots, who were busy collapsing their gliders for transport. He got out and walked to where the van's rear bumper sat crushed.

"Locals scare you, tourist?" The cook was chin-pointing again, this time at the van with a smile and tone Jesse could not read.

Jesse turned his back on the cook and moved over to Cocoza and started carrying parts to the van.

"Tell me what happened." Cocoza cut the tension as he stripped a rope with his knife.

"Apparently," Jesse said, his voice shaking from the adrenaline, "this guy must try to smash every car he sees."

"It's not one guy, it's all of them." Cocoza hesitated. "And only the cars that are on the road...or close to the road."

"Nobody bitches about it?"

"No, everybody knows it takes a fool to get in the way of a downhill logging truck." Cocoza let out his little laugh. "It's just the locals having fun, their way of saying I'm workin' here, get ta hell off my road. What color was the rig?"

"Blood red."

Cocoza stopped tying and looked up at Jesse, who saw nothing in his expression.

"That's Huntoon."

They packed and loaded everything into the van after removing Jesse's bike.

"We got breakfast a few miles up. You want some?" Za asked.

"Jesus Christ!" The cook spit on the ground and got in the driver's seat. "We got the van, you don't have to feed him."

"Yeah, I'll come," Jesse said and spit on the ground.

CHAPTER
SIX

Manaus, Brazil

Piper Brown came to life in Memphis. Her daddy was deep South, a second-generation physician.

She was, of course, a southern belle. Beautiful and cordial, she, like her kind, was hospitable to a fault. A cheerleader, campus socialite, and valedictorian at Tennessee, the family was hurt when she chose Northwestern to gain a master's in languages.

Then her mother cried when Piper told them she was spending the summer in some jungle in Brazil. Piper wanted to find her way in the world. Her mother blamed the damn Yankee influence.

Heat and sweat unlike any she had felt in Memphis greeted

Piper as soon as the airport door slammed behind her. The jungle was what she had told her mother...but she never intended to leave the city.

Manaus, a city of a million people, lay deep in the Amazon; it was civilization a thousand miles from the sea and mere yards from the jungle, even less to the cutthroat world of men.

She had come here because of the diversity of languages brought up the great river. But really, she came here to escape her world and to see the Teatro de Amazonia, the opera house built by the rubber barons in 1896 as a tropical miniature of La Scala in Milan, only with frescoes and statues of Amazon themes. The barons had illuminated the tall halls with French chandeliers. Piper had to see it.

And of course, she wanted to see the Mercado Municipal, designed by Alexandre-Gustave Eiffel after Les Halles of Paris. They built it with imported cast iron and slave labor, but now it was fabulous shopping, a sprawling stew of river life and trade. With aromas reminiscent of its Parisian parent, the market sold slabs of Amazonian fish, exotic fruits, and Indian goods brought on the boats that used the river as a liquid highway. Paris had been spectacular, and she hoped it would be the same here.

In the taxi, Manaus felt safe to her. The people were dark and well dressed. The streets were clean, but appeared chaotic and even a little wild.

She checked into the Taj Mahal Continental, the best hotel in the city, equal to the needs of a girl with her breeding. She ordered the finest bottled water to be delivered to her room. Piper dressed for dinner; she wore her mauve pumps because she loved the high click they made against marble floors. Everyone turned to see when she wore them, and they weren't disappointed. Piper cut an imposing figure in a place where American girls were expected to be brash, blonde, and beautiful.

The hotel's Italian restaurant engaged a jazz band that played quietly while the maître d' seated her. A middle-aged man in a wrinkled white suit sat across the room by himself, and one of the waiters sat at the ornate bar shuffling papers. Piper scanned the menu and wrinkled her nose. The waiter, dressed in crisp black and white, approached. "Have you made your choice, Madame?"

"Well, no," Piper replied. "How is your spaghetti?"

"Very traditional," he answered.

"What does that mean?"

"Madame?"

"Have you tried it?"

"Well, I have to admit this is only my second day here."

"Well, is it, like, SpaghettiOs?" she asked.

"I can assure you it is not like spaghettiOs."

"Well, that is what I want." Her words lingered in the best Tennessee drawl.

"Um, you would like…SpaghettiOs?"

"Yes."

He straightened his jacket. "I will check with our chef, Madame." He bowed and left her table.

In the kitchen, he yelled out, "Hey, Hefner, I got a lady who wants SpaghettiOs. What do I tell her?"

"Is she rich?" A short bulging man with forearm tattoos buried in jet-black hair twisted his head around, revealing a stogie burning under his upper lip.

"Very," the waiter said, lighting a quick smoke.

Hefner stood on his tiptoes and reached for a can on a stainless shelf. "Then you give her SpaghettiOs." He slapped the can on an opener and peeled the lid off.

"You got SpaghettiOs?" the waiter said.

"This ain't my first rodeo; a professional like me is prepared for everything." He poured the contents of the can in a bowl and set it in the microwave. "And unlike you, my friend, I know what rich chicks want."

"How many rodeos they got with rich chicks in Brooklyn?"

"When I was there? None, but you learn how to make a girl from Czechoslovakia squeal."

"All right, Hef, I'll bite. How you do that?"

"You cook like her mother. Some girls you make roast goose and some you make them SpaghettiOs." The microwave bell went off, and he handed the waiter the steaming SpaghettiOs.

The waiter grabbed a small loaf of garlic bread and exited through the swinging doors. He sat the bowl down at Piper's table, along with the garlic bread.

"What's this?" She picked up the bread. "It stinks, take it away." She handed it to him, pointing her head away from her outstretched arm. "I only eat white bread, no crust, and I want grape jelly."

The waiter bowed and hurried off to the kitchen. Soon, Hefner produced a basket of fluffy slices of bread with the crusts artfully removed.

"She wants grape jelly," the waiter said.

Hef tilted his head and shot a curious look. "That's a new one."

The waiter took the jelly and bread back to her table.

Piper smiled. "Thank you."

"Will there be anything else, Madame?"

"Not anymore."

Back in her room, the sheets had been turned down and a bath drawn. Piper slipped into the water, sipping on a chilled riesling from Napa Valley. The wine put her to bed right away.

Sunshine greeted her in bed. The first thing she wanted to do was sip cappuccino on the balcony. Swinging the tall doors open, she strolled onto the balcony. The midday sun and its heat caught her by surprise. Maybe she would skip the cappuccino. Still, it was such a great sensation; she was thousands of miles from anyone who knew her or could help her. For the first time, her father or, God forbid, her mother could not reach her. At last, she was on her own, empowered with newfound freedom. Piper made her first independent decision: she was going shopping.

The contents of her several suitcases had been loaded into the closets, but nothing in them appealed to her. "Well, something light and airy," she said aloud, strolling along the length of the closet. "Something white, and a hat too. Oh, a gold belt would be fabulous. That is where I will start." Dressed, she checked herself in the mirror. She lingered, feeling fun and sexy.

Downstairs, she enjoyed a wonderful breakfast of fresh imported blueberries and strawberries, along with muskmelon she insisted on substituting for the local fruit they normally served, and a side of bacon. She had to have her bacon.

Carrying only her little leather designer purse, she left the vaulted lobby through the revolving doors. She turned toward the sun and was off on her adventure. All on her own.

The shops near the hotel screamed Spanish architecture, but they were as sanitized as the ones on Rodeo Drive that she and her mother visited each Christmas. Only today, her domineering mother wouldn't bridle her.

There was security just inside the plate glass windows of the shops and the heavy doors held in the air conditioning. The sales clerks were well-dressed, aggressive, and spoke perfect English to her; she answered in Spanish.

Late in the afternoon, a growling reminded her she had not eaten lunch. The waft of aromas sent her searching for its source. Surrounded by cobblestone and a rusting handrail sat a little outdoor café trying very hard to be French. That's perfect, she thought. The menu was in Portuguese, a real delight for her, a student of languages who specialized in upper South America. It was her chosen education, just one of many things her father kept asking just what the hell it was good for.

Piper scanned the menu and ordered in perfect Portuguese. "Do you offer a hamburger and fries?"

"I will check, Madame," the waiter said, excusing himself.

Lingering in the shade of the canopy, she twirled her hair and passed the time, watching the city go by.

"Madame?"

Piper jumped.

"I have more wine than I can drink. Perhaps you could help?"

He was speaking in French and wore an old rust-colored beret. He had tan slacks and a button-down shirt under an ancient sport coat. The old man held a bottle of wine and two glasses. He shrugged his shoulders, tilted his head, and repeated the question with his eyes.

"No." She waved him away. "Wait, I'm sorry, that was rude. Please join me." I hope he doesn't kill me, she thought.

"I was seated at the far table and I thought, Gabriel, go and talk to that young woman and treat your loneliness." He sat down slowly, aligning himself with the chair before falling into it. "My knees no longer serve me, like bastard children."

He offered her a wine glass and poured from the bottle into hers and then his own.

"This café serves French wines, but that is the only thing French about it," he said. "The other places try to serve you wine made on this continent, but I will not drink it. It tastes like dirt and the cows that fertilize it."

Piper laughed. "Well, sir, prepare to be disappointed, I only drink rieslings from California." She tapped the red merlot in her glass.

"Have you not experienced the fine white grapes from Alsace along the Rhine?" He took her glass and drank it in a single gulp. He snapped his fingers and the waiter rushed to their side. "Trimbach Cuvee-Emile for the lady." The waiter bowed and left. "Today, we will make you a French woman." The old man smiled.

"What if I don't want to?"

"My beautiful child, every woman wishes she were French.

You only need to be exposed to that calling, which the Americans have buried away in your heart."

The waiter returned with the bottle and a wine glass. He poured a sample for her. Piper swished the glass and then put it to her nose to gather its bouquet. She touched the wine to her lips, but did not taste it. "It's good," she said, hoping his eyesight had faded. The old man smiled, and the waiter filled her glass and left the bottle. He returned with her burger and fries. The old man frowned.

"I am an American girl," Piper said.

"This transformation, I can see, will be long and tedious, but perhaps just as rewarding. Go on, eat, do not let me keep you from your sandwich of cow and soggy bread."

Piper dived into her burger with false gusto, ripping a piece from the burger.

He laughed aloud, and she did too.

"Every Frenchman wishes he had been born an American so he too could have a McDonalds around the corner," Piper said.

He laughed again and poured more wine into his glass. "Let us agree to learn from each other. I will start by asking your name."

"Piper." She bit into the burger.

"And Piper, why are you here so far from your McDonalds?"

"I am a linguist, I came to study language."

"Is that really why you came?"

"Yes."

"No, you daydreamed of discovering a language lost for many scores. You told your mother you were going to the jungle for shock value, but I think you never intended to leave the hotel district."

Oh my God, Piper thought. How does he know all of that?

"That sounds like the ramblings of an old man who has watched too many women pass by his favorite table at his favorite café," she said.

"Perhaps, but I learn a lot of things doing just that. You may not know why you are here, but I suspect I know the real reason you came to South America."

"And what is that? Piper asked.

"You study the words that allow people to communicate, but you are really looking for your passion in life. Does it really excite you? Ask yourself what makes you alive, what makes you toil and yet fulfills you. Can you tell me that, Miss Piper?"

"I think you should work on your methods for seducing girls."

"Shall we change the subject since you are offended?"

"Yes." She offered him a fry, but he refused.

"Then a story from the war, when I was both brave and my skill for seducing beautiful girls was equal to their attraction to me."

She smiled. "Yes, ramble away, I love a good story."

"So I shall." The old man entertained her until he had drank the last of his wine, and then he checked the time on a worn pocket watch. "I must go; my doctor has summoned me to listen to my heart while I lecture him on wine and sometimes women." He rocked forward a few times and then lifted his frame from the chair. "Please, Miss Piper, enjoy your visit to Manaus."

"Thank you, Gabriel. For the wine and the conversation." He kissed her hand and walked into the street.

Piper felt a little unsettled. He was right, she thought. She had gone to school because it was expected of her, and she had chosen to be a linguist because of a crush on a professor. Coming to Manaus had been to shock her mother because she would have no idea where the city was...or what it was. The old man told the truth—she didn't have a passion for anything...

"Madame?"

Piper jumped.

"More wine?" the waiter asked.

"No, check please."

Tired, she left the café with her bags, strolling toward the hotel. The shop windows were all so inviting; she loved the displays, the colors of the clothing, the urbane poses of the mannequins wearing impossible shoes and golden jewelry, romancing the images they sold.

She stopped at an intersection, waiting for the light to change. Her gaze circled the intersection, stopping at a bridal shop across the street.

There was a wedding dress in the window, and she could see her own reflection in the glass next to the gown. Setting down her bags, she sidestepped to the left a few inches until her image aligned with the dress. Standing on her tiptoes, she fit right into it. She smiled. She was beautiful. Even here, it was a happy world.

With her gaze still upon herself, a little girl stood next to her. Startled, Piper looked down, but the little girl was not there. Looking back across the street, she realized the little girl was in the window, or in front of it. Piper gathered her arms full of her bags.

She crossed the road to find a little form, perhaps three years old, naked and standing in a small pool of blood.

CHAPTER SEVEN

British Columbia

An old house that must have been built with a rich man's money stood among the pines. Now it was a neglected rental, slowly falling back to the woods. The house stood three stories tall with white sawmill clapboard siding. The window panes were wavy, so looking through them gave the surrounding trees the curious appearance of vibrating.

Jesse followed the van down the dirt driveway. The soil was acidic from the pine needles, loosely packed but never dusty.

His two hosts stepped out of the van empty-handed, leaving all the gear inside. Leaving his own gear on the bike, he followed Cocoza and the cook up several steps each in its own stage of dry rot but not yet giving up the ghost. The unlocked door gave a high-pitched squawk as it ground against ornate hinges. It slammed shut from the rusted spring adhered to it with several shiny and bent-over nails. Jesse, born of a long line of skilled tradesman, could not help but scoff at the roughshod carpentry.

Inside was the illusion of a weather command center on an aircraft carrier. Charts hung on the walls with topographic maps sitting under more maps. Wind charts penciled with latitude and longitude calculations were scattered over a large wood table, along with notebooks crammed with scratched handwriting.

The cook immediately began preparing bacon, toast, eggs, and potatoes, all at once. The kitchen was large even for a house of this era. It was covered in yellow wallpaper with white daisies leftover from some housewife of a long-ago generation. Everything you would find in a restaurant occupied the kitchen, well-worn cast-offs of the cook's trade.

Watching the cook, Jesse was awed by the sheer coordination of movement and beauty of someone doing a job with pride. The food landed on three plates all at once.

Cocoza slid a chair under the table that stood in the middle of the kitchen. Jesse did likewise at the head of the table.

"That's my chair, tourist," the cook said without turning around. "Get out."

Cocoza waved Jesse out of it so he took the chair across from Cocoza. The cook sat down at the head of the table and slid the plates to the other two.

They all dove in, the sound of silverware meeting Bakelite plates playing until they settled back into their chairs.

"What the hell is all this stuff?" Jesse asked, waving toward the piles lying everywhere except in the cook's kitchen.

The cook stood up and began cleaning up. Cocoza left and gathered an armful of papers from the table in the adjoining dining room. He plopped them down on the kitchen table, searching for a certain topographic map. "The cook found them first—"

"Your ass was last, Za," the cook added.

Cocoza didn't acknowledge the remark. "Hang gliders are powered by gravity. That is, they fall to earth and the air sliding under the wings moves them forward. But gravity always wins, until now."

Jesse put a bullshit frown on his face.

Za continued. "Look, man, today we started at the top and we had to find someone to come get us at the bottom."

"Thank you very much," Jesse said.

"The cook realized there are six peaks, or high points that all generate thermals on an unknown basis."

"Thermals?"

"An area of air that is warmer than its surroundings, causing it to rise instead of mix with its environment." Za held his hands palms upward to demonstrate. "Thermals can be found anywhere, but they are hard to predict, except near a rock face, usually a cliff side, where they can be predicted with some accuracy."

Za talked really fast. His wavy, dark hair only emphasized his Italian lover façade. His infectious and boyish smile drew women to him, but he had a knack for making them friends. You couldn't help but like him. "Here's the deal, the point where you found the van is the highest and most accessible of these points." Za brought his finger down on the map. "The objective is to begin here and end here. We think we can take off, fly to five different peaks and use their thermals to lift us to an elevation that will allow us to continue all the way back to Roundtop."

"And you've done this how many times?" Jesse asked.

"None yet, but we have gotten three points, er, peaks. We've taken readings for wind speed at different temperatures to predict when a thermal exists. And I got a hundred years of weather data to help. Beyond that, we have been doing experimentation on our model."

"You mean flying?" Jesse asked.

"Whenever we can, baby," the cook shot back.

"This seems like a whole lot of work just to save a ride," Jesse said.

Za hesitated. It was a question he had asked himself but never verbalized. He clapped his hands together. "Flying is way cool, man, and when you hit a certain confidence, you can experience things that are so much better than cool. It is a thing, a place, only a few get to have."

Jesse stood up, gesturing into the distance. "And the endorphins release, mixing with the adrenaline into the elixir of danger addicts. There is a utopia deep in the intellect that all covet, but only the ones daring enough to vanquish their fear would…could…ever know."

"Kiss my ass, Shakespeare," the cook said. "Who did you steal that from? And how would you know, tourist? You ever done anything dangerous? I say you're a pants pisser."

Jesse said, "You ever ride the twisties at a hundred-plus, dragging a knee? That will inspire you. It's not for pussies."

"Try a kite, tourist. It ain't nothing you can get from any land toy."

Za cut in, "The cook and I have been…maybe bored. Now we need to have more, go beyond, and this is something no one has done before."

"I want in," Jesse said. "Look, I can do the math for you. I have an architectural degree. You need to work out the rate of descent and the accurate distances to achieve it."

The cook stopped, wiping soapy hands. "You ever flown a hang glider, tourist?" Your degree won't save you out there."

"It's Jesse, Jesse Nickols, and no, but I can."

"Pah!" The cook exhaled through pursed lips, then walked into the next room and returned with a worn paperback. It said *How-to Hang Gliding* on the cover. "You read that, and I say you ain't got the balls."

"You won't know unless he can stay here," Za said.

"What?" the cook said. "Does he look like a stray kitten to you?"

"Oh come on, think about it," Za said. "Don't you want to be there when he pisses his pants at the launch?"

"Alright then, tourist, you start with the math, read this, and you got a job at the diner. Everybody pulls his weight, and dying out there is all on you."

Za slapped his hands together. "Come on, man, let's get your gear. You're now a proud occupant of a room with a view that costs whatever you got."

Jesse chose one of the bedrooms on the second floor. He set up housekeeping and returned downstairs to find both parties poring over another map. Jesse listened while they debated lift problems at a place called Backbone. Jesse knew they were both wrong in their conclusions. "What is the backbone?" Jesse asked.

Za stopped, sat in a chair.

"Aw shit," the cook said. "Now you damn sure asked for it, I'm outta here." The front door slapped shut, drowning the last words.

Za started right away with the confidence of a storyteller who loved his craft. "The six peaks each have their own difficulties and dangers. First, there is Roundtop, where you found the van. It's where we start and where we want to finish, thus the name. I named them all." Cocoza stopped, looking for some tribute from his audience.

"There are three launch areas depending on the wind, which is good, but only one landing area where you have to come in at treetop. It's also downhill and a little small, both of which are bad.

"The second peak is Flattop, where the cook and I found you sleepin'." Za laughed aloud.

Jesse gave him the finger.

"Flattop is a natural choice because of its proximity to

47

Roundtop. The trick to Flattop is to find which side the thermal is on, if at all. You need it to get back above Roundtop on the return trip."

The cook walked up the steps and gave the wooden screen door a kick to get their attention. "Hey, bring your tourist, we got work to do."

Za signaled Jesse to follow him. "Every few days we gather data from the mountains."

Jesse followed Za out to the van where the cook was waiting. Cook yelled, "Jesus, let's go, grandma." The pair jumped in, and they headed out the driveway.

"Where we going?" Jesse asked.

"Pintop," Za shouted back without looking. "That is the Pin." Za pointed. The tall peak was a good distance from anything else with any height to it.

They soon parked and the cook started toward Pintop with a backpack. Za grabbed a second one and followed the same unseen path, with Jesse behind.

Tall pines hogged the sun and carpeted the floor with needles, leaving few resources for anything save the jack pine and tall grass where the grasshoppers sang and sprang ahead of their every step, the clack of their wings distinctive and pleasurable. They walked in silence until they stood under the peak of Pintop; Jesse felt it was damn high. Coming in over the trees on wings and then breaking away to the top would be a thrill.

The cook removed a weather-protected laptop from a wood box that was staked to the ground. Za plugged in another laptop and downloaded information to take with them.

The cook pointed east. "It's an eastern approach, then you circle around until you can establish the thermal, manipulate it to a required altitude, and move west to the Backbone, the next peak, simple as that."

Za changed out the battery on the laptop. "Done. Let's move to the Bone."

"What's the Bone?" Jesse asked.

"The Backbone, the next peak, dickhead," the cook said.

"Like it was obvious, asshole," Jesse said.

Za cut in. "Jesus, man, were you two married in an earlier life? I could have stayed in Brooklyn if I wanted to listen to this."

They walked silently back to the van, the shadows from waving trees bouncing around their feet.

Back at the van, Jesse saw a ridge that ran north and south with a rounded peak on the south end.

"That's where we're going, the Backbone," Za said, getting into the van.

When the van stopped, the cook started along the trail that followed the top of the narrow spine.

A mile down the trail, the cook stopped, turned over some moss to reveal a hidden box containing another laptop. "So many damn tourists up here we have to hide the damn thing."

Za handed his laptop to the cook to download the data. "This is where we get stopped, man," Za said. "The Backbone, point number four. We come in from the Pin and you have to pump…"

"What?" Jesse said.

"Fly back and forth in front of the approach side of the ridge and climb the thermal over the top to where we are now. The problem is we have never found a weather combination that had enough lift to get up and over where we are standing. And everything else is on the other side. We can't get over the edge. Your air just stops. Even if you could get on top, you can't get over the trees on the other side."

Jesse studied the rock formation for a minute. He walked along the top, intently studying the cliff edge. "You're not crossing in the right place."

"What?" the cook shot back.

"You're not crossing in the right place."

"What the fuck do you know, tourist?"

Jesse stared back for a long moment, trying to keep his cool. "Take a look at this."

Za walked to the spot where Jesse was standing. "Hey, man, just come listen," he said to the cook.

The cook stayed put.

Jesse said, "This cliff face is mostly square-edged along the approach side. The shape allows the thermal to move upward, where it is swept back by the westerly wind that I suspect is constant here. There is a law of physics called the coanda effect. It states that moving air will follow a curved surface. Here, the cliff face is curved or rounded. The air comes over the top and follows across, carrying a supported object with it. The problem with the following edge is that it is also curved. This will cause the same air to follow the curve and slam a supported object into the ground."

"Like a hang glider?" Za asked.

"Very much a hang glider. But for a short space here, the pines are taller. They should break the coanda effect and allow the wind to flow west."

Za chimed in, "You could catch the west wind, flare for lift, and then dive again to gain westward movement, again and again, until the terrain drops off and gives you some room."

"You know this for a fact?" The cook wasn't biting.

"It's a theory."

"It's a guess to bullshit us."

"It can be done."

"By who? You want to try, boy?"

Jesse repeated, "It can be done."

The cook turned away. "You don't know shit about flying an' you got the answers, tourist? Bullshit."

Za shrugged at Jesse.

Jesse said, "How do you live with that much attitude?"

"Admiration, admiration for the flying skills and good chow," Za said.

They hiked in silence back to the van. Jesse was a little pissed at the attitude the cook was giving him. However, he had dealt with worse before, this was just a smoke screen. It was more bark than bite. Another ride in the van brought them to a trailhead that was another hour's hike to a great stone wall.

"Number five. The Horseshoe." Za held out his arms in a grand gesture. "It's shaped just as it is named. It is a lot lower than the Backbone so you can get some needed speed. This is where it gets cool. You have to dive and come in right up the gut full speed, aiming at the apex. There is always a thermal, man, but you have to be inches from the cliff face before you catch it. You have to flare—"

"Do what?" Jesse asked.

"Stop. Flare in this case means stop in midair. You have to stop right in the air. You have to flare really hard at the last second, to catch the ride up and over. Flare too soon and you miss the thermal and you die on the rocks below. Flare too late and you mate with the wall, man. This one has no room for mistakes. You do this one on instinct alone, baby."

"Like using your head but not your eyes," Jesse said.

"Yeah like that, man. Lotta times we've taken off from the Skull and come here to the Shoe. It's a ride, baby." Za was wearing the smile of a guy who had just bit the head off the devil.

The cook completed the laptop update. "He flies like he is chickenshit."

"Careful, the word is careful," Za replied.

The cook grabbed the backpack and started back toward the van.

"Got no sense of nature, that one. For all the time spent out in this beauty, no appreciation. Got giant balls of steel, though," Za said.

Jesse looked at Za with a puzzled look.

"Got no trace of fear." Za pointed to the north. "There it

is. Number six. The Cuchi, it's the place we all want to get to, man. Feels all soft and velvety, man. As soon as you top the Shoe, you cut north, and it's nearly a straight shot between two tall peaks, the Kneecaps."

Jesse let out a snort. "Not her kneecaps," he said, pointing a thumb over his back toward the cook. "She may have great curves, but the acid from her tongue makes me want to deck her. And I never felt that way about a woman before. What is her problem?"

Za smiled. "Yeah, it's like that, man. I don't know what made her mean, and I don't ask. Anyway, the Kneecaps, you can't get over them, but between them is a slot you can shoot through. It is tight. You have to line up and not waver at all for a thousand feet, but oh, what a feeling." Za rolled his arms up and thrust his hips forward. "Euh, baby."

"Better than the real thing?"

"Lasts longer. From there, it's a downhill run to Flattop and up to Roundtop. Hey man, we got to catch up. The cook isn't past leaving us behind."

Back in his bedroom, Jesse studied the book the cook had tossed at him. His engineering mind absorbed every word and every diagram. Here was something that was very technical and hopelessly full of danger. He absorbed terms like "best glide speed," "minimum sink speed," "ridge lift," and "SLT flight." The excitement opened his mind, allowing every detail into permanent memory.

This was what he craved: adventure. His road back at home had given him all the danger it could. But it had stopped calling, leaving Jesse the opportunity to listen for the song this road was singing.

Back home, though, his road still did have a call: Emma.

"Have you found a new boy to replace me?" he said over the phone.

"No, there is just one less at my door. Jesse, how are you?" Emma sat down next to the window, cradling the phone and the voice that was in it.

"You should ask, 'Where are you?'"

"I knew you had left when your butt stopped dusting my porch railing."

"So you want to know where?"

"Yes, unless you're locked up."

"I'm in British Colombia, hang gliding. Well, not yet, but soon."

Emma sat back in her chair. She felt the pleasure of discovery about to unfold. "Tell me everything, make me gush with envy."

He could hear the rustle of the chair as she settled into the cane rocker.

In his mind, Jesse could see her sitting by the window, beaming with the delight she got from his adventures, and the sound of her laughter enriched him.

He thought back to a simmering summer day spent in the sand, his toes in the water and that wonderful feeling of bliss a beach delivers. Sipping her Corona, Emma had spun her tale…

CHAPTER EIGHT

Manaus, Brazil

The little girl lay back down. A crude rope tied her ankle to a parking meter, her little ankle raw and bloody, completely void of skin.

At the edge of rich and poor, Piper stood holding her bags of excess, hovering over a little child without one thing in the whole world, not even her freedom. Tied to a post.

"Oh my God," Piper said, spinning around in a blur. "Where are the parents…*Where are the parents of this child*?" She shouted to the street, to the world. Dropping her bags, she knelt by the pathetic being.

She called to the little girl in Portuguese, asking her name. The eyes and the dirty face came around, staring with no expression at all.

Piper tried again. The list of languages flashed through her mind and dripped from her tongue. Still the dark eyes remained unaware of the world around her.

Piper began to despair. She could no longer think straight. She had tried them all…all except one that was thought to be just myth, just translated words written on notepaper lying on a shelf.

"What is your name?" Piper asked in this forgotten language. The face that had not flinched suddenly illuminated. The little form jumped into Piper's arms, wailing, "Tasan, Tasan!" In the whole city, only Piper understood: "Daddy, Daddy."

"Your name, what is your name?"

"Evenel."

Piper fumbled through her purse with Evenel clinging to her neck, looking for something to cut the rope that held the child.

"Hey, get away from her!" A man in a dirty white T-shirt put his boot on Piper's shoulder. He grabbed the rope, pulling Evenel off Piper's lap and thumping her across the concrete. Piper rolled backward from the force.

Evenel shrieked, "Tasan, Tasan!" pleading for Piper and holding her arms out for her.

The man lifted her in the air with the rope. Evenel dangled like a monkey on a leash. Tears fell to the concrete.

"This is my belongings," he said.

Piper clinched her fists against the concrete. "Then what is her name?"

"She got no Goddamn name, she's mine, you can bet that."

Piper stood up, bumping into a heavy woman wearing a stained orange dress who had appeared with the man.

"I'm standin' here, gringa!" She shoved Piper away, showing her yellow teeth, and then she shouted to the man, "Shut that little bitch up!"

The man kicked at Evenel, only grazing her and causing Evenel to spin in the air, wailing with fear.

The woman pointed at Evenel. "She's damn young, we'd haffa feed her for five years before we get anything back."

The man spit. "She'd get top dollar for fuckin' then, that young they like 'em. Hell, I might put in for first myself."

The woman snorted. "Fifty, that's all I give for her."

The man squinted in mock disbelief.

"I gets a hundred for her, like all of 'em."

Piper, stunned by the scene in front of her, came to her senses. She shook so hard she could not undo the gold clasp of her purse. She screamed in frustration over the sobs of the dangling child.

The dirty man smiled. "She wants to bid."

Piper concentrated on her hands and the clasp opened; she reached in and pulled out two bills.

"Two hundred dollars!"

The woman walked away without a word. The man grabbed the bills from Piper's fist. A knife appeared from nowhere. With a single swing, he cut the rope in two, victory in his face.

Piper faced him. "Cut the rope from her ankle."

He obliged and strutted away, kissing his new bills. Piper swooped Evenel into her arms, whispering, "It's okay, baby girl, I have you, I have you."

Piper, with the child in her arms and her bags abandoned on the street, carried Evenel, disappearing into the throng that was Manaus.

CHAPTER NINE

At the hotel, Piper ran a bath. She got in the tub with her clothes; the little girl would not let go for even a second. Piper washed the child's small face, and her tangled hair became silky black.

Afterward, Piper held Evenel in her arms and covered the girl with a great white towel that was as soft as hands could make. A long time they sat, wide-eyed. The little girl not emitting a single sound. The sun sank away and the moon shone.

The morning sun found two sleeping forms still bundled together. Evenel's belly growled them awake. Piper rubbed her eyes, and Evenel yawned loud and long. Piper giggled and Evenel replied with her own.

"Are you as hungry as I am?" Piper said.

Evenel looked puzzled, and Piper thought for a second, remembering the notes she had found in the dank annals of Northwestern in a dusty box dated 1939. Information collected but never finished. She had got lost in it, only to find there was not enough information to continue. Still, she had devoured it like candy. "Montotey?"

Evenel nodded. Piper nodded also. She reached over, picked up the phone, and dialed zero. "This is Piper Brown in 812. Would you please send up some strawberries and melon, no local stuff, just American fruit...no wait, we want local fruit, whatever you got, and some bacon too. Thank you." Piper hung up the phone, wondering what she had gotten herself into. She thought about the fact she did not know a thing about little girls. And she had to pee...and so must Evenel...who maybe had never heard of a bathroom...

A few minutes later, room service arrived. Piper tipped him and sent him away. They sprawled on the bed, each in a white robe, Evenel's rolled up at the arms and trailing like a wedding train.

Evenel took a piece of fruit and held onto it, looking curiously at Piper. Piper nodded and said, "It's okay, go ahead." Evenel bit into the flesh. Piper popped a strawberry in her mouth. "Try the bacon." Piper bit from a crispy piece and offered it to Evenel, who bit into it also and smiled in obvious pleasure. "See, I knew we could be friends. Wait till you try fried chicken skin." Piper laughed, and Evenel did the same. The sound melted Piper, and she hugged the little girl.

Watching this child of God in her care, Piper knew she would take the little girl back to her home, wherever that was. No matter what. She had a family somewhere out there, and Piper realized she had no idea how to find them and no means to do it with. She had never done anything like this, someone else always did things, her father...she stopped.

Her thoughts bit hard at her. She would do this herself. But how? Where in God's name would she start? She handed Evenel another strange fruit, and then wiped her hand of its juices. She took another piece of bacon. Piper knew Evenel must be from upriver. But there were many uprivers, rivers running hundreds of miles and branching again and again. She would need help, but she would procure it on her own. She thought about it as they dined.

Then Piper held her arms out to the now stuffed little girl. "Come on, baby girl, let's get dressed and go for a walk." Evenel held out her own arms, readily accepting Piper. She slipped a designer top over Evenel that hung to her knees and got herself ready in heels and makeup.

As she got ready, Piper quizzed Evenel with the words she did know from Evenel's dialect. Evenel was just as curious about English.

After Piper dressed, they changed and went downstairs to the lobby. They went shopping for new clothes for Evenel in the hotel mall.

Piper, with the waif in her arms, walked down to the Mercado. Down to the riverboats. At the edge of the city, the famous floating docks gave way to boards lying on near-swampland where the boats from the inner Amazon plied their trade.

Piper swung Evenel onto her back piggyback style as she made her way along the river. She tried to ignore the stench of dead things and old muck. Trembling, she squeezed Evenel's legs and thought about the advantage she had over any other white girl wandering the southern continent. She had the power of language, and that gave her some courage.

Several men labored, loading bags of what Piper hoped was flour but what she suspected might be more sinister onto a boat. They stopped working when Piper approached. They stood in the middle of the planks, forcing her to weave around them.

They called her names and brushed against her. She felt

grimy. The things they were saying terrified her, and she could not look at them. She didn't say anything, wanting desperately to get past them.

The jigsaw enigma of planks soon had her confused, but she kept moving, trying not to cry. She crossed numerous planks filled with men, each with a box or sack in his arms and a sinister smile or open scowl and blocking her way.

In the muck and shallow water that surrounded the planks, a reflected image stopped her cold: a row of dark-skinned men, their murky bodies surrounding a small face, held by a creamy skinned blonde woman. Piper moved her gaze across the landscape in front of her. Her gut stung at the realization of how strange she looked. How utterly vulnerable and visible. How her breasts stuck out as she carried Evenel on her back.

She moved Evenel around to her chest, hurrying along the narrow plank past the men and their sticky scent and grimy clothes. She walked onto the next and the next until at last she found what she came for.

One boat fit what she was looking for. She had no predetermined description of one, but she knew it when she saw it. It was forty feet of wood, a cabin painted in red and green rose above the deck. On the bow, it said Pantene. Piper knew the second half: tene loosely translated into "path to wealth."

Scanning the boat, she found the man whose aura signaled this was his boat. "Pan, is your boat for hire?" she asked in Portuguese.

Pan turned to her voice, his dark eyes emotionless. He jumped onto the shore, walked down the plank, and stood in front of her. He seemed to measure her worth in the time it took to get to her. "American dollars," he answered in near-perfect English.

Piper was taken aback; he looked like he had been born on this boat, she thought, but his English came from the Oregon coast. Piper put away her curiosity. "Alright. I...I...um, we need to get upriver…a long way. I don't know exactly where." Piper knew the quiver in her voice was making her vulnerable. She had already revealed that the two of them were alone, going upriver with money in their pockets. She was the ignorant white girl she looked like. She knew that he knew it too.

"I don't ask my clients why they are going upriver. It's not good business. But I sense I need to this time."

"I found Evenel." She pointed to Evenel. "In the city—"

"You bought her."

Piper hesitated. "Yes, I had to buy her. And I need to bring her home. But I don't know where that is, or what tribe she is from."

Pan took the shy little girl into his gaze. Her features familiar to a river captain. "I know where." Pan looked at Piper "She is Utay. That is not what she calls herself. It's what the outside world calls her valley. It means—"

"It means…no return." Piper finished.

Piper moved back through the gauntlet of planks. She had given Pan half the money, hoping he would still be there in the morning. She did not haggle over price, and she regretted that because it showed how vulnerable she really was.

She thought about the things she needed to accomplish as she walked back down the maze of planks. She started a list in her mind: call her parents, check out of the hotel, get some supplies and different clothes, find some bug spray and food—God knows what they served out there.

The man in a dirty white T-shirt scanned the planks from his usual place high on the hill where he stalked his prey. She stood out instantly. Her blonde head bobbed among the dark background of everything else.

"The American woman, with the purse full of cash. Got the Indian rat still with her too. An' she ain't downtown no more," he said to himself.

Here, on the river, he made his own law. The thought of stealing the Indian rat all over again made him grin. The gringa bitch. He would fuck her after he broke her neck, and he would use her money to buy more pussy. Some good stuff downtown just like her.

Piper, with Evenel holding her hand, walked up the worn stone steps rising from the river. They paid no attention to the dirty man standing on the curb. As they walked past the entrance of an alley between two brick buildings, the dirty man charged into them, knocking them both to the ground and into the entrance of the alley.

Piper skidded on her hands and knees, the skin peeling from both. She turned to see the silhouette of the man standing at the entrance, a large knife handle above his back.

"Evenel" she screamed. Piper scooped her up and ran down the alley. Her legs seemed concrete as she willed them to move faster. Fear-induced adrenaline choked her heart and lungs.

The footfalls clapped just behind her. Even Evenel's cries could not drown them. The alley turned and wound and dead-ended.

CHAPTER TEN

British Columbia

Jesse, Za, and the cook walked up to the diner, a dark and lifeless place on this, Jesse's first day of work. The brass bell on the front door sang out its warning as they pushed inside. The cook flipped a row of switches, and the fluorescent lights hummed in protest.

"Za, get your tourist busy mixing batter."

"My mama said I was Jesse. And you can talk directly to me when you need to."

The cook turned toward Jesse, shook an unfiltered Camel out of its pack, snapped open the cover of a lighter, and put its flame to the cigarette. "I don't need to." Gesturing toward the burning lighter, the cook put a finger on the top of the cover and closed it with a snap. "Got it?"

Jesse squinted, lowering his tone. "I could break that nasty habit."

She exhaled at Jesse. "The smoking or the asshole?"

"The asshole part."

"Yeah, that's what I thought." The cook moved past Jesse. "Now go find a spoon."

Za put an arm around Jesse's neck and patted him on the chest with his other hand. "Come on, I got a whole lotta work a bottom-feeder like you can take your anger out on." Jesse followed Za into a room in the back. Za pointed at a list stapled to the wall. "You mix all that stuff up. Then you do it again. Keep doing it until the cook says to stop. Got it?" Jesse nodded, and Za exited singing something.

The list started with a large bowl (under table) followed by eggs (in large cooler behind you) and continued on. Midway through the seventh batch, Jesse was pouring flour from a bag into the carnivorous bowl when the cook barked, "Stop. Get out front and bus."

"I'm halfway—"

The cook moved into the doorway. "Jesus, boy, you never work in food before? Get your ass out there."

Jesse threw the bag into the batch, splattering the counter. "I'm going to fuck you up—" but the cook disappeared before he could finish.

"Jesse!" Za came through the doors.

"What?"

"Get out here and bus tables."

Jesse pushed open the swinging French doors, slamming them against the counter. A guy wearing a dirty Skoal hat laughed out loud. "What's your problem?" Jesse growled.

"Why, it's you, princess," he said.

Za smacked a gray tub into Jesse's gut. "Clear off the tables, wipe them down, and wash the dishes in back. Do that till the cook says stop."

Jesse hesitated, taking it all in. Za clapped his hands in Jesse's face. "Jesus, you ever work food before?" Every table overflowed with dishes and T-shirted truck drivers, bearded men with grease stains and big appetites.

Hurrying, Jesse went to the first table. Four men were just sitting down; they picked up the leftover dishes and dropped them in Jesse's tub. Jesse got the dishrag from inside the tub. Before he could use it, one of the men wiped a ratty sleeve across the table, pushing the crumbs onto the floor. Jesse dropped the dishrag back into the tub and moved on.

Za came up to Jesse. "That's Johnny Huntoon you're picking a fight with."

"Which one?"

"The one who called you princess."

"He needed it."

"Well, first, that's the guy who ran you off the road, and second he is a paying customer. If that isn't enough, he's dangerous. You stay away from him."

"Move your ass, tourist!" the cook barked.

Jesse filled one tub and then another, until the tables were cleared. He glanced at Huntoon as he went into the back.

"You ever work food before, princess?" Huntoon called after him.

At the dishwashing station in the back, Jesse scraped the big stuff into an oversize garbage can, then sprayed the dishes down and stacked them. Over the next hour, Za would charge in, retrieving them while they were still wet and wiping them with his sleeve.

"Stop!" the cook shouted at Jesse. "Unload that garbage can. You can't lift it when it's that full. Goddamn it, tourist, you ever work in food before?"

Jesse grabbed the barrel by the handles, and it came an inch off the ground. It was twice as heavy as it looked. Duck-walking backward toward the door, Jesse ignored the strain that threatened to blow a nut.

Outside, the dumpster sat chest high. Jesse gripped the

handles, pulling upward with a mighty heave. The can rose from the ground and hovered well short of the dumpster's opening. The can hit the ground. Jesse jumped back, protecting his toes, and slime splashed on his boots. "Damn, that's disgusting." He scrunched up his face, staring at the napkins, eggs, hash, and other unidentifiable sludge.

Za slapped the door open and yelled, "I got no plates!" He went back inside as quickly as he had come out.

Jesse looked at the green-yellow snot in the barrel. He shoved both hands in to the elbows and pulled out what he could and dropped it into the dumpster. The snot ran down his arms and onto his back and chest. The stink overwhelmed him. He threw up a little in his mouth. He spit it into the barrel and dived for another load.

With the barrel half full, he took the handles and pulled, trapping the can against the dumpster. Putting a hand under the can, he strained with all his might. Slowly, the can inched up until the lip of the dumpster stopped it.

He struggled with the can, trying to bump it over the lip. More slime splashed in the air and landed in his hair. He yelled out and shoved with all his might. Finally, the can rose and fell into the dumpster.

He stepped back, flinging the slime from his hands and telling himself not to use them to pull the splashed gunk from his hair. Then he retrieved the can from the dumpster, wiping the outside with his hands. The can stink was bad, but the rotting food in the sun-drenched dumpster was ten times worse. He gagged, trying not to put his snot-covered hands near his mouth.

"Hey!" a voice rang out.

Jesse slowly turned to see two snickering truck drivers. "Ain't you never worked in food before, boy?"

❧

"Jesse!" the cook barked from the door. Jesse moved from the back into the front.

"Cleanup and lock down," Za said, turning the open sign around and slamming the door after them.

Looking around the diner, Jesse realized it was empty. The clock said four o'clock.

Jesse waltzed over to the front door, flipping his towel over his shoulder. He read the backward words on the glass: "*Weekdays open 5:00 a.m. to 4:00 p.m.*"

The white van pulled onto the pavement and headed up the mountain. Jesse gave them the finger.

Six showed on the clock through the front door glass when Jesse pulled the door shut. He shook the door, testing to be sure it was locked. He turned downhill, admiring his thumb. It or his boots would have to get him home. He had better finish that damn flying book soon, he thought.

CHAPTER ELEVEN

Sunday, first light. Jesse, Za, and the cook stood on top of Roundtop. The first rays broke over the horizon, rushing in, capturing their thoughts, reaching troubles, and locking them away.

The raptors glinted in the new light, elegant in the wind below them.

The valleys were coffee-colored, waiting for the dawn to awake the grasses. Above, the peaks' crystal blue indigo was edged with crimson light. Utter silence reigned as the singing insects awaited the warmth.

"First light is the best part of the day," Jesse said.

The cook exhaled. "Being right must be a new experience for you."

Jesse didn't reply, the morning magic having done its work.

"It's a great day to fly," she said. "Let's do it."

The trio unloaded the van and assembled the hang gliders.

Jesse had until this moment eagerly anticipated the thrill of human flying, the adrenaline sting, the thrill. Now moments away, his gut was turning.

The other two talked excitedly about the morning flight. Jesse said nothing. His instincts alleged that he had never jumped off a perfectly good cliff with nothing but an opinion some guy wrote in a book. His inner voice kept trying to reason with him, but he put it away only to have it surface again and again.

The launching point protruded out from the mountain, a good five hundred feet above the treetops below, just a flat rock where moss scavenged life from the cracks in the surface. The west edge rolled up and round, cracking away where a hundred-year-old pine battled the rock, each threatening to banish the other.

The cook and Za paid little attention to Jesse as they readied to launch. Jesse clumsily attempted to get in his harness. He caught his foot in the fabric and fell on his ass, glider and all. The aluminum pinged against the stone.

"Need a bunny hill, tourist?" the cook jeered.

"That's for pussssies," Za sang.

"He won't do it," she said.

Za replied, "He'll jump, might fly, might die, maybe get himself neutered. It's your turn to find another bottom feeder if he goes down in flames."

"I found this one," the cook protested, pointing at Jesse.

Za said, "My ass, I found him. You get another one."

Jesse struggled to his feet, hopping sideways to regain his balance, the glider tearing on the rock. He bounced onto his ass again. "Hey…fuck you two."

The cook smirked. "Let's go, Za, we need to be out of range of the blood splatter."

"But close enough to smell it, man," Za said, grinning back.

Za and the cook launched, shouting "COCOZA!" into the

budding day, the echo resounding back with the deep voice of the mountain.

Jesse was glad to be alone. He didn't want to jump, but he desperately needed to. Deep inside, survival lords over fear, and today survival meant not austerely coasting through life.

He took a mental inventory of everything he had read. His thought process stalled, and he had to start over again. Fear was doing its bidding. Harness attached. Wind direction, okay. Control bar at neutral position. What else...?

Jesse took a step, his legs numb. His heart thumped in his ears. Breathing, thunderous, shallow, drowning out all but the thump in his chest.

He had to swallow to set his guts back in place. A step from the edge. A beginning...or the end.

A crow flew past; the movement gave him the reason to stall. His knuckles went white from squeezing the control bar. He worked his fingers, but they seemed to hesitate. He blinked rapidly. Shuffled his weight. Reached down to throw a pebble out of the way. A long moment, he froze.

His mind in agony.

He snapped the door shut on his fear and jumped.

The canvas popped full, the frame creaking under the strain. The falling sensation stung his senses, pushing his panic. Instinct and reaction liberated him, and everything became clear and in slow-motion focus.

He pushed his control bar out. The glider stalled, shuddering like it was going to fold up and collapse. He fell like a stone. He pulled the control bar in to his gut, and the kite slid forward out of control.

The G-force pulled the blood from his brain, rendering his limbs useless. He was falling ferociously. Jesse forced the bar to the center. His weight settled into the harness, and the glider leveled off.

He was flying, and almost dying. The thrill he always

sought replaced the squeeze in his chest. The wind rumbled in his ears in a rhythmic chant. The scent of mountains coursed through his nostrils.

The great majestic scenes rolled past, streaking rivers sliced the green canopy into silver-lined stained glass, and the waterfalls sang their songs to him as they did the hawks and the eagles who soared with him.

His inner voice pulled him back, telling him to try his controls. Jesse leaned left carefully and the glider moved left. He leaned right. "It worked, thank God," he whispered.

Jesse broke into the same smile Za constantly had stuck to his face. He yelled "COCOZA!" Without the earth to drown it, the echo came back and thundered through him; the vibration lifted goosebumps along his arms. "That's why they do that," he said.

Jesse flared to a stop in the sky. This time, he enjoyed the sensation of falling, that slight moment without gravity before it pulled him down—only now he could cheat it.

He become harmonious with the wind, with the dive or stall, experiencing each new sensation flooding through him.

It's incredible, he thought. *Motion without means. Solitude without boredom. Serenity without peer.*

Below him, he saw the other two leaving Flattop. Jesse had been enjoying the excitement and not worrying about the landing. The first sin in the book.

He forced the book into his head. Again his thought process stalled. *Don't let the fear in*, he thought, and he squeezed his mind into action.

The plateau was maybe two hundred feet below, and he calculated how far east he had to tack to get within range of his descent. He cursed himself for not being prepared. The first thing you need to know when you launch is how to land. Take-off was optional—landing was not.

"Damn. I'm going to be short." He turned along the edge of

Flattop. "I'm too low, damn damn damn it." Trees like bayonets swayed below him. Pangs of fear pulsed along his torso.

Suddenly, the fabric groaned and the glider pulled toward the sky.

"The thermal!" he cried out, having forgotten about the uprising warm air along the edge. "Thank you, God," he said. "I won't be stupid again." By sheer luck, he was in position.

Aligning himself over the plateau with his book-taught knowledge, Jesse flared as he came over the landing.

He felt sure he was going too fast. Still ten feet over the plateau with the far edge coming fast, he had to drop fast or miss altogether. Pumping the control bar back and forth, he zigzagged down toward the limestone surface.

His feet met the ground. Sliding toward the edge, his forward motion refusing to stop. Panic tried to bubble into his head. He tripped along the rough surface as the glider caught the wind, dragging him through the thorns.

He grabbed for a branch, and the glider spun and rolled over, throwing Jesse into the air still bound into the harness.

The hundred-foot drop-off slid toward him at warp speed. The glider flopped over again. He reached out to grasp anything. The thorns raked him again along his torso and sliced his hands.

Red dust rose around him, and his sensation of falling subsided. When it cleared, he lay bloodied but alive on top of Flattop.

Jesse fought his restraints to free himself of the harness. He leaped, pumping his fist into the air, and he screamed his victory at the two distant flyers.

CHAPTER TWELVE

Manaus

"Oh my God, no, no, no." Piper slid to a stop and turned toward the man, hoping to run past him. He barreled into Piper, knocking her onto the ground. She lost her grip on Evenel, who rolled onto the ground next to her.

Piper's fear overtook her; she pulled her knees to her chest and crossed her arms over her face in panic. Evenel tried to crawl back onto Piper's chest, pulling at her arms, but Piper could not open them to her.

"Tasan! Tasan!" Evenel cried, trying to tunnel into Piper's arms.

The dirty man grabbed Evenel, pulling her away. Piper skidded backward on her elbows.

"Tasan...Tasan...help me!" Evenel screamed.

The cries awoke the lioness in Piper's heart. Her fear boiled over into anger. Evenel cried out again as she wrestled with the dirty man. Piper jumped to her feet.

The dirty man bent over Evenel, gripping the little girl's wrists. The machete sheathed on his back stuck out toward Piper. She grabbed it with both hands, withdrawing it from its sheath.

The dirty man let go of Evenel when he heard the unmistakable sound of the knife ringing from its scabbard. He stood up.

Piper felt the roar inside her swell to the surface, and she brought the great knife down on the man's thigh, cleaving it to the bone. She swung again at his face, stripping off his nose as the man fell backward, the screams of fear now his.

Piper gripped Evenel's wrist and swung the child to her breast. She hovered over the dirty man. He reached for his nose lying on the ground. Piper stomped it under her heel, the sounds of cracking cartilage bouncing off the alley walls. She turned toward the street, somehow no longer afraid.

At the street, they turned back to the river, the blood dripping from the machete in her hand. Her creamy skin was splattered, her hair streaming backward, glistening in its color, and the men on the planks rolled back out of her way.

"Pan...Pan, are you in there?" Piper called to the boat.

The shake in her voice cracked as the adrenaline drained from her bloodstream. Pan came out of the cabin. "I want to go now," she said.

Pan exhaled the smoke from the cigarette in his mouth; he nodded in agreement.

Piper stalked up the plank, Evenel in her arm, the sullied machete in her free hand. Piper jumped down onto the deck of the *Pantene*. She hacked the machete into the gunwale, and still holding Evenel, tossed the plank away from the boat. Piper gripped the machete handle and with a twist retrieved it into her hand.

Pan threw off the ropes, started the diesel, and motored through the boats, reeds, and debris of the river.

74

Piper carried Evenel into the cabin, she found a bunk in the back. Piper lay on the bed with Evenel still clutching her. Piper began to shake uncontrollably, the machete still stuck in her grasp.

The *Pantene* cut through the wide expanse of the great river. The sun had set, and the night was in command of the jungle. His clients slept now; Pan did not know the circumstances of their return to the boat. But he knew the river docks well enough to piece it together.

Usually he would hear of a creamy skinned woman hacked and dead, floating in the river, the body bumping into the boats until the creatures of the river finished it. This one must be hell on wheels.

Miles behind him, the glow of Manaus had gone; this was where he would begin to feel at home, in the jungle's river. Where the macaws sounded and the insects sang. Along the wilds, away from the laws of men.

Morning sunrise greeted the stern of the *Pantene*. Pan retrieved his machete and its sheath where it hung near the diesel. He opened the cabin door and walked in.

Piper awoke instantly. She spun to the floor, landing on her feet, the machete in her hands. Evenel lay behind her on the bed. Pan stopped, his face stiff and cold. He pulled his machete from its sheath. The lioness appeared inside Piper.

Pan tossed the sheath to her. "That thing will be easier to carry inside one of those." He backed out of the cabin.

Piper jumped at the sound of his machete thudding home in the outside wall of the cabin. Pan came back through the still-open door. He set down some fruit and hardtack. He smiled and left again, closing the door behind him.

Piper put down the machete. Evenel went around her and grabbed a banana in each hand. "I see you're okay," Piper said.

Evenel smiled. She handed a banana to Piper.

Piper looked at it. "There any ba-bacon over there?"

Days and nights the *Pantene's* diesel clinked upstream. To the unknowing eye, the river never changed, just kept moving along. Piper used the time to learn Evenel's language. But it wasn't easy. "Evenel come sit down, it's time for lessons."

Evenel sat with her back to Piper, rummaging through a wood box and examining bits of rope and old parts.

"Evenel, I know you can hear me."

Evenel stood up and wandered down the gunwale, pretending to be occupied by the passing trees.

Piper firmed her voice. "You know it's time for lessons."

Pan came around the cabin and picked up Evenel, poking at her belly. Evenel giggled and tried to push his hand away. Pan took the looped rope off the wheel, readjusted their course slightly, and put the rope back on the wheel.

"Why do you make her sit still for these lessons?"

"That is how you learn things."

"This is not Cincinnati."

"Tennessee, not Cincinnati."

"What is the difference?"

"Two states and the Mason-Dixon line."

Pan waved his hand in the air. "Whatever, this is not Tennessee. She has never learned anything by sitting for lessons."

Piper crossed her arms and stabbed herself with the pencil. "Ouch." She rubbed her side. "Then how do you do it?"

Pan put Evenel down and scooped some water from a bucket with a ladle. He poured some into Evenel's hand. "Water."

Evenel replied, "Lsse."

"We learned water days ago." Piper said. "How about drinking water, or pouring?"

"How about dipping?" Pan grabbed Evenel and dipped her head in the river.

She screamed and then roared with laughter as Pan spun her upright in his arms.

"Muj," Evenel giggled.

"That would be no," Pan said. He spun her around and held her by a heel over the side.

"Muj, ca etrc mipiu muj," Evenel cried out.

Pan dipped her again before spinning her in his arms again. "That would be, 'No! Don't dip me, no!'"

He put her down and she ran out of his gasp, shaking the water from her head. She smiled and came back and kicked him. "Usu!"

Piper laughed, "That would be bad."

Evenel repeated, "Bad."

The river branched again and again, each time becoming smaller, closing in on the *Pantene* until Piper could see both sides of the shore. Tall trees with white trunks skimmed the sky, and between countless green plants, some with giant leaves the size of elephant ears waved in the breeze. Strangler vines choked and clawed at the trunks of trees, each vying for the leftover sunlight. Still more trees and plants grew fernlike leaves, and seedpods hung from everything.

The riverbank constantly eroded away, leaving the yellow soil exposed, and roots hung in the water drinking life, and still more clung to the soil. They strained to keep the trees aloft until they too surrendered to the river, which washed them down, toward the next bend. Where the sand built sandbars, the river would eventually cut a new course, closing off the old riverbed and forming a U-shaped lake. Hundreds of times, the river left them abandoned in the jungle, never stopping or looking back.

Piper and Evenel peered over the gunwales, pointing at the trees and plants, listening to the buzz of insects and the cries of monkeys, repeating the words for sky, trees, clouds. They were like bandits upsetting Pan's work, and he seemed to delight in their mischief.

Sometimes Piper sat on the deck, recording the words and watching Evenel bouncing and running fore and aft so fast it seemed that any minute she would fall overboard. Piper loved the vernacular, its flavor, so derived from the earth, a language of nurturing.

"Piper…Pan! Moton…see…see!" Evenel pointed over the bow of the *Pantene*.

They came forward, and there racing alongside were the pink dolphins of the Amazon. They, too, seemed to be going home. "Moton-dolphin," Piper wrote in her journal.

Morning sun cleared the treetops when Piper pushed off from the side of the *Pantene* in the canoe Pan kept aboard. Now it was Evenel, her, and no one else. Pan had brought them as far as the *Pantene* could go in the shallow water.

The night before, she had begged him to go with her.

"This is your journey, finish it," he said.

"I can't, I don't know how—"

"That is why you have too. You will be afraid, and you will get bruised or worse, but you will find a way, and you will be the better for it."

"I don't need this…this trial by fire."

"Oh yes, you do."

She glared at him in the candlelight. "I paid you."

He laughed. "Your money will not change my mind out here. What good is it, out here in the wild? I won't go. So you can go back to Manaus, or you can take her home."

Now she was pushing a paddle on the biggest river in the world with a child in her care. She wondered how she had gotten here and if she would ever get back. She looked back at Pan on the *Pantene*. "Promise me you won't leave."

"I promise I will look for you if you don't come back."

"How will you do that? You don't have another boat to come get me."

"See, already you are asking the questions that will keep you alive."

"Pan!"

"I promise I will wait for you."

Piper put her paddle in the water and pulled it toward her. "You up there. Paddle."

Evenel cracked a smile; she turned forward and started paddling.

Piper kept repeating, "Oh my God, oh my God."

They pulled against the paddles, churning up river that whole day. Evenel had kept up a constant chatter in the beginning, but now she had been quiet for some time. She turned to Piper and asked, "Will Momma home?"

"Yes, she will be home." *Would the village even be there?*

The possibility had clouded her mind before. What if Evenel was all alone in the world? What if her family had moved or died? She shook it from her mind. Pan would have known that. The thought persisted, though, as the river turned and seemed to go nowhere. What if that is why he wouldn't come with them? If he abandoned them, they were doomed. He knew a lot about her, after all. During the long nights, they told their stories. Maybe that is what he did, find out who you were, then leave you to die, then ransom…

"Piper, look!" Evenel pointed ahead. A village rolled into

view. New energy ignited their muscles. Fatigue forgotten, they quickened their pace.

The huts sat away from the riverbank, but the shoreline was void of anyone. "Is that your village, Evenel?"

"Yes!" she replied. "My house."

Piper felt butterflies spinning in her gut. She suddenly realized she was going to lose Evenel. Her heart tore through her lungs and her throat and into her soul to pool into a forever void. Still she went on because the excited little girl was paddling holes in the water.

Piper and Evenel landed the canoe. The village was still a short distance from the river's edge.

Evenel jumped out, taking a few steps toward the huts, but she turned back and grabbed Piper's hand, pulling her down the small path with the grasses swishing across her arms and legs.

"Come on…Piper," she implored. "Go fast."

Hand in hand, they trotted to the village.

"Momma, Momma!" Evenel called out.

The path opened into a circle of huts. A woman, her back to the river, stopped her weaving. She whirled around to see her only child. She cupped her face.

The entire village came to their feet, and with Evenel's mother, rushed to Evenel, surrounding her in a sea of motion and emotion.

Her mother hugged her lost child. Evenel sobbed tears of relief, of home, of family, of that which only a mother's touch can release.

Piper stood outside of the circle with tears streaming down her cheeks. She had done it, and her reward played out before her now—this feeling, this precious memory, would never leave her.

CHAPTER THIRTEEN

British Columbia

She pulled open the door and stood in the doorway. The sun came through the opening, illuminating her form beneath her skirt.

Strutting past the stools, she circled a table and came back to where Jesse and Za stood in front of the counter.

She slid onto a stool, crossed her legs. Za was staring; Jesse felt like a stud who had just found a loose mare.

She was nineteen with jet-black hair cut at the breast… where the boys were stuck staring. All of five-foot-three, she was not petite, but she wore a voluptuous cut that flowed over her moneymaker and down to her exposed calves.

"Danny Cocoza." He put out his hand, forced his eyes to hers—they were caramel.

"Really? Then I've got the right place. Hallie Morgan."

Za said, "It became the right place when you got here."

Hallie pretended to blush. "Why, Rhett, how you do go on."

Jesse laughed, followed by Za and Hallie in succession.

"I'm Jesse, start with some coffee?"

"Um…yeah, that would be great."

Za gave Jesse a "get lost" head jerk. "Jesse would be happy to get it." Za slid right in beside her.

Jesse cursed his poor positioning. He went around to the back of the counter and grabbed the coffee pot. He poured her cup just as the brass bell tied to the doorknob rang, and in marched Ed and three other regulars. "You're late," Jesse said to them in a time-worn greeting. "I'm docking you an hour's pay."

Ed settled on his usual stool. He thumbed his nose at Jesse as he said, "I'm retired. I answer to no clock."

"Then why are you here at the crack of dawn every day?"

"Because the crack of Dawn is at home, and it ain't a pretty sight no more."

"Oh, you're going straight to hell for that one, Ed."

Jesse looked at Za and gave Jesse another "get lost" head jerk. Jesse left to take their orders.

Za turned on his stool to face Hallie. "I'll try that again. Why is this the right place?"

"Because I'm from Utah, and I hang glide," Hallie answered.

"You fly?" Za lit up like a candle. "But I don't get the connection."

Hallie sipped her coffee, flipping her hair over her shoulder. "Well, I'm waitressing at this job I've had all through high school. And this guy comes in, and we start talking. Turns out he's a truck driver, and right away we're talking about me and my flying."

"Hang gliding?"

"Yeah, three years now…anyway, the truck driver tells me that he just came from Canada where this guy talked about hang gliding and how they were going to be the first to fly these mountains in British Columbia and the guy had a stupid name like Googoodoll or Cocopuff."

"It's Cocoza." Za held his arms out in front of him. "Chicks love it."

"It's so hot." Hallie cooed, a teasing smile on her face.

Za stuck his great smile on his face. "British Columbia is a whole lotta ground. How did you find me?"

"Some detective work and a working knowledge of 'chicks with needs.'"

"What?"

"I just look really innocent and lost, and you guys are ready to drop everything to help my kind."

"A little tease, huh?"

"I prefer flirt." She smiled at him. "My whole life has been about getting out of my town. So I thought why not? I loaded my pickup and came to check it out."

"I've got fans, this is great."

"So how about a job? I've got experience." Hallie flipped her hair and looked away, flicking her eyelashes.

The bell rang out again, and customers poured in. Za handed her a menu. "Read that, order some breakfast, and when you finish, you can wait on the counter here. Jesse will take the tables."

"Hey, thanks, Danny."

"It's Za, short for Cocoza, but you already figured that out... yeah, um, let's talk flying after the morning rush."

Za got up and went over to Jesse. "She flies, man."

"Flies what? Planes?"

"Kites, you tourist. She flies hang gliders."

Jesse moved along the counter and picked up two plates full of eggs and toast fresh from the kitchen. "How long?"

Za grabbed two more and they delivered them to Ed and the others. "Turns out three years. She might be good, man."

"I'd say she'd look good doing it."

"She talks the talk, man. She's been around."

A customer sat next to Hallie. She started talking to him. He burst out laughing.

"Did you hire her?" Jesse asked.

"Yeah." Za put his hands in his apron pocket, staring at her.

"Oh, you are in so much shit."

"She's good, look at that guy, he is ready to kiss her ass."

"That would be twice today," Jesse said.

Hallie slipped around the counter, picked up an order pad, and wrote in it. She winked at them. They both gave a little wave. She turned to the order window and put the ticket on the turn wheel. "Order up!"

The cook came over to the wheel and slapped the spatula on the Formica. "Za! Come here!"

Hallie asked Jesse, "Who's that?"

"The cook."

"Why don't they call her Cookie?"

"You'll see."

Two more truckers came in. They looked around, and the first guy tapped his buddy on the shoulder, pointed at Hallie, and went around the empty tables to the counter.

When Za came out of the kitchen, the diner buzzed over the new waitress.

"Jesse," Za called out. Jesse picked up his gray tub and walked over to Za. "She's moving in with us," Za said, offering his hand for a high-five.

"Nice," Jesse said, slapping Za's hand. "I'm just impressed you're still alive. Is the cook jealous or just pissed?"

"I'm the new bottom feeder," Za said. "But I figure the way you fuck up, that won't be for long."

They, like everyone else, were watching Hallie. She crossed her ankles and leaned over the counter, winking at her customer.

"Worth every minute, man," Za said.

That evening, Jesse sat on the steps of the massive front porch of the old house. A small cooler sat beside him.

Hallie had moved into one of the bedrooms just down the hall from his. Cool breezes wandered back and forth across his face, trying to find a singular direction. Darkness overcame the pines, and now only the peaks pointed at the crescent moon. Jesse got up and walked to an evergreen tree. He stripped some needles from a branch and carried them to the steps. He sat and broke the needles into pieces. Fresh pine scent emitted from them.

He had showered and slipped into a favorite shirt. He slid toward the porch post, leaving just enough room for one more.

The brass hinges of the screen door sang their annoyance. Jesse opened the cooler and brought out two longnecks. They dripped on the porch steps, enhancing the pine needles. "I got everything but the girl here," he said without turning around.

A smile broke over Hallie's face. "Coronas, my favorite," she lied. She took one and sat down.

Jesse opened first hers and then his own. "A good friend got me started on them."

"A pretty friend?"

Jesse hesitated. "Yes, a pretty friend."

"Well then, here's to pretty friends on hot summer nights." Hallie clinked her bottle to Jesse's so hard he thought it would break. Hallie tipped her bottle and pounded down a swallow. Jesse did the same, not wanting to be outdone.

"My God, it smells good out here. Is that you?" She leaned into Jesse's collar and drew a deep breath.

"Essence of stud. Makes the chicks horny."

"It's pine needles, smart ass," she said. "Za! Come have a beer with Jesse and me."

Za came out of the house, and because there was no room

next to Hallie, he sat down next to Jesse. Za opened the cooler. Nothing but ice.

"Yeah, we're out," Jesse said with a gotcha grin on his face.

"Yeah...um, can't be out of beer, man." He moved off the porch toward the van. He dug in his pocket for his keys, then turned back, "Hey, want to—"

Jesse gave him a "get lost" head jerk.

"Right. So Hallie, what's your brand?"

"Corona!" she whooped, swinging her fist in the air. "Make baby loco!"

"Why do you fly?" Jesse asked after Za and the van were lost to the dark.

Hallie giggled. "You're going to laugh at me."

"I promise." He pinched his lips tight with his hand, then burst out laughing. "Wait." He shook his head and pinched his lips again, mumbling, "I promise."

"Okay, I had to write a paper on it once so I really thought about it...fly...you promise?"

Jesse was still holding his lips shut with his fingers. "Mmm-ummm." He clamped his other hand over his mouth.

"Flying is about the breath of the land, the scent of the landscape, the bold color of the ever-imaginative sky, as free as angels to soar in my ailing heart."

Jesse sat motionless and silent.

Hallie said, "What?"

Jesse picked up some of the pine needles by his feet. Rolled them in his fingers. "Flying is edgy, time stopping and powerful. Only the music of the dance is with you, turns flow as liquid. Gut-wrenching drops secrete adrenaline, mixes with the endorphins. Utopia feeds from me into the wind and I am truly alive."

Hallie turned to Jesse, met his eyes, and burst out laughing, spilling her beer over both of them and slapping at his arm. Jesse followed suit.

"Sorry," she said, mopping at the beer on Jesse's arm. "What you said…that is so over the top and so true. Did you just make that up?"

"No, I wrote it down right after the first time I flew."

"When was that?"

"Few weeks ago."

"Oh my God, really? Here in the mountains?"

"Yes, just started, but I am the brains of this outfit." He poked a thumb into his chest.

"Oh really, how's that?"

"All right, Miss Nonbeliever. You got the story from Za today about the six peaks?"

"You're not going to tell me again, are you?"

He bumped her shoulder with his, sending her sprawling on the steps. "You're all sass."

She laughed really loud and sat up. She slid over, smacking her hip into his and trying to knock him over. "I'm the girl your mother warned you about."

"You want this story?"

"Yes." She chugged from her bottle and flipped her locks back.

"Well, I calculated the distance between all of the peaks and the altitude needed to get there with different wind directions and wind speeds."

"How'd you do that?"

"You just be quiet and I'll tell you."

Hallie nudged him in the ribs.

"Ouch. Jesus, you are a fireball."

"And?"

He pointed with his bottle. "It's possible to get from Roundtop back to Roundtop…on paper. It's possible on three of five days by leaving from different directions, using different winds."

"How far did you guys get?" Hallie asked.

"Two peaks."

Hallie jumped up. "Woo hoo, I am going to be the first one to do it." She flicked her hair again and held her arms out.

"That's pretty cocky."

Hallie put one hand on her hip and the other behind her head. She rolled her hips around and banged them to the side. "That's me, baby!"

CHAPTER FOURTEEN

The Amazon

Piper wiped her nose on the back of her hand while Evenel hugged her mother like she would never let go. The crowd swelled and engulfed Piper in the ebb and flow of the group. She became part of the celebration.

Shouting and singing, the circle rotated in a swirl, pulling Piper to the center. She jumped up and down with the rhythm, laughter bursting from her lungs.

Evenel reached out and drew Piper in. She put an arm around Piper's neck and the other held her mother's. Piper burst into tears again, and the three cried and hugged and held on to that human phenomenon that is family, that which could not ever be taken again.

Slowly, the crowd dispersed, and Evenel and her mother, Deza, retreated to her house along with Piper. The house was built of log uprights and poles lashed together with rope, palm fronds layered over the poles formed the roof.

Hammocks hung from the poles and functioned as the only furniture. The aroma of campfire and soil, humidity and plant, circulated through the open structure. Sun and heat dominated all things, even in the twilight of day.

An old woman stopped to congratulate Deza. Her arms and chest were tattooed, and grey hair lay on her shoulders. Deza introduced her as Nokai, her best and oldest friend. Between the many interruptions of other well-wishers, Piper told Deza how she had found Evenel tied to a pole in Manaus and what transpired to return her home.

The procession reminded Piper of her own home, where her mother's friends dropped off homemade baked goods or even entire meals whenever Piper came home from college.

When Piper had finished her story, Deza said, "Evenel, I have to cook so you have to let go."

Evenel nodded her head and crawled off her lap. She moved to Piper's lap.

Deza ambled over to the fire pit and placed a pot full of water in to prepare the evening meal.

"Can I help? I mean, will you show me how to cook?" Piper asked.

"Do you not cook in your village?"

"No." Piper felt hot pangs of guilt. "Someone else makes it for us."

"What is your value then?"

"I um…learn about other people."

"A gossip."

"No, I learn about people and why they do the things they do."

"A gossip," Deza demanded, and then she laughed aloud. Piper did too.

Deza placed dry leaves on the embers in the fire pit. She blew on the embers, and a small flame burst from the leaves.

She fanned the flame gently with palm fronds, adding wood until a small fire burned vigorously.

"What are we making?" Piper felt the pleasure of discovery overcome her, directly followed by dread. The food on the *Pantene* did not leave an impression, and she had lived on canned peaches and peas. At any rate, she was sure it wasn't SpaghettiOs.

Piper put Evenel down, took her hand, and followed Deza to a tree near the hut where a dead monkey hung from a rope. She handed the monkey to Piper. Flies buzzed from the carcass.

"Oh. It's not what I expected."

Deza said, "Burn the hair off."

Piper stood with the monkey in her hand, wide-eyed at the request. "How?"

Deza put her hands on her hips. "You have never burnt the hair from a monkey?" "No."

"You eat your monkey with hair?"

"No, I do not eat my monkey with hair on it. I do not have monkeys where I live." Deza looked stunned. "Take it to the fire and hold it over the flames."

Piper did as instructed. The smell was instant. She coughed involuntarily.

"Is there no burning hair in gossip?" Deza broke into a hearty laugh.

Evenel giggled too. Piper stood with one hand on the monkey and one covering her face.

"What?"

"Is there no burning hair in gossip?" she said bouncing on one leg, covering her face like Piper.

Piper waved her hand in front of her face, hacking away. "Oh my God, it stinks." She threw up in her mouth a little.

"Lay it in the fire," Deza said.

"What?"

"Lay it in the fire," Deza repeated.

"Just let go?"

Evenel took the monkey and dropped it in the flames.

"A gossip," Deza confirmed while Evenel nodded agreement.

Away from the smoke, trying to occupy her mind with anything but her culinary options, Piper looked around the circle of huts and the twenty or so people in the village. "Where are the men? I only see women and children."

"Now turn it," Deza instructed.

Piper stood dumbfounded, not wanting to touch it or see the little face connected to the monkey. Deza reached into the flames, quickly picked the monkey out, and flipped it over in the fire. A trio of kids called to Evenel and she trotted off.

"Are the men away?" Piper said.

Deza poked at the fire, turning the logs. The flames roared. "Our valley is a dangerous place. Many times men go into the jungle and never come back."

"I don't understand. Why don't they come back?"

The monkey hair smoldered. "A year ago, the village across the river had a killing. The man who was murdered was their headman. The man who killed him is as evil as a man can become. Bring it over to me now," Deza instructed.

Piper hovered over the monkey, determined to do this.

"Just grab it," Deza said.

Piper reached in and grabbed a foot, yanking the monkey smartly from the fire. She gagged again.

Deza pointed to the ground, and Piper dropped it. Deza gave Piper a flat stone with one sharpened edge. "Scrape the hair from the hide," she instructed, motioning with her hands.

Piper kneeled over the smoking carcass and slid the stone hesitantly across the burnt hide, scraping away the hair. She scraped the same area several times.

"Push *hard*," Deza said. She took the stone from Piper and demonstrated the correct motion.

Piper began again and Deza corrected her again, then she said, "Under the arms and the crotch too."

When Deza was satisfied, she took the carcass and tossed it on top of the embers. The scent was better, but the still-attached head stared vacantly at her from the embers. Deza pushed at the carcass with a stick. "Our men go to hunt and never return. Now all are gone, and we have no one to hunt. We fish nearby, and sometimes we trap a monkey close to the village."

"Are you saying someone killed them?"

"Yes." Deza pushed at the carcass.

"Well, have there been..." Piper searched for the translation. She rolled her hands together and finally just used her English: "Um um, arrests?"

Deza shook her head in confusion.

Piper realized there were no arrests out here. Murder must be served with murder. She gasped. For her, that only happened on cop shows. "You mean all of them...dead?" Her skin crawled. "Even your, um, um, headman?"

"The devil tricked him and sent word to us that he should come meet the new headman Tohanna. And they killed him. This is not something we talk of with outsiders."

"Why?"

"Respect your elders. It is not your place to ask after this."

"Yes, I am sorry," Piper replied.

"Our headman told us when to hunt and said when the rains will come and when to plant manioc. Now we have no headman, and it is hard. Nokai, my old friend," Deza pointed to the old woman with the tattooed arms, "her husband was killed in front of the waterfall. Nokai and he had crossed the river to gather roots. They came out of the forest and slaughtered him.

"Every night I have a dream. In my dream I run from hut to hut, and everyone is dead, their heads crushed, and I scream. But I sometimes feel that is better...better than waiting until there are no monkeys and no fish left to eat. I don't know what we are going to do."

Deza reached into the fire and pulled the monkey out. She split the monkey open with a worn knife, removed many of the innards, and placed them in the boiling pot along with some of the meat and the head. She put the rest back on the fire. "Evenel came back to me, and because of that, we have hope that others will return."

"They can't all be…gone. How long have they…the men in the village been gone?"

"The last one? I don't know, months ago, many widows there are. Some of them are killed, like Nokai's husband, in front of their eyes, and some never come back."

"Someone has to do something. Why hasn't someone done something to stop it?"

Deza waved her hand toward the huts. "Those who did something are dead. They have left us to pay for their foolishness."

Deza poked at the monkey with the stick again. This time it slid in easily. "It is time to eat."

Evenel showed up, rubbing her belly.

Deza handed the monkey to Piper, offering her the chance to take the succulent pieces.

"I don't know what to do," Piper said.

Deza took the monkey and twisted an arm. It peeled back like a Christmas turkey drumstick. She handed it to Piper and then took the other for herself. Deza then dipped a bowl for each of them from the pot. Evenel expertly opened the monkey's skin with her fingers and stripped meat from the bone.

Determined, Piper gripped the meat between the bones with her fingers and hesitantly pulled if off. She brought it to her mouth and forced it in. It didn't taste like chicken. Evenel picked pieces out of her soup bowl and chewed them. Piper wasn't going there. She picked at the monkey, more picking than eating.

Deza cut the stomach from the monkey and split it open. She scooped out the contents and deposited them into a bowl.

She added water and swirled it around until it looked like green oatmeal. Chunky green oatmeal with a biting odor. She drank from the bowl and then handed it to Evenel, who poured it down her throat, slurping away. Piper hoped and prayed that Evenel had the capacity to finish it, but Deza snapped a warning and the bowl passed to Piper.

Piper swirled the bowl. Under closer examination, it looked just like vomit.

Two little girls ran over and waved for Evenel, yelling, "Evenel, come and play." Evenel stood up and took a step.

"Evenel," Deza snapped. "Sit and eat your monkey."

She sat down and gave her playmates a frown. Piper quickly handed the bowl to Deza, nodding her approval. She hastily picked up her soup bowl.

Deza scooped the monkey head from the pot, an eyeball hanging from its socket "for our guest," and plopped it in Piper's bowl.

Piper lay in the empty hammock next to Deza, who slept with Evenel in her arms. She wondered if this hammock belonged to the man of the house. To Evenel's father, her *tasan*. Outside, the jungle teemed with noise. She wondered if she should be afraid, for nothing sat between her and the insects, the snapping twigs, or the killer Tohanna.

Deza slept soundly with Evenel burrowed under her arm. The stars endlessly dotted the black sky; the air was hot and Piper could smell her own skin. Sleep came deep in the night, after her mind had been made up.

The next morning, Deza and Evenel set off with Piper in the canoe. Deza sat in the front. "My husband," Deza said, "he left with Evenel down the river and never came back." She dipped her paddle once, then again. "Did you find my husband?"

Piper stopped paddling. She thought about how to say this. For a long moment, she said nothing. A bird lifted from its perch. She paddled, splashing outward.

Deza turned to her, her face ready.

The word rolled from Piper's lips: "No."

Deza turned and resumed paddling. Sobs drifted back to Piper. Evenel moved forward in the canoe and put her arms around her mother, hugging her back. "Mama Mama Mama" she whispered, laying her face against her mother's back. "Tazan tazan tazan." She wept with her mother.

The river turned again and again, and the soft wind brought scents of the jungle to them…dark scents and flowing water and salty tears. "I cried for him and for Evenel because they were lost. Now I cry for him because he is dead." Deza looked toward the trees and up to the canopy. She wiped her tears with her hand and swiped them across Evenel's face, collecting her tears also. She put them in the water upon her palm and she lingered there, the three liquids as one. She put her labor to the paddle, and the canoe cut the river, ever forward.

The current brought them to the *Pantene* near mid-day. Pan sat on the deck, repairing one of the many ropes, his fingers expertly weaving the fibers.

Evenel called out to him. "Pan? Pan? Are you sleeping!"

Pan stood up and grinned. "I'm working, Little Bandit." He held out the rope as proof.

The canoe glided alongside the *Pantene*, and Pan reached over and caught them. They climbed aboard, and Evenel jumped into Pan's arms, charming him with her signature giggle.

"You found her people," he said.

"This is her mother, Deza."

Pan nodded. "They coming with us?"

"No." Piper went inside the cabin and lifted the lid of a trunk. She had hidden several one-hundred-dollar bills between the pieces of the delaminated trunk. She retrieved the bills and returned to Pan.

"I need to pay you for the canoe, some supplies, and our original fee."

Pan waived her off. "You pay me in Manaus."

"I'm not going to Manaus."

Pan put Evenel down and lit a cigarette. "You are not from here. You have no idea what you have to do to survive here. And I don't mean that it will be tough. I mean that you will die."

"I'm staying, Pan. You don't know what has happened to these people, they need me."

Pan snorted. "They need you?" He pointed at Deza. "Has it occurred to you that you are just a burden to them?"

That had never occurred to her. She crossed her arms. "You can't talk me out of it."

"I can make you," he snapped.

She held out the money. "No money in that."

He snatched the money away and threw it on the deck. "You are a stupid gringa."

Piper picked the money up and put it in his hand. "I am a stubborn gringa."

He pulled the stub from his mouth and exhaled. "The jungle is hard, and people die every day. I don't know why I should care." He walked toward the cabin.

"I want canned peaches and canned peas. And lots of hardtack. You won't believe what I ate back there."

He turned and came back, pointed in her face. "I can kill a pig and eat it and the fleas that crawl on it, because I am born in the jungle. When you can do that, then you will earn your keep with them. You learn and you follow what they tell you to do, before your meddling gets them killed."

"And I need to write a letter to my family. And you have to mail it for me."

He folded his arms.

97

"Please."

"Be sure you tell them you did this on your own account, gringa."

Piper sat on the stern; she struggled with what to say to her family. She couldn't tell them the truth—that she was living in the jungle—because her mother would send the marines. At the same time, she didn't want to lie. Her family had to realize she was grown now and doing this of her own free will. She thought about how she had stood up to the dirty man twice, and Pan too. But they weren't her mother.

Finally, she crossed her fingers and her toes and began writing.

Pan let Deza shop from the supplies on the *Pantene*, and then he loaded the canoe along with Piper's machete. Afterward, Pan moved to the stern and put one leg on the rail. "The canoe is full with you three. Nothing else will fit. Deza cleaned me out."

She folded the letter, reached in her pocket, and removed the roll of American bills. She added the letter to them and held it out for Pan. "Thank you."

He took the money and the letter. "When you are ready to go home, if you are still alive, come back to this spot and wait. Every few months, I go past…You know, if you need help, I can't help you…not me or anyone else."

Piper heard his words but slapped them from her mind before they could reach her. "I know."

Deza and Piper climbed into the canoe. Pan was holding Evenel. He kissed her cheek, and she bear-hugged him the way only little girls do. He lowered her into the canoe.

Piper pushed off the side of the *Pantene*. She turned the canoe around, and the three pulled against the great brown river of their home.

CHAPTER FIFTEEN

British Columbia

As usual, the cook left first from the south approach. Music in its most fluid form is how you would describe her flying a hang glider. The glider fell, then corkscrewed on the way to Flattop. It would be a flight without mistakes, as always.

Hallie leapt from the sheer face seconds later. She belted out "Cocoza!" as she followed the cook toward Flattop.

"Love it, man." Za grinned at Jesse and then fell off the cliff. "CO-CO-ZZAAAA!" trailed behind him.

Jesse checked his wrist altimeter, visually inspected his harness and the canvas, then checked the setting on his altimeter again. Here he was again, stalling, unable to make that leap. He pulled a deep breath. "Okay, I jump off Roundtop, fly to Flattop, circle, and find the thermal to gain elevation, then on to Pinhead, repeat the thermal. Then fly to Backbone, rise on the thermal and look for the sweet spot to get on top." He pulled a long breath and jumped. "CO-CO-ZZAAAA!" he wailed and felt the rush that grabbed his ass after stepping off solid ground into space and the unknown, everything speeding by, negative G's sucking on his brain, giving him fear, falling, and adrenalin coursing through his veins. "*Co-co-za!*" echoed back, hit the raspy rock, and vibrated in stereo. Shivers pulsed through him.

He pushed out on the control bar, and the glider caught the wind, defying the earth's pull. The air was as cold as the first plunge into a mountain lake.

Jesse thought Za was having more fun than God intended. He was flying reckless, looping and banking, pulling off stunts Jesse couldn't do.

A minute later, Jesse dipped along the side of Flattop, moving ever closer to the edge and searching for the lift. The glider jumped skyward in the thermal at the same instant the sunlight hit Jesse, rose-colored through the red fabric.

A hundred feet above Flattop, Jesse turned into the sun in order to stay in the thermal. He could see the western sky and the Pin.

Jesse couldn't see Za above him, but he could hear Za whooping and singing Queen's "We Are the Champions," cluelessly out of tune. Jesse checked his wrist altimeter; he had gained the minimum altitude the chart said he needed to reach the third peak, Pinhead. The glider flexed with the sound of metal and canvas, signaling that he had hit the top of the thermal. He cut for the Pin.

Across the full breadth of vision, silver coated lakes reflected the sun, decorating the forest with abstract shapes. Clouds nestled between peaks. Every mountain was adorned with tamarack, cedar, and resilient pine climbing the peaks until the icy air cropped them and exposed gray basalt, serrated rock spearheading to the heavens. The irregular terrain rolled past him, up and down, like a jade dragon.

The trees kept getting closer, the Pin rushing toward him.

Jesse came in from the east, circling the Pin to the west, all the time the trees getting closer like needles pointing at him. He had one chance to catch the thermal before he would be in the trees.

His muscles stung with alarm, his brain screaming out the looming danger. Coming around to the west face, Jesse moved closer to the rock face of the Pin, searching for the thermal.

The thermal swirled upward, the glider creaked again under the strain, and Jesse felt the stress fall from his muscles.

Twice more he circled back to the face and out again, each time the thermal lifting him toward the top of Pinhead.

The next pass was always the worst, right under the rock where the thermal hung close to the boulder. You had to fly under the rock outcrop and then somehow float back around it and stay in the thermal. Jesse came once again toward the rock face, this time the shadow of the overhanging face blanketed the cliff.

Suddenly he couldn't see. Full-blown fear rifled through him. He jerked quickly left. The glider stalled and dived.

It took all his power to draw a breath. He felt like he had to concentrate to keep his heart beating. His chest squeezed so badly it hurt. The glider caught the air and bounced, the aluminum singing in pain.

Terror raged through him, shaking his body and sending his heart cutting from his chest. *Run away*, he thought, *go back, get out of here.*

The trees went for miles, and without the thermal, he would never get back or high enough to reach the clearing at the Backbone.

Jesse put his fear in a bottle and corked it. Time was running out. Another few seconds and he would be below the thermal.

Turn. Do it now. The glider wobbled toward the rock face.

Three times he circled, climbing in the rising air. Each turn brought him closer to the black shadow. The anticipation of facing the dark threatened to overwhelm him, rushing toward him like a plague.

He had to fly into the rock face blind, stall in the thermal, then turn before he hit the stone and fell into the trees.

He felt nauseated. The shadow crossed him, and his pupils strained to adjust to the shadow. Icy air stripped him of confidence. He retched abruptly, and the vile contents of his gut blew into his mouth and out. He wiped his mouth with his hand, and the glider reacted, pitching him sideways.

The rock face sped toward him again. He put his arm out, bracing for the impact and disturbing the load. The glider banked and scratched along the rock, bouncing him back into the thermal and lifting him over the top. The sun struck him, and he gained control.

Like an angel's embrace, the sunshine flooded him with warmth. He concentrated on his breathing, taking deep breaths, deep breaths; his altimeter went off and startled him. He was sure it was wrong. He had to be higher, a lot higher than he was now. He ignored the damn thing.

He kept circling high above Pinhead, climbing until he recognized himself. Never had he been that terrified. He didn't want to move if it meant challenging another rock face. Not ever...he would stay on the ground after this. *After this*, he thought. But right now, the choices loomed: get to the Backbone or punch into a tree.

The thermal gave out, and the glider creaked and fell. Panic bit again, freezing him as the glider fell, losing altitude. He concentrated on his arms and regained control, steering for the Backbone.

As Jesse sailed toward the Backbone, his heart calmed down, but something inside was gone. All he wanted was to get out of this thing. Ahead, he saw the other gliders swimming in front of the Backbone, climbing to get over the top. No one ever had.

The cook moved along the top edge, waiting for the moment. Banking suddenly, the glider ran at the top, lifted, and the winds swept it back.

The cook folded with the glider and fell like a stone before swooping to a recovery. Jesse thought a fall like that couldn't be recovered. The glider fell below the trees and landed.

Jesse had no idea how to save himself from that. A sharp sting ran down his spine and hollowed out his gut.

Hallie and Za tried, and they too fell like a shotgun folds a dove.

Jesse, a prisoner caught in a sling, watched. He sucked for wind to cry out but nothing came.

Both of them pulled out before the ground crushed them.

Jesse came over the top of them. They were out of their harnesses, and Hallie waved at him. He banked along the wall, his kite rising in the thermal and the wind buffeting in his ears. He passed back and forth, flying along the cliff and climbing toward the top, until his mind screamed, *Land before you get yourself killed!* He veered away from the cliff, out of the thermal.

"Chickenshit!" shouted the cook.

Pride and anger blew through Jesse on a hot wire. He hated her and he hated Hallie and he hated Za. They wanted him dead, fine, then he could deliver.

He banked hard, back into the thermal, and pumped back and forth along the face of the cliff, lifting higher and higher.

Near the top, he saw the one spot he had said would put a glider over the top.

One more pass and he would be high enough. Jesse banked at the north end and turned back, afraid to get too high where the wind sweeping across the top would blow him away from the cliff.

The sweet spot was coming…he tried to concentrate, but his mind wouldn't move. The closer the sweet spot came, the less he could think. Panic grabbed his throat.

The sweet spot raced toward him. Jesse steeled himself, he burnt it into his mind, but reason was running away on him. He turned sharply, directly toward the wall in front of him. He pushed out to lift, the rock face coming like a bullet.

He froze, surrendering his well-being, handing the rest of his life over to leprechauns and pixie dust.

The glider floated up and over the top and deposited him on top of the Backbone in a heap, skinning his elbows and crushing his fingers into the rock. Lying on the ground, fear coursed through him in lightning bolts.

Hallie and Za screamed his name like he was Elvis. He had been right: the Backbone could be flown.

Jesse inched his knees under him like a caterpillar and stood up. He waddled over to the side of the cliff and jumped. He glided down to his reception, hitting the ground hard in a cloud of dust, unhooked and tossed the glider away from him.

"You son of a bitch, what a ride!" Hallie jumped on his back. "I want a ride like that!"

Jesse flopped on the ground. Za pile-drived them, forcing grunts from both of them. The cook hesitated, then fell on the pile.

They celebrated rolling around, bringing the moment and the sunshine inside. Hallie kissed Jesse and then Za. The cook rolled off the pile. "Come get it, baby!" Hallie called out.

The cook squinted back. "Fuck you all. Get this shit loaded up."

"Hey, this is how friends are made," Hallie said.

"This is how good life in the fast lane is, man," Za added. "The next time we all get over the top, then we are gonna shoe the Horse."

"What horse?" Hallie asked.

"The Horseshoe baby. The next mountain in the way." Za snorted. " Hey, Cookie, that damn horse is gonna bite you in the ass, and while he's chewing you up, I'm gonna fly right through."

"I'm not carrying your shit out. Move your ass," the cook said.

Jesse saw his chance. He jumped up. "Hey, Hallie and I will go get the van while you lovers quarrel." Jesse grabbed Hallie's hand and scooped her onto her feet and down the slope before the cook could take over.

CHAPTER SIXTEEN

Jesse led Hallie through the woods on the way to the van. "Woo hoo!" Hallie shouted. "I feel like I can fly...oops, I already did that!" She jumped over a log following Jesse. She knew he was smart and he kept his ass taut—two things she liked in a man. "Hey, Chuck Yeager, how did you know you were going over the top? When you got to the Bone, I said to Za, 'He is gonna smear his ass all over that cliff.'"

Jesse pulled a branch back and said, "I thought, 'If I don't make it, Hallie will have to wipe my ass off that cliff.'" He let go of the branch so it sprang in her face.

"Aaahh!" she yelled, busting him to the ground. "I'll put a boot in your ass!" Hallie pushed Jesse's face into the dirt. "Eat it!"

Jesse pushed himself up to his knees and stood up, still carrying Hallie on his back. Hallie felt surprised and pleasured by his strength. He swung around like a madman, trying to throw her, but she squeezed his waist with her legs just like a girl from Utah oughta.

She shrieked her pleasure as Jesse swung around, trying to dislodge her. She swung around to his chest and found herself face to face with him. Both of them giggled like kids.

"Give?" Hallie asked.

"Never!" He reached for her arms, trying to pull her off.

Hallie grabbed a branch and pulled Jesse off balance, tipping him over backward. She landed on him, her curves fitted to him. She pinned his wrists down, yelling like she had just ripped up the 101st Airborne. "Now you give?"

"You promise you'll stay where you are?"

"Damn, you're cocky. Now tell me how you knew you weren't going to die on that cliff."

"I didn't."

Hallie rolled off him to sit on the ground. "Really?"

Jesse hesitated. "That's not entirely true. I did accept it could kill me, but once I turned into the cliff, I panicked, froze up. I was so scared. It was up to somebody else if I died. Beforehand, I knew where I could get over the top; it was a mathematical certainty. But when I got on the glider I lost all that, it was not up to me anymore." Jesse rolled and sat up next to Hallie.

"Right now it's not something I want to do again." He plucked some grass and ran it through his fingers. "But if I don't—"

"You won't be you again till you do."

"Yeah."

"So don't. Who cares if you don't fly? It won't define you."

"Like you would quit. I say being a man-killer up there defines you."

"Well, yeah, I get my rocks off up there, and I like to crush a few balls. Not like they don't need it."

"Well, I got some pride too. Got some alpha dog in me. I

may be the new kid out here on the mountain, but I won't quit."

"Alpha? The cook's got all the alpha from what I see."

"That's because I got a brain. They have something to teach me, and I am smart enough to lap it up. I can follow orders when the situation calls for it. The cook's not the first drill sergeant crawling over me."

"Alright, puppy, who are you anyway? I mean why are you here?"

"That's a long story, I should save it for a wine and a moon."

Hallie felt a hot ping run from her head down to her hips.

After making their way to the road, they hiked toward the van. "Hey, I hear a truck coming," Hallie said. She stuck her thumb out and struck a pose. "Watch this." The rig slowed and pulled over.

"Aw, crap," Jesse said. "It's Huntoon."

Air brakes hissed and country music wafted out from the cab when Hallie opened the door and crawled in. She rolled onto her hip on top of the console between the seats while Jesse sat in the passenger seat. Then she slid over onto Jesse's lap. "Thanks for picking us up."

Johnny Huntoon was indeed impressed. "Can't pass up a specimen like that, honey. You got more curves than a mountain road." He spit out the window. "Where you two goin'? Hitchin' to the diner?"

"No, we are on our way to pick up our van."

"Well, I never did figure you hash slingers to be flyboys. That is, I can't believe you work, course it don't take much to wait on people."

"We enjoy helping people, even the one's who can't make change. And who run people off the road," Jesse said.

Huntoon's eyes narrowed to slits.

Hallie jumped in. "Everybody just wants to have some fun." She gave Jesse google eyes.

"Fun is for little boys and girls with dolls. A man has to work. Hard work. Doin' a job meant for women tells a lot about some people."

Jesse shot back, "So does a job where you don't have to be any smarter than the truck."

The jake brake sounded through the cab, slowing the rig, shutting off conversation.

Huntoon swung for the turn that would climb up the mountain. The diesel took over on the uphill and blasted through the cab with its distinct knock. Huntoon pushed the radio past the knock. "You ever have a real job? Or I suppose you a college boy." He shifted, and the cab lurched under the strain. "I asked you a question. You too good to answer me?"

Jesse stared ahead. Hallie elbowed him. "Yeah, I went to college, and I own a share of a construction company. I do steel jack work too. Before that I slaved on a farm."

"You don't look it to me. If you all that high and mighty, why ain't you there?"

"I like the scenery. Too bad the place is polluted with shit-kickers and inbreds."

Hallie broke in, "Damn, is it me or is there too much testosterone in here?"

Huntoon shifted, spit in the can next to her foot. "You smile pretty and talk when you talked too. Ain't nobody want to hear a woman babbling their nonsense. I swear they ought to make aprons long enough so you can gag 'em with it."

Hallie lifted off Jesse's lap, but he pulled her back. "Well, fuck you, you ignorant dick. Let go of me, Jesse!"

"Jesus, she a mouthy bitch. I guess you ain't man enough to control your woman. Too soft to bitch slap her? I bet you wear that apron around the diner 'cause she says to. Am I right, Nancy?"

"Stop this thing." Hallie opened the door. "I want out before I kick his ass."

Huntoon smirked. He stomped the brakes. Hallie jumped before the rig stopped. She hit the ground and rolled. Jesse jumped after her, but the rig had stopped. Hallie got to her feet.

Huntoon said, "I got a load right up the road a piece. You get home right quick before I come around. Sometimes this rig don't want to stop."

"Yeah, I know firsthand," Jesse said. "Asshole." He slammed the door shut.

"What a prick," Hallie said, checking for cuts.

"You all right?"

"Yeah, I'm fine."

"Just another redneck." Jesse shrugged. "Forget about it. Another mile or two to the van, we can walk it and you can cool off."

After they got the van, they drove to the Backbone and picked up the cook and Za.

Za grilled Jesse about the Backbone all the way to the house, his excitement bubbling over tomorrow's flight.

The cook started supper while the others pored over maps and weather data. Soon, chicken fried steaks and fried potatoes crackled in the kitchen. "Set the table, tourist," she barked.

"I got it," said Hallie. She went to the kitchen and put the mismatched dishes and tableware on the table.

"Tell me your entire approach, man." Za unrolled a map.

Jesse went through the flight as Za grilled him for details and plotted the next flight.

"Eat!" the cook slapped a spatula on the table.

"Jesus, that gets old," Jesse yelled.

"Yeah," Za said, "but we don't have to cook it, so who cares? Let's get it." They went into the kitchen, where Hallie had already dug in.

"Huntoon gave us a ride to the van," Hallie said.

"So what?" The cook stabbed a steak from the plate when Jesse attempted a piece for himself.

"So it was intense...I say he makes a scene at the diner tomorrow."

"What happened?" Za said.

"Nothing happened," Jesse said.

Hallie pointed her fork at him. "You call that nothing?"

Za went to the fridge and brought back four Corona's. "Well, it might not be business as usual tomorrow. I will be all right, because I am a master bullshitter, with good looks and charm. And Hallie, she has a secret weapon."

"I do?"

"Great tits." Za blocked the oncoming fried potatoes. He continued, "But Jesse, he is lacking all these traits...so watch for him to make a scene."

Jesse gave him the finger. "Eat me."

It was late morning when Johnny Huntoon strolled in. He sat down, bumped the trucker next to him, and yelled, "There's gonna be trouble, and that pretty bitch waitress is how I'm goin' to get it."

He turned on his stool and put his feet in the aisle.

Jesse came out of the kitchen carrying a gray tub.

As Hallie walked past Huntoon, he took her by the waist and put her on his lap. She broke free with a good elbow, but the baiting was done and Jesse was on his hook.

"You don't want this trouble," Jesse hissed right in his face.

Huntoon stood up.

Every glass and plate in the place went still. Johnny was their boy, but Jesse was plainly up to it. The place was vile with the stink of violence, and everybody wanted it, right down to the players.

"I am this trouble. You go back to your tables with your apron now, while I pork this little bitch waitress," Huntoon said.

Hallie screeched with anger, lunging at his side. Huntoon caught her in midair with a fist low in the forehead; she hit the floor, bounced back to her feet, and came again.

Before she got there, Huntoon swung at Jesse. Jesse slipped aside and grabbed a handful of hair. Jesse used the momentum to slam Huntoon to the floor.

Hallie landed on top of Huntoon, punching and clawing. Huntoon swept her into the stools.

He stood up, gushing blood from his nostrils and with fire in his eyes. He rushed Jesse to tackle him. Jesse moved aside and folded Huntoon with a knee to the gut, putting Huntoon to his knees.

Huntoon stood up.

Hallie attacked him, yelling, "Fuckin' redneck bastard!" She roundhoused him, but she missed and fell against Huntoon. Huntoon grabbed her hair at the roots and brought his fist back to deliver.

Jesse smashed his fist into Huntoon's face. Huntoon fell back, taking Hallie with him. His head caught the countertop and bounced, and then he slipped to the floor.

Jesse spit on him. "Get him out." He pointed at two men standing in the circle that had formed around the players. "You two."

He looked for Hallie, but Za picked her off the floor and sat her on the counter. She was still on fire; he had to hold her down. "You have to learn not to lose your temper, you get your ass whipped that way." Za said.

"Let go of me, Za."

He still held onto her.

"Za, I will kick your ass." She busted loose and jumped down.

Za put his arms up in a surrender motion. He held a wet bar towel out at arm's length as a peace offering.

She hesitated for a second before taking it. "I am so pissed off."

The two men picked up Huntoon. "You got your trouble, boy, didn't ya?" As they dragged him, his boot tips vibrated on the floor. They pulled him through the door and dropped him onto the pavement.

Jesse moved to the door, but the cook pushed past him and poured a bucket of water on Huntoon. He woke with a start.

"Get out of here; I don't want you bleeding all over the place."

"Get off me! Get away," Huntoon staggered against the wall.

"Nobody's got you. You heard me, get your ass in that rig."

Huntoon gathered his wits and weaved to his truck.

The cook went back inside and the whole place watched out the window. "Sit down and eat. You think you're the only customers I got? You get to work, tourist."

Everyone sat down, and the glasses and plates started their chiming again.

Jesse picked up the gray tub, looked outside, and said, "This ain't over."

CHAPTER SEVENTEEN

Jesse took Hallie by the hand and led her to her Dodge pickup.

"Supplies. We're going into town," Jesse yelled to the other two, who were walking up the porch stairs. "Get in quick," Jesse said to Hallie. Jesse jumped in the driver's seat and retrieved the keys from the visor. After closing the diner, Jesse knew he needed a beer and a night on the town.

Za turned toward them, but Jesse got the truck started and out the driveway in time. Za kicked at the stones in the driveway.

"Oh, he's pissed," Jesse said, looking in the mirror. He turned to Hallie and planted a megawatt smile on his face. He winked at her, impersonating Huntoon, and said, "Can't pass up a specimen like that, honey. You got more curves than a mountain road."

She laughed and smacked him in the arm. "He got his ass kicked."

Jesse pulled up in front of Stanton's, the only store in a one-horse town. The bell placed above the door a hundred years ago sang out when the front door opened.

Stanton's had one main aisle and hardwood floors gullied out from the years. A wood ladder on wheels ran along the wall, providing access to cloth, axle grease, and varnish with Indian heads on the label.

Nails, toys, and shotguns, along with groceries, crowded every corner and cranny, and a sun-faded Radio Flyer sat in the front window.

"Hey, Jesse."

"Hey yourself, Belley."

Belley Stanton didn't have the feature his name suggests, but he had the good fortune to have married the town princess and his high school sweetheart, Belle.

"Hey yourself, Ali." He nodded toward Hallie.

"It's Hallie."

Jesse grunted with amusement.

Belley leaned on the counter, his anchor tattoos emblazoned on his forearms. "It's a small town, fight stories travel real quick, and if I got the right version, you must be the little lady with grit."

Hallie went shades of red. "I lost that fight."

"That was the version I got."

"Well, Belley, tell me the whole story, and we'll straighten it out for you."

"Sorry, Hallie, I'm sure the real version won't be nearly as good as the one I heard."

"It was that good, huh?" Hallie said.

"It was a doozie." Belley laughed, rubbed his eye and chanted, "ALI…ALI…ALI!" He shadowboxed and spun on one leg like a ballerina.

Jesse joined him.

"Yeah, yeah, I'm gathering the stuff we need now." Hallie moved to the back of the store.

Belley said to Jesse, "Hallie, she got some steam, jumping on Johnny Huntoon, but you be careful. He was in today with his face all messed up…"

Hallie climbed the ladder on her toes, stretching and extending her body, the sunlight from the window exposing her curves through the linen white sundress.

"He came just to buy rifle shells. It scares the hell out of me. It should scare the hell out of the both of you."

"What?" Jesse still staring at the girl show.

"Huntoon came in to buy rifle shells. It scares the hell out of me. It should scare the hell out of you."

"Is that unusual?"

"The way he was acting? You bet it wasn't normal."

Jesse wondered if Belley watched too much TV. "He'll cool off."

Hallie called out, "How about some help over here?"

Jesse walked over and took the items out of her arms.

"Do we need seam sealer?" she asked. "We need charcoal too. Damn, I wish I had the list from the house. Do you know what was on it? The cook is going to bitch if we miss anything."

Jesse picked up a bag of charcoal from a shelf. "Yes, no, yes."

"The batteries are over there." Hallie pointed toward the back.

A few minutes later, they returned to the counter with their arms full.

Belley rang up their purchases, his fingers playing tunes on the cash register, bagging their goods. "Hallie, you got some steam, jumping on Johnny Huntoon. He came in today. I saw your handiwork on his face. He was here just to buy rifle shells. It scares me. You be careful, watch out for him."

Hallie glanced at Jesse. "That's good advice, Belley. Say hi to Belle."

"Sure will, right after I tell her about the fight!"

"This time I get to win, though."

116

"Of course." Belley waved good-bye, then waited for the snap of the screen door before returning to his work.

It was the kind of place you would call a biker bar, where once inside, the outside world did not exist.

Hallie led the way across the barroom floor. Jesse watched the eyes slide across the room as she strutted to the bar and sat down. He sat on the barstool next to her.

"Two Coronas," she said to the bartender.

He pulled open the door of a 1960s Norge refrigerator, brought out two bottles, and closed the door with a boot. He opened the beers with a bottle opener nailed to the bar. The caps clinked on the floor, joining a hundred others.

"So, tell me your story," Hallie said.

Jesse took a long swallow from his bottle. "I was born with great hair."

She slapped his arm. "Ass, you know what I mean."

"You want this story?"

"Skip ahead until you were twelve."

"Why twelve?"

"Because men are just twelve-year-olds without their mothers to watch them."

"Don't try to change it." Jesse clinked her bottle. "What about you? Why are you here?"

"Don't change the subject. Tell me why you are here."

"I like to hang in bars."

"You know what I mean. You grew up on a farm?"

Jesse wondered if he should give her the sanitized version. "I got a dirt bike when I was twelve. And I did my best to live on that thing. I would race through the morning chores so I could spend ten minutes riding it before the bus came. My dad would raise hell about jumping that thing and breaking it or flipping it on some hill.

"My mom said I was born to drive. And I would say, 'It's ride, Mom, born to ride.'" He laughed. "I miss her."

"Both your parents gone?" she asked.

"Yes, recently."

"Ouch, I'm sorry to hear that."

"It's…a part of life. Just…"

"Just what?" Hallie put her hand on his knee.

"Nothing you want to know about, bad family blood."

She tipped her bottle back, drank a long swig. "Don't stop on me. I just got inside."

"That's what twelve-year-olds do." He picked up his bottle and imitated her motion. "That, and scare the girls." He kicked her stool out from under her and pulled her off it and into his lap in one movement.

"Whoo!" she screamed, grabbing him. The stool rattled across the floor, and the bar went silent, then abruptly went back to business. Astride his lap, she put her arms around his neck and kissed him long and rough, pulling on his hair.

He pushed her off his lap, his face suddenly cold. "Huntoon." Jesse stood up, took Hallie by the arm. "Stay close to me and don't you start anything."

Huntoon stood by the door, scanning the room, then locked eyes with Jesse. He stormed across the floor.

Jesse pulled Hallie behind him, stepped forward, and then heard the ratchet of a shotgun cocking. Huntoon stopped.

"I'll be doin' the shootin' in here," the bartender said. "Huntoon, hand me that iron."

Jesse turned to see the bartender holding a shotgun. He returned his gaze to Huntoon. Huntoon pulled a pistol out of his belt, set it on the bar.

"Now you. Turn around, boy."

Jesse felt the barrel punch into his back. He turned toward the bartender. "I'm not carrying a gun." He held his arms up proving so.

The bartender picked up the pistol. "I got a liquor license to protect here. You boys want trouble, you do it without this."

"Well, come on, little dick!" Hallie said, moving past Jesse. He grabbed her, held her back. She kicked at Huntoon. He flinched. The entire bar roared in laughter.

"Let the skirt go!" someone shouted. Jesse picked her off the floor, trying to contain her. Huntoon took a step forward, and Jesse responded. Huntoon jumped back, covering his face. The bar roared again.

Hallie got loose and attacked Huntoon. He retreated, with Hallie wailing on him.

"Hallie!" Jesse got a hold of her and picked her up by the waist.

"Come on, pantywaist, I'll kill ya!" she screamed.

Huntoon made a move, but Jesse stopped him with a look.

"Chickenshit bastard!" she screamed, struggling to get loose.

More laughter boomed from the crowd. Huntoon froze. He started to shake, red-faced.

"Get out," Jesse growled.

"You better hike your skirt up and run before she gets loose, scooter!" Someone in the crowd shouted.

Huntoon turned in a circle, all the faces laughing at him. He turned and stomped out the door.

Jesse carried Hallie back to the bar and sat her on a stool. The crowd applauded her, whooping her name.

She jumped on the bar, her little sun dress swirling, and slammed her beer. "It's a party now," she yelled out. "The beer is on me!" The crowd went wild.

The night wore on, and Jesse got a little drunk and very attracted to the wild girl in front of him.

They went out to the gravel parking lot, and Jesse took the

wheel. Hallie slid all the way across the seat and sat with her hip against his. Her scent was wonderful, like morning rain, the touch of her body even better.

She ran her fingers through his hair and nuzzled his neck with her lips, then moved across his earlobe. She pulled up his T-shirt and slid her hand across his chest. She sat back, tossed her hair back with her hand, and passed out.

Hallie woke up when the tires hit the gravel driveway. They went inside. "I'm taking a shower," she said, moving up the stairway.

Jesse thought she added some extra bang in her backside. He went to his room, which happened to face the bathroom door. He left his door open. Undressing quickly, he locked his eyes on the doorway, then hurried into bed and shut off the light.

He heard her shoes come off and drop to the floor in her bedroom next to his. He heard footsteps coming down the hall.

In the dark, her form looked uncovered; he felt a jump in his throat at the thought of it.

She moved through the bathroom door, switched on the light, and left the door open just a little. Jesse wondered if she had done that for him.

The running water made the room steamy, and he could feel the moisture flow to him. Jesse could smell the steam, her female fragrance.

He told himself to turn away from the door, but the excitement would not let him. Moments later, the shower stopped and the steam began to clear.

He could hear a towel moving across her skin. A bottle top opened. She stretched her legs into view of the doorway, and he could hear the movement of her hands lotioning her body.

His heart beat, a lump in his throat choked him, and he felt like he would burst from the tension.

The light went out, and he still could see nothing.

"Goodnight." Hallie, by the sound, was in his doorway, but he couldn't see a thing.

"Hey," he said, hoping to keep her there until his eyes adjusted to the darkness. "Feel better?"

Jesse could see her form now and she appeared to be naked—or was that just hope?

With a giggle, Hallie slipped away into the darkness and her door swung shut behind her.

Jesse thought he should follow her, but the click of the door closing changed his mind. It was a decision he would revisit many times that night.

CHAPTER EIGHTEEN

The Amazon

Piper caught the pole on the bounce, using the bounce to lift it and then drop it again and again against the giant wooden bowl.

Satisfied the roots were properly pulverized, she knelt in front of her work. For an hour, she had worked to reduce the roots to manioc flour...or maybe two...time really had no meaning here. Only the sun and the dark were clocks.

She thought about the weeks she had been here, since she had left Pan with a letter to her parents. She wondered if they had gotten it yet.

She was amazed at her transformation more than the transformation the village had undergone. Pan had it right; she had been a burden to the village at first.

Today, sifting the flour through her hands, she realized she no longer was the spoiled-soft girl. Her body tone contrasted with her sun-bleached blonde locks. Her eyes were incredibly blue against her sun-dark skin.

When Deza had mentioned that the manioc fields were ready for harvest, Piper went to each mother and encouraged them to leave the next morning on the day-long hike to the fields. Many were afraid to leave the village, but she convinced them, and everyone harvested the fields. They carried the harvested roots in baskets woven from *zaciree* palms. The baskets slung on their backs and attached to their foreheads with a headband made of the same palms. Even the young girls knew how to make them, and they taught Piper the old art of a thousand generations.

She knew everyone now, where they lived, who their family was, and who their cousins were. Old Nokai, who gossiped, and Lesise, a teen who seemed older than her years, with beautiful eyes just like her brother Hada; both were superstitious. And Penan and Sotee and Viteen...Evenel's playmates who loved to run in the rain.

She also found a sense of community and family here. Not that it wasn't strong in her own family, but here it was amplified.

She had her favorites, of course Evenel, the giggle bandit. And Xting, a young boy, tall and thin, with moppy hair who lived and breathed curiosity about her and the world beyond the trees. She told him of the world for hours on end, of planes and skyscrapers and candy. She talked of fishing poles and cities of people who were light-skinned like her and slept with soft pillows.

"No wonder you are so weak and soft if you sleep on feathers every night," he said. Piper smiled, recalling his words.

Deza came from inside the hut. She too scooped the flour into her hand and let it fall between her fingers. She smiled at Piper. "The flour is soft and good, you have done well."

"I want to give it to Nokai."

"Why?"

"I noticed Nokai needs flour and…I don't know if she is strong enough to make her own."

"You have a good heart, Piper. Come, let's bring her the flour."

Piper poured the flour from the wood bowl into a smaller clay bowl, tapped one bowl on the side of the other, and then brushed the last of the flour into the smaller bowl; she and Deza moved across the clearing to Nokai's home.

"Piper has flour for you, Nokai," Deza said.

Nokai smiled and nodded. Piper handed her the bowl, and Nokai poured the flour into her own bowl. "Thank you," she said.

Piper noticed that Nokai grimaced when she gripped the bowl.

"I brought you some medicine," she said. Piper took a white bottle out of her pocket. "These will help the pain in your fingers. Eat two of them when you eat, Nokai." Piper put the bottle in her hand and closed her fingers.

"What is this?" Nokai asked.

"It's called Tylenol—"

Loud shouts came from the river. "Piper, come," Deza said.

Piper sprinted behind Deza. *My God she runs fast*, Piper thought, and then the urgency of the shouting bit her gut when she saw Evenel, Sotee, and the little boy Viteen pointing down the river. Tears cut streaks in their dirty cheeks.

Stende, Fopan, and Xting dragged a body upstream toward them.

"It's Penan," Evenel said. "We couldn't find her!"

"We found her in the water," shouted Xting.

Piper rushed into the water and met the boys. She took the limp form and carried it to shore. Deza knelt in the sand, and she shrieked with horror.

Piper put the limp body on the sand and rolled the girl over, pumping the water out of her. Penan's face was blue. Piper rolled her back and listened for a breath. Piper inhaled and cupped the little mouth and blew small breaths into the child. She pumped Penan's chest, the compressions shaking the little girl's body.

Deza and the others stood hovering over them. Piper heard a voice call out, "What is she doing? Is it witchcraft?"

She waited a second and again she blew and again.

"Stop her, the child is gone."

Penan coughed and vomited.

"Penan!" Piper shouted. "Penan!"

The little girl sucked in a long breath and then chortled and gagged.

Piper turned her on her side and rubbed her back vigorously.

Penan coughed and took one wheezing breath, then another, and her color became golden brown.

Piper picked her up and handed her to Deza. Deza looked shocked, but she took Penan and held her tight. A smile broke through.

"Penan!" Her mother Jenra rushed through the onlookers and grabbed her child in a death squeeze.

"They found her in the river," Deza said. She returned her gaze to Piper. Piper smiled and hugged her.

"She's safe," Piper said to Jenra. "Hold her awhile and keep her awake. She will be all right." Jenra looked at her with relief and thanks. She carried Penan back toward the village, both crying.

"You can bring the dead back to life?" asked Deza.

"No, I know how…I was taught how to make a person breathe again. She was not dead, just not breathing. I got her breathing again. I will teach you how to do it."

"Will I…have to die first?"

Piper spent some time talking with Nokai, explaining what she had done. Then she returned to the mortar and pestle. She had lost all interest in making flour.

"Piper! Piper!" Xting ran to her and tugged on her arm. "Look!"

Piper looked in the direction he pointed. From the river came six men Piper had never seen before.

Deza looked to Xting and said, "Take the children and run to the forest."

Xting did not move but stood frozen.

"Now!" snapped Deza. "Take Evenel with you." Deza took Xting's arm and said, "You stay with her."

Xting nodded.

"Go!"

Shouts rang out, and fear bled from every face.

He came ashore like evil itself.

"It's Tohanna," Deza said.

Piper's first instinct was to walk out and greet him. *No, don't show any weakness*, she thought. Piper steeled her spine and tried to talk, but nothing came out. She forced it out. "Don't be scared," she said, willing herself to control her voice so it did not shake. She physically lengthened her spine to be as tall as she could be.

Piper scanned the village. It was empty except for Deza, who stood beside her with an uncaring, stone face. Piper was grateful she was there.

Piper studied Tohanna as he came toward her. He seemed to wear a permanent scowl. His face was scarred and his mouth unusually small. He wore his hair cropped short, and the shells and jaguar teeth that adorned his face and body appeared to have been carefully chosen. He moved toward her with confidence and arrogance.

And his eyes…they never looked into her, but through and past them. They were round, brown pebbles that never wet and never spoke an emotion. The devil himself wished he had them.

His followers had the look of hardened men, but they were careful to stay behind Tohanna.

"I am Tohanna," he said loudly. He pointed at her, his arm straight out, his finger an inch from her mouth. "I am the headman. I am the headman of all the land. I am the headman of you." He pounded a fist into his chest violently. He held his mouth open in a scowl, his head pointing upward and cocked toward her while the evil bled from his hard eyes. "I can take from you anything. Anything I want. Leave you to bleed, woman."

"My name is Piper. I am from America, a land so large you could not find the end of it." He had pissed her off, like he was a rooster in her henhouse. Piper burned inside. "I am the woman who helps the people in this village—"

Tohanna scoffed and stuck his finger in her cheek.

She shoved it away.

He put it back. "A woman? What can a woman do for them?"

"Everything a man cannot." She slapped his hand away.

He slapped her with his stone hands.

Tohanna took Piper's hair, wound it around his fist, and brought her to her knees. "I will kill you, woman. But for now I will leave you here to show I am right. Only a man can save them from the jungle. Look at me! I will wait until they beg me to drown you."

He released her.

She stood up wild with rage and struck his face. He did not move at all; his face felt like iron and her entire arm went numb.

He scoffed, like she was just another insect. "You are weak." He slapped her again.

Piper fell to the ground, the pain was incredible. The men laughed.

He turned and walked away, the other men following him.

Piper trembled with anger and felt outside her own body.

127

She wanted to scream at him, smash his head with a rock, but her arm still rang numb. Her strike didn't even hurt him; instead, she may have broken her arm. So she stood and seethed and did nothing. Nothing, she thought with shame.. She looked at Deza, who was pale and trembling, her arms hanging limply by her side.

Slowly, everyone returned to the village. They picked up their work where they had left it.

Piper went to the river to fill a water bowl, and even the water seemed dark and angry. As she passed back through the people, they stopped, and she felt they looked at her differently. Had she condemned them? What if the killings started again? Would he kill women and children? She really felt he would kill her if he wanted to. Her stomach churned. She felt like the girl who comes to a new school halfway through the year, hoping desperately to have new friends. No one spoke to her, but she caught their stares when she passed by.

That evening, just before the sun settled away, Piper felt— no she knew—she had been abandoned, or maybe condemned. Her emotions were raw, and her anger from the incident was pent up inside her. Her jaw ached too, and it was turning colors.

She had done nothing, nothing. She repeated it over and over. She wouldn't cry, but she desperately needed to cleanse her emotion. She dropped another pulpy root into the bowl. And then the skies opened, and the rain ruined the flour. She struck the pestle. Torrents of rain joined the numbing work of pounding roots to flour and salty streaks poured into the bowl.

CHAPTER NINETEEN

British Columbia

On Saturday, Jesse stood on Roundtop at first light, and the chickadees scolded him to jump.

Za and the cook had already launched. Now Jesse waited for the trigger to let him go. He had dreaded this moment every time since the episode with Pinhead. Now he had to shame himself in order for the trigger to fire.

"COCOZAAA!" Hallie's voice cracked the morning silence as she sped downward.

Jump, he thought, *you're supposed to be her wingman*. He would never catch up with her now.

He checked his wrist altimeter again, turned to check the wind again, and thought about Hallie ripping on him for being late—it was enough humiliation to move his legs and jump off the edge.

The wind in his face erased the ugly feeling in an instant, and pure ecstasy coursed through him all the way to Flattop, where he floated in the thermal until he broke loose to Pinhead.

His joy left just as suddenly with Pinhead approaching. Dread built in him like a sonic boom. But the sun had moved with the season, and he was relieved to see that the shadow did not hide the rocky face of Pinhead today.

Jesse put on his game face and weaved in and around the Pin till he got above it where he could breathe again. *Three down, here comes number four.*

The ride to the Backbone presented a pink dawn that nearly glowed.

Jesse watched each of the trio pump along the Bone and over it in the sweet spot.

Jesse turned; the glider went into stall and then fell. Fear cut through him.

The glider wavered off course. He could not move a muscle, his mind stalled. His life was in the hands of fairies. The glider veered left, and Jesse got his senses back but not his nerve. At least Hallie had chased Za so she couldn't see him turn chicken.

He glided toward the road, feeling like he had been squarely beaten about the head. The others would get back to Roundtop for sure. He dreaded their taunts. They would have to come and get him like always.

Lost inside his head, he clipped a tree branch, spinning him around. He hit the ground, sliding on his belly to a stop. His wrists, elbows, and chin were bloodied. "Jesus H Christ! What else you got!" He pulled at the harness, his fingers numb. He tore at the restraints, tossed the glider as far as he could, ran over and kicked at it, then picked it up over his head and threw it at a tree. The wind caught it, and the glider flew back into him, the control bar punishing his ribcage.

Startled, a snake slipped through the grass.

"Aaa, bastard!" He chased after it. The snake slithered into the end of a hollow log. He dived, fell to his chest, reaching inside. ""Come on, you slimy bastard." Jesse jumped up and wrestled with a branch, trying to break it off. The branch twisted and twisted. He pulled, gritting his teeth. "Damn it!" He slung the branch away, but it came back and swatted him. He fell backward on top of the log. Pain ripped across his ankle.

Jesse gripped one end of the log and pulled upward. The end wavered a foot off the ground and then crushed him to the ground, smashing his finger. Pain fired across his hand, and he collapsed.

Biting for breath and sucking on his finger, he wondered what had happened to him. *I'm the guy who would try anything. I craved the danger. Now I'm the only one who didn't have the balls to do it. What's happened to me?* He thought about the snake. Where the hell did it go? He gingerly got to his feet, testing the ankle. He limped to the glider and collapsed it.

He thought about the other three. Having accomplished their goal, they would be ready to party. The thought made him sick. A hundred thoughts raced through his head. Hallie chasing after Za…that didn't seem right. Za could have her then. Not like he had to settle for her. As soon as his ankle felt better, he would fly the whole thing. See if that made them happy, shut them up. *If I had a better damn glider, that would have made a difference.* It wasn't like he had been flying forever, like them.

He limped into the turnaround where they picked him up last time. He dropped the glider and folded onto the gravel, raising arid dust. He flopped to his back and awaited his chastisement. The hard stones under his back began the process while he waited.

When the white van pulled up, Jesse didn't even stir. The tires rumbled on the gravel, then slid across the stones to cover him with more dust.

He raised his head—only Za was inside, thank God.

"Jesse!" he shouted. "We heard you didn't make it, man."

Jesse still lay on the gravel. He raised his right hand and flipped him the bird. "Who told you?"

131

"You did, man. Could hear you screaming like a bitsy girl."

Jesse flipped him off with both hands.

"Ha ha! I knew you would take it well. It was great, man." Za got out of the van and shut the door. "We left from the van, flew for an hour, and landed right back at the van. You should have been with us, man. What happened? Come in too low?"

Jesse took it. "Yeah, should have been higher at the Pin." Jesse stood up. "Got a little crashed too." He limped a step and held up his bloodied forearms.

"Well, come on, it's early yet and we're going to launch again. You get another chance at it, son."

Jesse thought he would throw up. Jesse was quiet during the trip back to Roundtop. That was easy because Za wouldn't shut up. "This is a great day. Two years we have been working toward flying the NRN."

"What?"

"No rides needed."

"Why didn't I know that?"

"'Cause you never got there man." Za put out his hand for a high five from an imaginary friend.

Jesse gave him his own sign language.

They pulled up to the launch site at Roundtop. Jesse opened the van door to step out, but Hallie pulled him out and planted a huge kiss on him.

"I thought you would like to taste a winner," she said. The other two burst out laughing.

"Oh, that's funny. Bring it, let's go." Inside, Jesse wanted to pack his things and run away.

"So was it stupidity or just chickenshit?" the cook said.

"What's it to you, bitch?" Jesse shot back.

"I wasted the last hour waiting for your sorry ass, and I want it back. Asshole. If you can't cut it, then go home, tourist."

"What is it about you that makes you so...so acidy? You

look normal, but you attack and belittle everyone like a damn black widow spider."

"You ever been poor, tourist? No, you got it poured on you like water. Well I have, and I've been beaten. It's you, rich boy." The cook picked up a rock. "You're never going to step on me 'cause you're chickenshit. Not you or nobody."

"Jesse!" Za pulled Jesse's glider out of the van. "Come help me get your glider checked out and set up. I would rather be flying than listen to you two express your love."

"Amen," Hallie added. "Let's fly."

Jesse turned to help Za, leaving the cook standing and pointing at him.

"Chickenshit." The cook tossed the rock.

A half-hour later, the three others took off with Hallie in the lead.

Jesse stood alone on the rock again in the harness, trying to make himself jump. It was not happening. The trigger simply would not fire. *Screw this*, he thought, *and screw them. I don't have to do this today, I can do this tomorrow. Hallie will understand, and I will fly the whole thing after...after I sleep on it.* He turned away from the cliff face, disgust pouring into his bloodstream. He looked down the path toward the van.

In that path stood Johnny Huntoon and his rifle. Huntoon jammed the bolt shut.

The sound unlocked the trigger in Jesse's head. Jesse turned, ran, and leaped into the air. The fabric snapped taunt and the aluminum sung out; a gunshot cracked, and the air split with a shrill cutting edge.

"Son of a bitch!" Stunned, Jesse felt a fire light in every muscle. "Goddamn it. Nowhere to hide...think, think. Should I turn back toward Roundtop and get past the edge of the cliff where he can't see me?" He banked, turning hard toward Huntoon.

Huntoon stood with the rifle to his shoulder and fire came from the barrel, followed by the crack of the gunshot.

Jesse dove for speed. Hanging in the harness, he waited on the seconds to sloth past, fighting his mind as panic edged in and he waited for a bullet to blow his entrails out his torso.

Jesse saw the far edge where he would be safe. The hang glider, ever falling downward, was below Huntoon now and Jesse could not see him. Twice more the gunshot boomed above him.

"Go, go, go." Jesse's airway constricted his voice. "Come on, faster!" Safety was so damned close. The rifle blasted again; Jesse's control bar broke in half. The hang glider wobbled up and down, slowing. Jesse grabbed the bar, but all he could do was stare at it. It looked like it had exploded in two. Gripping the outside edges of the control bar, he managed to put the glider back into the dive. He wondered if the bullet had pierced him.

The glider slipped around the edge where Huntoon could not see him. Jesse looked along his torso in the canvas harness, looking for blood. *No blood, unless he gut-shot me.*

Panic blew into the last corners of his mind, seizing control; the glider swung wildly, the tail trying to pass the front. Jesse concentrated all his will, forcing the panic back out and gaining control.

He had only bought a little time. Huntoon could run across the top of Roundtop to the other side and finish him off. It was only a hundred feet across the top to the other side, where Huntoon would have Jesse in sight again.

Should I dive and crash into the trees below, or turn toward Flattop and put distance between me and Huntoon?

The question ran through his head a hundred times as he lay in the harness. "Do something," he cried to himself.

134

Jesse saw movement. He looked and Huntoon running downhill on the steep slope of Roundtop facing Jesse.

The small jack pines shook violently as Huntoon hurtled some and plowed others. He fell and rolled down the hill, sliding and twisting around while clutching the rifle. He slid to a stop among the brush. Like a dart on target, Huntoon got up and ran full speed toward the edge.

Damn it, Jesse thought, *when Huntoon gets there, he'll have a level shot right at me.* Jesse banked toward Flattop, exposing his entire length.

Jesse saw Huntoon reach the edge, slamming into a tree to stop his momentum from hurtling him over the edge. He put the rifle bead on Jesse.

Jesse hung in the harness, watched as a rooster watches the axe raised to strike.

Huntoon lifted his head from the stock, and Jesse saw him smile.

Huntoon returned his eye to the gun sight and his finger spilled over the trigger. Jesse froze in time, his fate assured.

A voice cracked the air and Jesse saw Huntoon turn and stare for a split second. Huntoon swung the gun around and his shoulder recoiled the same instant the cook slammed into him with the hang glider.

Jesse lost sight of them. He barrel rolled, straining to find them, but the world just spun around and around.

Throwing away all value for his life, Jesse dove for the trees below. The glider crashing through the pine branches, chunking off pieces of the glider and spinning Jesse wildly until he hung above the ground. His face and arms were cut and bloody.

He tore the remaining fabric away and dropped to the ground in a thud. He rolled down the ravine, finally stopping against a rotting log. He sprang to his feet and peered through the trees toward Roundtop.

His ears were singing in pain. He gulped a breath to stop any noise and listened. The only sound in the forest was his heart. He ran up the hill, slowly at first, his mind racing with everything he did not know.

Then his determination gathered itself, and his legs pumped against the incline rapidly. He reached the road leading up to the place where Huntoon had stood poised to kill him when the cook had come to his rescue, crashing right into Huntoon, hang glider and all, at full speed. Jesse played it again in his mind. He hoped they were still alive.

But now with the open road in front of him, the pavement went on forever.

A wave of guilt flooded Jesse. He had gone out of his way to hate the cook. He had never looked to see anything good inside. He had never lifted a hand to help. Jesus, he had never said a single kind word. And she had saved him from death.

He strained to cover the distance, his shoes pounding the asphalt. He rounded the last corner and cut through the trees toward the spot he had last seen Huntoon and the cook.

As he ran and slid downward toward the edge, he caught sight of Hallie and Za. He heard fragments of speech and saw Hallie kneeling over someone on the ground. Her forearms were dripping red. The cook lay on the ground, thrashing, and Za struggled to hold her still.

Jesse tried to stop, but in his panic he slid past them, wildly grabbing at anything to keep him from falling over the edge. A desperate grip on a root spun him around, and he stopped with his head and shoulders suspended over the edge.

Below him lay Johnny Huntoon impaled on the rocks.

Jesse pulled himself up and crawled back toward his friends. His hands and knees slipped in the cook's blood. He stumbled to his feet and stood over the cook. She stopped struggling slowly, her gaze fixed on Jesse. The life faded from those eyes squarely focused on him.

Jesse dropped to the ground. The wind swept his hair and planted the smell of death deep in him.

"I didn't…don't know her name."

Hallie looked at Jesse. "What?"

"A person died to save me, and I don't even know her name."

Za looked at Jesse, and then at Hallie. Her expression asked the same question.

Za held out his arms and stared at the blood covering them.

"Mar…" Za formed the word, but his voice went silent. "Mary. Her name is Mary Ellen Morrison."

CHAPTER TWENTY

The Amazon

"Piper, wake up."

Piper stirred out of her dream. It was a damn good one too, she thought. Blueberry muffins were steaming and topped with honey butter. She could taste them.

"Xting, why is…?" Her sleepy mind was slow to form the words of her adopted village. "Why am I awake?"

"We're hunting today, you agreed to come along."

"Oh…yes." Piper nodded. She knew the privilege of the invitation. She swung out of her hammock; Xting went to gather the others.

Evenel slept, emitting a little snore. Her little arms were folded under her torso, her butt in the air. In the weeks since Piper arrived, she'd managed to convince the mothers to let their sons return to hunting, as long as they stayed on their side of the river. This was the first time she had been invited to hunt.

She stepped outside; Nokai fanned the coals in the smoldering fire pit. The flames appeared, and she added another log. The sun held fast below the horizon and the first light seeped across the village. It promised to be hot again. Nokai's role in the village was to keep the fire. It was an important role handled by the most aged members for millennium.

Xting returned with his younger brother, Stende, and Fopan his best friend. All three boys, long and gangly, were perhaps ten, or maybe even twelve years old.

Xting handed Piper a bow and a quiver with a dozen carefully crafted arrows. The enormity of this gift was not lost on Piper. She had watched Xting create them, not knowing they were for her. He had scoured the jungle for miles, choosing the right tree. He then shaved the wood for days with the upper jaw of a monkey, until the bow and the arrows were just right. He glued the feathers on with glue gathered from fir trees and kept the glue a perfect temperature over the fire. He made them one at a time and judged the balance and the weight of each arrow over and over again, shaving the excess away. Each arrow was five feet long, very light and an exact specimen. Piper thought that when it came to launch such a perfect thing, she did not know if she could let go of it.

She turned her eyes to Xting. She opened her mouth, but no thanks came out. The gesture hit her like nothing she had ever received before.

She could not cry. Her emotions and her actions belonged to the village now, not to her. The eyes of Xting expressed the emotion she felt and that was enough.

"Thank you." She bit her lip to keep it from quivering.

Xting beamed. She hugged him as he said, "You will take me to America? Show me the great airplanes?"

"Yes, I promise."

"Let's go," Stende said.

The party followed Xting into the jungle. Piper saw no sign

139

of a path as the village quickly fell into the jungle. Relieved that they traveled west, away from the Tohanna's territory, she let her mind absorb the jungle.

The three boys carried a bow, arrows, and a blowgun, along with a pouch slung over their shoulder. Piper brought up the rear with her new bow and quiver strapped on her back.

Xting led them through a Tarzan movie; every turn was a growing adventure. Green permeated all things, under the hundreds of types of tall trees in the Amazon. And water was everywhere. It seemed they were constantly either alongside a stream or crossing a dribbling brook or cooling off knee-deep in a small torrent.

Piper said, "Jungle pretty, it natural."

The boys laughed. "The jungle is naturally beautiful," Xting corrected.

Crap. She prided herself on her language prowess, and she reminded herself how far she had to go. But she felt the jungle even if she could not express it correctly. It was the attitude the jungle put in your face that attracted her to its beauty. The jungle could do whatever it wanted to you. There was no one to stop it. If a pig wanted you for a meal, he just had to come get you. Of course, you could kill the pig too, she reminded herself, holding onto her new bow. She felt afraid yet freed of everything, all mixed together. It was a damn good feeling, and she felt herself strutting. Piper wanted to ask about the trees, the bugs, the sounds, and the smells, but the boys were silent. She told herself to keep quiet.

Another hour passed before Xting stopped at a trail that intersected their path.

Xting conversed for a minute with the other boys, and then both left for the cover of the canopy. Xting turned to Piper and said, "We are going to set up a trap," before disappearing into the forest himself.

Piper stood alone wondering how she would get home if

they didn't come back. *What if they are playing tricks on me? Trying to scare me.* Real dread came over her. *What if this is a test? What if they really did leave me here?*

Something crashed though the forest toward her. Her demeanor began to come unglued just as Stende returned. She breathed deep, hoping her fright went undetected. She scolded herself for being such a sissy.

He had something in his hand. "What is it?" Piper asked.

"Bark from a breadfruit tree," Stende answered, and then he set to work. The other two returned with more bark.

From their pouches, each retrieved a fist-sized stone and began beating the bark into pulp. "Piper, cut the big leaves from that bush," Xting directed, pointing.

Piper pulled her machete from the sheath Pan had given her. She cut the leaves and brought them back to the others.

The pulp from the bark soon yielded its purpose. A white sticky paste began to surface.

The boys spread the glue on top of the leaves and then laid them in the trail. They sprinkled small leaves over the top.

"Glue trap? Yes?"

"Yes, it is a glue trap," Xting corrected her again.

At least this time they were too busy to make fun of her. "What are we going to catch?" Piper asked slowly, being sure to use correct grammar.

"Things that are stupid," Xting said. He pointed and said, "Ahead there are monkeys to hunt."

The boys picked up their weapons and continued their trek westward. Twenty minutes later, Xting stopped and scanned the treetops. Stende and Fopan did the same.

Piper looked too, but she had no idea what to look for. She could not contain herself any longer. "What are we looking for?"

Xting smiled. "The monkeys heard your clumsiness and ran away."

She mocked. "Ha, I was just as quiet as you."

"I have another plan," Xting said. "But first we eat."

The boys sat down and pulled out manioc bread from their pouches.

Piper hadn't thought to bring anything with her. *Christ*, she thought, *you walk into the jungle without a thought about food. Idiot.*

Xting broke off a piece and handed it to her. She waved him off, but Stende and Fopan did the same.

"Thank you."

"Is there really a place," Stende said, pointing at Xting, "he says called America. Where huge villages full of wonderful things exist?"

Fopan, who had sleepy eyes and a cowlick, added, "I think he is telling crazy stories."

"Well, I traveled here in a canoe and before that a boat that paddles itself and before that a machine called a jet that flew me here through the air."

"He is not crazy," said Stende. "She is crazy."

Stende seemed older than his years because he was always serious.

"No, she's not," said Xting. "We see the jets all the time in the sky."

"You mean the birds with long tails that fly so high?" asked Fopan.

"That's not a bird. It is a machine that a man built and flies high in the sky, like the one that brought me to Manaus."

"Where is this Manaus?" Stende asked.

"A couple weeks down the river."

"Tell them about the ice cream," Xting said.

"Well, it's white like snow…um, like the peeled manioc roots."

"And it is cold like the coldest river," Xting said, "and sweeter than anything you ever tasted."

They lay in the shade and conversation flowed until Stende stated his disbelief in all of it. But Fopan had converted.

"See, I told you?" said Xting. "It's time to get moving." He got up, gathered his stuff, and started walking.

Fopan stepped in line next to Piper. "Tell me more about your village."

"I can tell you about the girls."

He blushed.

❧

Xting stopped at a small river. He moved downstream to a place where two huge trees had fallen across the river next to each other, forming a good platform.

Fopan slipped into the jungle. Xting and Stende reached in their pouches and brought out what looked like oversized lures. The boys tied these to the logs with thin rope made from palm leaves. "Our father made these," said Xting. "Tie the lines tight so we do not lose them, Stende."

Stende nodded.

Fopan returned with several insects.

"I hope that is fish bait," Piper said, folding her arms. "And not lunch."

Xting stared at Piper.

"What?" she asked.

Xting reached toward her hair and plucked a strand.

"Ow," she blurted. "You could have asked me."

He plucked another. "I need more."

"Ouch!" she grimaced. "All right, but I do the plucking," she said, stepping away from him.

Stende and Fopan each held out a hand. Piper kept plucking, wondering how much more she had to give up.

Xting tied the bug with a strand of her hair to the lure. He kneeled down over the platform and slipped the lures into the crystal river. The sun penetrated the water, and the rocks reflected on the bottom.

Stende anchored the lures to the platform and tied them near the tails so their heads faced downstream. The bug squirmed in the water, held by Piper's hair, a foot in front of the decoy. The expertly carved lures oscillated easily in the shallow water.

The tree platform sat about two feet above the water and each of the three boys nocked an arrow.

"Now I know what's going on," Piper said, placing an arrow on the string and nocking it. She had been an all-conference archer in college. But they didn't know that.

A ripple from the shoreline caught her attention; it became a streak of light and movement. Piper's instincts took over. She swung on the target, the trigger in her brain fired, and the arrow streamed from the bow. The splash rippled; the arrow was still there but not its target. An instant later, Xting pinned the fish with his.

Rage mixed with disappointment spiked in her.

Xting beat his chest with his fist, a smirk on his face.

She ignored his boasting. She nocked another round on her bow. Concentration had been her forte in competition. She narrowed her mind to one focus. A fish shot from the bank. Piper fired and predator became prey, victim to his hunger in the last second of life.

She whooped with delight. She turned to her competitors. "Woman!" she shouted, leaning toward them and thrusting her thumb into her chest.

Xting said, "The power of the fish now is in you. And you are now stronger by its spirit."

Piper nodded, she pulled the fish from her arrow, "Thank you for your power, I will use it wisely. There's another one!"

Four arrows flew as the next predator shot forward. It struck the bait, carrying it away. They all missed. The fish disappeared in a streak of color.

"You shoot like a girl," Xting said to his little brother Stende.

"I shoot better than you. You only have one fish. You are no better than her."

Fopan fired an arrow. "I got it!" he said, leaning down and retrieving his arrow with a silver six-inch fish attached. "I am the best hunter of all time!" he shouted, usually quiet and reserved, beaming with victory.

Piper turned to Fopan. "Hold up your hand," she said to him, holding her hand stretched above her head. He did as she showed him. She slapped his hand with hers. "High five!" she shouted in English.

He laughed and replied, "Hifi!"

"High five!" she repeated.

Xting scored another strike.

Piper turned to him and held up her hand high.

"High five!" he shouted, slapping her hand. Everyone broke out in festive laughter. Piper nocked another arrow, straining to see first, to strike before her friends. She fired and said, "Hot damn. It's fun to be an assassin."

Two hours later, the boasting and the friendship poured from them as they wrapped the fish in large leaves and put them in baskets to carry them on the trek back. The glue trap sat empty when they returned to it.

She said, "That's disappointing. I had hoped to see something stupid caught in the trap."

"We have the fish," Xting said. "The monkeys would be better, though."

Piper knew the hunters carried home the very thing that would keep their families from hunger. She could see the shining smiles of the children when the great hunters returned home. The sweetener of life.

CHAPTER TWENTY-ONE

British Columbia

Sheriff Tom DuPage sat across from Jesse, inside the embalming room at Fedlers Funeral Home. Tom was not a local, but he had grown up in a logging town himself.

"And that's when I called 911," Jesse finished his story.

The sheriff rolled his hat in his hands. "Johnny Huntoon was spitttin' poison all over town about you last night. Most people said it was the beer talking. Me, I've seen his kind before. Every little town up here has got a tough thinks he's entitled to putting his own brand on the law. I wish I had found him first."

"What happens now?" Jesse asked.

"Well, your story checks out with the other two witnesses. I contacted Mary's parents in Vermont, and they are going to take the body home for the funeral seein' as she didn't have any of her people around here. 'Cept you three, of course."

Jesse nodded. "So what about us?"

"You're free to go. But some advice here. Johnny Huntoon was a local, and that counts for a lot around here. He was not the only one around here who could do something crazy. And I ain't going to have this happen twice on my watch. I think you should move on. See some new territory."

"That just advice?"

"That's marching orders with a smile," the sheriff said. "I got to fill out all them damn forms. How 'bout you three be packed tonight and get an early start in the morning? I'll be there to say good-bye."

The sheriff stood up and put his hat on.

"We'd like to wait for her parents, talk to them."

"I guess that's reasonable. They will be here tomorrow noon. I'm going to meet them at the airport."

He opened the door and motioned Jesse into the hall where Hallie and Za were waiting.

"Time to go," Jesse said.

The sheriff repeated, "Time to go." The sheriff walked down the hall, his phone ringing.

In the hall, Jesse said, "The sheriff wants us to clear out in the morning."

"He told us the same thing," Za said. "That's bullshit, man, and what about the cook?"

"Her parents are coming to take care of her and the diner and the house, they were rented in her name."

"Well, I think we should stay and take care of things. Explain what happened," Hallie added.

"I agree, they're flying in at noon," Jesse said. "Look, our gear is still on Roundtop. We need to get it and then go back to the house and decide what to do."

Za and Hallie both nodded.

It was nearly dark when they got back to the house. Za brewed some coffee. The three settled around the kitchen table. Za said, "Jesus, how we going to eat without..." The phone rang and he answered it. "It's the sheriff. The diner's on fire."

They pulled up in the van minutes later. The sheriff's squad car sat in the road with the lights flashing. Flames roared through the roof, sparks swam skyward, and heat blasted Jesse from a hundred feet away. "Oh my God, I can't believe this," Hallie said.

"The bastards set it on fire, man." Za threw a stone at the inferno. Sirens wailed from down the mountain, and the sheriff waved the trucks in.

Just twenty minutes later, the shell stood empty, stark and steaming. Hallie embraced Za, and Jesse leaned against the van with his arms crossed and a stunned look. Hallie said, "She didn't deserve this."

The sheriff came up to them. "I sent my deputy over to your house. He says it ain't on fire yet. I only got one deputy, and I can only spare him one night. I want you cleared out in the morning."

"What did we do?" Hallie said. "We're the victims here."

"My job is prevention first. With you gone, I can start being proactive instead of reacting to crimes already over with. I'll relieve my deputy at seven sharp." He put his hands on his gun belt. "I won't be happy if I see you three again." He turned and walked toward the fire chief. "Bill, you 'bout done over here?"

"This is bullshit, man. We got a right to wait for her parents."

"Za, did you ever meet them or talk to them?" Jesse asked.

"No."

"Then what are you going to say? That she is dead and we are sorry? Besides, we leave or they can talk to us from a jail cell."

"Do you think he would really do that?" Hallie asked.

Jesse thought about his conversation with the sheriff. "Yeah, I think he would, but more likely he would herd us over the border and dump us off. We should pack and just go, contact the cook's parents afterward. Maybe go to Vermont where they live. Hell, we have to go somewhere."

"You still here?" the sheriff bellowed. "My deputy can't watch you from here." He waved his hand toward the road.

When they got to the house, the deputy sat in the driveway, his windows down. He nodded when they went inside.

They flopped down in the living room. "So where do we go, man?" Za said.

"Well, don't even suggest Utah. I spent my whole life trying to escape," said Hallie.

"Maybe Vermont?" Za suggested.

"We need to think big, really big." Jesse said. "My friend Emma had a story—"

"Oh good, I love Emma's stories," Hallie said. "I could use one tonight."

"Emma told me a story about wanting to fly. She told me about waterfalls, deep in the jungle, and she said…"

"If ever I wanted wings, it was there." Emma's weathered voice filled the open porch where the sun danced over Jesse and the surf sang. "To soar out and past the falls, into the rainforest. But there is where the story ends, not where it begins.

"Like many stories, this one begins with money and deceit. Louie Jodong was a Chinaman living in Hong Kong, but he probably came from poor stock, perhaps the Loess Plateau or another remote place, as he was considered odd even in Hong Kong. I would say he was charmingly slimy, like a wet lap dog. His value lay in his connections; you see, Louie could walk among the thieves and the Fuk Yee Hing, or the dignitaries and the right kind of police.

"Johan and I bought jade and such things from him and

149

sometimes sold diamonds to him. And there is the catch. It seems Louie Jodong needed to remove himself from Hong Kong, but quite a lot of other people's inventory got caught in his slime and went with him. Enough that he needed a few oceans between him and his pursuers.

"That's about the time Johan, who was a hard man, the kind Mae West talked about, had pissed me off. And I may have been what I call spirited and he called impossible. Anyway, we were apart when I got a call from none other than Louie Jodong.

He was looking for Johan, but I told him I did the deals now.

"So two days later, I strolled in the sunlight of the romantic architecture of Manaus. So metropolitan and so wild, like the French married a Spaniard and never quite got the jaguar chained. Gorgeous buildings fringed with dark beautiful women colored in brilliant blue and yellows. Suggestive eyes and kindly smiles. And every street with a Roman fountain and the scent of local cuisine grilling over open flames. Everywhere shirtless men with sensual eyes. Edgy danger and adventure oozed into your senses. Beware or be stung. Mmm, I loved it.

"I met Louie Jodong at a bar in the old town. He wore a white suit and fedora, crisp and tailored, trying to be European, you know. He removed his wire frame sunglasses, and I remembered the scraggly hair he tried to pass off as a mustache. He had a dragon tattoo that ran down his right arm and onto his palm, so that when you shook his hand, you stuck it directly into the mouth of the dragon.

"After a little small talk, he launched his attempt to bed me. I played along, but only to bait his pocketbook. He said he had the stones at his house, of course. In the safe in his bedroom, of course. I said the offer was tempting, even sweet. But I slammed my drink and told him I would be more open to an offer tomorrow.

"A girl has to be desirable and out of reach, but barely so. I pulled my blouse off my shoulder and used my sensual voice, told him to meet me in the morning at my hotel for a stroll and to bring the stones.

"Lying in my bed that night, the ceiling fan moving the mosquito netting lazily about, it reminded me of the many nights I lay with Johan under the stars and under just such a fan. I missed him as if my soul had left with him. I had lost track of him by then. He never stayed anywhere for long, you know, and being romanced by Louie Jodong reminded me just how good a man Johan was. Maybe I took that trip to show him I could do without him, or maybe…I still don't know. Maybe I thought he would find me in Manaus.

"Well, the next morning I got the stones and something even better. Louie knew a painter named Alejo Diego Maradona and took me to his home. Alejo had the best Chilean wine, and his home and studio, just like the man, were magnifico. We ditched Louie, and I spent a few days there…it still makes me smile; we toured the city and we lived a thousand days in just those few. Anyway his work, his paintings, they were gorgeous scenes of huge waterfalls and smoky cliffs bursting with life. Huge masterpieces so large it took two men to move them. He painted the birth of the river where it fell from such high, dusky places it seemed from the sky.

"But one piece in particular held my thoughts and my wants. Alejo had climbed atop all the land and painted what God had put before him. And if ever I wanted wings, it was there. To soar out and past the falls into the rainforest."

Two hundred miles off the western shore of Canada, the *Santa Fe*, a thousand-foot container ship, pushed through the Pacific.

"Captain, incoming phone call for you."

The captain took the phone. "Vic Morgan."

"Hello? Uncle Vic?"

"Hello, Hallie! How's my wild little filly?"

"Hey, I need a lift."

"And you're calling me?"

"When will you be in Seattle again?"

"I dock there on Thursday."

"Like this Thursday? That would be perfect!"

"And where are you going?"

"The Amazon! Is that cool or what?"

"The Amazon, Lordy Jesus. Well, call me Wednesday night; I'll give you the dock number. You remember where the docks are, don't you?"

"I sure do. Oh, and I got two friends with me. Bye!"

Vic Morgan hung up the phone. All he could do was smile. His niece was always telling him she was going to hitch a ride with him somewhere someday. He wasn't surprised she was really going to do it. Like himself, she was plagued with the adventure bug.

Thursday morning, the three friends found the *Santa Fe* at dock 1215. Hallie bounced with anticipation. "I'm so excited to see Uncle Vic. He's one of my favorite people. He has all these old stories of far-off places, and this time I'm going to be an actual part of one."

"Hallie!" A barrel-chested man with a frayed Jung seed-corn hat moved toward them. He swung one leg a little when he walked and was missing half an ear and two fingers.

"Uncle Vic! Come get a hug!" Hallie ran to him. He swung her round and round. "Uncle Vic, these are my friends Jesse and Danny, but everybody calls him Za. I have my hang glider too."

"I bet you have more than one and a whole truckload with you."

"Of course."

"I made room for all of it. But I got only one cabin. It's got four bunks. I hope that's all right." He looked at her and then scrolled across Jesse and Za with a scowl that only a ship's captain could muster.

"Yes," Hallie said, "we're old friends."

"I have to unload and load a boat here, so I will see you tonight for supper in the captain's galley. The time is posted, along with the location for your gear. Ask for Tom Powers when you get on board, he is expecting you."

Vic Morgan's warmth turned icy as he turned back toward the ship and Captain Vic Morgan, barked, "Where's the fookin' dock master. I'm not waiting for the ruddy bastard all day. Find him!"

Za turned to Hallie and said, "You are a spoiled brat! I see you can do nothing wrong in that man's eyes."

"Yeah, that puts me in command over you two swags, so get moving, you've got gear to haul."

That evening, the three visitors were gathered in the cramped galley when Captain Vic Morgan arrived. "The rest of the crew is busy loading the ship for a 5 a.m. departure; if the bastards keep to the schedule," he said, sitting at the head of the table. The cook sprang from the kitchen and served them.

"All right, Hallie, who are these guys?" He flicked his hand at the two men. "And where in Sam's hell are you going? Last I knew, your dad said you went to Canada hang gliding." He took a long swig from a stained mug. "Said you went up there on a whim. He cussed me out for it, said you was going to turn out just like me." His eyes twinkled and he grinned until his dimples came out.

"Well, I went up there to find these guys." Hallie smiled at them. "They were doing some cutting-edge flying there. Then we, um…got fired from our jobs all at once, and well, we needed a new direction and Jesse has a friend who spent some time in South America."

"Fired, huh? Give me the long version."

They recounted the summer and the murder as they dined on prime rib, potatoes, and Coors.

"And then," Hallie finished, "Jesse's friend Emma told us about a place where man was meant to have wings. So I call my Uncle Vic, and here we are."

"That's a hell of a story. Makes an old tub captain jealous. Part two, what do you know about this place your going?"

"Well, it's not a place yet, we are kind of winging it. Kind of makes it a bit of an adventure."

Vic Morgan settled into his chair. "We got state-of-the-art access to information for every piece of terra on this ball right inside the bridge. My mate, Tom Powers, is up there. I'll tell him how much he would love to talk navigation with you." He picked up the phone. "Tom! My guests need some information. You deliver whatever they need." He hung up.

Jesse and Za lit up like a bulb.

"You two go and see him." He waved them out. "I am going to catch up with my favorite niece."

CHAPTER TWENTY-TWO

Pacific Ocean

Hallie slept in a long tee, trying to fight off the night heat—the first reminder this was a freighter and not a cruise ship.

The sunlight crossed her face, awaking her for the morning. She could feel the slow wobble of the propellers through every inch of the great ship. She sat up, stretching her arms and legs and was interrupted by a great yawn. She crawled across the bunk and peered through the porthole. Za and Jesse leaned over the rail, with their butts pointing right at her. She had to judge.

Za wore cargo shorts, nice and round, very sharp, you had to like it. However, Jesse…rock hard and just so taut in his blue jeans. It made her go wow.

"Oh, they have coffee." She scooted outside and robbed Za of his cup.

"Hey! You know what they do to pirates on the open sea?"

"Do they look like this?" she spun around, exposing her Hello Kitty panties.

"Okay, okay, just save me some."

Jesse said, "Here take mine. A pirate who looks that good can have all my treasure."

"My pleasure." She wrinkled her nose, took Jesse's cup, and flung Za's cup over the rail.

"Arrrr…you little tart." Za picked her up and sat her on the rail. "I'll put you over, wench."

She squealed with delight.

"While you were asleep, we helped launch this ship," Za said. "So?"

"So the crew invited us to a party tonight. And the best part is a lot of them are Brazilian. They might know something about what we're looking for. Only you weren't there, so you weren't invited, baby."

Jesse snorted. "She wears that and she can get invited."

"You think?" Hallie asked with a wink.

Za had his hands on her hips holding her on the rail. He stared at her tee and what filled it out. "Enjoying the view?" she asked.

He lifted her off the rail and sat her feet on the deck.

"What a great day to start an adventure." Za said. "Helps with, you know, the cook and everything."

"You think she would have come with us, I mean if we decided to take this with her?"

No one answered.

The full-bodied ocean breeze held a slight tinge of salt, bringing the sun in with it, into your senses. "I know what Emma meant now," Jesse said, moving to a new subject. "She used to say how she wished it was salt air. Always wished the breeze was salt air."

The day wandered on with nothing much to do except get some sun in their loungers—for a while anyway, then Hallie got bored.

Za said, "You know they got some really good navigation toys on this tub.

Hallie wasn't listening. She thought of her judging that morning. She didn't have to be bored. She said, "Why don't *you* go play with them?"

Za droned on. "You know, Jesse, that bothers me. What if we don't find a place?"

Jesse never moved a muscle. "We meet nearly naked Brazilian women who think we're Gods. What's not to like?"

"You mean we don't get to fly?" Za looked truly deflated.

"I think you need to do more research." Hallie had already declared a winner; it was time to thin the herd.

"You're right, I should try to find out more," Za said. "I'm going to the bridge." Za got up and went inside.

"You're not even trying to be subtle," Jesse said.

"A girl has to know her men."

"And what does a girl know about this man?"

"A girl has to acquire some things."

She stood up, her back against the rail, the sun breezing all around her again. She looked just like the first time he saw her at the diner. She was inviting then, but now that he knew who she was, she was damn delicious. "What's to know? I'm young and single an' I likes to mingle."

She laughed, "I saw that movie too, you know."

"So?"

"Lame! That all you got?" She slipped back inside the cabin.

"Nice job, dimwit," he muttered to himself. "Get your game on and think before you say anything stupid."

Hallie latched the door to the cabin behind her when she came back onto the deck. She wore a thong and a mismatched yellow bikini top, designed for maximum sun exposure. "I bet you could help me with my tanning oil."

157

She sat down, her back to him. She swept her ebony locks off her back, holding the oil behind her back.

He took the oil, stood, and moved around to sit in front of her. "I prefer to start with the legs."

"Oh." She thought he would do her back, but this was a pleasant surprise.

He pulled his shirt over his head, took her leg, and placed it across his thigh. He warmed the oil in his hands and slid it the length of her leg before he began to work it into her pores.

He labored long minutes before moving down to her foot, working the oil onto her heel and toes. Hallie thought he had great hands and an innate ability to sense her pleasure.

I'm in heaven, she thought. It wasn't just the physical pleasure, it was the view. She liked the movement of the muscles in his chest and the way his forearms pulsed back and forth. Chills ran down her arms and torso.

He oiled her arms, her belly, and caressed her ears and face before massaging her head. *He's unique*, she thought. *Usually quiet but witty and explosive when pissed, though that's hard to do. Very bright, even boring when you ask him to explain something, like a little boy with a new toy airplane, all enthusiasm and lost in its wonder. Attractive? Oh yeah, somewhere between pretty boy Brad and...*

"Turn." Jesse stood and twirled his finger, indicating it was time for the backside. Hallie turned over onto her belly on the lounge. He started with her neck and shoulders, moving the oil with firm pressure and melting her muscles.

Hallie debated silently whether he would push his fingers under her bikini strap or, she hoped, remove it. She didn't have to wait long. He undid the hook, and her straps fell to the side.

He poured the cold oil on the small of her back. She shivered. "You little bastard," she teased. "Are you having fun?"

"I was hoping you would have the courtesy to stand up and take a swing at me."

"Bite me."

"Where?"

She lifted her arm and pointed to her cheek.

Jesse sunk his teeth into the flesh of her butt.

"Ow!" she shrieked. Hallie jumped to her feet, trying to hold her bikini top with one arm. She chased him up and down the deck, beating him with the other arm.

He picked her up and put her on his shoulder. "I'm going to toss you over." She grabbed the rail and pulled him off balance. He nearly dropped her as he fell.

She rolled over him, got up, and slipped in the spilled tanning oil. Her arms went out to catch her balance, the bikini top in her hand. "Whoops!" she said, gaining her balance and trying to cover up with her top and her arms, giggling.

"Do it again," Jesse said.

She charged him and he ran for the cabin, their laughter echoing down the steel walls of the ship.

The night breeze engulfed Jesse and Hallie. They held hands as they moved toward the rear of the ship. Jesse found Za near the door with a Corona and a shot in hand. They were late. Twenty or so men crowded tables around a room decorated with well-worn paper lanterns and faded paper mache ships. Wartime pinups hung on the walls. Old dust and stale beer smells wafted out.

"What's going on?" Hallie asked.

"They're celebrating the last cruise of Simon Lee. A retirement party," Za said. "Where did you two disappear to?"

Jesse looked at Hallie, shrugged his shoulders. "What did you find in the bridge?"

Za frowned, hesitated. "Lots. There must be a thousand pieces of stone to fall off of and fly. I bet nobody ever flew them before."

A big man with a bought-and-paid-for belly whistled everyone quiet, then he started reciting a poem:

Today we celebrate the last cruise of Simon Lee,
forty years he prowled the sea
never lost a leg, but he always be a pirate to me,
it was the rum that made him dumb,
not the clap you see,
a face like that,
the whores wouldn't do him for all the lost gold in the sea.

Laughter erupted, along with shouts of approval. Another
man stood up and waved everyone quiet. "That's Bertram from
the bridge," Za said.

Bertram gave a poem of his own:

The last cruise of Simon Lee,
soon we will send him home to his wife;
it's the last of him we'll see,
but give it a week, and his wife will go off to sea!

All the bottles and glasses clinked together. "To Simon!"

Bertram continued, "May he be drunk on his ass by mid-
night, and stay that way for a week after he's home."

"To Simon!"

"Our guests aren't drinkin,'" the big man shouted. "Pass
'em a beer and shots!"

Two beers and two shot glasses with amber liquid passed
to Jesse and Hallie.

"To Simon!" Hallie shouted and slammed the shot. "Let's
get this party started!"

CHAPTER
TWENTY-THREE

The Amazon

First light hung over the forest when Piper felt someone stir her out of her sleep. "Xting, what is it?"

"Hunting today, wake up and kill a monkey."

Piper nodded. She rolled out of her hammock and wanted desperately to roll right back in.

She went outside, the air was still and quiet. The sounds would begin in moments; light transcended the jungle, holding all things mesmerized in its innocence.

She went inside and got her machete and her bow with its quiver.

Xting returned with his younger brother Stende, and his best friend, Fopan. Each carried a bow and a blowgun, along with a pouch slung over his shoulder.

The party walked into the jungle, and the whole world changed its clothes.

Pushing back leaves and stepping in mud from yesterday's rain, they moved slowly.

Xting led the way again, with Piper in tow behind the other boys. She fought back the urge to constantly look behind; she couldn't help herself—too many Tarzan movies.

An hour later, they crossed the trail she now recognized. Xting and the boys went to look for breadfruit trees, and Piper did also. She found one in just minutes. She pulled her machete free, and a few heavy strokes yielded her harvest. She sleeved the machete and carried the breadfruit bark through the jungle. Back at the trail, she retrieved the stone from her pouch and set about making paste.

Shortly afterward, the boys returned with more breadfruit tree bark. Each retrieved a fist-sized stone and began beating the bark into pulp until the white sticky paste surfaced. Xting gathered large leaves, he put the glue on the leaves, then laid small leaves over the top.

"What are we going to catch with this?" Piper said aloud.

"Things that are stupid," they said in unison.

Xting laid the glue trap in the trail, along with some raw dough from the roots they had harvested last week as bait. The group continued down the trail, leaving the trap in place. They spent several hours hunting for monkeys to no avail. They turned back toward the village, the hunt over and no longer a need for stealth.

Piper thought of the other hunts. She had harvested a couple monkeys and a capybara. The capybara had tasted…well, it sucked. It tasted like leaves and roots and charcoal. However, it was better than monkey. All the supplies from the *Pantene* were gone. She dreamed of ice cream and…and…well, all of it.

Xting stopped. Piper bumped into Fopan, and everyone jumbled together. The glue trap had worked. In the trap was a rat.

Just then, a snort came from the jungle a few yards away.

The group took cover just off the trail, Xting and the other boys using their hands to communicate.

Piper recognized that snort immediately. It was the same sound all hogs make. It was a *tajecu*, or wild pig. Quietly, Xting opened the pouch he carried and unwrapped a tightly rolled leaf. It held brown paste. He dipped the tip of a dart into the brown substance, carefully wiping the dart on the leaf so he applied only the smallest amount. He rolled the leaf back up and returned it to the pouch. Piper thought that whatever the brown paste was, it was dangerous and precious. Xting slid the dart into his blowgun.

The pig sniffed the air, moving toward the rodent. Xting, using the skills of a seasoned hunter, waited for his shot. Piper thought he seemed to know where the pig would show up as it wandered on and off the trail. Everyone sat still waiting. The pig wandered onto the trail and rooted at the ground. Xting pumped his lungs and blew the dart so fast Piper never saw it.

The pig squealed when the dart bit into its fleshy back. For a few seconds, the pig continued to root in the dirt. Xting stood up. The others did too. Then the pig began to waver like a drunken man, grunted excitedly, and then it became very quiet. It sat down on its butt and fell over. Xting walked right up to the pig, wrapped a rope around its back legs, and dragged the pig over to where the others were waiting.

"It's alive," Piper said, fascinated. "Like a zombie."

"It will be fine in about an hour," Xting said. "We will take it back to the village and tie him up until we need it."

Piper's face lit up. "You guys know how to make bacon?"

A growl rumbled through the jungle. Piper jumped. She felt it as much as she heard it. She looked at Xting.

"Jaguar!" Xting said.

They slipped into the jungle.

"The jaguar must smell the rodent," Fopan whispered to Piper. "Or the pig."

Piper moved back, away from the pig, and hid behind a tree, staring down the trail. The cat wandered around the corner at the far end of the trail. The rat, still caught in the glue trap, sat between the hunters and the jaguar.

Yellow, with crazy black lines and eyes that turned her to stone, the jaguar saw the rat caught in the glue trap. The big cat froze, its lines well defined by the contour of its muscles on alert.

The cat seemed to grow as each muscle wound up like a spring, its stomach almost on the ground. The predator inched forward a few feet, concentrating. Twenty yards out, he flew through the air.

Quicker than her eye could follow, the cat landed on the rat, its claws and mouth seizing it. The rat squealed for a few seconds and then went quiet. The cat ripped the rodent in two and gulped it down quickly. Piper thought again about the pig that lay in the grass almost beside her. What if the jaguar smelled the pig? Or her? After witnessing the lightening quickness of a jaguar, she knew it could sink its claws into her before her mind told her to run.

She felt the wind ever so slight in her face. It was keeping the cat from them now, but if the wind switched…the jaguar stood up. Piper could feel her heart beating. They wouldn't stand a chance.

The cat lifted its paw; the leaf stuck to it. He tried to shake it off, but it held like glue. The cat stood up, and its whole underside was stuck with the glue. The more the cat turned, the more glue he was covered with. He wasn't caught in the glue, but the glue that clung to him obviously irritated him. He tried to clean himself with his huge tongue.

If she were not so scared, Piper would have laughed. The scene reminded her of Spanky, her mom's cat, sprawled in the sun on a lazy Sunday afternoon cleaning its fur. The jaguar bit at the leaf litter, only to find the leaves stuck to his mouth and whiskers. He tried to lick away the leaves and then sat up and used its hind paws to scratch. It just got worse. The feline instinct to be clean was in high gear, and the jaguar worked feverishly on the problem.

Piper thought this was cool, although she wanted to get the hell out of there. But twelve-year-old boys are the same the world over.

Xting and the other two boys stood up in the grass and moved onto the trail, carefully watching. The jaguar acknowledged them like a guy sitting on the same bench waiting for the subway.

"The jaguar is more interested in being clean than he is in us," Stende said.

"Are you sure?" Piper got out from behind the tree and cautiously moved onto the trail with the boys. She felt vulnerable. She drew her machete from its sheath. The fact was, the village was on the other side of the cat. "This has got to be the weirdest thing ever…and the coolest," she said.

"How do we go around to get back to the village?" she said softly. "I mean, circle around him."

Xting spoke up. "I won't run away and cower to the jaguar. A boy is a man when he tests the jaguar. If the jaguar blocks my way, then the jaguar is in danger."

"Don't be stupid. Come on, let's go around…waaaay around him."

"Xting is right," Fopan said.

Stende nodded. "Our fathers talked about facing the jaguar."

"You're not going to try and kill it, are you?" she asked.

"No, the jaguar is our ancestor, an old grandfather who has come to test us," Xting said.

The cat sat in the trail, which was maybe ten feet wide, still working on the glue that now covered most of its fur.

Xting looked very intense and bounced on the balls of his feet.

"Now wait—" Piper said, but Xting charged toward the jaguar. Xting ran along the very edge of the trail, the leaves slapping him loudly as he ran.

The cat hissed, but he continued to clean himself. Stende and Fopan each sprinted toward the cat.

"Stop!" Piper cried.

The jaguar froze, tensing its muscles, but again it only hissed at them.

Piper found herself on the wrong side of the cat, alone. She stared wide-eyed at the boys.

"The pig!" Xting pointed. "We forgot the pig. Pick it up and bring it with you."

"Are you crazy?" She stomped her foot and flung her arm forward with the one-armed finger-point. "You come over here and get me!" She stomped up and down with both feet, her fists clinched beside her. "Right now!"

The cat roared his annoyance at her. "Aweeee!" she hid behind the tree. "Don't come back! Stay where you are."

"Put the pig on your shoulders," Fopan shouted.

"I'm not putting that pig on my…"

The jaguar looked up again.

"Damn it. I should kick their little asses. Making me carry the pig," she muttered. Piper put her bow across her torso and sheathed her machete. She took both hands and gripped the pig by its legs. She picked up the forty-pound pig. Flies were already crawling on it and it smelled like it had crapped itself. "Ewwww!" She put it across her shoulders. "Now what?" she said, trying not to be too loud.

"Bring it here."

"I am not going past that jaguar. Tell me how to go around."

"He won't hurt you, he is cleaning his fur. Besides, he only eats children, not adults."

"And pigs!" Stende added.

"Tell me the way around or I swear I will kill all of you."

They laughed at her. "Come on, Piper, bring the pig."

The cat licked at his paws, pulling glue from between his paws and then using his tongue, trying to clean his whiskers.

It looked like the time she had fed Spanky peanut butter.

"Tell me the way around!" she shouted.

The boys started to leave. "Good-bye," they mocked.

"Noooo!" Piper looked at the cat and tried to picture Spanky. She started forward.

"Run!" they shouted.

Piper pumped her feet as hard as her heart pumped. If the big cat came after her, she would run, just run and run.

At the last second, the cat's tail swung toward her and brushed her leg. "Eeeeeee!" she screamed.

The great cat wheeled around and gave an evil hiss. He got to his feet and bellowed at them. Still facing them, he went back to work on the paste.

Piper plunged into the boys, screaming at the top of her lungs. The boys screamed and shouted, making lunging moves at the cat.

"Holy shit!" Piper whooped. "That was awesome."

"Yeah, baby," Xting said, high-fiving Piper and the others.

Piper and the pig were both shaking; she dropped the pig to the ground and hugged Fopan. They looked back and the jaguar was gone.

CHAPTER TWENTY-FOUR

Pacific Ocean

Captain Morgan found his guests lounging on the deck, the sea-salt breeze awash in sun. "Hello, little miss."

Hallie waved. "Hey, Uncle Vic," she said, careful not to move her head.

The captain smiled. "Tom said I should come see the damage you poured down your throat. I must say I am impressed. Nothing half-ass about a Morgan drunk."

Za cheered slowly.

Captain Morgan turned to Jesse and said, "I understand you're an engineer, Hallie says a good one too. I'm gonna make you earn your keep."

"Actually, I'm an architect, but I have experience with engineering."

"I'll take it. I have some ideas that would make this tub better, but I don't know the application to make them work."

"You know," Jesse said, "being way smarter than my traveling companions, and seeing as they are not able to stimulate a brain wave this morning, I will earn our keep. In fact, that would make me the boss of you two." He pointed his finger at them. "Wouldn't you say that's right, Captain?"

"That's how the captain sees it."

Low groans came from the two friends.

"You two swags tote my laundry down and wash it."

A barely audible "Aye-aye" was returned.

The captain and Jesse left for the engine room. Before they were out of sight, the other two were snoring.

Hunger brought Za and Hallie out of their slumber. The sun burned high and their heads were better, but their stomachs grumbled. The slow roll of the ship mixed with the low growl of the engines vibrating through the steel.

"Are you thinkin' we should raid the galley?"

"I'm with you, Za."

The galley sat empty, exposing its stores to the raiders. Stainless counters bolted to the floor, each with a lip surrounding the table edge to hold whatever sat on them from sliding off. Big pots and pans hung overhead; Za thumped a copper pot large enough to hold five gallons. "Betcha you don't want to get cold-cocked by this in a high sea."

He opened a fridge. "Leftover pizza."

"Score! Apple pie," Hallie said, opening a glass case.

Za clapped his hands together. "All right! What else you got…?"

Clang, clang sounded on the steps. Hallie gave Za the devil's grin. He grabbed the pizza while Hallie rattled through the silverware drawer.

Za swung his arm in a circle, saying, "Come on, we gotta go."

"What about the pie?" Hallie asked.

"Take the whole thing."

The footsteps stopped just outside the door now.

"Run," Za whispered.

They took off for the other end of the galley, running up the stairs and into the passageway, then jumping through the watertight doorways.

"Which way?" Za stopped and Hallie ran into him. The pie upended and flipped. Za caught it as it uprighted again.

"Oh my God," Hallie said, then both of them burst out laughing. "This way," she said, taking the pie back and sprinting down the hall.

Za banked into the wall with his shoulder. "Ouch," he yelped, but he saved the pizza. He ran on her heels, ducking through the watertight trippies. Hallie burst through a door and onto the deck. She stopped to catch her breath, but Za grabbed the pie and ran away, cradling it and the pizza.

"None for you, missy!" He ran down the deck and the stairwell onto the main deck.

"I will kill you!" She sprinted after him onto the stern. Minutes later, they leaned on the rail on the top deck overlooking the ocean, enjoying their booty.

From what they could see, they were the last two people on the whole planet. The wash from the ship gave way to the stillness of the sea, the distance erasing any sign they were ever there.

After the pie, the two friends took in the serenity of breeze and salty sea scent, the slow roll of the ship, and the vast beauty of the blues and greens.

"Za, I'm getting bored."

Za was lying on his back, slowly roasting in the sun. He rose up on his elbows and gave her that sly smile of his. "Come with Za, baby." He sprinted off to the bow.

"Wait for me," Hallie said, giggling. She ran after him, their shoes clanging on the steel deck and sounding all the way into the sea.

Hallie had no idea what he was up to, but she followed behind him, climbing down the steel ladders. Za read the numbers on the containers as he moved up and down the rows. He stopped at one, turned to Hallie and pinned on that smile of his.

He moved to the locked door at the end of the container. Za pulled a piece of wire out of his pocket.

"What are you doing," she asked.

"Outsmarting a lock."

"You can't do that. This is my uncle's ship; he'll put me ashore and probably kill you."

"I'm not takin' anything, I'm just showin'."

"What if they see us?"

"They're not going to see us." The lock popped open.

"Jesus, any other talents you haven't told me about?"

"I could show ya." His eyes gleamed.

"What are we doing?"

"When I was on the ship's computer, I kind of came across the bill of lading. Seems we got some really good stuff with us."

"You can't steal it!"

"Not steal it, see it."

Za pulled the door open slowly, allowing the sunlight in.

Inside, he moved around, searching boxes, shaking them. "Here it is." He sat it down, cut open the cardboard and opened the top.

He pulled out his lighter and held it over the box. "Take a look."

"I am not sticking my hand in there. I don't trust you."

"Come on, I thought you were a little tough from Utah."

Hallie wondered what he was up to. If something jumped out at her, she was going to beat him to a pulp, she thought. Still, she couldn't stop herself. She moved the packing straw

171

aside, and the box began to glitter in the small reflection under the lighter.

She ran her fingers through them, enjoying the magic feel that is diamonds. She squealed, "How did you know?"

"I got Italian blood." He grinned. "The bill of lading said it was clothing from Belgium to a certain address in New York. An address a guy in my family would recognize."

Hallie's hand found something soft in the bottom of the box; she pulled it out and held it to the light. "Shazam, it's a whole dime of weed." She put her hand up for a high five in the darkness before she realized he couldn't see her. "There's a note inside."

"What's it say?"

Hallie read under the flicker of the lighter. "Hey, Buddy, I put a little bonus in the box for you."

Za looked at Hallie; Hallie looked at Za. "It's not going to be Buddy's day," Za said. "Look, there's rolling paper too."

"Somebody down there?"

Za closed the lighter, "Shit, put the packing back in the box and close it."

Hallie giggled.

"Hurry!"

Hallie closed the box and put it back in its place.

"Who's there?" Boots started down the steps.

They locked the container and raced to the other end of the ship. Hallie spun open the lock on the watertight door and they stepped through and reclosed it.

"Take the stairs, head for the deck," Hallie said. Minutes later, they fled in the sunshine. Za ran ahead of Hallie to the stern. He climbed up each container until he reached the top of the highest container on the stern, then he reached down and helped Hallie onto the roof. He pulled her down on top of him. They laughed. "Shhh," she covered Za's mouth. He bit her. "Ouch!"

"Shhh," Za said, holding his finger to his mouth.

Soon, the smell of their contraband wafted out to sea. Low laughs gave way to belly squalls.

"So of all these talents, what is your favorite?" she asked.

"The ability to make the ladies scream my name when suspended in the air."

"Yeah, I love the way it echoes."

"I mean when they're not wearing clothes."

Hallie fell over sideways, cupping her hand over her mouth. Her sides ached from his antics. "I think clown is your best talent."

"Just give me a chance, baby. I can make your world spin."

"First you have to talk to me."

"Talk? How 'bout I dance!" He jumped to his feet, doing his best John Travolta and shaking his ass.

Hallie burst out. "Stop…it hurts!"

"Your funny bone?"

"No, your dancing!"

He fell on top of her and tickled her ribs. She squealed and thrashed around, trying to escape. "Oh, you are in so much shit now, boy."

"Yeah? What you gonna do?"

She took her right hand and grasped the family jewels.

Za froze. "You have my attention."

She let go and broke into another fit of giggles.

Za stood up, grabbed her hand, and lifted her to her feet. He took her waist and pulled her whole length against him. Holding her hand high in his, he waited a full count until her eyes met his and then he began to tango. Turning and spinning in the sun, Hallie's mane shined as it flew. She began to lead, giggling over the stupid pretend stare he carried.

"I want music," she said.

He spun her out to arm's length and pulled her back. "You don't want me to sing."

"Oh? A talent you don't possess?"

He dipped her.

"Did you get all these talents from your mother?"

"My stunning good looks are from my father." They switched arms and danced across the roof of the container.

He stepped on her foot and she tumbled backward. He landed on top of her.

"I learned that from my old man too."

"Dancing?"

"No, get on her and stay on her."

She rolled him off and sat on top of him, straddling his hips with her legs.

"Oh, a topper, huh?"

She slapped his chest. "Talk. I want to know where you're from."

"New York, New York. Italian, big family, cops and fire-fighters, all hot Italian blood, little miss on-top-of-me."

She rolled off him. "Keep going."

"The talking or the begging?"

"The talking," she said, emphasized the *ing*. "I never got to know you. I mean, every time we are together, it's always with the whole crowd, you and Jesse and the cook...Mary." She stalled for a second. "And Jesse's always finding a way to take off without you along...Do you ever feel, you know, guilty, about Mary?"

"I still call her the cook. She liked that for some reason. Not guilt, just loss I guess." He sat up, but remained quiet.

Hallie sat up beside him. The sun rolled off the shimmering steel in the ocean air, the breeze cooling their sides. "You think they had the funeral by now?"

"Sure, well maybe. I feel like we ran out on her too. I sent an email to her parents when I was on the bridge. Kind of explained why we weren't there. The sheriff and all. Promised I would look them up when we got back."

"How did you meet her?"

"I caught a ride with a buddy to Vancouver. He had a software job out there. I got a job waiting tables downtown, and one weekend I wandered into the mountains with some borrowed backpacking gear.

"I found the diner, and she must have been pissed at the last guy because she fired his ass on the spot and hired me. She taught me to fly, and it was all good. She had a hard exterior, but I knew she was a straight shooter. No bullshit, told it straight to your face. We got along."

"You two never got together?"

"No," he lay on his back. "She was like a big sister. And she loved to fly so much, it was an obsession for her. Fly or die, she said. Guess that was true."

He rolled over on his side, swung a leg over hers. "Tell me about you."

"What's to know?"

"Who taught you to fly for one?"

"Uncle Vic."

"Really?"

"Yes. He gets back every once in a while, and he's a big flyer. He strapped me on with him when I was five or six. I freaked the whole time, and when we landed, I wanted to do it all over again. We kept it secret from my parents until I was twelve. Then they found out, and we were both in trouble."

"How about boyfriends?"

"Yeah, lots of them."

"Lots? Can't keep a man? You have an odor problem, or was it the corrective shoes?"

She smacked his arm. "I broke up with them all. I kept one thing in mind and that was escaping my one-horse Mormon town. Nobody going to tie me down. We weren't Mormons, but it was a Mormon town."

"Kind of stifling?"

"I made them earn their salvation."

"I can see that in you. I like that."

"I never can wait to see what's on the other side. I guess that is how we ended up on top of a boat in the middle of the ocean."

"Me too, I can't wait to see Brazil and the river and fly a huge cliff in the middle of something so wild. I get goose bumps."

❧

Hours passed on top of that container, until the sun was setting. "So you think they found the trespassers, or did they give up?" Hallie said.

"They should have checked the last place on the ship. They might have found us naked."

"Oh yeah, what went wrong, big boy?"

"Just when I had you in the palm of my hand, I no longer just wanted to bed you. Well, that's not true, but I wanted to know more, know everything about you. Somewhere in there, I just wanted to take you in my arms, lie down, and just listen."

After the sun cycled away in all its splendor, they climbed down from the container. Za led the way and waited on the ship's deck for her. He put his hands on her hips, guiding her the last step. His touch firecrackered across her torso. She stepped down to the deck, and he spun her to him. She looked in his eyes, and they whispered the same song her desire shouted.

She lost her gaze when his kiss captured her, spinning her mind in devious, delicious directions. She slid her arms across his back, trying to pull him closer. Hallie pressed with her lips, seeking him, seeking the masculinity that streamed from his lips to hers and rocketed through her. The feeling overwhelmed her and she had to move, run, or she would explode.

She pulled away and ran down the deck, energy and desire driving her release. He caught her, pulling her into his chest, and she kissed him hard and wrapped her legs around him. The yearnings were unleashed in her, exploding with so much pleasurable pain…she had to burn it, run, move, fly down the deck.

She ran to the cabin door, and he again caught her and pinned her against the steel, lifting her with his power, kissing her, touching her, seeking her. Hallie pulled his hair, she needed to scream…

He opened the door somehow and lifted her, looked into her eyes, and swept her inside.

CHAPTER TWENTY-FIVE

Atlantic Ocean

Sunlight found the two of them entangled in the sheets. Jesse banged on the door. "I'm coming in!"

The previous night, Jesse had returned to the room after a full day on the bridge updating the GPS system. As he had approached, the room echoed with mating noises. "What the hell?" He listened again. "Damn it." He swung his foot back to kick the door, but he stopped in midswing and thought better of it. *Freakin' Za*, he thought, left alone for one minute and he jumps right on it. He felt his face flush and burn with anger. Hallie and he were just getting to know each other and now this? What kind of a friend does that?

He walked away from the door to escape the noise. *And where am I going to sleep? I sure as hell am not sleeping on cold steel for those two. Maybe I should ask her uncle where I can sleep, let him come listen at their door.* Then he thought better of that.

He went to the crew cabin and bummed a bed next to Mac.

Now, as he came inside, Za and Hallie woke with a start. "I came to get some clothes."

He had intended to grab his shower stuff and a change of clothes, but seeing the two of them together in bed changed his mind. "Fuck it," he muttered. He stripped naked, hoping Hallie was watching. Grabbing his shaving kit, he stepped into the shower.

His head was full of swirling thoughts all ending with, "See what she is missing." He stepped out of the shower, stood in the doorway, and toweled off. He glanced their way. Hallie had covered up, and her tangled hair rested on Za. He grabbed a shoe from atop the dresser and threw it at them.

"C'mon, man," Za said. They stayed in bed, stuck together with glue.

Jesse dressed, gathered his stuff, tossing strewn clothing at them as he did so, and left the room.

The *Santa Fe* met the Amazon delta at first light, 160 miles wide when it meets the Atlantic Ocean. Jesse, on the bridge, could not believe the sheer size of it. They were still a thousand miles from Manaus, but he could have been midocean except for the traffic.

Another three days passed before Manaus graced the horizon. In that time, Jesse slept in the crew quarters and stayed busy on the bridge. It kept his mind occupied except for an awkward meeting in the galley.

Halfway through his lunch, Za and Hallie had come in. They nested on the far end from where he sat and giggled and fed each other. Jesus Christ, he hoped he had never put that display on. He still thought about her whenever his mind ran idle. *Really, I miss her company, but not in a lover's way*, he thought. *To tell the truth I miss the cook too*. It had been an ideal summer, well, except for the deaths.

They laughed aloud.

Too fucking loud and annoying, he thought. Things were great before they fucked it up. Literally.

Hallie looked up and waved.

Jesse scoffed. That must have been the first time she realized there were other people on the love boat. He stood up, tossed his tray in the kitchen, and walked out.

Now, Jesse put the final changes on the GPS system and installed the cover plates on the bridge.

"Looks like your timing is perfect," Captain Morgan said. "This is an unexpected bonus, getting this done. Thanks." He held out his hand to Jesse.

Jesse grasped his hand and shook it. "Really, I enjoy the puzzle, glad to do it."

"Well, your indentured servitude is complete. Thanks again."

Jesse stepped outside the bridge as the city slid past the ship. Manaus went as far as the eye could see. With such an urban setting, he wondered if there could be any adventure left in the waters from wherever the river came from. A tug came to greet them and brought them into the dock. The port smelled of petroleum.

Skyscrapers bounced from land that was as flat as Kansas. Ships laden with grain, containers, and unknown wares filled every dock. Smaller craft moved between them like bugs swirling around a rhino snout. Jesse wondered if anyone knew where all the ships were at any one time or if not getting squashed was left to the skill of each captain.

An hour later, Jesse said his good-byes, carried his personal gear down the gangway, and sat it on the dock. Hallie and Za came down and piled their gear a few feet from his. Hallie sat down on the gear. Jesse stood silent, ignoring them.

"Hallie!" Vic Morgan came to see his girl off; he gave her

a great big bear hug. "Sorry I got so busy I couldn't visit with you. Did you have a good cruise anyway?"

"The best." She shot a glance at Za.

Jesse saw it. He recognized the affection in her eyes. He never saw it when she looked at him. It stung in his chest.

Morgan said, "I have to tell you to be safe because that's my job and if you get hurt, I can't go home again because your father would shoot me and he'd never speak to you again."

"We'll be careful."

"I'm damn jealous. I gotta get back on this tub and you, you're going on an adventure."

He handed her a piece of paper. "I arranged for a boat to take you upriver. An old friend who sailed with me. Mac and Steve are going to deliver your gear from here to his boat. I called him a couple days back, and he's going to outfit you. He'll have everything you need."

Hallie hugged her uncle. "Thank you. This is more than you had to do."

"No, it's required." Vic Morgan pushed her from him, held her arms, and searched her eyes. "If I ever want to see you again."

"You make it sound perilous," she said.

"This is the jungle. Remember that it can be a nasty place, but the real danger is the human kind. The worst people on earth are here…and the very best. Getting back here depends on recognizing the two of them. That is the best advice I can give you."

Hallie saw worry in his eyes and in his voice.

He looked past Hallie at Jesse and Za. "You two hear that?"

"Yes, sir," they answered in unison.

He softened again, hugging her like a rag doll. "Make it count."

"I will," she said.

The three Americans walked down the dock and stepped

into the Third World, to a place where cruise ships came to shore, to an inviting street that was bright and planted with the local culture, tourist style. Vibrant shops, laid out by corporate designers, welcome the money. But behind the facade, where the corner met the cross street, the bricks turned to dirt.

"Why is all this trash piled up everywhere?" Hallie asked.

"That's what we call it," Jesse said. "That tin and cardboard is actually a house. I saw the same thing in Acapulco. The children and their parents who live there most likely beg for coins and have to rummage for food with the rats. Yet they're the lucky ones. They're families with parents and siblings all pulling for survival and hopefully the essential presence of love.

"The unlucky ones are the orphans. They sleep in the dirt, waking to beg at the sound of a person's approach. They fight the gulls and each other for what is thrown at them. No one teaches them how to be human, shows them that the world is more than cold and pain.

"The Third World is where opulence and poverty brush past each other without leaving anything on the other."

They walked quietly for several blocks, feeling rather fat and guilty.

"Damn, there are people everywhere, I came here to see the jungle."

"Don't worry, Jesse." Za put his arm around Jesse's neck. "I bet there is a lot of jungle left, probably something for you to kill too."

Hallie snickered and said, "Feel free to smack him."

"Oh, now you own me? Giving permission to get my ass kicked, huh?" Za asked her.

"No, I like your ass, it's the other end that needs help."

Za ran at her and scooped her off the ground. She squealed and kissed him.

"Hey, does anybody know where we are going?" Jesse asked.

Nothing looked familiar, but it was a city same as the rest.

Somebody sold the fish, somebody cleaned the sewer, somebody fixed the cabs, and somebody was lining their pockets. Along the working river, whitewashed brick buildings stood three stories tall; an old woman fanned herself on a balcony. An old man peddling stiffly past, his bike burdened with potatoes.

Another street overflowed with street vendors selling fish and a hundred kinds of native fruit. Still other stalls displayed cloth and factory-made goods. Beef sizzled over oil drum grills, and gas cylinders fired pots full of steam and unknown ingredients. Maybe it was lizards or maybe rats fried on sticks, along with bugs and snakes. People crowded and clamored and the air was scented in the way only a market can smell.

As they moved along, leaving the market behind, the pavement gave way to wood and then to dirt, as did the people they passed. Shirts, shoes, and trousers were replaced with torn and dirty gym shorts.

Then the dirt also gave out where the streets ended, where the regular vendors stopped. Hand-sawn planks thrown over swampy bogs provided just enough footing to reach the place where the boat people displayed their wares. Each family held a little high ground linked by the thrown-down boards, so their clients could reach them. Some sold goods from crude stands. Some sold services, dirty deeds you had to come here to obtain. This is where the tides ruled. A thousand miles from the sea, Manaus floods and recedes with the tide. The boat people were here because this was the only place no one had figured out how to collect rent from. Mooring their boats to a small piece of ground, the tide comes, and they get in the boat and wait. When the tide leaves, their customers come back.

Jesse, Za, and Hallie moved among these people along the planks.

"What are we looking for?" Jesse asked again.

"That." Hallie pointed at a boat.

"What was the name again?" Za asked.

Hallie opened the paper. "The *Pantene*."

Their gear from the *Santa Fe* sat on board, along with a few crates and some cartons of canned goods.

They walked up the rotting plank that ran to the gunwale of the *Pantene*. The second they were aboard, the plank fell to the water and the *Pantene* pulled out.

"Jesus, I hope we got on the right boat," Jesse said. He wanted it to be the right boat. She was perfect. The *African Queen* and the *Bounty* all rolled up in one. Not in appearances but in the way she smelled, and the way she slid through the water, she would be scary if she wasn't so grizzled. Her diesel might not outrun anyone, but the stealth of her captain could.

The captain stood in the stern, steering with throttle and rudder. Pan's face and skin looked native, but the rest of him was salt from every sea the earth held before he came back to the river. Home was a powerful mistress.

"How did you know it was us?"

Pan answered, the cigarette in his lips bouncing, "Captain Vic told me to look for two Americans under the command of a beautiful woman."

Hallie's laugh crackled through the boat.

"Jesus, I thought we left your command on the last ship."

"It's forever, baby."

"I'm Jesse, this is Za, and Hallie." Jesse waited for a response. "Your name?"

"Pan."

"Pan, okay, so you usually ferry people?"

"I bring things upriver. Supplies, tourists who want a hard vacation, tourists who want to see the jungle while buying a Coke from a Coke machine with American quarters. Whatever pays the gas to get there."

"Get there?"

"Upriver. The trip back is better money. Exotic birds, plants, things that used to be plants, people. I can get you to the open sea without the police or the banditos, which ever." He pulled a pack of smokes and a stick match from his pocket, shook one out, scratched the match across the wheel, lit the cigarette, and put out the match between his fingers. He grinned. "And the balls to get my money from the clients."

The *Pantene* moved upstream, passing heavy river traffic, day tourists, trade boats, and fisherman. Pan steered her tight, within inches of some. Jesse thought he was showing off until someone on a passing boat laid three backpacks onto the *Pantene's* deck as they rubbed easily against each other.

Jesse turned to Za. "Did you see that?"

"Yeah," Za answered with a worried tone.

Pan piped up. "A delivery for an old friend."

"This friend, he one of the banditos?" Jesse said.

Pan waved the cigarette offhandedly.

Pan steered toward the middle of the river. The traffic gave way to open water and the shadows grew long. Dusk came and swallowed them and the river whole.

"Where do we bunk?" Hallie called from the bow.

"There's only one. Take your pick," Pan said. "Me, I like the hard deck and the stars."

"Well, Jesse, it seems you too enjoy the hard deck and the stars," she said, moving toward the small cabin.

"Maybe I'll learn to smoke," he replied, kicking at a dragonfly sunning on the deck.

They were far enough out into the river that the lights from shore fell behind and darkness reigned. They glided rather lazily into the evening, the sound of the river cut by the worn boards of the bow.

Pan brought them warm beer and some dried fish. "Welcome to riverworld."

"God, no wonder they all smoke. The food sucks," Za said.

The stars covered the sky when Pan cut the diesel. A full moon cast its refection over them.

"So are we okay?" Za asked.

"Okay with what?" Jesse said.

"C'mon, man."

Jesse looked at Hallie sitting on a pile of bags. She looked like she could kick his ass and he would like it. He cracked a smile. "Yeah, we're good. If you two can still walk. I'm not going to carry either one of you sons-of-bitches through the jungle."

"Thank God," Hallie said. "I really want all of us to still be friends..."

The diesel clinked to its death.

"Why we stopping?" Za said.

Jesse stood up. "Don't know, but I don't like it. Hallie, whatever happens, you keep your cool."

"I am not that volatile."

"Whatever." Jesse scanned the darkness.

The boat coasted along on the flat canvas of the river. There seemed to be no noise whatsoever. Pan scratched a match along the cabin. It flamed, and he lit a cigarette. The awkward sulfur smell was familiar when nothing else was.

In the dark, three boys treaded water in the obscurity of the river. The moon and Pan's cigarette broke the black air.

The *Pantene* floated alongside the boys. Pan discarded his smoke stick and lowered each a backpack into the water.

They signaled with their fingers, rolling them together.

Pan smiled. He pulled out his pack, tapped three sticks partway out of the pack. He gripped them all in his mouth. Took a match from his pocket and slid it along his thigh. It flared, and he waved it under the tobacco sticks. He inhaled, and all three glowed afire.

He bent down and placed one in each of the boy's lips. They put the backpacks on and began swimming toward the ocean, the river dark swallowing them.

Pan fired up the *Pantene* and throttled toward the interior of the continent.

CHAPTER TWENTY-SIX

The Amazon

Piper sat around the fire with Evenel's mother Deza, Lesise, her brother Hada, and Nokai, the old woman who tended the fire after an evening meal of manioc flour and wild pig. Evenel was asleep in her hammock, emitting little snores.

Piper breached the question again. She hoped that, little by little, the trust between her and the others had matured. "Why did Tohanna want to kill all the men in the village?"

Deza looked to Hada, and he looked at Lesise as if to ensure her permission.

"It's alright," Lesise said. "It is part of me, us." She turned her gaze to Hada, and he nodded. Hada was a tall, slender boy with calm eyes and a dimpled chin, born minutes before Lesise. They shared traits of temper and mannerism. Lesise, however, wore her dimple on her cheek, so when she smiled her beauty blossomed twofold. She always knew what he was thinking, and he always knew when she needed him.

Deza said, "Nokai, I will be silent if you wish."

Nokai poked at the fire with the charred tip of the ever-present fire stick, turning the logs. "My story too is part of the clan and if never told, it will no longer be so."

Piper thought she should thank Nokai, but then thought better of it.

Deza hesitated, fingering the bright shells of her necklace, then she lengthened her neck to check if Evenel was all right. "When Tohanna was a young boy, maybe ten or twelve years, he followed his older brother into the woods to gather firewood. Tohanna returned, but not his brother.

"His father asked him where his brother was. Tohanna said, 'I am now the oldest, and you should forget him.' Tohanna's father slapped him to the ground and immediately went to find the older brother. Tohanna's mother found Tohanna upon the ground and consoled him.

"But her sympathy, her weakness, her feminine touch enraged and disgusted him. Tohanna told her only one son could there be, and he told her where to find his brother. Therefore, when she went down the path her husband had taken, Tohanna followed her and shot her in the back. He took his gringo hatchet and cleaved her head in two. Watched her die in the dirt.

"Tohanna hid in the tall ferns, and when his father returned, he carried the dead boy. He fell to his knees over his dead wife, and Tohanna leapt from his lair and cleaved his father's head in two."

Piper held her hands over her mouth, shocked. "Really, he killed his family? Why?"

Deza held her hand up to silence her. "The shaman said Tohanna was possessed. Only the jaguar could cure this, he said. The gut of the jaguar would destroy the evil. The headman expelled Tohanna from the tribe into the jungle." Deza waved her hand toward Hada.

Hada said, "Our father found him in the jungle nearly starved and an inch from death.

"My father and the rest of the clan had heard what he had done, of course. However, my father took mercy on him and gave him a home. But I always felt the evil in him. Even as young as I was, I...we knew that only wicked things lived in his thoughts. So did my father, I believe.

"The elders said that all the men in the village were to lord over him, to chase out the evil in him and find the good that must be there. Life was hard for Tohanna as everyone tried to harness him. But power and his lust for it blinded him, and he never accepted authority. Instead, he used sly craft where needed and outright intimidation when he could.

"He was relentless in beating anyone who stood in his way. Most of all, Lesise and me. We were many years younger than he, and we shared the same bowl and the same home, but whenever we were alone with him, he whipped us and told us we would never see adulthood, nor would our parents grow old.

"My father was a powerful man, and Tohanna feared him, or at least he respected his fists. He hunched behind my father like a rat, staying just out of reach, and planned his revenge. That is what he talked about, how he would prevail over the *cajobs*—and we all were *cajobs*."

Bastards, Piper translated in her head.

"He pretended to be friends with the boys who were stronger than he, but in the end, he betrayed them all when his time came. Some boys disappeared, and I believe he was responsible."

Piper sat with her mouth open, wishing she had not pushed the question and at the same time fearing they would stop.

"Then the day came when the sixteen-year-old boys were to become men, in a ceremony held every summer," Hada said. "We were in the hut with my father and mother. My father refused Tohanna, told him he was not yet a man, that he needed to learn wisdom and humility."

Lesise said, "Tohanna grabbed the spear. My father said to him, 'The truth shows in you, threatening to harm your own family.' My father spread his arms and said to him, 'Do you wish to kill the only things that love you?' Tohanna thrust the spear through my father's heart, and then he turned on my mother and cut her womb, the womb that never bore him.

"I don't know why he did not kill us too. Perhaps he did not fear us, or he wanted to leave a witness. He took my father's weapons and ran into the jungle. I was too stunned to move for a moment. We fell upon our parents, and I held my father and he said, 'I am sorry to bring this upon our family. I was wrong to think I could save a monster. Be strong, my child.' And then he left us."

Lesise continued, "Tohanna returned to his old tribe and the headman who banished him, who had a four-year-old son. Tohanna stole the child away and hung him from a tree at the edge of the forest. He cut the child to make it scream, setting the trap.

"Tohanna ambushed the headman and killed him with the hatchet. Cleaved him until the blood and the gray brains mixed on the ground. He brought the head into his old village and assumed power. He quickly used his charisma to recruit young warriors, and they systematically killed his enemies, beginning with the shaman who had sent him to die in the jungle.

"Then, over the next two years, he began to attack our men and kill them one by one. Every man who was his superior and every boy who had reached fifteen years. Many men went to seek him out, to stop him, but all of them died." She hesitated. "My brother Hada will be fifteen this year, along with Stende, Xting, and Fopan."

Piper said, "We will stop him. Or bargain with him."

They looked at her as if she were crazed.

190

Hada said, "How do you bargain with a dragon?"

"His power is intimidation, not magic," Piper said. "Surely we can do something, there is always a way." They didn't look convinced.

Deza turned to Nokai and touched her hand. "Nokai's husband was the oldest person in the clan. Many years past his days as a warrior." Deza waved her hands in a circle around the camp. "They were married before any of us were born. One morning they went to the waterfall to do laundry and catch fish. Tohanna came out of the forest. He walked toward them, picked up a stone, and smashed his skull. Again and again. Nokai said rage, blood thirst, and lust possessed Tohanna. Then he stumbled back into the forest drunk on his success. The last elder was gone. Dead or gone."

Nokai sat upon the ground, a tear running down her face, sadness and longing reflected orange from the flames upon her face and the moon continued across the sky, never able to stop or to change.

CHAPTER TWENTY-SEVEN

The Amazon River

The morning rays found them far from the shore. The traffic had ceased, and each mile looked more like the jungle they had imagined. The day lingered into late afternoon, the passing water and the rhythmic sounds of the *Pantene* smoothed Jesse's worry over the near future. Anything might happen, and that unknown appealed to him.

"So, Pan, you have a waterfall picked out for us?"

"Captain Vic told me what you were looking for. I got just the place." Pan had chosen it not because it had everything they wanted, but because it had the things he wanted. "I got it plotted on a map in the cabin."

Jesse smiled. "We're going there for the flying, but some adventure would be icing."

"The place has a reputation for keeping its visitors..." Pan stopped, he squinted upriver, holding his focus for a long minute. "You guys got any guns?"

"No."

Pan moved past Jesse to the back of the boat, retrieving his machete from its resting place hacked into the wall of the cabin. A quick chop to a rope opened a wooden crate.

Pan pulled out an AK-47 assault rifle. "That's okay, 'cause I do."

Za and Hallie stood up when the gun came out. They stood frozen in the bow.

Pan hooked a rope on the wheel and came forward with Jesse in tow. He read the concern on their faces. "Don't get excited, I ain't your trouble, we got a bigger problem. There's a boat ahead, and they're going to want to board us."

Hallie scanned the horizon. "Why? Are they robbers?"

"Pirates, honey. On the water, you say pirates." He pointed toward a budding spot on the horizon. "Come with me." He went back to the stern. He pulled belts of ammo and a grenade launcher out of the crate. Pan handed the ammo belts to each of them. "Put 'em on. We need to show some fire power. I get the grenade launcher. You three sling a weapon over your backs and get another in your hands." He pointed toward the crate. "Everything is loaded so check the safeties."

Hallie looked at Za and then Jesse. "What do we do?"

Za replied, "We put on the guns."

Hallie turned white.

Jesse felt his heartbeat ratchet up. It was that tightening of his throat again. What used to be thrill was now stifling fear. He took one ammo belt from Pan and placed it over his head. It was heavy and uncomfortable, biting into his ribs. He put another one around his other side.

Za moved past Pan to the crate, the others following him. Za brought out AK-47 assault rifles, shotguns, and pistols.

"Jesus, man, you got enough to supply a small country in here."

"Put on everything you can," Pan shouted. "Hallie, you stay in the stern. You other two, spread out on the bow. Nothing will happen if they think we can kill them."

"What do we have that they want?" Hallie asked.

"They want the backpacks," Jesse answered, looking at Pan for a reaction.

Pan dug under a tarp and brought out three backpacks. He hung them up half-hidden among the other cargo. "They have to think we still have them."

"This is your shit; we got nothing to do with this," Hallie said.

"This is your shit right now."

"Who are they?" She kicked the crate. "We need answers."

"You need to shut up and listen." Pan shook his finger at her. "They're banditos, and that ain't good for gringos. Now get in place 'cause they're watching us with binoculars." Pan took the grenade launcher, wrapped the carrying strap around his arm, and moved to the wheel.

The oncoming boat was bigger and, judging by her growl, could out run them too. She was wood and carried five crew-members from what Jesse could tell.

"Pull the safeties off," Pan called out. "But keep your fingers on the side of the stock." He swung around and demonstrated. "If you fire a round by mistake, this whole thing is going to take off. Stay calm and look real committed to keeping your boat. Nothing will happen."

"Then why are we taking the safeties off?" Jesse asked.

"Because that's how they will know we're committed to keeping our boat. It's the same with us."

The other boat broke its course and steered toward them. Jesse felt the first drop of sweat roll down his back. *This had better be Pan playing cops and robbers with us*, he thought.

As the two boats converged a few feet apart, he saw they

194

were locals, no gringos. They wore stone expressions and rape-your-daughter ruthless attitudes. That is, except the man wearing a weathered Stetson—he flashed a smile, revealing small teeth as black as his struggling chin bristle. He spit his chew.

They were showing their firepower too. They had automatic weapons, plus mounted in the bow sat a cannon with a two-inch barrel. A shirtless man wearing jeans that were too short and a sweat-lined straw hat pointed it at them.

Pan greeted the other boat, grenade launcher slung ready across his chest, "Hello, Andrés, you get to steal anything today?"

The man in the Stetson slid his eyes along the whole of the *Pantene*. They lit up, and he stumbled across his words. "No, Señor Pan, we only fisherman. Or maybe we have to scavenge if the fishing is no good."

"Such is the river," Pan answered. He struck a match and lit a smoke.

Jesse felt relief flood through him as the boat passed away.

Pan put a grin on. "Everybody stay still and keep quiet. Voices travel a long ways over the water, especially late in the day like it is now, when the river creatures go quiet."

As the boat began to shrink in the distance, it turned back toward them. "Shit, they're coming for us," Pan said, throwing his smoke into the water, the sizzle amplified in Jesse's fear-flooded head as it hit the surface.

Jesse's gut twisted into a rope. Hallie stepped to Za. He put his arms around her, pulling her so tight to him she exhaled her terror.

Pan hit the throttle. "We got enough firepower to keep them from getting too close. They'll use the cannon to reach us." He steered toward the shore. "We have a better chance against the shoreline than we do as a lone object on the water. And put those safeties back on."

Jesse stared at the boat. "What is happening here?" he

yelled out to Pan. "Whatever you got going here is putting our asses on the line. I say we tie those backpacks to a float and get the hell out of here."

"This ain't the States where you call 911," Pan said. "This is the river where you live smart or die dumb. I give them the fakes, they don't stop there. They still come get us. And trust me, you don't want them on this boat with you."

"So what do we do?" Hallie asked, fear bubbling in her voice.

"We stay away from them, run for cover, and try to lose them in the dark," Pan answered.

"How far can that cannon reach?" Jesse asked.

"It's a three-pound Vickers. British, 47 mm, WW II vintage. Kill your ass at two thousand yards."

"They must be half of that now."

"They can reach us; I don't know if they can hit us."

"Hit us? Jesus, man, that's it," Za said. "You put us on shore and we are out of this."

"They get me, they come get you, no witnesses. I lose them, they come get you to find out what you know, and you had better know something."

"They would have to catch us," Za said.

Pan laughed. "Out there, you would be begging for them to kill you, keep you from being food." He jerked a stubby chin toward Hallie. "You want to see her half inside a croc?"

"We ain't so easy."

"You ain't too hard either."

Jesse knew Pan was right. He looked at the other two. They looked scared, the kind of scared that doesn't think right. The same scared he had.

Pan looked at them. "All right then, we do this."

"What's in the backpacks?" Jesse demanded. He threw one at Pan's feet.

"Palm leaves."

"Not these, the ones the boys got," Jesse snapped.

"I tell you that, and you can't get off this boat. Not alive. Any of you. So don't ask."

"This is crazy. You want to mix it up with them?" Jesse said, waving his arm toward the other boat. "You saw those guys. You want to get in a firefight with them? You ever have to kill anything?"

"Like you have," Za said.

Pan raised his hands, slapped them together. They all stopped. "We don't fight
    them, we lose them."

Jesse stared at them and then at the boat. They all nodded.

Pan swung north to put the *Pantene* directly in the sun. The pirates countered, switching their course, trying to find the *Pantene* in the low sun hanging just off the water.

"Be dark in a few minutes." Pan cut hard again, the *Pantene* sang out its strain, and crates toppled over. "Clear that out, tie it down," Pan boomed. He expertly weaved toward shore, never allowing them to get a good look at the *Pantene*.

"How far to shore?" Hallie asked, desperation plain in her voice.

A water geyser erupted from the river a hundred paces starboard. The concussion wave rolled past them, blanketing them with pressure and spray, and the boom followed it.

Hallie screamed, while Jesse's gut sucked inward in fear. Za seemed froze in time, stuck where the sound of the muzzle blast had passed through them. All eyes looked at the pursuing boat just as a flash burst out of the bow.

CHAPTER TWENTY-EIGHT

Where are they?" Hallie asked.

Pan shut the diesel down. The *Pantene* floated to a stop. The world pitched into blackness, the night dead quiet and the moon absent.

"They're listening for us, so keep your voice down," Pan answered.

A spotlight appeared out of the dark. Hallie let out a small cry.

"It's okay. They can't reach us, it doesn't have the candle-power," Za whispered.

The light scanned back and forth searching for the *Pantene*. "They must be a half-mile away."

The pirates started their engine.

"We row," Pan said, pulling out two sets of oars and placing them in the oar locks. "While they run their motor, we row. But when they stop, we stop. Softly, row quietly, and don't drop your oar in the water, set it in."

"They can't find us in the dark? Can they?" Hallie asked.

"We'll make it," Za assured her.

"Then row," said Jesse. Jesse and Pan took the starboard side; Hallie and Za sat across on the port side. Jesse pulled on the oar, setting the rhythm the others fell into. He lifted his oar, slowly set it down until he felt the weight of the oar fall away, and pulled hard. On the second pull, the *Pantene* began to move forward. His fear worked on the oar. Facing the pirate boat, it looked like an illuminated ghost floating in air. The cabin and front deck lights showed yellow, contrasting with the bright white spotlight.

"When they get closer, I'll start the diesel and try to lose them again," Pan said.

"Don't you mean if?" Jesse whispered back.

"This is the real shit, gringo, they is gonna find us…listen," Pan said. "Stop rowing." From upriver came the clink clink noise of a diesel. The spotlight spun toward the sound, and the pirate boat turned away from the *Pantene* toward the sound.

Thank God, Jesse thought, *now that there are witnesses, they won't be able to harass us anymore.*

Pan jumped up and hit the starter. Nothing happened. "Holy oh no." He went into the cabin and opened the manhole built in the floor.

The others moved to the stern, watching for long minutes as the spotlight scanned the dark river, moving away from the *Pantene* and toward the center of the river. Jesse and Za went to the cabin and looked into the cramped space housing the engine.

"What is it?" Jesse snapped.

"Like I know yet, gringo. Get back to the deck."

The clank of wrenches followed them out to the deck. "What happened?" Hallie asked. "Can he fix it? God, if he can't, then what?"

"He'll fix it," Za said, hugging her again. He mouthed concern toward Jesse.

A mile away, the darkness suddenly split with instant light and then seamed back together. The sound of a cannon shot bellowed past. They all jumped. The spark and recoil of a hundred rounds followed the cannon volley. Screams and shouts came to them. Followed by a command: "Kill them!"

Jesse swallowed. Someone was dying his death as he fled from it. Still, relief ran rapid over remorse inside him. "Holy Christ," he whispered.

The light bursts begat cracking sounds, spaced seconds apart. "They're executing them," Jesse said.

The sound of each execution cut like a whip, forcing whimpers from Hallie. Za wrapped her in his arms. The river turned silent. Splashes sounded as the dead were tossed overboard.

"Start rowing," Jesse said softly. He bit his lip and put his anguish into the wood that resisted him. He was glad it was too dark for the others to see him, glad he could not see their faces. The searchlight began hunting again.

The *Pantene* made it to the shoreline an hour later. Pan dropped an anchor overboard slowly and tied it off. "We have to hope they go downstream looking for us. Then we can hide in one of the tributaries upriver."

"What if they don't?" Jesse said. "What if the diesel still won't start?"

"We don't know until I hit the starter, gringo."

The spotlight continued relentlessly hunting the *Pantene*. Their engine cut out every minute or two, listening.

"Jesus, this is impossible," Hallie said. "I can't sit here anymore, this is bullshit."

"Shut her up," Jesse said, pointing at her. He realized his finger was shaking. The full moon and stars were out and showed jarringly in the dark night.

The pirate boat worked the river like a matrix, back and forth. Sooner or later, they would flush the *Pantene* out. "What do we do now?" Jesse said. "They're working right toward us."

"You shut up, gringo," Pan spit over the side. "You people need to start listening to me and stop jawing. Or you gonna die. Now row."

"It's too late for that now, they have us boxed in—"

The pirate boat shut down again, listening, drifting. They were quiet as stone. The flip flip of bat wings hovered over the river, insects hummed, and the scent of long-dead fish puffed past them. The pirates restarted the engine.

"Look what they did to those innocent people on that other boat. You think they will just let us go? You had better fix this now," Jesse said, pointing at Pan.

Pan slapped Jesse's finger out of his face and fiddled with an unlit smoke. "Alright, gringo, we attack them. Shoot out the spotlight and fight our way out."

Even in the dark, Jesse saw the others go white. "Are you nuts?"

Pan took his oar and pushed against the shore, shoving the boat away from the land. He pulled the anchor. "You're dead right now. It's only minutes away." He pointed toward the spotlight. "You need to find a way to get alive again. I'm what you got, all of you. So start rowing. The moon is getting higher, and that is not good for us."

Jesse stood with his fists clinched, his mind awash in fear and rage.

"Sit down, Jesse," Hallie said softly.

He did, and they rowed out twenty yards. Pan put the anchors down, adjusting the boat so the bow faced the middle of the river. "Put on the ammo belts. Keep one AK-47 on your back. If we have to go in the water, you have a weapon with you. Stay under the water as long as you can. Keep moving." He stopped, looking for confirmation. They were as quiet as the night.

He pointed toward the cabin. "Move all the ammo behind the cabin, we have some cover there. Make sure they're fully loaded." He picked up the grenade launcher and shook it.

"When they get in range, I'm going to put a grenade in their rudder. When I do, Za, you take out the spotlight. Jesse, you start the diesel and get us out of here, keep us on their stern. Their cannon can't get us if we're behind them. The rest of us have to put all the firepower we got into them to keep their heads down. Surprise is how we win. So no one move until I do."

"What if the diesel doesn't start?" Za said.

Pan ignored him, swung the grenade launcher around to his back, and picked up an AK-47. He pulled the clip out and ratcheted out the live round in the chamber, catching it in midair. "You shoot in small bursts, pull the trigger and let go, retrain on your target and repeat. When it goes empty, the chamber will lock open. Pull the lever here, the clip will fall out. Grab a new one and shove it in. Then pull back on the bolt and let go, you're ready to fire again. Got it?"

"What about—" Jesse blurted out.

Pan cut him off, "Shut up!"

The river went quiet again, only the bats and the nocturnal sounds from shore broke the night. Something splashed. Deep in the jungle, timber snapped and the stars reflected off the water. Then the whirl of the starter, followed by the growl of the pirate's diesel and the splash of the propeller.

"Practice your loading till you can do it without thinking. It's important. Your life depends on keeping them pinned down."

"The spotlight?" Jesse continued. "Can we somehow put water on it? Break the hot lens. If we shoot it out, they will locate us. If we don't shoot, we will have a better chance. Slip away while their motor is running."

"What if they have another one?" Hallie said.

"If there were two, they would be using both," Pan said. He fingered the cigarette pack in his pocket. He took one out, put it to his lips, but didn't light it. "I got an idea." He removed his weapons and slung his machete over his back and slipped into the water.

"We need to get the hell out of here," Za said. "We take the weapons and just go."

Hallie nodded. "We should swim to shore and run. We have no part of this. I am not ready to get killed for whatever Pan is mixed up with."

"We can't run," Jesse shot back. "We don't even know where we are. And they're locals, they would hunt us down."

"Well we sure as hell can't fight them," Hallie said.

"We're already dead, no other options, so start practicing," Jesse said. "Our best chance is with Pan, like it or not."

They stood contemplating. Jesse dropped a clip out. Hallie and Za stood frozen. "Do it," Jesse snapped, putting the clip back in.

A few minutes later, Pan returned. He slipped on board easily with a woody reed cut from the riverbank. He trimmed the reed into a pole to about four feet long with his machete. Dipping the pole in the water, he put his thumb over the end, withdrawing the reed and holding the water inside. He took a deep breath and blew a stream of water six feet across the river.

"Great, how do you get close enough?" Jesse said sarcastically.

"You swim to them."

"Me? Why don't you swim over and get your ass shot off?"

"Because without me those two don't stand a chance."

Jesse stared at Pan, then at his friends. "Fuck." He grabbed the pole roughly from Pan. He dipped it in the water and pulled it back out. He blew hard. The water tricked out the end.

"Try it again," Hallie said. Jesse dipped the pole again and put it to his lips. The water shot out six feet from the hollow tube.

"New plan," Pan said. "Jesse takes out the spotlight, hopefully they won't figure out why, and swims back. We run for it. With luck we lose them before daylight."

"It's up to you Jesse," Hallie said.

Jesse exhaled roughly. "Alright."

"You better get going," Za said, looking nervously at the approaching spotlight a quarter mile away.

Jesse stripped down to his boxers.

"Wait," Hallie said. She took some rope and, using Pan's machete, cut it six feet long. She tied one end to the pole and slipped the other end around Jesse, tying it at his waist. She looked straight into his eyes. She was biting her lower lip to keep it from quivering.

He slid into the water while Hallie held the pole. She lowered it into the water quietly. She touched his hand. "Come back. We won't leave without you."

He managed a smile. The water was warm and pleasant. He decided not to think about what else might be in the water with him.

The pirate boat was a quarter mile away, working the river back and forth in a zigzag pattern toward the *Pantene*. Swimming easily to stay silent, scenarios ran through his head. All of them bad. *Concentrate*, he told himself. *Plan your assignment.* His mind seemed stuck, unable to force his thinking forward, returning over and over again to what had put him in this mess. He thought about where he had to position himself to get in the path of the boat and hope the engine was running when his chance came.

Jesse stopped swimming where he hoped to intercept them. He untied the rope from his waist, and the hollow stick floated to the surface. Treading water, he turned to look back at the *Pantene*. It was lost in the dark; he was no longer sure where it was. Loss and despair flooded him. He was as alone as Crusoe.

The pirates turned and headed right for him. He adjusted his position as it approached. He wanted to be close but not so close that the wash sucked him in. *And the propeller, don't forget the propeller*, he thought. As they approached, his thoughts focused. The task became clear, and he suddenly knew exactly what to do.

A hundred yards out, the engine stopped again. *Good, they'll restart the diesel again by the time they get to me*, he thought. *They won't hear the water shot, and hopefully they will think it was just a splash. As soon as the light goes out, I'll drop under and swim for it.*

Sound from the bow cutting water came to him. He paddled backward, he was too close. Just as quickly, he felt he was too far away. He swam forward two strokes.

Lifting the pole out of the water, he let the water run out. He dipped the far end into the water and put his thumb over his end. He let out a small amount trying to judge just the right load. They were really close, and the boat seemed huge.

The bow appeared, reflecting light from the spray. *I'm too far away*, he thought.

He struggled to get closer, waving the tube in the air and trying to hold it above the water. The reflected light bounced off the pole.

A voice from the boat shouted. "Look!"

Jesse put the tube to his mouth, but sank below the surface. He kicked frantically to rise back above the water. He popped out and blew with all his worth into the pole. But something knocked the pole out of his grip. The metallic click of weapons came to him.

He dropped back below the surface, turning to dive. Suddenly he was tugged backward to the surface. He bent at the waist and grabbed for his leg, a gaff hook buried inside him.

Hooked like a tuna, he struggled against the gaff as he was hauled into the air. He screamed out.

A rifle-burst broke over him and the searchlight blew apart. He fell back into the water. He stroked hard, diving downward.

Bullets sailed around him, cutting the water with a zipper sound. In seconds, his lungs burned. His fear was no longer able to suppress their demand to fill. Still he stayed deep, stroking again and again. His lungs bit at him. His consciousness began to fade.

Jesse surfaced, and a burst of light came out of the dark. A huge explosion sounded just behind him, the heat and force so close that he jumped. He turned to see the pirate boat on fire, the stern blown apart.

Pan must have gotten his shot.

"Jesse!" a voice shouted from where the burst of light had come from.

"Jesse!" the voice repeated. It was Hallie.

Weapons fire erupted from the *Pantene*. He could hear it smack into the wood of the pirate boat, splintering it as a hundred rounds shredded the cabin and gunwales.

Jesse swam toward the *Pantene*. He stroked and he stroked toward the light dots streaming from the *Pantene*. His foot clacked against the gaff hook. Pain smashed through his mind. He reached back and gripped the handle, quickly ripping the gaff from his leg and screaming in pain again.

Blood trailed behind him in the water. He thought for a second about what was following him in the unseen water. He stroked again, the fear of invisible teeth propelling him.

He swam toward the mayhem. Bullets pummeled the *Pantene*. Bursts of gunfire came from behind the cabin. Jesse dived and then leapt upward, grabbing the side of the boat.

A hand gripped his, pulling him onboard. Jesse looked up to see Pan hauling him out of the water, a cigarette in his mouth.

Jesse dropped onto the deck and scrambled toward the safety of the cabin. The knock knock knock of lead beat the walls. Jesse stepped on his wounded leg and fell flat. Echoes vibrated back from the jungle.

Jesse reached out, and Pan gripped his arm and began pulling him toward safety along the edge of the boat. Jesse stared directly into Pan's face, his expression set like stone. Suddenly, Pan convulsed violently. He drooped slightly, his expression never changing. The cigarette still clenched, Pan toppled into the water.

Jesse crawled the remaining distance to the cabin. Hallie and Za crouched behind the cabin, each ejecting a clip and scrambling to put a new one in. Their barrels glowed in the dark, emitting red onto their faces. Terror read across them.

Jesse hit the starter button. Hit it again. Panic and despair rolled over him. He hit it again. The diesel spurted to life.

He forced the throttle down, the propeller pushing them through the water. The two rifles spitting light and thunderous cracks. Wood splintered around them with equal ferocity.

"Stop shooting!" he yelled. "They can't hit us if they can't see us."

Seconds later, the gunfire stopped. Shouts came back from the pirate ship. Large splashes, panicked shrieks, and curses punched the air. The cries of a sinking ship. The pirate boat glowed afire.

Hallie dropped to the deck and vomited. Za reached for her and squeezed her brutally, the two of them a great heaving ball. And still the barrels glowed red.

CHAPTER
TWENTY-NINE

The Amazon

The falls thundered, and their spray enveloped Piper and Evenel fifty feet away. The cold mist tingled their overheated skin. "Piper, can we always be friends?" Evenel asked, wading ankle deep at the river bank where the mist's sparkling blues, purples, and reds hung in the air.

"We will always be friends, baby girl, even when you are tall."

"How tall? Will I be as tall as the trees?" She jumped in the air throwing her hands to the sky.

"Maybe the little ones," Piper laughed as she started dressing. "As tall as your mother for sure."

"As tall as you?"

Piper picked up her basket of freshly washed clothes and stared toward the village. "If you eat and eat and eat, you can be as tall as me."

"Really? Then I can run fast!" She sprinted ahead of Piper. "Pokey!"

Piper smiled at the word. She had called Evenel that just a day ago, and now Evenel used it. Such a smart little whip, she thought.

Piper chased her back to their hut. She saw that the entire village had gathered at Nokai's hut. She had felt tension in the air since last night when she had asked about Tohanna and why he terrorized the tribe.

She set down her basket and stared at the group. No one but Evenel wanted to go to the falls with her this morning, awkwardly making excuses. Now she knew why. This council must be about her. She had crossed the line, she thought, her aggressive words last night tilting the balance of her worth to the tribe. She didn't want to go, didn't want to leave her new friends and this new life, one she'd never imagined and loved.

The crowd opened, and Deza walked toward Piper. As she passed, the members fell in-line behind her: Hada, Lesise, Xting, Fopan, Nokai, everyone.

Deza walked with purpose, her head up and her hair awash behind her. They came, all of them erect and looking right at Piper.

Piper stood rigid. She instantly felt ashamed for putting them in danger. *To be run off now would crush me*, she thought. She loved the warmth of their community and family, the way everyone treated each other with respect, how everyone knew each other like their own sister.

The crowd stopped in front of her. Everything fell silent. Piper's ears hummed with tension and her heart raced, telling her to run, to dart away before they said she could not be one of them anymore.

Deza spoke: "Once, long ago, it is told a black jaguar preyed on the children of our village. It would come in the light of day and steal the children away. It was said the black jaguar was a spirit, because the men in the village hunted the jaguar but could not find it. Some of the men left the village to never return and the village suffered greatly. The clan called to the spirits of our ancestors to deliver us from the black spirit. This was told across the jungle.

"One day, a woman came to this valley. She was tall and strong, and she wore a green stone around her neck. A beautiful stone that only a great Amazon warrior could wear. It is said that only after an Amazon proved herself worthy would the old ones guide her to the place, a great lake, where she would find her stone. Diving treacherously deep into the clear waters, her stone awaited her. It would reveal itself to her. And if she lived, she wore the stone always. As a sign of her great strength and courage.

"She slayed the black jaguar. Our people knew the old ones had sent her to us. The people asked her to guide the clan and the village prospered as never before. And when she died, the old ones said that one day she would return.

"This has been said to me and to my mother and her mother for generations. We have decided that you are sent to us."

Deza fell quiet. She held her hands in front of her, cupping them together. She stepped close to Piper and opened her folded hands to reveal the green stone reflecting brilliantly in the sun.

CHAPTER THIRTY

Amazon River

The trembles began slowly along Jesse's arms and quickly moved to his legs. He felt cold and on fire all at once, and he raced through his emotions trying to justify everything. No longer able to stand at the wheel, he slipped the rope noose over one of the spokes to keep the boat going straight. If they hit something, so be it.

He tumbled down onto the deck, his energy used up.

Za and Hallie still held each other. He wondered if they had been hurt, but he could not move enough to ask. He looked at his own blood beating a steady drip onto the deck. If it bleeds out, so be it. Long minutes went by before Za and Hallie rolled apart and turned to Jesse.

"Are you alright?" she asked. Jesse nodded. She reached for him and hugged him. Warm liquid and blood scent covered the deck. "You're bleeding," she said. She moved her hand along his arm and chest. "Where is it coming from?"

"It's not a gunshot wound. It's my leg, from a gaff hook or something."

She put her hand on his leg. Blood covered from the calf downward. She winced. "I'm going to find something to treat you." She stood, moving toward the cabin.

"Are you hit?" Jesse asked Za.

His voice cracked, "I don't think so."

Hallie came back. "I don't see a first aid kit. Za, ask Pan where it is." Jesse stared at her, and she realized Pan was absent. "Pan? Where's Pan?" She stood up. "Za, find Pan."

Za twisted his head back and forth and then went to the bow. "Pan, are you hit?" He looked inside the cabin and came back to the stern, where Hallie held her hand over Jesse's wound. "He's not here."

"They shot him," Jesse said quietly. Za and Hallie froze. Jesse bit his lip and said, "In the course of one night, Pan was one of several who died the death meant for me." He grimaced. "Pan pulled me on deck, and I fell trying to get to cover. He came back for me. He grabbed my hand and was dragging me. I was looking right at him, and his chest just exploded. He never even winced. He was dead standing there...he fell into the water." They both slid down to the deck beside Jesse.

A bird crowed. Another answered. First light pierced the air, and the black gave into that day's dawn.

"It has to be stitched," Hallie said. "Za, baby, find a first aid kit, there has to be one." Za went to the cabin. "What do we do, Jesse?" Hallie asked.

He hesitated, then he said, "The cook, those innocent people on that boat, and now Pan are dead because of me." He looked at Hallie and her eyes streaked tears, washing crevices through the gunpowder on her face. She sobbed, and he took her to his chest. Bitterness, self-pity, and injustice bit into his heart and they cried together.

The sound of overturning bags and boxed goods came from

the cabin. Za returned, fell to his knees, and laid his hands on them. Hallie sat up.

"I found one."

"It has to be stitched," she said again. She found a needle and thread. She held it out in front of Jesse.

"Do it," he said.

"What do we do now?" Za said.

Hallie pierced a spot on Jesse's leg, next to the wound. He gasped and bit his lip. She pulled on the needle and his flesh closed together.

"If we go back, ouch!"

Hallie stopped. "Shit, I forgot to clean it first."

"Don't stop, get it done before I can't handle the pain."

"We have to. Za, find some alcohol or something."

Za rummaged the cabin again and returned with a bottle of rum.

"Splash it on," she instructed. Za poured it over Jesse's leg, then soaked the needle.

Hallie pushed the needle through again, her hands shaking, followed by a great sob. "If we go back, they won't believe us. We're not in the States, we're foreigners. Christ, we're here illegally. What do they do to you when you jump off a freighter?"

"And when we show up without Pan, with the boat all shot up? They will put us away."

Za said, "I agree. They're going to think we killed Pan. The guys who attacked us don't operate where they can be seen. Who is going to believe us?"

"And what if the people...Ouch, Jesus mother of God that fucking hurts." Jesse jerked his leg back.

Hallie pulled his leg forward. She started again.

"And what if the people who want the backpacks are upriver? I mean, who else wants the backpacks?" Jesse clenched his teeth. "These bastards wanted them real bad. And we don't know what they are after. Or who else is looking for them. And we still don't stand a chance without Pan."

"They're looking for us," Hallie said. "They know the back-packs were on this boat and we were on this boat and the trail stops here. If we go back to Manaus, like Pan said, we had better have answers."

They fell silent to the sound of the thread hissing through Jesse's leg again and again. Hallie tied a knot and bit the thread in two. She covered the wound with an antibiotic cream and wrapped it in gauze.

"I'm glad that's over," Jesse said. "Thanks."

"We go to the falls, hide the boat, man. Wait it out," Za said. "Pan mapped the route. It's in the cabin."

"Can we do this without him?" Hallie asked.

Jesse looked to Za and then her. "We have a boat and a big place to hide in."

"I say we give it a day and see how we feel then." Hallie said.

"You're right." Jesse said. "Za, get the GPS, and let's put this behind us."

Two weeks passed. The decision to continue upriver to the falls was rehashed again and again. In the end, right or wrong, they felt that the falls were better than the alternative. Only they would have to do it without Pan.

The flora and the river went on and on. Hot and sunny days, punctuated with rain, repeated over and over again. "Look!" Hallie said, pointing. Hundreds of macaws, their color flash-ing reds, yellows, and blues, maneuvered against glistening green parrots, both roosting and circling in front of a fifty-foot riverbank.

"That's really beautiful, baby," Za said. "Jesse you see this?"

Jesse looked up from the map. "Wow, what is that?"

"I read about this," she said. "The flooding of the river erodes under the banks and carries away the trees, and the entire fifty-foot high bank is exposed. The birds gather to eat the exposed clay, an antidote for the poisonous nuts and berries they eat." The air crackled with cries and winged art, as if Van Gogh sat on the opposite bank, palette and brush in hand.

Later on, Jesse called out to Za. "According to the map and our current heading, the mouth of our river should join up… in another half-mile."

"Hallie!" Za called out.

Hallie came out of the cabin with a rag drying a bowl. "If you're going to bitch about my cooking again, we can skip my turn."

"No, it was really good today." He turned to Jesse and stuck his finger in his mouth as if he was gagging. The bowl caught him square in the back. "Hallie, baby, you know I love you." He held out his arms, and she jumped into them, the two of them giggling.

"We're almost to the last turn," Jesse said.

"There it is," Za called out to Jesse. "Starboard." He pointed at the open space in the riverbank ahead. This branch of the river was just as brown as the Amazon itself so it was impossible to tell what was below the surface. There was a solid wall of green along the shore; even close to the shore, you could not see into the vegetation.

The river opened up. It was sixty feet wide and wild; lichen-colored rocks littered the shore; giant lily pads with yellow flowers scented the air.

"How far is it now to the falls?" Hallie asked.

"How far to the falls?" Za yelled to Jesse.

"Ten miles." Jesse steered into the river. "How deep does it look?" Jesse called out.

"Can't tell, man."

"Stay there and keep a lookout. It could get shallow real quick." Jesse's blood was up. "Za! You see anything up there?"

"Like what?"

Abruptly, the *Pantene* jerked to a near stop, throwing Za onto the deck and nearly out of the boat.

Jesse crushed into the wheel and down onto the deck. He clutched his left thumb, rolling in pain.

Hallie came out of the cabin saying, "What the hell was that?" She pulled the throttle down, and the engine stalled.

"We ran aground." Jesse put his thumb to his mouth to suck on it.

"Smooth move, Captain. You need a chick to do the driving?"

Jesse got up, shaking his hand. "I jammed my thumb." He held it up.

She slapped it.

"Ouch! That really hurt."

"Pussy." She grinned. "Need your mama?"

"Za, come get her before I throw her over."

She slapped his thumb again, laughing.

"Ouch!"

"Like you can. Now both of you get out and push. I'll back this thing up."

Two hours later, they were off the sandbar and Jesse steered into a cove big enough to fit the *Pantene*. "Alright, we have to hide this thing. We need to cover her up in case somebody comes looking for us."

"We passed dozens of river branches, do you really think we need to?" Za said. "Probably not, but it's late afternoon, and we have to walk the last four miles. We can't start until morning, so we got the time."

"How's your leg?" Hallie asked. "You able to make it four miles?"

"Good as new."

"You should have let me take out the stitches."

"No. Doing it myself means I'm in control of the knives."

"Means you're a pussy, man." Za gave them each a machete. "Let's get it."

By nightfall the boat was hidden with leafy branches.

"We just take our personal backpacks tomorrow," Jesse said as they ate. "Scout the falls first before we haul all the gear in."

"Do you think we should hide Pan's backpacks in the jungle? I mean, instead of leaving them on the *Pantene*?"

"Why bother? They're fakes," Za said.

"Maybe they're not fakes. Maybe he just separated the plunder into two halves."

"Bad idea," Jesse said. "We risk our lives knowing what's inside those packs. When we get back, that would make us just as guilty as Pan was."

"How do we know Pan wasn't working for the government?" Hallie got up and brought the three backpacks to where they sat on the deck.

"Good point, baby." Za picked up one of the packs.

"Bad idea," Jesse said, his voice drowned out by the zipper.

CHAPTER THIRTY-ONE

Jesse, Hallie, and Za stood in the jungle, an inch from the dark river and enclosed by the green abyss. A black bird with yellow tail feathers whistled his opinion of them.

"Hot damn, this is the life for me!" Za whooped, rolling his fist in the air. "This is what I imagined the jungle would feel like."

Jesse slapped a bug on his neck. "Yeah, it's the jungle." A green bug as thick as a broom handle with huge eyes gripped his thumb. "Jesus, let go!" he screamed, trying to fling it from his finger and using his free hand to fend off his attacker.

"I can see its teeth buried in your thumb," Za said.

"Get off!" Jesse yelled, dancing on his tiptoes. He tried to pull the bug off. "Ouch! Jesus, my thumb is coming off."

"Quick! Stick it in the water," Za yelled.

Jesse started for the water, but his feet tangled in the roots and he plunged into water up to his waist.

Hallie grabbed Za and buried her face in his shirt to stifle a laugh.

Jesse burst out of the water, the bug still ripping into his thumb.

"Go back!" Za yelled.

Jesse stuck his hand back in the water. Hallie still tried to control her mirth. Jesse lay on his chest with his hand in the water up to his elbow.

She bit her lip to stop, but it came out of her mouth the second it hit her brain. "Piranha!"

Jesse jerked his arm out of the water and pulled his feet under him in one motion.

He teetered on the very edge of the riverbank, flailing his arms and trying not to fall into the water. Panic bloomed across his face. He bent at the waist, putting his hands on the ground regaining his balance.

She put her boot in his ass, and Jesse toppled into the river.

Za broke out in belly laughs. Jesse shot out of the water like a cannon. He stood on the bank like a wet toad.

"Hey! Bug's gone!" Hallie said. She tore along the riverbank as fast as her legs could take her, Jesse two steps behind.

Za tried to quiet himself, talking to himself, "Wait for it, wait for it…" A shriek and a splash followed. "Ah, there it is."

An hour later, Jesse had the lead, working his way along the bank. He had stripped to his shorts after he got soaked. And he was hot.

Hallie followed in the same attire, and Za pulled up the rear. Her wet little rear was making him randy. Hallie skinned off her shirt, tied it around her waist, and wiped her face with her forearm. Howler monkeys bellowed from the far end of somewhere. The wind was dead and hot.

The plan was to find a base camp near the falls and return for their gear. It felt like they were the only people for a thousand miles. The jungle's sounds reminded Jesse of the Tarzan movies he spent watching on rainy summer afternoons. Huge moths big as young sunflowers flirted past. The world was not just green and brown but many shades of it, most of it glimmering with moisture. Lush and wild, it was as fun as hide-and-seek on the Fourth of July.

"Jesse, I got to stop," Za said. He lay on the grass.

A couple weeks on the boat had taken their toll, and the going was hard. Jesse sat on his butt, the reeds holding him almost upright.

"The heat zaps you right away," Hallie said. She plopped on top of Za.

"Hey, I'm hot here," he moaned.

"You think I want a flesh-eating bug stuck to my finger?" Hallie asked. "You better get used to me being on top of you till we get back to cabana boys and room service."

"Man, I been wishing for that since the moment I laid eyes on you, and now...I can't even move."

She kissed him.

They rested a few minutes before Jesse said, "Let's go. Adventures await."

Piper leaned against a large rock in the ankle-deep water burbling across the stones, lathering her legs in the water. She stood with her right leg tiptoed as she soaped along her calf, up and past the knee, and along the curve of her thigh. Her motion was fluid and confident. Her blonde hair hung to her shoulders and lightly flowed over her creamy skin. A light glimmer covered her in the full sun. Her eyes were as fiercely blue as the Viking queen who bore her line.

Voices caught her attention. She looked up to see a bare-chested man in the jungle. His hair was dark and wet and pulled back; his arms thrust against the grasses.

She shrieked. The sudden sound forced a retreat: he behind the grass, she around the rock. She felt a hot pang run from her brain and land in her heart. Piper stood with her back against the rock. She called over the rock. "Hello?"

"Hello, I'm Jesse. And, um...I have friends with me."

She put on a torn and once-white gauze dress. It clung damply to her. She came around the rock. "You kind of surprised me." She crossed her arms. "Who are you?"

"This is Za and Hallie."

"Tourists, we came to see the falls...are you a ranger or something?" Za said.

"What?"

"Ignore him, I'm Jesse."

"Yes, you already told me." She tried to suppress a smile. *He is gorgeous*, she thought. Her eyes ran up and down him despite her effort to resist. She turned toward Hallie and smiled.

Hallie returned the smile. "We're acting surprised because, well, we didn't expect to find a white face out here and an English speaker besides."

"Really, why are you here?" She knew she had to be cautious, but God, what a specimen of a man. She slid her eyes over Jesse again.

Hallie said, "Really, we are tourists. We came to hang glide from the cliffs at the top of the waterfall. Just a little adventure."

"You came without a guide?"

"Well, we were referred to here by one."

"Are there more of you?"

"There were—"

"Just the three of us came this far," Za finished. "Just the three of us. Old friends. "Are you a missionary or something?" Hallie smiled again, feeling awkward.

"I live in a village upstream. I'm here to study their...I'm helping them with...really, I am learning from them."

"Got a name? Or is it Jane?" Za said.

"Piper, and yes, I am queen of the jungle." She felt silly and shy, thinking about how bad that line was.

"What about your bath?" Jesse asked. He tried to eat the words as they fell out of his mouth. "I mean…I didn't mean you should continue to take a bath while we're here…"

Hallie turned to Jesse. "Smooth operator, dude."

Piper replied, "I'm done now."

"Is this the way to the falls?" Hallie asked.

"Yes, but first…" Piper hesitated, wondering if she could trust them. "Um, you have any weapons? You're not armed, are you? Or sick? You can't come any further if you have any diseases." She waved her arms. "The people in the clan have not been exposed before."

"No and no," Hallie answered. "You live in a native village? That must be cool."

"It's," she said, nodding, "been enriching." Thoughts of Tohanna rushed through her head. She decided to keep quiet about that.

Piper noticed Jesse gaping at her like a teenager. "Why are you staring at me?"

"Yeah, Jesse. Why are you staring?" Hallie said.

"I'm not, just, um, looking, um, sorry." His cheeks turned red.

"How did you guys get here?" she asked.

"We have a boat downriver, too shallow to get this far—"

"You have a boat? So you have supplies? Do you have some bacon? Or, God, tell me you have SpaghettiOs."

"Um, I have some chocolate," Jesse offered.

"Where?" She grabbed Jesse's arm. "Give it to me. You don't know what I have been eating."

Jesse took off his pack, opened a side pocket, and handed her a candy bar.

"Snickers! Oh my God, you are a savior." She tore the wrapper off and wolf-bit the candy.

"I've been carrying it in there for about a year—"

"Oh, it's so good!"

"So it may be kind of…stale."

Piper chewed voraciously. "How much you got?"

"Enough for two months or so, but no, we don't have SpaghettiOs."

"She means candy, dummy," Hallie said. "God, where is your brain?"

"That's okay, what supplies do you have?" Piper said. "Bacon? Never mind, no refrigeration. Wait, how about jerky? I had jerky on the way here. And you never did say how you got here."

"In a boat," Jesse answered.

"I know that. I mean how? And did you ever think it might be dangerous to come here?"

"Yes, that's why they call it adventure."

"So tell me your story." She shoved in the last of the candy bar. "Oh God, I am going to die now."

"Can we visit the village?" Hallie asked. "I would really like to see that."

"I suppose that would be alright. It's upstream a ways, and you look normal." Her instincts told her she could trust them; she hoped it wasn't lust.

"Good." Hallie decided to skip the part about the backpacks and the shootout with the pirates. And the part about Pan too. The entire tale fell out of them before they reached the village.

CHAPTER THIRTY-TWO

The Amazon

Evenel sat on a tree branch watching for Piper to return from her bath. She had wanted to go with Piper, but her mother had chores for her. Now she smiled anticipating Piper's return. She waited and waited until the sun and the breeze put her to sleep. Then voices below awoke her. "Piper!" she exclaimed, standing on the branch above them. "Catch me."

"Don't you dare!" Piper said, shaking a finger at her. "You sit down before you fall."

The little girl crouched, ready to take wing.

Piper took a step to save her. "Evenel, don't!"

Evenel tumbled out of the tree with a shriek.

Jesse reacted to catch the falling girl. They both tumbled to the ground.

"Evenel!" Piper shouted. "Are you alright?"

Jesse was on his back with Evenel sitting on his chest. She

let out her little giggle. "You're a wild one," he said, smiling at her. Evenel beamed.

"Are you trying to scare me to death?" Piper scolded.

Evenel nodded a yes. Piper picked her up and began to tickle her. Evenel's laughter brought the rest of the children out from the village, who ran up and hugged the newcomers.

"Isn't this just awesome?" Hallie cried. "I feel as if I'm a long-lost sister returned."

Jesse saw the admiration the children had for Piper. He wondered how had she won their hearts. She wasn't something Jesse expected on this trip, but certainly a welcome surprise.

Jesse sat on the ground near the fire, fascinated with the food preparation. He elbowed Za. "Can you believe this? Feels like I'm in a movie."

"Yeah, just remember any minute you're going to eat it."

Deza put some wiggling white grubs in a leaf and set it beside her. Then she placed a manioc pancake on top of a flat rock that sat in the red-hot coals. She returned her attention to a brown stew of animal parts in a pot in the fire.

Jesse swore he saw beaks and claws as she stirred.

Hallie read the look on his face, herself a little green. "Hey, when in Rome." She shaded her eyes from the afternoon sun. "Thinking about the cook?"

He nodded, thinking about the cook and how she had held court in her kitchen and that he had never made friends with her. Here, the clan had been standoffish at first, but they warmed quickly when Piper explained they were from her homeland.

"Me too. She would have hated all this, you know."

"Probably so."

Deza passed the leaf with the white grubs to Jesse. He looked to Piper.

"Take one, pass them around."

He selected one and gave the rest to Za. Jesse rolled it in his palm as the grub curled around his finger. He tossed it inside his mouth and bit before the grub did the same to his tongue. Watery liquid and oil burst across his mouth. The taste of old lettuce and older dirt mixed across his palette, and the skin felt like raspberries and caterpillars. He put the thing past his tongue and down. The other two stared at him, each with a grub in their fingers. He smiled purposely and gestured in delight.

Evenel sat at the end of the circle and took two. Deza handed Jesse a rough-hewn wooden bowl filled with brown stew and, buried below the surface, unknown bounty from the jungle that might have crawled or slithered or bit.

He noticed Piper had not selected a grub. His travel companions were in combat with their own throats, their fingers empty and clinched. A flat manioc bread followed. Deza held it before him, and he took the bread. His fingers cried out to his brain, "Hot, hot, hot!" He dropped it in his lap and sucked his fingers.

Deza picked another bread right from the stone and handed it to Za. He did the same as Jesse.

Jesse watched Piper lay a leaf in her hand, and Hallie seeing this, she did the same. Deza set the next bread there. Jesse looked next to him and saw a pile of fresh-picked leaves. He remembered Evenel carrying them earlier, bouncing across the courtyard, a few raining behind her.

All the bowls were passed out, and fine scents wafted from them, reminding Jesse of country gravy and sourdough bread. Piper and the others fished in the bowls and retrieved meaty parts falling off the bone, then sipped from the bowl. Jesse dipped in and put the meat in his mouth, fingers dripping. Unique flavors flashed in his brain, pleasure tumbling over his palate, and he ate like a growing boy.

He noticed Piper begrudgingly eating from her bowl like a bratty kindergartener separated from her cotton candy.

Hallie smiled politely, selecting carefully from her bowl, and Za bit at the small pieces on a bone. Evenel and Deza chatted like they were at a park picnic.

After the meal, the clay bowls were scoured clean with dirt and rinsed before being returned to the open-air hut. Jesse reached into his backpack and pulled out a candy bar. Evenel squealed with delight, but Piper beat her to the candy.

"Oh my God, you don't know how much I missed candy." She tore open the wrapper and bit into the chocolate. Her eyes rolled over in her head. She broke off a piece and gave it to Evenel, who was mauling her. "How long will you be here?" Piper asked.

"A few weeks," Jesse said.

"Then you had better have more of these. Or else."

Jesse snickered. "Or else what?"

"I might have you killed."

Evenel chewed, sucking on the sweet caramels.

Jesse pulled out another candy bar and gave it to Deza. She sniffed it and was about to taste it when Evenel, still chewing, took it from her mother and opened the wrapper. Evenel held it up, explaining the treat to the group that had surrounded her. She gave it back to her mother, who bit off a piece and handed it down the line.

"How far to the top of the falls?" Za asked.

"I don't know, I never went there."

Za gave her a look like she must be crazy.

"Okay, I was busy." She licked the candy wrapper.

"Za, you're being rude, again," Hallie said.

"No, I'm being direct," he replied.

"Rude."

"Ah, direct."

"Rude."

"Alright, I'll find out how to get there," Piper said.

227

"When?" Za asked.

"Tomorrow."

"How about now?"

"That is rude," Piper said.

"Directly rude. But effective." Za gave her his best little-boy grin.

"You got payment?"

"Payment for what?"

"Evenel," Piper said. "Go and get Xting. Ask him to come here." Evenel left. "Five Hershey bars. It's not a fee, it's a translation expense." Piper flashed her Southern bell charm, her eyelashes and fingertips fluttering.

Za threw up his arms. "Somebody help me here?"

Evenel returned with Xting in tow. "Xting how do we get to the top of the falls?"

"I can show you way, two hours' climb."

"Let's go in the morning," Za said.

"Can't," said Piper.

"Is this a quiz?"

"We have to harvest roots tomorrow."

"Roots? How long will that take?"

"A few days."

"Don't you have somebody to do that for you?"

"Yes, yes, I do. So glad you came."

"What?" he said, throwing his arms up.

"Welcome to the jungle, big boy."

"You *are* queen of the jungle," Jesse said, laughing.

"It comes with the stone," Piper said, fingering her necklace with the green stone.

"I was going to ask you about that," Hallie said. "It's beautiful. I love the way it sparkles in the sun."

"It's been kept in this village for a long time, generations." Piper took the stone in her hand, rolling the stone over and over. Shaped like a rough arrowhead, it was worn smooth from many pondering fingers. Parts of it still showed the coarse and irregular surface where it had broken away from its mother. The color was uniform and unchanged, even where so many hands polished the stone. It was brilliant green in the sun, with subtle yellows seeping away from the rays. Four monkey teeth gripped the stone, and a leather cord fashioned from soft jaguar hide circled her neckline.

Piper told the ancient story as it was told to her, how the stone came to her. "Za, now I want my Hershey bars."

"I think a delay in delivery of said request requires a substantial reduction of said fee."

"Oh no you don't, pay up."

"I believe she is the police," Hallie said.

The next morning, they joined the working life of their hosts. Xting held the machete ready while Jesse strained on the viney root, jerking it from the ground. A potato-like tuber pulled from the dusty soil.

Xting chopped it free from the vine. He picked it up and set it in a basket. "There," he said to Jesse, grabbing a plant and pulling on it.

"How can you tell? They look the same."

"Is darker, is dry, leaf is old, chop here." He pointed.

Jesse chopped at the ground a hundred times with the wooden hoe, exposing the vine. He sat down to rest.

Xting took the hoe and opened the hole with expert blows. "You no eat," he teased.

Jesse rolled to his feet and pulled with Xting on the vine, yanking it from the ground and spitting dirt into their eyes as the tuber appeared.

Jesse dug around it while Xting cut it away and moved it to the basket.

Evenel and her little friends, Penan, Sotee, and Viteen carried the baskets, which were made from woven fronds, back to the village. They placed the long handles across their foreheads and laid the baskets over their shoulders so the baskets hung down their backs. Jesse put his hand on each as they labored by and shook their heads, eliciting a smile and giggle from each of them.

He wiped his brow and gazed over the field, which held as many trees and bushes and vines as it did manioc. "You say you planted these roots? Why didn't you clear out the field and then plant them?"

"Bugs attack. Then next plant, then next plant. Manioc too close. Plant far apart."

"That's pretty smart."

"Piper tell me, America, you tell more." He thumped his chest and handed Jesse the hoe.

Jesse could see Hallie and Za working with Hada the quiet boy, Piper with Lesise, Hada's sister, and all the others working in the field. "Alright, I can tell you about snow."

"Snow?"

Jesse chopped with the hoe. "Snow. When water becomes so cold that it becomes solid like wood. But you have to tell me something you know about Piper."

"Water hard as wood?"

Jesse chopped at the soil. "Water hard as wood."

"Piper, why you ask?"

"Because she is a pretty girl."

"So?"

"I want to get to talk to her. She's always busy with somebody, doing something."

"Just a girl," he said. "Talk a lot, talk talk talk. You tell Xting this snow?"

❦

Three days later, the Americans were dirty, blistered, tired, and supremely satisfied. The harvest done, the manioc stored, and the field replanted, they fell into the delicious river face-first.

"Oh my God, that feels good," Hallie said surfacing. The entire village frolicked with them.

"She's a slave driver, man," Za shouted before dipping his head again.

"She's not a slave driver," Jesse said. "Every group of people needs a leader."

"My back and my hands," Za said, holding up the blistered palms, "say she's a slave driver."

Piper squealed as she splashed water on Lesise and Evenel.

"I want to get to the falls, man," Za said. "You can hear the roar the whole time you're in that stinking field, and it's a reminder were really close. I say we get our gear from the *Pantene* and go flying."

"Enjoy some culture, you lout," Hallie said.

"Yeah, well, enjoy some mud in your face." He dived on top of her.

They left at first light the next morning, their gear still on the *Pantene,* for the cool, windswept top of the falls. Xting led the way, along with Fopan and Stende, his friends and hunting companions. The four Americans came next and then Lesise with her brother Hada.

Jesse whirled his head, fascinated with the jungle and all its life. He struggled to pull it all in, but there was so much to see, each tree and vine struggling to overcome the other. Ants and beetles hustled about their business and the sounds of life piqued his curiosity.

Mist drifted down the rocky cliff, where stone steps had been carved into the steepest spots, ancient and worn. Vines and mosses clung to the stones. The path was wet and slippery, threatening to spill them down and past the spectacular views. At the bottom, roaring rapids interspersed with roiling waters. The clean scent of wild and forgotten things permeated all.

Despite the beauty, he kept returning to the sight of Piper, who walked behind Stende. He loved the way she moved. To him, she was perfect. Powerful muscles flexed in her calves and thighs, topped by a perfect butt. Ever since he met her, he'd been trying to get her alone and talk to her, but she always seemed to have a village to run—and she had him working dawn to dusk.

The hike cut into the jungle and out of the valley, winding upward toward the top of the falls. For the first time, they could see above the green abyss. The emerald canopy ran until the cotton-clouded sky devoured it, the soft sounds of the falls building to thunder as they neared. The sun moved across the sky, and it seemed that time had vanished because they had no more trail to climb, no more trees in their view, and the green foliage became smooth stone beneath them.

It was just like Emma had said. This was a place where you wished you had

wings; it was immense, beautiful, and wild. And no man had ever flown it before. No one on the entire planet.

CHAPTER THIRTY-THREE

The sun shone upon the travelers as they gazed over the jungle from atop the cliff. The flat stone surface spanned two hundred feet before being sawed in two by the gurgling river, then the waterway roared over the cliff. Upriver, the water cut a path through the jungle until the mountains bounced to the sky in the vastness of continent.

"Hot damn! Hallie come on," Za said, running to the edge of the cliff beside the waterfall. "It's wild, man, crazy, crazy wild, just look at it."

"My God," Hallie breathed out. "The jungle goes on forever. Let's get the kites right now."

"Kites?" Piper asked.

"Hang gliders," Jesse said. His attention was focused on the long view over infinite canopy and distant horizons, past the limitations of man.

"Oh, hang gliders," Piper said, blushing a rosy pink.

"Jesse! Man, come look at the edge," Za called out. "If that ain't a breeding ground for a thermal, I don't know what is, man. We can climb, fly, climb the thermal, fly again."

"Emma," Jesse whispered. "She was so right."

"Emma?" Piper asked.

"A friend, well, really the whole reason we got here."

"Jesse!" Hallie ran over, took his arm, and dragged him toward Za. "This is so cool! Come on!"

Piper sat down on the grass, letting the breeze flow over her locks. Hada and Lesise joined her. The visitors pointed and gestured, discussing the flying for half an hour.

The three of them came over to Piper and the siblings.

"We were going to wait until tomorrow," Hallie said, "but we want to speed things up. It's early yet. We could get the kites from the boat and get back here yet today."

"We could get the food too, like real food from a can?" Piper asked.

Jesse smiled. "We got peaches in heavy syrup."

"Let's get going." Piper stood up. "We can spend the night here, on top of the world." She started down the trail and Jesse jumped in right next to her.

Midday found them walking along the river a few miles past the village. Za and Hallie had taken the lead, then came the locals, with Piper and Jesse following behind and carrying a conversation. "You're kidding," Jesse teased, "SpaghettiOs? Every day?"

"I could eat them every day. Bacon for breakfast, sliced thick and fried." She jumped in the air and twirled. "I've even dreamed about it since I have been here. Last night I couldn't sleep wondering what you had on that boat."

"You're a foodie."

"I am not."

"I don't dream about food. You're a foodie."

"Wait till you have to eat what I do, and I don't mean for a few days, I mean for months."

"If I did dream, it would be something good, like a juicy burger and fries or perfectly ripe strawberries in June."

"It's my fantasy."

"Food fantasy? That all you got?"

"I have fantasies."

"About what?"

"A lot of things."

"How about a dark and handsome man?" He put on his bad-boy smile.

"No, not that," she sighed. "My fantasy has his nose buried in a book and talks dirty to me in French."

Jesse opened his mouth to say something but Hallie interrupted.

"There it is!" Hallie called out. She pulled off one of the branches covering the boat.

Piper stopped short. "That's the *Pantene*."

"You know this boat?" Jesse said.

"Where's Pan?"

Jesse paused, then said, "You know—"

"Where's Pan?" Piper demanded.

"We had a problem on the way here—"

"Tell me where Pan is!" she shouted, pushing Jesse in the chest.

He grabbed her wrists. "Calm down and I will tell you."

She ripped free of his grip. "Tell me! What did you do to him?"

"We didn't...We were attacked by pirates. They wanted... let me start over. We hired Pan to take us upriver. Just outside Manaus, Pan stopped the boat and there were some boys swimming in the middle of nowhere, and he gave each one of them a backpack with something in it."

"And?"

"And later on we ran into this other boat and they wanted the backpacks." Jesse hesitated. "Pan showed them some fakes so they thought we still had them. They chased us and cornered us. We had to shoot our way out."

"And Pan?"

Jesse hung his head. "They killed him."

Piper looked to Hallie and Za. She could see the truth in their eyes. Piper bit at her lip and fingered the green stone. She wiped at her eyes and turned her back. The entire party stood silent.

Lesise put her arms around Piper and they moved away from the others. "It is the way of the river, Piper. Be strong. Use the stone to be strong."

Piper nodded. "It's hard. He was so good to Evenel."

"When we lose someone, we have to go on. Tomorrow and its hunger will come whether we want it to or not."

Piper nodded. "Alright, Lesise, yes." She turned toward the others. "We have to get back. Gather the things we need."

Later, when they arrived at the village, the group set about storing the items from the *Pantene*. "Keep the kites over here," Jesse ordered, "along with the stuff we need. Hallie and Za, check over the equipment."

"What are you doing?" Piper asked.

"We're going to the top of the falls," Jesse said.

"After this, after Pan? You are still going? Going now is… is just stupid."

"Then why don't you come with us?" he said, inspecting his gear.

"Well you don't have to be pissy about it," Piper said.

"How is that pissy?" He looked at her, then continued inspecting his equipment. "Look, I take this real serious. I wasn't saying you're stupid, I meant I want you to come with me."

"It didn't sound like that."

"Let's talk about this after I check this equipment over. I have lots of things to get ready here. I can't do anything else right now."

"Fine, I'll just go and find some tea to gossip over! While you play with yourself." Piper stomped off.

"It's not like that," he called after her. He shook his head, then returned to his work. They inspected every inch of rope and the hang gliders, then set up and mated every piece, ensuring they were compatible and each function was working properly. Then they did it all again, before breaking them down for transport.

Afterward, Jesse sat on his haunches, feeling a deep pit in his stomach. He walked over to Piper. She was carrying palm fronds to Lesise, Deza, and several of the women who were making baskets.

"I'm sorry, I—"

"No, don't…It was me, I was feeling, just being stupid." She crossed her arms. "I just…I really don't want to screw up and I don't know why I did that and I don't know why I am talking so fast right now."

He took her armful of palm fronds and kissed her. "Come with us? Please?"

"Go, Piper," Lesise said. "We will watch over the village. If we need you, I will send Hada. Take Xting, Stende, and Fopan with you. They are excited to go."

Jesse smiled, took her hand, and pulled her toward the others.

CHAPTER THIRTY-FOUR

It was two thousand feet of vertical stone, so sheer that the water cascading over the top never touched the rock face. "Where will you land?" Piper asked. From the top of the falls, the jungle went on as far as the eye could see.

"In Rio."

Piper looked at Za, her eyes wide. "Oh you ass." She grinned. "I bet Hallie could make it. She doesn't have to haul such a big ego with her."

"Ouch." Za cupped his heart. He stepped into his harness, pointing with his chin, and said, "Your village lies there, where the smoke hangs."

Piper looked. "You can get that far?"

"Piece of cake. There's enough of a clearing to get on the ground there."

"You were supposed to be digging roots, how do you know that?" She crossed her arms. "What if you don't make it?"

"That's flying, baby," Za said.

Piper punched him in the shoulder. "Jerk," she said, smiling. She turned her attention to Jesse, who was working with Xting, showing him how to set up the hang glider and the harness.

Hallie said, "The river has two sandbars next to the village that would work nicely, so recovery will be easy. That gives us three options, with the river itself being the safety."

"I got chills just lookin' at it," Jesse said. "Get in the harness and let's do it."

"Wait," Piper said. "There are rules."

"Rules? What kind of rules could there possibly be?" Jesse scrunched his shoulders.

"Stay away from that area over there." She swept her hand over the far eastern sky. "There's a tribe there, and they are dangerous."

"Could you be a little more specific?" Jesse swung his arm in a wild arc. "You just painted out half of our playground." He buckled his harness.

"Their village is east of the river. Just stay close to the river and the cliff."

"Because?"

"Because we leave them alone and they have left us alone. You don't know what happens here."

"Well, I would love to hear about it, but really, I'd rather jump off a cliff."

Hallie first then Za and Jesse jumped into the sky. "COCOZA!" vibrated over the jungle three times.

Jesse pulled the control bar back and fell like a stone. He jerked the bar back hard and that old familiar fabric and aluminum groaned under strain, the snap followed by singing metal. The sudden exposure of the wings to the wind sucked G's and his mind mushed like it was being compressed. This was quickly followed by a swirl back to consciousness, like a top winding up.

God, it's awesome, Jesse thought. He used his speed to curl back in front of the falls. He ran across the front, so close that water poured off the fabric like an umbrella. The staccato sound announced danger and conjured magic memories of thunderstorms and downpours. He circled and dove again, racing the fluid down, gaining speed. He dropped until the water stood still alongside him, falling, falling, and yet the droplets hung in the air with him.

He broke away, and as far as he could see spanned the untamed forest. A rainbow begged to be chased down and just maybe flown through. The moist heat wrapped around him as he came closer to the treetops. The ride already over, he flared, scoring a perfect landing along the riverbank next to the village.

Hada and Lesise, along with the entire village, greeted him like a rock star. His fellow fliers came in right behind him.

"That was quite a dive, man," Za said, high-fiving Jesse.

Hallie ran over and jumped on both of them. "This is awesome! What a ride."

Two boys picked up the gliders and started running, trying to soar away. "Hey!"

Jesse said. "We better grab the kites before they break them."

"Come on, let's do it again," Hallie yelled, jumping around and clapping her hands.

They collapsed the gliders. Lesise said, "Sarten and Czondi go with you." She pointed to two adolescent boys with bushy hair. "Everyone wants go, but we work to do." She looked toward a sullen Hada. He drooped his shoulders and kicked at the sand.

"There will be a next time," Jesse said.

"I'll wait up here again," Piper said. She was smiling but her

tone was a little dejected, like she was the only little girl standing by the ice cream truck without a dollar. Jesse stood in
the harness, demonstrating the controls to Xting and the
other boys.

"We'll be right back, one more flight, and then we'll make
camp up here. Right atop the falls and close to the stars," Jesse
said with a wink.

"Follow me," Hallie said as she leaped into the air.

The two men jumped almost together. Hallie swung back
toward the waterfall and grabbed the thermal close to the
rock. Jesse watched her rise above the elevation of the cliff face.
Hallie circled in the thermal above where the waterfall left the
rock and the water plunged toward the blue pool a thousand
feet below. She turned upriver, and the sudden change of two
thousand feet of drop to a few hundred as she crossed over the
face of the falls was a rush in itself. Hallie waved at Piper as
she passed over, going upriver.

"You're my hero, Hallie," Piper yelled, waving at her.

Hallie swung over the campsite atop the cliff and the sun-
baked stone that ran right to the riverbank.

She flew a quarter mile upriver and then turned back downriver, descending slowly above the river toward the waterfall.
Za stayed close to Jesse, swerving at him like playground bul-
lies. They, too, waved at Piper as they followed Hallie's path.

They swung around and over the river, mimicking Hallie.
She dropped to a few feet above the water, following the river
and heading for the falls. Then she fell right over the edge.

Jesse whooped. "Did you see that, man?"

"That's why I love her," Za shouted back. He swung in front
of Jesse, cutting him off. Za headed for the falls before disappearing over the edge of the roaring torrent.

Jesse floated just above the water almost to a stop, about
to collapse into the river. When Za cut him off, he scrubbed
some speed and hung in the air. He dived for speed until he

was inches from the rushing liquid. If he fell into the water, it would drag him in and he'd tumble over the edge of the falls to certain death.

His brain sent the message he wasn't going to make it. "No."

Electric snaps of fear crackled through him. Pulsing wave after wave of fear ran from his center out to his fingers and toes. His heart hammered his torso.

Just as quickly, the edge of the waterfall passed under him and he fell into the sky.

He dove straight down as if he had gone over the falls, a roller coaster times ten.

His mind screamed fear and thrill and the pure pleasure of living in the passing lane with a truck coming. The liquid vaporized to mist before he swung away, down the river.

He scanned the sky. Hallie and Za were back in the thermal and climbing. Jesse followed, circling as they climbed. She circled wider, waiting for them to meet her elevation.

"How was that?" she shouted.

"Fookn' awesome," Jesse yelled back.

"You're my hero, baby," Za shouted. They were as high as the thermal would take them. Hallie slid out of formation and flew in an easy glide toward terra firma.

So many things to see, Jesse thought. The contours and the color changes beckoned from the west and the river alone called to follow it to the very end of the earth. A wafer of scent came to Jesse. Smoke.

Jesse scanned the sky, and there it was. In the east, smoke climbed from the canopy. Must be the village on the other side of the river, he thought.

He whistled to Za and Hallie. "Hey, check it out!" He pointed. "Follow me."

Jesse moved over the canopy, curiosity pulling him. They approached the clearing in the forest and he could see several huts. He saw people and heard their shouts. Some of them had stained their bodies head to toe, red or yellow. A sizzle cut past him, then another.

"They're shooting at us!" Hallie shouted.

Jesse looked down and saw the bows bent backward, then popping straight. Arrows sang past. He shifted his weight and swung away from the village, looking for Hallie and Za. They had followed his lead. He flared a little, and they came beside him.

Za looked over at Jesse. "That was crazy, man!"

Hallie let out a scream. "Oh my God, that was so cool!" She rolled her kite. They all burst out in nervous laughter.

CHAPTER THIRTY-FIVE

As soon as they hit the ground, Jesse called to Za and Hallie. "Don't tell Piper. She'll rant about disturbing the neighbors."

"I don't think that's a good idea," said Hallie.

"Hey, what she doesn't know won't hurt her," Jesse answered. "It was nothing."

"It's your relationship. You want to mess it up?"

"What relationship?"

"Denial? Or are you really just stupid?"

Jesse rolled his shoulders with his hands out. "I'm just hanging out, having fun gettin' shot at with my friends."

"Yeah, man," Za grunted.

"Show her some respect while we're here. She's gone out of her way to help us."

"Not like we have to lie. We just avoid disclosure."

"Come on," Za said, "we can get another jump before she makes us do chores."

"See?" Jesse said. "No worries." Hada ran up to them. Jesse continued, "I'll go to the village and get the black bag of equipment with Hada. You two collapse the gliders, and pack them for the climb back to the top."

When Jesse and the others got to the top of the falls, he dropped his pack on the ground.

Piper said, "I better get back to the village."

"That's a great idea. You're coming with me, baby."

"What?"

"I brought the tandem harness."

"And what does tandem harness mean?" she asked in a suspicious tone, twirling her hair.

"It means you're jumping off a cliff today."

"No."

"Oh, yes. Come over here."

Piper started backing away. "No…"

"Let's get her!" Hallie said.

Piper turned to run, but Za picked her up off the ground and put her on his shoulder. "There's nothing to be afraid of. Just a little flying."

"Put me down!"

"You going to jump off a cliff then?"

"Yes, no, maybe…"

"Put her down," said Hallie.

Jesse took out the harness and, facing her, reached out his arms and pulled the straps around her. "You're shaking," he said in a calm voice. "It's perfectly safe."

"Compared to what?" She bit her lower lip to stop the quivering.

Jesse tugged the straps tight as she fell against him. He looked into her eyes and saw fear mixed with excitement. "You're going to be right beside me. All you have to do is hang on and enjoy the ride."

Minutes later, she shrieked like a little girl. The glider leveled off, and she stopped screaming. "It's…beautiful and it's wild and…I'm flying!" She screamed again in exhilaration. "Oh my God, this is the craziest thing I have ever done."

She leaned over and kissed him, and the glider banked hard left from the weight transfer.

"Whoa," Jesse said, fighting for control as the glider fell hard left. He kissed her back.

She screamed again. "Woo! This is awesome!" The glider leveled out as Jesse caught the thermal. The floating feeling gave way to a pop that lifted them like an elevator.

"Are we going up?"

"Very good," he said sarcastically.

She smiled. "You are such a smart ass. Lucky you're so cute."

"Don't forget your life is in my hands."

"I'm not worried. I've got feminine power."

"What?"

"That thing men can't resist and I keep it with me wherever I go."

He kissed her again, swung away from the thermal over the forest, and floated toward the village.

"Come on, dive this thing."

"Alright, you asked." The screaming started up as Jesse delivered a proper carnival-thrill ride.

After repacking the harness, Jesse and Piper hiked back to the top of the cliff with Piper firing off questions and reliving her first flight.

Xting and the other boys descended upon the flyers like ants and excited boys as soon as the Americans reached the top of the falls. "Jesse, please take me flying," Xting cried.

"Me, take me!" they all shouted.

"Tomorrow," Jesse replied.

"We have to work now," Piper said.

Xting grabbed Jesse's hand and said, "You promised me a lesson when you got back."

"Ten minutes, then you both cut some firewood," Piper commanded.

"Then we fly like birds tomorrow? You promise Jesse?"

"Yes." Jesse tussled Xting's moppy head. "I promise."

"Za, go with Fopan, Stende, Sarten, and Czondi and get some firewood. Hallie, you and I are going to make the best Spam and beans ever," Piper said.

Soon the machetes thudded rhythmically as they gathered firewood. That set off the howler monkeys with their warnings. Yellow butterflies the size of pennies floated by, a hundredfold at a time. Morpho butterflies, perhaps the bluest things in the world, iridescent and metallic, like sapphires brilliantly engorged, touched the greens and browns of the forest.

They dined on the stores from the *Pantene* and answered endless questions about flying and canned food until the light faded and the small band settled onto their grass mats.

Jesse stared at the night sky. The locals drifted off to sleep, although Xting confirmed Jesse's promise first. The stars sparkled from horizon to the far away horizon. He rolled over and looked at the other Americans; they watched the sky too.

"The sky is different," Za said. "It's the stars, they're not the same ones."

"What do you mean 'not the same ones?'" Hallie said.

"Well, they're in a different place."

"Like you can tell."

"It just looks different. It's so big and so beautiful."

"More than me?"

Za stood and reached for Hallie's hand. "Let's find a secluded spot, and I will demonstrate the difference between your beauty and some dumb ol' stars." He pulled her to her feet.

He turned around, and Hallie jumped on his back. "Promise nothing will eat me?"

He grinned. "I can't promise, but I'll be there."

"My hero." She feigned a faint.

He trotted off beyond the firelight, Hallie giggling in delight.

247

Piper and Jesse tended the small fire alone. It emitted a flickering light that alternately showed her face and then lost it as if photo strobes flashed in slow, romantic motion. Black moths with ovals of dark-green upon their wings fluttered by.

Jesse said, "So tell me how you ended up on top of the world with a handsome man."

She cupped her chin in her hand, considering. "The long story or the really, really long story?"

"We got time…look, a shooter." He pointed, tracing a streaking star.

"It's like fireworks off in the sky," Piper said. "You know what I want to do someday?"

"What?"

"I want to be on an airplane on the Fourth of July and fly over all the fireworks in every town and see them from above, exploding all over the night sky."

"That would be cool. I love fireworks."

"Really? Me, too. It's my favorite holiday. The family picnics and music and fireworks and all."

"Is that how you ended up on top of the world with a handsome man?"

Downriver, near the falls, a slight laugh sounded over the sizzle of the waterfall, followed by a squeal of delight. The moon appeared.

"Mmm, mating noises and stars and a crackling fire, and here I am with the most beautiful woman I have ever met." Jesse pointed toward the sky. "God has picked me out as his favorite man."

She laughed.

He thought that was the most sensual sound he had ever heard. Jesse was fascinated with her. The way she used her hands to illustrate everything, her pleasure in learning about him. The way her eyes were big and gorgeous. He put a log on the fire and stirred the coals.

She was absolutely striking, beautiful, and charming, and she was articulate like a scholar. She was a sexy one with generous curves who wore the green stone comfortably.

"You haven't told me your story," he said.

"You have someplace to go?"

"There's a chick behind every giant ceiba tree." He put his hands behind his head.

"How 'bout I leave you out here to the fire ants?"

"You really don't want to tell me this story. Must be embarrassing."

"If you would close your mouth I would tell you." She leaned back with a smile and put her hands behind her head. Then she spilled the story of how she found Evenel in the streets of Manaus.

"Wow. It took a lot of balls to do that."

"I would have thought that too, before it happened to me. I rose to the challenge, and I am proud of that."

"You should be." He tossed another log on the fire. "Quite the coincidence...we both hired Pan and we both ended up here."

Piper lost her smile. "I really didn't know him that long, but something about him, well, it made him special."

Guilt rolled across Jesse like lake water. Two people...that was the number who had saved him. Two people lay cold and dead for him. He pushed it aside before his feelings got a hold of him.

"I don't think it was coincidence that brought you here. Pan brought you here, hoping you would bring me back."

"Am I?"

"No, I can't leave now. You don't know what has happened here."

"I know I'm freezing." He let out a violent shiver. "Where did all that heat go?"

Piper said, "Come on, I'll show you how a native warms up." She stood and walked toward the river. Jesse got up and followed her.

She stopped at the water's edge and pulled off her top. Piper stripped down in the starry darkness. Turning back to him, she stood in silhouette. "Coming?"

Her sudden disrobing caught him off guard, and he froze just staring at her, cursing the lack of light.

"Are you coming?"

Her voice snapped him back. He yanked off his shirt and flicked his shorts in the air with his foot so they landed on top of the shirt. That ink did not seem very inviting until they toed the water. It was much warmer than the air. She jumped into the river and disappeared in its blackness. He jumped too, and the liquid brought vigor to his whole being. He swam hard toward her, and in so doing, brushed his arm along her outer thigh. He felt a hot pang. She let out the sexiest little sound he had ever heard. Then he lost her in the dark.

He treaded water, searching for some sign of her. He felt a nibble on his toe. "Shit! What was that?" he said aloud, his mind rattling through all the unknown, unseen things that eat you in the water.

He spun in the water and some God-awful thing hit his foot. Tap tap tap.

Jesse kicked at it, and whatever it was, it was big. He stroked through the water as fast as he could. "PIPER!"

The water burst in front of him. Something landed on top of him, forcing him under. It screamed, and he realized it was her. He kicked to the surface again.

She let go and swam toward the shore.

"Game on!" Jesse put his head down and reached for her legs, but she was powerful and fast. He doubled his stroke, determined to get her. The water boiled in front of him from her strokes until at last he caught her foot. He pulled violently, yanking her back and toward him.

She turned, facing him and slipping both her legs around his waist, her face and her eyes to his. He felt the sand bottom

250

under his feet and he stood up, standing half out of the water and holding her to him.

That man-to-woman nakedness pressed along his whole length flooded him. Liquid drops ran along her face, across her cheeks, and dropped on her breasts and his chest.

In her eyes he saw her lust—the same sin, the same virtue that swelled him. He brought his lips to hers, and she sought his kiss. Fireworks went off inside Jesse when they touched. Sensuously bonded together, she wrapped her hands around his face holding that kiss forever, burning it into his memory.

He fell forward into the shallow water, and he kissed her again deep and hard. Water slipped across his back, washing ever toward the falls. He held her tight, pulling himself upright with her clinging to him, never to let go. He stood, easily lifting them from the water.

With a quick step, they fell upon the bank still engulfed in the hot wonder of each other. She rolled on top and stretched out upon his entire length, her feet sliding along his legs until they met his. She felt along his arms, the long and hard arms, until she clasped his hands, intertwining her fingers with his. She was completely supported over the earth by this man. She lowered her mouth to his and ever so lightly brushed his lips with hers.

All the fires lit, and Jesse let his passion for her rage unchecked. He cupped her face and kissed her lips and along her neck, searching her passion and treasuring her curves. She responded to his touch, seeking him, his masculinity. Pleasure and pain, so delicious, so unique to man and woman, pulsed and exploded between them. All the world went absent, only her and he under a tidal moon atop the world.

CHAPTER
THIRTY-SIX

Jesse stirred out of his sleep. Someone was shaking him awake.

"Jesse, awake, wind very good, fly now, fly now," Xting said.

"Okay, I'm awake."

Jesse rolled away from Piper and stood upright. He stretched his arms upward and yawned. He thought about the first moment he had gazed upon her, how he had felt that morning, and last night's memory glowed wonderfully.

Xting pulled on his arm, nearly dragging him toward the glider. He said, "Last night I called to the wind, a song to come to the falls."

Jesse waved him permission to move the glider to the take-off spot next to the top of the falls. Xting bounded toward the edge with the glider.

"Whoa, hold up there partner," Jesse said, strolling over to the cliff, still shaking the sleep from his frame.

He stood on the edge and looked into the sky. It was just past black, almost a new day. The wind blew stiffly into his face. "Xting, it's no good, the wind is wrong. We have to wait."

Xting's face fell. "I sang well, we fly now?"

Jesse put his arm around Xting. "No, in a few hours maybe." The beams of first light struck them, its warmth soothing. The expanding color rolled over the distant canopy, awakening the jungle. Jesse could see that Xing wanted to launch the second the sun peeked over the other side of the world.

Jesse stood on his tiptoes and stretched again. "I'm going back to bed."

Xting dropped his shoulders. "Today?"

"Maybe today." Jesse returned to Piper, slipped under the blanket, and curled up behind her, spooning her and enjoying the feel of her body. Debating whether he needed sleep or some morning pleasure, he cupped her breast in his hand.

She raised her head and turned to kiss him.

"Miss me?" He kissed her.

"I already miss any minute without you."

He laughed low and quiet. "I missed all the minutes since day one."

"Well, I guess I can tell you now, I had the hots for you at the rock. It might have been because I was naked. I never met a man while taking a bath before." She giggled. "Yeah, that's all it was."

Jesse heard running footsteps. He looked up and saw Xting in the air with the raptors. "COCOZA!" he yelled.

Jesse burst to his feet. The glider was gone. He ran to the edge and his gut rolled. Xting wobbled wildly in the wind. "Za! Hallie!"

The tone of Jesse's voice brought them out of their blankets and on their feet in one motion. "Come here! Hurry!"

They rushed to the edge of the cliff.

"Xting just took off," Jesse said.

"By himself? He doesn't know how," Hallie said.

"The wind is all wrong. He can't get to the landing zone," Jesse said.

"Like he knows how," Za said. He felt the wind in his face. "Goddamn it, man! It's going to take him across the river, he can't get back."

The entire party assembled at the edge, watching Xting swing wildly through the air, his shouts of joy floating back to them. Chilling fog hung in the air, hiding the glider from view.

"Where is he? Xting! Xting!" Piper shouted.

Her voice echoed back to them. The fog passed and the blue glider appeared. Hundreds of birds lifted from the canopy, their cries and wing beats reaching them in slow time.

"Christ," Jesse said. "He's going to smash into a tree. He can't even steer. Look, he's going down."

The kite fell through the green canopy and was gone. "Did he get down to the ground or did he hang up in a tree?" Hallie said.

"I think he got down, but I can't tell," Za said.

"What the hell was he doing?" Piper asked.

"I told him we couldn't fly this morning. The wind was wrong," Jesse said.

"You were going to let him fly himself?"

"No, in tandem. I never thought he would just take off—"

"He's a kid, use your head," Piper snapped, throwing her hands in the air.

"I said no to him." Jesse pointed toward the abyss.

"How far is he?" Hallie asked.

"I would guess about two miles," Za replied.

"That's a long way in the jungle," Piper said. "It will take a while for him to get back."

"Him? What about us?" Jesse pointed at his chest with his thumb. "It will be hours before we can get back to the village and get started after him."

"You're going after him?" Piper asked.

"Why wouldn't we go after him?" Jesse said.

"You know why. The other tribe. Besides that, he was born here, he can get back on his own."

"Without my hang glider."

Piper stood with her mouth open, gaping.

Jesse wanted those words back before they even reached her. "For all we know he is hurt, hanging in a tree," he said.

"You don't get it. That is not just the jungle; it's the other side of the river.

"You can't go."

"Oh yes we can," he snapped. "We haven't bought into that evil empire crap. We're going." Jesse looked at the other two for their commitment.

"We should think about this, Jesse," Hallie said.

"Christ, not you now. I would think you would be first in line here." He turned to Za and said, "Don't you puss out on me too."

"I'm with you, man. If he's hurt, we should go." He glanced at Hallie. "We really should."

"Let's pack up, we can get what we need back at the village. Stende, Fopan, do you know the area where he went down?" Jesse asked.

"No! You can't take them. Tohanna will not stand for it. It's too dangerous for them," Piper blurted.

"That is not up to you. It's up to them. And who is Tohanna?"

Piper grabbed the two boys and stormed off toward the trail.

"Hallie, go talk to her. Please?" Za said. "We'll pack and meet you at the village."

"Look, you two need to shut off your macho bullshit. She asked you not to go out there. She must have her reasons."

"You think we should let him die out there?" Jesse said.

"Shut up, Jesse." She took a step toward him, shaking her finger. "Don't think you can bully me. I just want to know why we shouldn't go, that's all."

"Please talk to her," Za said, nodding toward Piper. "Please?"

"Pack it up," Jesse said. "I want my damn glider back."

At the village, they quickly gathered supplies and loaded them into dugout canoes. "Stende and Fopan are going with us?" Hallie asked. The two boys carried their bows, walking toward them. "Why did Piper let them go?" Hallie asked.

"She didn't, they came anyway," Jesse said. "Once we cross the river, we'll need them if we're going to find my glider. Stende, Fopan, hurry up." He waved them in. "Are we ready to go?"

They started to shove off when Piper ran up to them.

"Don't do this. Xting will come back."

"I can't believe you're an American. Where is your compassion?" Jesse said.

Piper put her hand on Jesse's arm and said, "I am asking you not to do this."

"I can't."

"Then you have killed us."

CHAPTER THIRTY-SEVEN

They crossed the river in the dugouts and stepped ashore on the other side. Every inch was covered in swamp. The trees grew six feet apart, the bark arduous and dark. Small humps of stained slime-moss and fungus protruded from the ground. Black water pooled between the humps, covering the swamp with mosquito larvae.

Jesse stepped on one of the humps and it gave way, like stepping on Jell-O. He fell forward, his jaw, mouth, and nose dipping below the ooze.

He struggled to recover, splashing about. Hallie burst out laughing. The slime stained his face as if he were wearing a veil. He spit out dark plops of gunk. "Gross." Hallie stopped laughing.

Jesse took another step, setting his foot between two humps. His leg sank until he was knee deep. He took another step, and the rest of the team followed his lead. Each step disturbed the water, sending waves of sulfur rot stink up to gag them.

Hallie gripped a low branch and pulled her foot out of a hole. The disturbed tree swayed slightly, and thick slime plopped on her hair and shoulder. "Shit, what is that?" she asked.

"It looks like bird shit," Za said.

"Well, get it off me."

Za grabbed at the tree next to him, and it rained down more thick slime.

"Stop, don't touch the trees," Jesse said. "This can't go on forever. Just keep going and we will walk out of this." He stepped forward, and the water released with a sucking sound when his foot escaped the mud. The stink of gas boiled under his face.

The team plunged on in silent misery until they crossed the swamp. Now they moved in dim light under tall trees that closed off the sun. Vines and thorny brush blocked their way. Stifling heat pressed upon them. "This place feels...I don't know, evil I guess," Hallie said. "And nothing lives here except ugly bugs."

"And snakes and caymans and piranha," Za added. "I can see why the people who live on this side of the river are a little testy."

"Well, I'm not real happy either, so they best not mess with me," said Jesse.

They trudged on in silence, feeling disgusting in the heat. The residue from the swamp stuck to them, attracting biting gnats that swarmed their heads and flew into their eyes. Then the grasses became so thick they had to cut a path with machetes. The blades of grass cut their faces and fingers.

They began to string out when fatigue and boredom set in. Hallie stopped and looked back. "Jesse, hold up. I can't see Stende."

"Well, where was he?"

"He was last, but he was right behind me." The group gathered around Hallie. "So you think he went back?" she asked.

"Ask him," Za said, pointing to Fopan, who was leading them.
Fopan stood silent.

Za pointed back the way they came from. "Stende?"

Fopan shrugged. He suddenly seemed the young boy he was.

"Do you think he went back?" Hallie asked.

Jesse shrugged. "Maybe. Let's take a break here, see if he catches up, if not, he went back."

"What if something happened to him?" Hallie asked.

"I doubt it," Jesse said.

They sat down. After a few minutes, Jesse stood, "Okay, we can't sit here forever. Let's get going."

Hallie looked at him, worried.

Jesse said, "Yes, I am sure he went back to his mama. Everybody up, come on, let's go."

Hot and close, they waded deeper into the jungle. Late in the afternoon, they reached the spot they had calculated the glider should be. They spread out and searched the area.

Jesse scanned the trees and the ground ,hoping to pick up any sign of Xting or the glider. He yelled out, "Xting!" Everything went silent in the jungle. "Xting!"

They stood still, listening, a few dozen yards apart.

Suddenly Za jumped. "What was that? Something moved out there, man!"

"Like what?" Jesse asked.

"I don't know, man. Something big."

Jesse scanned the jungle. "It must be Fopan. Where did he go? Fopan!"

"It wasn't Fopan."

"Well, he's the only one not here. Fopan! Where the hell did you go? Fopan! Answer me, boy!"

"Fopan!" Hallie called out.

They listened for a long minute, their eyes scanning the green abyss.

"There it is again!" Za said.

"There too!" Hallie screamed. She ran to Za. They huddled against each other.

All around them, the jungle held something just beyond their senses.

"It's the wind," Jesse said.

"Something is out there, man," Za said. "We should have brought the fucking guns, man."

"Fopan!" Jesse called out again. Nothing came back.

"Fopan! We have to look for him," Hallie said, her breathing erratic.

"We go together then," Za said, gripping his machete.

Jesse moved over to them. "Which direction did he go?"

Hallie pointed. "That way."

"I'll take the lead." Jesse swept the grass back with his machete. Nothing there. He called out to Fopan, then waited, then hacked a few yards. The grass and vines and thorns grew thicker. "Fopan! Xting!" He moved ahead. The jungle opened up. "Fopan! Xting!" Nothing.

"What could of happened to him?" Za asked.

"I don't know. He hasn't been missing long enough to get beyond shouting distance."

"Did he go back to the village?" Hallie asked.

"Why would he run now after we got all the way here? He would have taken off before this," Jesse said.

"Then whatever was out there must have got him," Za said.

"You mean a jaguar?" Hallie asked. She trembled, her voice shaking.

"No, baby, not that." He drew her closer. "What if it was human? What if Piper was right?"

"Then why are we still alive?" Jesse said.

"I don't know. Maybe they are waiting to get us one at a time," Za said.

"Shut up! We don't need that hanging over our heads," Jesse snapped.

"You shut up!" Za said. He pointed at Jesse with his machete.

"There is no such thing as the boogie man." He used his machete to slap Za's away. "Not back home and not here either. The chance of them even knowing we are here is zero," Jesse said.

"Well, nobody says you're right. I think they know we are here. And I don't think the boys went back. They must have gotten them," Za said.

"Bullshit."

"How do you know?" Za said, raising his voice.

Hallie pulled on Za's arm, trying to pull them apart. "Stop that, both of you. We have to go back, right now, to the village and get help to find the boys and Xting."

"Alright," Jesse said, not taking his eyes off Za. "But we stick close together."

"It's going to be dark before we get back," Hallie said.

"You want to stay and sleep?" Jesse said.

"God, no!"

"That's what I thought." He moved past them, toward the river.

Each step was a race with the sun as it fell across the sky toward the looming sunset. Browns overpowered the yellows and greens as the light bent ever more, falling to earth, trapping them in the chasm of the jungle. They moved faster, and the thorns cut deeper, the vines pulled, and the creatures called. The trip to the river was measured in miles and the light failed them, choking their eyes as the candle-colored light flickered, turned to smoke, and was gone. An indistinguishable cloak descended.

They rested, so close together their hips touched. Their breathing was harsh and stinging. Their chests pounding, legs heavy and drained. The flashlights were off to conserve them. They sat in the black water and muck, fatigue fully in command after the long dash through the night. Hunger and thirst pulled at them.

"Is this, this, this...the swamp next to the river?" Hallie asked, trying to keep from passing out from fatigue.

"Yes," Jesse answered, his voice harsh. "It has the same stink."

Za turned on his flashlight. "The evil factor is doubled, man." The flashlight poked holes in the enveloping darkness. "The worst part saved until last, man. Must be a fucking mile to the river." He looked at his watch. "It will be sun-up by the time we get through this shit."

Hallie slid her head across his chest; asleep. He caught her, struggled to set her upright again. He dropped his flashlight in the muck. He retrieved it, wiped it off, and shined it into the dark. Movement crossed in front of the stunted beam.

"Ahh!" they both screamed.

Hallie, startled awake, cried out.

All three thrashed about in the muck, rolling to their feet with machetes gripped and flashlights switched on. One, two, and then the third cut holes in the dark.

Water splashed, moving swiftly behind them. The light beams turned, and all three shrieked out.

Jesse pointed the flashlight. The light trembled and his gut contracted, pulling both ends inward. "Wh-what is it! Fuck!" He could hear his voice cut through the trees. He remembered the machete and brought it up.

Dead silence. Their breathing came fast and choppy. Dead silence. He swung his flashlight, looking, looking. Silence. Jesse felt his brain return to function, the fear subsiding a little.

He scanned with the flashlight again. The beam moved across dark trees and muted vines. Fog drifted across the light, obscuring tree trunks, some a few feet away, others ten feet away. Moss, stringy and slimy, hung from the bark.

Forms crept into the light and disappeared as the beams moved. Water droplets reflected back, dancing in the artificial light. Jesse felt something in his psyche and spun around. The light beam cut into the dark and a set of eyes reflected back.

Jesse stumbled backward into Hallie and Za. He bawled out as the three of them fell into the swamp, the black water claiming the two flashlights. The mud sucked at them as they fought to get up, to stand.

Jesse lost his machete as he fell, and the light stabbed at the sky. He rolled to his hands and knees, trying to find it, but his flashlight plunged into the muck. The cloak of darkness tightened like a rope around his throat.

He groped in the mud for the machete. His mind pounding, screaming as he scrambled in the mud. Suddenly he was lifted from the mud.

"Jesse!" Za pulled him upright.

"I saw it! It's coming!" Jesse shouted.

Jesse broke free and dived for the machete, his hand somehow landing on the handle. He jackknifed to his feet, machete and flashlight in hand. He stabbed the light into the jungle. The other two shined with his, their beams muted from the mud. They turned again, and the light beams illuminated vines that still swung in the trees right in front of them. They all screamed. Hallie fell. Za picked her up and leaped through the potholes, splashing wildly. "Something was right there, man!" Za said.

Panic gripped Jesse, and he ran after Za and Hallie, desperate not to be left behind.

Za fell in a hole and teetered backward. Jesse hit him like a linebacker, and Za popped out of the hole with Hallie beside him.

Jesse swung his flashlight while leaping and running through the sludge-filled potholes, slime raining from the trees. Pain and fatigue bubbled below fear-fueled adrenaline. Ahead, Za was appearing and disappearing in the light beam as Jesse leaped and plowed forward, swinging the light, until he plunged into deep water.

It engulfed him and he sank, feeling the muck and slime cover him. He stroked for the surface and burst out, sucking for air. He swam a few yards and bumped into Za and Hallie, both struggling to climb onto the bank.

"Za, Hallie, stop." They clung to the bank, shaking and gasping. "We have to be quiet. Listen."

The swamp fell deadly still. Long, aching minutes passed. Fear exploded inside Jesse. *Be calm, be calm*, he thought. He whispered, "You have your flashlights?"

"No."

"Hallie?"

"No."

"Machetes?"

"No."

"No."

Jesse thought for a minute, his brain having trouble with reason. "I have mine." He forced his mind to work. "We're going to stay here and be dead quiet. Hide out until daylight. We hang on to each other. But if something happens, we dive under and follow me. When we get to the other side, we get out and run. Understood?"

"Was it a jaguar?" Hallie asked. "Not a jaguar. God no, not a jaguar." She sucked in a quivering breath.

"Maybe."

"God no no—"

"It won't come in the water after us," Jesse said, trying to sound calm.

"That's right, baby," Za said. "Cats don't like water."

They fell silent, and the water quivered, sending ripples out into the dark abyss.

❧

"The canoes are still here. Another twenty-five yards of river and we're home," Za said.

Hallie stumbled into the water. "Thank God, I can't stand another minute on this side of the river. Goddamn evil."

Fog hung over the water, and the wind was dead. Soon, the only sound came from their canoes gliding through the river.

They came ashore next to the village. A single form waited for them. Piper lay in the sand, with Evenel beside her, both covered with a blanket.

The sound of the boats sliding ashore awakened them. Piper stood and ran to Jesse hugging him tight. "Thank God you're back. Don't ever leave me again," she whimpered. "Bastard."

Her presence and her strangulating squeeze broke his dark mood, and all his emotion slapped at his eyes. He crushed them together, held her, felt her trembling. Overwhelmed, his feelings for her poured from him.

"Bastard," she wept, her body heaving. "You have to listen to me."

Evenel hugged their legs, reaching for them. "Me too." They pulled her up, and Hallie and Za joined in.

"Did the boys…they come back?" Jesse asked.

A cry erupted from the other shore. It was a scream bathed in terror, followed by another.

They turned to the river, and several men appeared in the shifting morning mist on the far riverbank. "Tohanna!" Piper gasped.

Fopan, Stende, and Xting called out. While the Americans crossed the river, the boys had been strung by their feet upside down from the trees.

Tohanna shouted a command. Arrows sprung from the jungle behind the boys and landed a few feet in front of Jesse. He let go of Evenel and Piper and picked up his machete.

Jesse stared at the arrows. They were dripping in blood. His instinct said to run, until he looked back at the terrified boys, and then he knew.

These arrows were not to kill him. They were a delivery. The blood was fresh. The arrows had pierced the boys' lower abdomens where it was soft, then sent to him as a message.

Tohanna yelled to them.

Piper answered.

Tohanna shouted a command back into the forest and more arrows hit the boys. Some crossed over and hit the shore in front of the Americans. The boys cried out in pain and horror.

People ran from the village to the river, attracted by the screams. Xting's mother, recognizing the voice of her son, plunged into the water. An archer took aim at her and an arrow stuck her in the chest. She fell beneath the water.

Za and Jesse rushed in. They dragged her from the river. Some of the women shrieked, and still others held people from running into the water.

The boys cried out. Tohanna shouted an order, and another round struck the boys. Now their screams gurgled with the blood that dripped from their mouths. They swung wildly, holding onto the arrows that pierced them, until one by one they fell quiet.

Jesse quivered from his helplessness, fear, and anger. And then he knew. He knew he had brought this. He had brought this day to the village. His strength abandoned him, and he fell to his knees.

Tohanna shouted at them. Jesse could not interpret the words, but he knew the message.

Tohanna stood under the boys, tilted his head back, and caught the blood, drinking it. The blood splattered upon his face, and he used his fingers to trace patterns across his chest.

He unsheathed his machete, and he swung, hacking into Xting. He swung again, butchering Xting, slicing him open. The thuds reached across the river, biting into Jesse's ears. Women screamed. Tohanna dug inside and ripped Xting's heart out, cutting away the ventricles. Tohanna held it toward Jesse. He turned and faded into the jungle.

CHAPTER THIRTY-EIGHT

Cries of anguish and fear, of anger suppressed by grief, sang out over the river.

The young victims hung still on the other side of the river as the morning mist lifted away and the sun rose for another day.

Jesse lifted himself from the sand and waded into the river.

"Jesse! No!" Piper shouted. "It's a trap." She handed Evenel to Deza, ran out, gripped his arm, and tried to spin him around.

He jerked free. He didn't look at her but waded on. He swam slowly, sometimes sinking below the surface, allowing gravity to pull him down. He sank, struggling. It was a death dance, a time to pay, to sacrifice himself for the lives he had taken, the ones who died his death. The air left him, and the liquid poured into his lungs.

But life is strong, and it is the master. Pain beat on his chest, and his legs jerked for the surface. His stomach retched as he boiled to the surface. He broke through and breathed. Jesse swam ahead, Piper behind him.

He buried his mind in the work and he moved toward the shore until his arm struck bottom and he rose, exhausted, with Piper beside him. He grabbed her and embraced her roughly.

Great heaving sobs came from them as they sank to the ground. Za and Hallie pulled up with two canoes. They slid them ashore and collapsed, gripping Jesse and Piper.

"We have to cut them down," Piper said several moments later. They nodded. Za dropped his arms from the group and pushed himself upward like a gorilla. Jesse followed, staggering. Piper and Hallie continued to hold each other. Hallie wiped tears from Piper's face with her palm, leaving grains of sand on her cheek.

Za pulled Jesse's machete from his sheath. He looked to Jesse. Jesse stared at Xting, hanging by a foot. Blood dripped from Xting's mouth and ran into his open eyes. It coagulated in the sockets of his skull. It was a face that had been embroiled in agony and terror when life flickered out. Za waited, still staring at Jesse and at nothing at all. Jesse could see in Za's face that he was struggling to do this. The same as him.

Jesse took a breath and the hot blood odor filled him. Sticky and liquid in his nose. The warm puddle squished between his toes. Jesse wrapped his arms around Xting's shoulders and torso. Flies lifted off the body. He heaved, and the arrows inside Xting poked Jesse like sticks in a bag. Upward he lifted, and Za swung hard.

Xting fell sideways, and Jesse instinctively grabbed an arrow to catch him. It pulled out, and Xting thudded to the ground. Jesse stood with the arrow, a long string of flesh and blood connecting him to Xting. He threw the arrow. Then he ran and picked it up and broke it in two and then he broke it again and again. He raged when the shaft was too short and he could not break it anymore.

Jesse, Za, and every male older than five stood a few miles from the village. Hallie had gone alone to the top of the falls, unable to sit in the village and unable to go with the men. Jesse wanted to remain in the village, but Deza and Nokai assured him that a full lunar cycle of mourning would be observed. Even Tohanna would respect that. The males carried the bodies to this place to be buried. It was not a beautiful place, but high enough that the river never flooded here so it could never carry away the dead.

As was tradition, the dead boys had been prepared in the village, and now the men brought them here and dug the graves. They would bury them and then return to the village, and the women would come to grieve. As the crude shovels labored away, Tohanna stepped on the shore of the village.

Tohanna leaped from the canoe as it slid ashore. He marched with bold determination in front of his small band of warriors. They wore feathers weaved into their hair and they were streaked with bright blue clay. Arrows and long bows rode across their backs. Spears swung with their steps, each soldier careful to stay behind Tohanna. He wore a machete across his back in a steel sheath. Feathers and shells adorned his neck.

Piper sat in the middle of the village, near the large fire pit. Evenel sat on her lap, whimpering quietly. Piper's thoughts were on the burial, wishing she could have gone along. She didn't notice Tohanna until he appeared a few yards in front of her. She jumped to her feet, sending Evenel sprawling onto the ground. Piper grabbed Evenel's hand tightly, pulling the girl to her feet. *He has come to kill her*, she thought. She pushed Evenel behind her.

Tohanna strutted, quickly covering the last steps that separated them. Piper's instinct wanted to turn and run. Something inside steeled her. The lion rose, and she barked at him in

English: "Get away from me!" Her panic steadied and she switched to the native language. "You are not allowed here! Go back! Leave!"

Her anger surprised Tohanna and took him back just a step. He shouted, "Why have you brought warriors to my land? You thought I would allow this? You thought these birds would frighten me? That I would run away? I spared your life, and now you attack me?"

"We did not attack you—"

Tohanna slapped her. Piper wavered, almost falling from the blow, momentarily dizzy and angry. Evenel began to wail, gripping Piper's hand. Suddenly, Piper worried that Tohanna might steal Evenel away.

"I will talk, you will listen," Tohanna said. "You have made a war, and I will punish you and these people. I will not kill you first. I will kill you last, after you suffer the deaths of these wretched people." He pointed at her. "You have brought this upon them."

"We won't have a war with you. I will not be threatened into allowing you to slay these people. Now go, and leave us alone."

Tohanna slapped her again. Her face went numb and pain spiked across her torso.

Rage boiled in Piper, but she would not be his victim. "Never! Nothing you can do will make me send these people to slaughter."

In a single motion, Tohanna pulled his machete from its sheath. Piper remembered that unmistakable sound. She told herself not to blink, not to waver, but to die. Die and deny him his pleasure.

Tohanna leaned back with the knife until it was high above him. He stretched his calves, raising his bulk up upon his toes, and he brought the razor edge down.

The blade bit into the arm, severing it. Piper leaped sideways and fell to the ground. She still held Evenel's hand. Piper raised it up and looked past Evenel's hand. She saw the petite forearm, Evenel's elbow, and blood pulsing out and falling upon the ground in a fountain. Piper pulled Evenel to her, but only the hand came to her embrace.

Evenel stood looking at Piper, stunned. Her frail form spurted red upon the ground.

Evenel's mother Deza shrieked from behind Tohanna. She charged toward him with a spear. He turned and grabbed the shaft just as it struck his chest, biting in a half inch. He raised the machete and struck her. And he raised it and he struck her and he struck her. Deza crumbled to the ground. Tohanna gripped her by her hair and watched her life expire.

Tohanna reached inside her wound and cupped her blood in his fingers; he brought it to his mouth and sucked on his fingers. He turned back to Piper, who was still holding the stump in her hand. "You did this." He turned and walked away.

CHAPTER THIRTY-NINE

Piper rushed to Evenel, the girl's severed arm still in her hand. She scooped Evenel up. She stared at the limb she held. Somehow she could not put it down.

Evenel stared wide-eyed at her stump and gasped, breaking her silence. A great wail came from her, calling out to her mother. To help her, to fix her, to make her a person again.

Piper rushed her to a hut, where several palm strands lay ready for weaving. She lay down the severed arm and took a strand to tie a tourniquet on Evenel's arm to stop the spurting blood. She laid Evenel on top of the palm strands.

Evenel reached for her severed arm. Piper pulled her away, and Evenel screamed in despair, "Put it back…put it back on!"

She tied the tourniquet around Evenel's arm. "It's okay, baby girl. It's okay."

Evenel cried out for her mother again, reaching past Piper with her hand and the stump stretching.

Piper let herself cry. She let herself sob. She let herself wail while the other women came back from the jungle, collapsing around Evenel's mother.

Jesse and Za followed the other boys down the trail back toward the village. No one spoke.

Jesse had never buried anyone before. His own mother and father, yes, but he did not have to throw the dirt on them. He pictured the first shovelfuls falling on the boys' faces and splattering across their foreheads, stopping in the eye sockets and mouths. He expected it to be expelled as they gasped for breath. But nothing happened. A weevil sat on the wall of the grave waiting his turn. Each measure of dirt took them further away and covered who they used to be.

Jesse could not tear his mind from the burial scene until the wails coming from the village bit his gut.

Piper walked in a circle holding Evenel, both soaked in blood. Jesse ran to her, not knowing where or whose blood covered them. And then he saw the stub hanging over Piper's back and the stain running down her back. "Piper!" he yelled as he came near her.

Hallie kneeled among the women doubled over in grief, and Za ran to her.

Fear of the unknown gripped Jesse, and his mind raced ahead. Piper turned to him. Her expression cut him to the quick, her expression of utter despair and hopelessness.

"What happened?" he said as put his arms around her and Piper collapsed at his touch. They slid to the ground.

"Tohanna," she said in a whisper, her voice used up in her grief.

Jesse cradled Evenel's head. She pulled her head back and tried to wrestle away from Piper. She jerked away the cloth covering her wound, and it began to spurt blood again.

"Evenel!" Piper yelled, gripping her harder. "You have to be still."

Evenel cried out, "Mama, help me, help me. It hurts! It hurts! Why won't you help me? I want my mama!"

Jesse held her in an iron grip. Piper reattached the cloth and applied pressure to stop the bleeding. Evenel faded and lost consciousness.

Piper held on to the stub, her hands shaking and her eyes raining.

"He killed Deza and...he cut off my baby girl's arm." Piper sobbed uncontrollably.

Jesse held her and said, "You're safe now."

"Safe?" Piper cried out. "My baby girl is not safe, and she will never be whole again." She jumped up and pulled away from him. "I wanted her to be happy and safe, and I brought her here and now she is not even whole anymore."

"We're here now. I won't let anything happen again. I promise we will never leave again."

"No," she snapped. "I want you to go. Take my baby girl back where no one will hurt her again. You take your boat and you take her out of here."

"She needs medical help. We can take her, all of us."

"I can't leave. Ever. He's going to kill them all...You take her out of here." She buried her head in his chest again and cried harder than Jesse thought possible.

"I won't leave you, Piper." He held her face. "I won't leave you here."

"Evenel has to...has to have help."

"I know."

Za and Hallie left for the boat. Hallie carried Evenel, while Za led the way with his machete. They walked quickly down the trail to the *Pantene*. Hallie remembered the anguish in Piper's face. Nokai and Lesise, with Hada beside her, supported Piper as she swayed. Evenel's playmates, Penan, Sotee, and Viteen, were there, with tears washing tracks down their dirty cheeks.

Piper held a still-dazed Evenel, whispering to her, the clan touching Evenel, saying good-bye forever. Piper's shoulders heaved, her breathing was hard and shallow. Her blazing blue eyes were dead and extinguished; hate and regret, heartache and angst, defeat clouded them. Never to be whole again. She collapsed as she let go of Evenel and Hallie took her away. Piper's screams of revulsion, of ruinous loss, enveloped Hallie as she took the steps that would take Evenel ever further from her.

Za led the way and approached the boat with caution. He jumped aboard and then returned to the shore where Hallie waited. "It's clear. You get inside the cabin with Evenel and break open the medical kit while I'll get us under way."

Hallie handed Evenel to Za and crawled on board. Za handed Evenel back to her. He then began clearing away the brush they had used to camouflage the boat. He worked as fast as he could. When he was done clearing the boat, Za pulled the choke out, pushed the starter button, and the engine fired. The jungle erupted as howler monkeys screamed and birds burst into the air. Za jumped and said, "Holy-o-shit, man. Scare the crap out of a man." He pushed the choke off and went to the stern.

Za flipped open the crate with the rifles. He took out two AK-47s, slung them around his back, and found two ammo canisters. His dripping sweat splashed onto the metal. He brought the weapons to the edge of the boat and jumped overboard. He landed hard and grunted, the air biting his lungs as he ran.

I shouldn't have started the engine before I was ready to leave, he thought. *What if they heard it?* Za carried the rifles and the ammo canisters twenty-five paces due north as Jesse had instructed him to do. Jesse would have to find a way to get them and not leave Piper's side. He quickly covered them with leaves and ran back to the boat.

Za removed the lines mooring the *Pantene*, heaving with all his might. Slowly, the *Pantene* moved into the river. Za clambered on board and went to the wheel. He idled the diesel down and engaged the transmission. She clunked, and the *Pantene* responded to his commands. She backed away slowly. He pulled the throttle to an idle again and shifted the long-throw lever forward. Smoke curled up from the smokestack as he cranked the wheel. She clunked again, and the boat churned in the water, then began to turn downriver. He steered toward the middle. Relief flooded him.

He called to Hallie. "How you doing? How is she?"

"She's awake but groggy. She's really weak, and she's cry-ing out...her pain." Hallie hesitated, then said, "I found some morphine, but I don't know how much to give her."

"You have to decide. She needs it."

Hallie bit her lip and plunged the needle into the bottle. "Don't kill her," she whispered.

"Piper," Jesse said.

Piper had made sure everyone was accounted for. She went from person to person, comforting and attending to needs. Now she stood in the middle of everyone. She seemed a little lost.

"Piper, I think we should head downriver with everyone and pick up the rifles Za left. Get everyone out of here and find a safe place somewhere."

Piper did not answer. She took his hand and led him away from everyone else. She had the look of a desperate person. "I know what has to be done. Everyone here is marked for slaughter. He won't stop. We can't run far enough to get away. And we can only go where there is food. We can't move fast enough to stay away from him."

"Then what do we do? We have to get the rifles, even the odds."

"Guns won't save these people."

"What do we have without them? With the guns, we can stay here, we only have to stay until Za and Hallie come back with help—"

"That will be months. Everyone will be dead before then. And who is going to help us? This is just a little war to the outside world."

"Then let's leave. I know you don't want to hear this, but this war was going on before you got here…"

She stopped him. He could see she would not run away.

"I won't leave without you," Jesse said.

"I know. But there is a way."

CHAPTER FORTY

Piper took Jesse's hand, wrapping her arm in his and pulling him tight to her. She moved through the whimpers and cries of the women and the hopeless expressions they wore. She did not look at them. Not now.

She kept moving slowly along the huts and the cooking fires, out onto the path that led to the river. She clung to him as if he were a child who had disappeared down a dark street and just now found. At the river's edge, she stopped.

"Piper, it's dangerous out here. We should go back."

"No, Tohanna wants us to come to him. He wants his people to see him impose his power."

"How do you know that?"

"Otherwise he would have killed us already." She pushed her hair behind her ear with one hand as she tightly held his hand with the other. "And right now, I just don't care." She crossed her legs and sat down in the sand.

He did the same, still watching her, comforting her. She kicked off her sandals and dug her toes in the sand. He slid off his shoes and did the same, curling his toes into the cool interior of the sand.

His childhood returned. He remembered hot, sweaty hours in the haymow followed by a few minutes before the chores had to be done, spending those minutes swimming in the bay that lapped at their yard. The cool shock of diving in, cleansing the chaff from your hair and neck. The pleasure of water and sand.

They sat hip to hip, his hand still in hers.

The falls sounded along with the insects and the soft sounds of the river, always moving and changing, joining the bank yet keeping the complete separation of land and water. Two vastly different worlds, each joined and held by the other, mixing their scent and color, each giving up some of its self to the other in order to live.

"I know how," she said, "to stop this craziness." She turned to him and looked into his eyes, running her fingers along his jaw, over his neck, and through his mane, gripping the thick locks at his neckline. His hair was long and dark now, despite the hours in the sun.

"When I came to Manaus, I just wanted a little adventure. Some shopping and language, maybe some romance. Then I stumbled upon Evenel. And the crazy thing is, the Piper who left Tennessee would get on a plane and insist her daddy come and fix all this. But I want to…no, I *need* to fix this. Myself. I could never run away now. It's like I don't know who I am, but I would never go back to my old life. Here I have purpose, and it feels much better than when I lived without any real reason." She scanned the sky and cleared her throat, the emotion causing her to cough. "But at the same time, I'm so scared."

Jesse turned to her. "It's the same for me," Jesse said. "Since I left home, this has been a trip I never imagined. I'm afraid too, but what's even stranger is...I want to fight back, protect what is ours, not let him win." He stopped, searching her expression for hope, trying to plant the seeds of it in her.

Piper stared across the river for a time. "I have a way," she said.

He waited, watching her, a thousand scenarios running through his head. They could take everyone to Manaus. Or they could start walking west for a hundred miles. Maybe they could get help from someone, the government...

"I need an assassin," she said.

He realized she was looking directly at him now.

"Jesse," she said. She brushed the sand from her calves and looked down the river. Slowly, she turned back to look him in the face. "I have been here long enough to realize that respect and power are what drives aggression in this culture. When a man kills someone from another tribe, the closest relative must avenge that death or he will lose the respect of his people."

"So how does that help us?" Jesse asked, watching her intently.

Piper was silent. She looked away, refusing to meet his gaze. A dragonfly buzzed around them, landing on the sand in front of Jesse. Its drone stopped. Brilliant green, its lacewings sectioned by purple lines, shone in the sun. Jesse waved his hand, forcing it to fly, to buzz again to cover up the silence.

"I need an assassin without ties to this tribe," she said, looking him directly in the eyes. "I need you."

"Me?" He jumped to his feet. "No." He stood in front of her. "I thought this would be kind of a war thing where you fought battles. I never considered the...I never really thought about the actual...I mean, I can't just kill someone."

She sat looking at her feet in the sand. She picked up a handful of sand and let it sift through her fingers.

It reminded him of an hourglass, their time together slowly but surely running out.

"You're the only one, Jesse."

He dropped to his knees and lifted her chin. Tears cut through the dust on her cheeks and ran into the corners of her mouth.

"There's got to be another way," he implored.

She shook her head in mute denial.

Jesse rocked back on his heels. "If I do this for us, then we go home."

She tore away from him, stood up, her fists clenched. "Don't you see?" she cried.

"See what?"

"We can't be together. Not now, not ever. I have to be here or these people will die." She fell to her knees, her head in her hands. "And you can't stay here."

"I can't hear you," he said, crouching down beside her. "What did you say?"

She bound her arms tight around her torso. "You can't stay. Not after you…kill him."

Jesse tried to hold her, but she pulled away.

"No. You have to stop this. You have to kill him. And you have to leave or the killing will never end."

"I can't leave you," Jesse said. "What about—"

"There is not another way to fix this."

"What about us?" Jesse asked.

"Us? Us is the most important thing to me! Jesse, I love…" she sobbed so hard she lost her breath. After a long minute, she said, "I love you, but us is not big enough to save these people."

He reached for her and held her tight.

"I'm…sorr…so sorry," she said, her breathing episodic. "I'm so sorry." She leaned against him, still distraught, and shook in his arms.

She seemed to calm in his embrace. She blew her nose. He stroked her hair and realized how much he loved her. He wanted her; he needed to hold her like this everyday. She had become everything he wanted to live for.

Abruptly, she looked at him, her cheeks red and her eyes watery. "Oh my God, what if...he kills you? I didn't think about that...Jesse, oh my God, I can't do this..." She looked to him and her eyes pleaded.

He took her face in his hands and kissed her hard. He let her go and pulled her back to him and squeezed her, holding her in a long embrace. He brushed her hair back and sought her eyes. He wondered how they could be so blue and so beautiful. He kissed her lips hard once more, not stopping, not caring about anything else. If it was the last, then it was the best.

Then he turned away and forced his feet forward. He could hear her calling his name, but he beat his feet into the ground as he headed toward the place Hallie and Za had left the guns.

CHAPTER FORTY-ONE

One purpose, one focus, he thought. There was no room for anything else, at least until this was over. Then they could…

Shit, there it was again. He had the worst task conceivable in front of him, and its purpose was to take him away from her. "Stop," he said aloud, shaking her out of his head.

Even though his legs burned, Jesse kept up a steady run while his thoughts raced. *I have guns, but that only evens the score. This is his turf. He could be waiting for me right now, here.* He quickened his pace, pushing harder. "Focus, one cause," he said softly. *Or you will end up dead. Not video game dead, but really dead.*

The concept ran in and out of his thoughts. He never really thought he would truly die. This time, it was feasible. He had avoided death three times since he left home. Other people had died in place of him. Sweat poured onto his brow, and he wiped it away.

If I get killed, it would be justice.

And there it was, the true cost of losing.

If I lose, so will Piper. My death equals Piper's death.

That was the plan all along, he realized. *Tohanna is playing with us. Kill me first and then Piper. I'm only the pawn. Tohanna only wants to kill me because it will crush Piper. Then Tohanna will kill her...or worse.* His gut lurched. A man like Tohanna enjoyed the process as much as the kill.

I can't lose. If I get killed, I'll have to take Tohanna with me.

He steeled his mind, mashing his resolve until his brain hurt. One choice, one result.

He slowed his pace now that he had settled it. "I'll get the guns, set up a kill zone, and shoot him down. Shoot them all... it doesn't matter. They're the aggressors. I'll wait them out, set up a defensive position, and bait them. Kill them from two hundred yards. Put a bullet in every head. I have the advantage."

He wondered if he had enough ammo to get them all. Every last one of them. Then he could still be with Piper. "Yes, every last one of them. Even the women? Yes. Every last one. I have the power. It's my choice."

He could kill them all, wipe them out, and no one could stop him. He smiled. He felt like the weight had lifted from him.

He thought about the aftermath, his chest filling with air and bursting with pride as he surveyed the scene of dead, a field of annihilation by his own hand.

The intoxicating sense of power floated him above the ground, making his steps light and powerful. He imagined the gun in his hand. Gray metal, the grip so solid, the killing weight balanced just right, the solid feeling, even when it recoiled a hundred times a minute. The first little bastard who stepped into range...

"Stop," he said aloud, children's faces running across his mind. He recognized the evil inside him. How easy it was, he thought, how easy it was to be just like Tohanna.

Then he thought of Piper's words: "Us is not big enough." She was right. They were not big enough to commit genocide. "Us is not big enough," he whispered. But it would get him the very thing he wanted most.

He ran on past the grasses, panting and stirring the dragonflies, past the green life surrounding him. He reached the place where they had left the boat. He quickly paced off the agreed paces. "There! There it is." A pile of leaves lay only a few feet away. Christmas never felt better. He pulled off the leaves, digging down, and there they were. They were beautiful. He kissed each of them.

He took the first rifle and opened the bolt; it was empty. *Load immediately*, he thought. Then he would have the advantage, the power. He took the first ammo canister. Written on the side was, "1440 rounds, 30 caliber, full metal jacket." He opened the canister. They were gorgeous. Boxes and boxes of killing rounds. He opened one and pulled out the brass and copper projectile. So precise, so exquisite, and still so deadly.

Jesse pulled the clip off the rifle and began to load it. He fumbled with the round. It would not go in. He calmed himself, realizing he was shaking. He looked around, back and forth. "Steady." He jerked his head up again, scanning for movement. "Get it loaded and you're safe." He tried again. Then again. He could not get the round to go in. He removed the clip from the other rifle. He tried again with the second one. The round would not go in the clip. He turned it over. On the side, it said, "7.62 x .39 only."

Jesse picked up the box, it read, "30 caliber, full metal jacket." He put the clip next to the box. The clip read, "7.62 x .39 only."

He stopped. A cold fist knotted him. Za had left the wrong ammo.

His instincts shouted, "They're watching you! Load it! Load the fucking gun!" He began jamming the bullets, trying to force them into the clip. He threw down the clip and pulled open the bolt on the rifle. His hand shaking wildly, he set a bullet in the chamber and tried to shut it. The bullet jammed in the chamber. He shook the bolt, trying to get it back open. Stuck tight.

Jesse ran to the nearest tree and smacked the bolt against it. The bolt came open. The bullet casing had a large kink in it. Useless. He threw it down, sprinted to the box, and took another. The box spilled onto the ground. Jesse grabbed the other rifle. He opened the bolt, put another shell in, ran to the tree, and jammed the bolt against it. "Come on," he cried, "shut, you can shut." He danced to another tree and swung the rifle against it. The bolt broke off. The jungle erupted, and the howler monkeys cursed him, crying out their warnings that he was the outsider, that he had best heed their warnings or suffer the consequences.

Jesse collapsed. His own survival collapsed with the broken rifle. He cursed Za and everything he stood for. "How could this happen? I needed this more than anything in my whole life, and someone else's fucking idiot move has screwed me royally when I needed it most! How could Za fucking do this to me? I have no chance in hell now—"

Something went snap in the jungle. Jesse burst to his feet in a single move, running blindly into the jungle, stumbling and falling, sliding on his chest and face. He got to his feet again, running. His guts twisted and his mind ran like a whistling arrow. He sprinted until he could not run anymore. Wheezing and spent, he fell down, shaking on the ground. "I can't save her now," he cried out. A cool breeze flowed over him. The jungle sat quiet and flickering its color.

Slowly, he calmed, and his mind began to work. He had a machete and a bow, the same as Tohanna. But Tohanna had a killer's training and he liked it. He was a butcher.

What would Pan do if he were me? He seemed to be able to make long odds into something. Until I got him killed, Jesse thought.

I have to find a way to do this, to use my strengths to gain an advantage.

Jesse rolled into a sitting position. He plucked a fern, tore it down the middle, and sat in thought. "Use Tohanna's pride, use his arrogance to kill him," he said aloud. "All of us have the capacity to be a natural-born killer. Stop suppressing mine and find it."

CHAPTER FORTY-TWO

Jesse stood up after several minutes of self-damning. Now that he was standing, he still had no idea what was next. "Turn toward the river," he whispered. "Where the hell is the river?" He stared ahead. Insects buzzed, the wind blew. He moved his head in slow motion, the sun spotting the sky in a bright ball. He cleared the roadblock in his mind. He stepped forward, then stopped. He turned around and stepped forward, then took another step.

He began to feel his environment again, his thoughts clearing like fog lifting and returning to the bulldozer grinding forward, relentless and unstoppable. It was a Jesse trait, the trait that took him from operating a shit shovel to being a good architect.

Stumbling, pushing back walls of foliage until he got back to the river, he picked up the machete where he had left it in his panic. Jesse cursed himself, vowing to never panic again.

He would never again part from his weapon until the next time he could see a Starbucks.

The steel that formed the machete gleamed in the sun, scratches feathered into the steel here and there, nicks punctuating the wooden handle. The brass rivets that married the two elements reflected brightly, adding color to the brown and gunmetal gray. Battle-worn and banged up, just like him. The blade was as effective now as when it was new.

He looked along the spine of the great knife, up toward his own forearm and to his shoulder and across his chest. He, too, was just as effective as the knife. He flickered the machete back and forth. Steel shimmering in the sun. Jesse took it in both hands and swung it over his head and down, slicing clean through the brush and the grass. Not as good as Xting and Fopan, but he was dangerous with it. He would avenge them.

He had the bow, too, but no training. He would have to be close to them to use it. Jesse slipped the bow and quiver over his shoulder, put the machete in its sheath.

He waded into the water then dived. The liquid flowed past him, cool and invigorating. He swam, and the very purpose of movement felt good. It energized him. His muscles warmed and he could feel his heart pumping life and strength, his system regaining confidence. Each stroke was more powerful than the last. The creature inside stirred, woke from its slumber. By the time he reached the far shore, the creature stood up, focused, confident, bearing no scars and no qualms.

Kill 'em all, let God sort 'em.

Jesse slogged inland through the disgusting swamp that lined the shore on Tohanna's side of the river. The stink from the disturbed water engulfed him. Rats splashed as they fled. The scum dropped out of the trees and grit rolled between his teeth.

He slogged forward. *Always go forward*, he thought. *Always keep going. Your reward awaits.* He pictured a bloodied Tohanna, pictured how he would snuff out the evil. At last, the swamp gave way to solid ground covered in dense vegetation.

A plan, I need a plan, he thought. Jesse did not have military training other than Sunday afternoon war movies.

He would control the arena, battle Tohanna, and kill him without emotion. Jesse unsheathed his machete. He imagined swinging that thing, battling Tohanna. Using the butt of the knife to strike and break a clench, spinning and slicing, biting an ear off, arms bulging, gritting teeth, expressing his own evil, and then delivering the kill blow. He threw his chest out, pulsed his biceps.

Jesse swung the machete, slicing through a tree thick as his thumb. He put the machete in both hands, held it waist high, scowling at the world. He brought his eyes forward…two young boys stood watching him.

Panic hit him hard in the heart. His core hurt from the constriction as fear produced adrenaline. He turned and ran, crashing through the brush, branches cutting his face, leaping over logs, sprinting wildly.

His quiver caught, and the strap whipped him around before breaking. Jesse abandoned it, continued sprinting, turning with no direction, just running away. Finally, his mind caught up with his racing body and stopped him.

He hid behind a tree, his heart threatening to blow apart. He looked back, staring. His thumping heart not allowing him to hear and even giving away his hiding place.

He stayed still as stone.

Nobody came, nothing moved. Still, he stayed concealed. He held the machete, the tip vibrating in his hand. Time passed…he had no idea how much, just that it was being wasted.

He stood up, recouping. Jesse walked forward again. "I have no idea where the damn quiver went," he whispered. He searched to no avail. "Stupid, stupid. No guns, no arrows, idiot.

"There's one choice, just go forward. Make a plan, any plan, just some fucking plan." He couldn't think of anything that gave him a fighting chance. The problem swirled like dust inside him, never showing him a solution. Only one thing was clear: he would have to be close, hand-to-hand.

Not that he could win such an encounter. But he could tie. He had to find a way to strike the first blow, one that would eventually kill Tohanna. That was what he had. He had to save Piper. Pan had been right, he thought. He was already dead; there wasn't a way to get back alive.

That acceptance numbed his very core, but it calmed him. Panic no longer applied somehow. Time no longer mattered. Death was accepted and waited upon.

The sun scattered through the leaves so everything flickered as if it were fire. The birdcalls and the whisper of wind mixed scents with the sound of moving waters large and small.

All of it was lost on him.

He moved forward for a long time. Moving west, he came to a trail that had human footprints on it. That scared him, knowing it must lead to Tohanna's village. But bushwhacking through the woods had him sweating and tired. Little cuts and abrasions, bug bites, and a fog of vegetation had defeated him.

Reluctantly, he followed the narrow trail, trying to read any sign of anything, but soon realized there was little to see with his untrained eye.

Jesse stopped cold. He thought he heard voices ahead. He was sure of it. He moved into the jungle and laid flat on his stomach, completely still except for his heartbeat and a noticeable shaking. He felt exposed; he grabbed leaf litter and covered himself as fast as he could.

Three dark men passed by him carrying blowguns and spears. Jesse held his breath. He studied each face, looking for a sign they had seen him. Jesse gripped his machete and his heart pounded. What would he do if they had seen him? Maybe he should attack them. That would be stupid, he thought. He waited a long minute for them to be gone.

Suddenly, a heavy blow struck the middle of his back, knocking the air out of him. He rolled over, his chest aching. A foot came down over his throat and a spear jabbed at his cheek so hard it felt like the bone would break. Blood ran out.

Adrenaline burned through him as he tried to spring into action.

Jesse went into full panic. He kicked, trying to jump to his feet. His body was starved, gasping for air.

They rolled him over and bound his arms behind him. Jesse tried to struggle, but not one of his muscles would respond. His wind returned, calming him a bit.

They yelled at him or each other, he couldn't tell. They stomped on him and punched him with the spears. The burn and the pain became worse. They dragged him to his feet and threatened him, jostling, slapping, and punching with the spears. One man was taller than the other two, and his nose and ears were pierced with bone. Paint was smeared across his face and legs and his eyes were crazy. He inflicted the most pain on Jesse.

He realized they were not killing him, just enjoying him like cats with a live mouse. One of them put a rope around his neck and pulled, another struck him in the calves with the spear tip. It cut in and drew blood.

His mind now wholly occupied with the pain. The third one took his machete and slapped Jesse across the back with the flat side of the blade. Jesse cried out, the pain writhing through him. He turned, but the rope jerked tight around his neck and he couldn't breathe. He stepped forward, and a second later, the leash loosened so he could breathe again. Struggling to keep the leash loose and trying desperately to avoid the beatings from behind, Jesse was a bridled mule.

Have to find a way out, Jesse thought, gasping as the rope didn't allow him a full breath. *Maybe I can knock the asshole with the noose down, get him to drop the rope and then run into the jungle before the other two caught him.* With his mind struggling for clarity, he tripped on a root and fell forward. The leash throttled him, and his lungs burned. His face hit the dirt. *Stand up!* his mind screamed out. *Stand up!* Jesse brought his knees under him and raised his head. He gasped, sucking for air. He saw the rope man move his mouth, but he couldn't hear anything. Spots swamped his vision as they traveled across the jungle.

The rope man pulled. Jesse stood, and the rope relaxed. Jesse gasped, and a blow in the back drove him to the ground again. The leash squeezed, and Jesse felt pressure upon his legs as they stabbed at him again. But that pain did not penetrate his mind. Only the ability to breathe counted, to pull in the air and shut off the constriction. He struggled to his knees, and the rope man pulled him to his feet, the fiber cutting into his skin.

Jesse gasped, wanting to use his bound hands to loosen the noose. He gasped again and sucked in a restricted breath. The rope pulled and Jesse stepped, struggling to stay upright. He was reduced to struggling for breath and nothing else.

Half an hour later, a village appeared. As soon as the three captors entered, they began to shout. People came from their huts to see the prize, and young boys poked at him with sticks or scratched him with their nails before darting away.

And then Tohanna stood before him. The man looked hard as nails and wiry.

Tohanna paid more attention to the audience than the prize calf he had on display. Jesse noticed the way Tohanna enjoyed how he controlled everything in his world. How this stranger from another planet was his play toy. How he could do anything that he wanted, and he wanted to amuse his audience as long as he could. Tohanna took Jesse's machete from his captor and cut the rope around Jesse's neck and wrists. Sensing Tohanna's game, Jesse felt a hot pang in his gut. *I can do it now. Kill him, before they can stop me.* Tohanna circled Jesse, inspecting him. *Do it now*, Jesse thought. He lunged at Tohanna, putting his head in Tohanna's chest and knocking both of them to the ground.

Jesse was seventy-five pounds heavier and half a foot taller. He crashed Tohanna to the ground. The adrenaline filled Jesse, and he knew he had him. He could strike a killing blow before they could get him off the little bastard.

Jesse brought his elbow up to smash Tohanna's Adam's apple. But before he could swing his elbow, Tohanna flipped Jesse over onto his back. Jesse spun to his feet, crouching to attack. But Tohanna was standing already.

Jesse lunged again and Tohanna somehow stepped aside or jumped, thumping Jesse to the ground, stepping onto Jesse's back like a crowned champion. The crowd cheered.

Jesse's nose hit the dirt and he went numb, the dust choking him. He rolled onto his back, and Tohanna stepped on him as if he was rolling a log.

Jesse grabbed for Tohanna's feet, but Tohanna just kicked his hands away each time. Now Jesse heard the laughter and saw Tohanna smirking. Tohanna stepped off Jesse.

Jesse got to his knees. He stood, realizing his nose was bleeding into his mouth. Tasting his own blood, Jesse wiped his face. Rage flooded him, and he attacked again.

In an instant, Tohanna gripped him in a headlock. Jesse wrapped his arms around Tohanna and lifted him off the ground, spun and tossed the small man. Tohanna came down on his feet like a cat.

But Jesse had scored. The laughter turned to oohs. Jesse stood tall. He rose with his power and renewed breath. Tohanna lost his smirk. *I have him now*, Jesse thought.

Tohanna kicked him in the gut before Jesse saw him move. Jesse doubled over and fell back on one hand.

Tohanna kneed him in the face, and Jesse toppled back, stunned. The sky, blue and white, blurred and focused again. Jesse got up, his head swirling.

Tohanna walked around Jesse, smashing him in the kidney, and Jesse buckled, paralyzing pain stole his breath. Before he could fall, Tohanna kicked him again. Jesse lay on the ground. Tohanna struck several times more. Jesse thought of Piper. He curled into a ball and hoped to survive.

Jesse felt all the pain his brain could deliver. He prayed he could endure. Guttural grunts and wails escaped him with every blow. His mind seemed to stop. He was only processing pain, not smell or sound or even the blunt force, just copious pain as Tohanna beat him. Darkness closed off the agony.

His brain began to process another input and he realized someone had taken his legs and was dragging him face down. His chin and mouth bit and bumped into the dirt and filled his mouth, but he could not force it to close. There was no taste, just volume, and he choked, excreting the dirt. Then blackness covered his mind.

He awoke still staring at the ground. Ants were crawling over his face and out of his nose, feeding on the blood. He moved his head, and globs of blood full of ants fell out of his mouth. He spit them out, using his tongue and teeth to expel them. Darkness consumed him again.

It was dark when he woke. The ants were still running over him and a bird was working the stab wounds on his calves. He managed to roll over and pain streaked from his brain and he screamed—but all that came out was a gurgle. Blackness again.

Heat blistered him when he opened his eyes once more.

The parasites covered him. He willed himself to roll onto his side and look up. The sun blinded him. He brushed at the bugs feeding on his wounds, but this time he ate the ants. His entire being hurt and stung. He struggled, sat up, and saw that he was tied to a tree on the edge of the village, a rope looping around his feet. He flopped on his back and prayed to pass out again. A shadow covered him. Jesse could not lift his head to see. The shadow became form, and Tohanna stood over him. Jesse tried to speak, then he realized Tohanna was pissing on him. Jesse jerked forward and pain coursed across him and consciousness fled from the pain.

He wavered in and out, never able to escape the fogginess in his mind, never able to lift above the stupor, and each time the dark engulfed him once more.

A day later, Jesse snapped awake. He sat up with great effort. The moon was full. He looked at the ropes around his ankles, the ones they had used to drag him here and tie him to the tree.

Jesse examined the knots. He could not focus enough to untie them. His calves had bled onto the ropes thanks to the birds that had opened large wounds in them, and the ants were eating the blood-soaked braids. He squeezed open the clotted wounds and dripped it on the ropes. He fell back, exhausted.

Every movement required a monumental effort, and it felt like even his lungs were bruised. He had no sense of smell; his eyes worked, but only barely as they were nearly swelled shut. He slid toward the tree, gritting his teeth so as not to cry out.

Slowly, he rubbed the rope against the bark. *Stay alive*, he thought, *just fight the pain, and you will stay alive.* He pulled on the rope and then back again, the ants biting his forearms, neck, and face. "Little biting bastards," he whispered, and the thought came to his overloaded mind.

He pulled himself forward with all his strength and inched forward. He put the rope into his mouth and bit. His jaw hurt, sharp and intense. He struggled to not cry out. He tried again, gripping just a single strand in his teeth. He bit through; it tasted like blood and ant shit and rope. The ants continued along his torso now. He separated another strand and bit again. He could feel the ants run over his tongue as he fumbled for another strand.

The moon fell behind clouds and rains began beating him. Still he worked the rope, and the night wandered on until the last strands of the rope gave way.

He crawled, dragging his cheek on the ground, not able to lift it from the mud. He kept just one thought repeating: *Arms pull, arms pull, arms pull.* His hand caught a pole. He pulled himself to it. He rolled to his back and looked up. The rain blinded him. He sheltered his eyes. He was in the village. "No, damn it, no," he cried out. "How did I do this? Why..."

Then he caught the image. Hanging on a post was his machete in its sheath. Determination welled up in him. He dragged himself forward, toward the pole, his arms shaking with the effort.

He struggled to stand, crawling up the post and biting his lip not to yell out. He got hold of the machete and fell in a lump back to his knees then onto his belly, crying out softly on the hard ground. He couldn't move, his body rejecting his commands. The rains became a torrent.

He tried again. Slowly, he crawled for what seemed like hours, crawling through the trees and over downed logs, across thorns and mud. *Have to move faster*, he thought, *have to stand.*

With all his will, he cursed himself to his feet, struggling with the thousand knives stabbing his entire being. He stepped and fell down, splashing into the mud. He got up again, stumbling into the jungle. The rain stopped, and the moonlight reflected in the fog lifting from the warm jungle earth.

He found a stream and dropped into the crisp water, washing away the blood and the mud, and a hundred welts burned. Kneeling in the shallow water, he dug mud from the bottom and covered his wounds. "Don't want nothing to smell my blood," he said slowly.

He struggled upright again, and the speckled moonlight allowed him to find his way over the roots and the fallen trees and the razor sharp grass. *Keep going,* he thought, *keep going.*

CHAPTER FORTY-THREE

Amazon River

"Think think think," Za said aloud. "Fuck fuck fuck," he muttered, beating the wheel with his fist, beating his knuckles across the weathered wood to make them bleed. It was his punishment for running away.

"The whole thing, the whole trip, everything is bad. Bad in every way," he said. "I should go back. Hallie knows how to operate the boat. I could help Jesse and get them the hell out of there."

Evenel wailed from inside the cabin, bringing him back to reality. Hallie's sobs punctuated Evenel's cries. Never had he felt so helpless. He could not help their pain, and he could not stop. He could not go back.

Za imagined several canoes downstream. "What if they try to board the boat?" he whispered. "I'll...I'll kill them all. He put the rope on the wheel to keep the boat on course. Za threw off the lid of the storage crate that hid the weapons. He grabbed an AK-47 and loaded it. Set it beside the wheel. Then he loaded another and another. He scrambled back to the crate and grabbed as many clips as he could carry, dumping them by the wheel.

He readjusted the boat's course, picked up the nearest AK-47 and held it, scanning the river ahead. What if they could catch him? What if they could paddle faster than he could get the *Pantene* to go? He whipped around and stared back down the river.

"What if the Goddamned gun doesn't work?" He grabbed for the safety, but his hands could not make the safety fall. He gripped the barrel tightly to stop shaking. He tried again and the safety came off. He shot a burst into the jungle.

Hallie screamed, Evenel let out a bloodcurdling spurt like she were about to die. He cursed himself...

Za stood at the wheel of the *Pantene*. Along each side, the jungle glided past as it had for days.

"Here, some coffee, babe," Hallie said, handing him a cup.

"How is she?"

"She could not be any better for a little girl who lost an arm. We were lucky. I don't see any sign of infection."

"Is she awake?" he asked.

"Yes, but I don't know how much longer I can keep her in bed. Unless I tie her limb from lim..." She stopped and winced. "Za, what are we going to do? I mean, what are we doing? Where are we?"

"I've been thinking about that—"

"And what about Jesse and Piper? I still can't come to grips with leaving them behind."

He put his hand on her shoulder. "They will be okay. They

got firepower. Enough to give them the advantage. We have to do our part. Get Evenel help."

"It appears she won't need help. By the time we get back, she's going to be doing cartwheels, you watch." Hallie pointed at the cabin. "She amazes me." She turned and looked toward the cabin. Za noticed a dreamy look roll over her eyes and onto her lips, parting them into a beautiful smile. He loved her dimples.

"How are Piper and Jesse going to get out?"

"I don't know if they will leave."

She frowned. "I never considered that."

"Do you think Piper will ever leave?"

"Well sure, I guess," Hallie said. "I can't...go on forever not knowing what happened." They sipped their coffee in silence. The sun rose above the canopy and the first rays landed on Hallie's face.

"I love you," Za said.

"What?"

"I said we are a family now. You, me, Evenel."

Hallie looked shocked. "You never talked about us in forever terms before."

"I knew it was forever from the first moment you walked through that door at the diner."

She hugged him tight. Evenel peered out of the cabin, looking to Hallie for permission. Hallie held out her arm, and Evenel came to her and hugged them both.

"We have to talk about this," Za said. He looked downriver and gestured ahead. "We go to Manaus and find a doctor, a real doctor, and do whatever we can for Evenel. Find a safe place for her. That's first. We can hire a plane to fly over, no, we get a floatplane and we go back and get them, or at least make sure they are safe. We could bring them supplies."

"And then?"

"And then we go home. We get Evenel in school, get her a cool little backpack..."

"Za, where is home?"

"Let's decide that when we are back in the States."

Hallie opened her mouth and then hesitated. "What about the pirates?"

"I don't know. Maybe they're gone, or dead."

"What if they're looking for us in Manaus?"

"Who? The cops or the pirates?" he said.

"The pirates."

"That depends on how valuable those backpacks are. They were willing to kill us for them. I don't think they are going to just let us go."

"Then we go to the police right after we find a doctor." She turned to him and her dimples were put away, replaced with concern. "Za, how do we know we can trust the police or anybody?"

"I don't know." He contracted his mouth in thought. "We'll call your uncle. He'll know who to trust.

"Hallie!" Za called.

She came out of the cabin with Evenel in tow. Evenel was chewing on some jerky.

"Do you ever stop eating?" Za asked. She handed a chewed end to Za; he took a bite and smiled at her. "Thanks, Squirt."

She squished her nose at him. "You're welcome, Za."

"Ahead is where the pirates attacked us on the way to the village. I think we should hold up here and wait for dark."

"Like that worked last time."

"We are one great big target in the daylight." He gestured.

"Well, running into something in the dark will not get us home. We have to stay to the middle and run through as fast as we can go."

Za hesitated. "I don't like it."

"Chances are they won't be there. Why would they wait for us here?" she said.

"Because this is the last known spot we were at. That's all."

"I say we keep going." She folded her arms.

Za looked down the river as far as he could.

Hallie said, "Look, if we go now, we will be past it before it gets dark. Right?"

Za hesitated, checked the throttle. "Alright, we do it your way—"

"Always." She looked to Evenel, and they both squished their noses at each other.

"But I want both of you out here watching."

"Okay." She kissed his cheek. Evenel climbed up on a box and kissed him too. "Alright, kid, take my hand and come with me." She led Evenel to the front of the boat and sat down. Za could hear Hallie saying, "Okay, chicken butt, you watch for boats and you call out if you see anything at all. This is really important. Do you understand?"

"Yes."

"I will be right beside you and I am going to watch too."

"I bet I see it first."

"No, I will see it first."

"Are you watching?" Za called out.

"Yes!" they both answered in unison. Laughter flooded back to him. He smiled, shaking his head. "This is serious," Za called out. "I hope they're gone." Za throttled up the diesel and split the river in two. The diesel blew smoke and clinked its disapproval. The *Pantene* left the mouth of the river that led back to the village. The water opened a thousand yards wide.

Za looked back. Nothing. Ahead lay the place where their trip went to Hades in a handbag. He bumped the throttle with his palm to make sure it was wide open. "Wide ass open," he murmured. "That's how we do it."

For thirty minutes, the *Pantene* ran straight ahead with nothing in sight except the false images that popped up in his head every minute. Spots on the water that lifted off and became birds as he closed in on them. His finger was sore from rubbing the safety on the AK-47. "Jesus," he muttered. "Just get it over with, get past this spot and run home."

Not that there wasn't a lot of river left, there was, but the last encounter here was a bad chapter and he did not want to do that again.

He was sure his lookouts were not doing their job. "I bet they're playing cards, man, I bet they snuck them with them, or worse yet they're asleep." It was up to him and...

"Jesus, what is that shimmer ahead? It sure has a lot of mass."

He looked down to grab the binoculars. That is when he noticed the one gauge the *Pantene* had. It was pinned in the red. "Noooo, not now, baby, don't you cook on me now." He pulled back the throttle, and the engine stalled instantly. He turned the *Pantene* toward the shore. He did not want to be adrift in the middle.

"What happened?" Hallie came around the cabin.

"She's too hot!" he yelled. "Get some buckets; we have to cool her down."

Hallie disappeared into the cabin. Za could hear her moving items around and the hard tick of the hot diesel straining to hold together under pressure.

"Where's Evenel?" he called.

"I told her to stay in the front," Hallie said, coming out of the cabin. She stopped. Her face turned cold. "Look!"

Za turned to the stern, and maybe a mile away, a boat was coming. Za felt his guts clamp all the way to his balls. He took the buckets from Hallie. "Come on! Dip these over the side and keep filling them." He filled the first one and opened the hatch to the hold. He jumped in and stepped over to the hot steel of the diesel.

He started to throw the water, but stopped. The water flew up and out of the bucket and fell upon him. Evenel screeched next to him. He grabbed her and said, "Jesus, how did you get here? Get back in the cabin!" He threw her toward the hatch.

Hallie came up beside him, ready to throw her bucket of water on top the diesel.

He grabbed her arm. "No!" The bucket swung round and the water hit only a small part of the engine. Steam and crackling noises bounced off the black steel. "Too much and it could crack!"

She pulled back. "Then what do we do, asshole?"

"Fill the buckets and bring them to me." She went back outside, leaned over the side, filled one bucket, and then went to dip the other.

"No! Bring that one to me first!" Za ordered, his head sticking out the hatch.

She carried the bucket to him, and he grabbed it and stepped back up to the steaming diesel. He poured some water along the oil case, trying to guess how much he could use without cooling it so fast it broke in two. The water turned to steam as he poured.

Hallie handed the next bucket down. "The boat!" she snapped.

"What can you see now? Use the binoculars," he said.

She ran back to the wheel and put the binoculars to her eyes. "They have guns!" she said.

"Fill me a bucket!" he yelled.

Hallie rushed to the side and filled the first and then the second. Za was pouring faster now. "What does the heat gauge say?"

"Where is it?"

"By the wheel."

She ran to the wheel. "Where?"

"By the wheel!" he said, slamming the bucket down and grabbing another.

"It says…I mean it is just inside the red."

"Try to start it."

"I don't know how," she screamed at him. "You come and do it!"

Za jumped onto the deck. "Pour water on the engine. Only on the bottom. Only on the bottom." He moved back to the wheel while Hallie took the buckets to the side and filled them.

"What is the bottom?"

"What?"

"What is the bottom of the engine?" She stomped her foot, splashing water from the buckets. "You said just the bottom of the engine. What part is the bottom?"

Za stole a look at the boat. It was still coming, and he hoped that, just maybe, they were not after them. "You are going to have to figure it out. Go!"

"Asshole!" She stomped off and disappeared into the hold.

He hit the starter and the diesel wound around once, twice, three times, and sputtered alive. He snapped the transmission into gear, and the entire diesel let out a crack.

But she churned forward. Za hit the throttle so hard it jammed his thumb. "Keep the buckets full!"

Hallie scrambled out of the hold and said, "I can't asshole! We're going too fast."

"Do it!" he barked at her.

"You do it!" she screamed at him, coming toward the wheel.

New sounds flew past them. They were eerie and familiar, but they did not register until the cabin splintered and the knock knock of lead sounded around them. Bullets sizzled past.

He tackled her to the deck. With his feet, he swung the wheel, pointing the *Pantene* toward the shore. "Hold it with your feet," he told Hallie.

"Where's Evenel?" she yelled.

"In the cabin."

Hallie rolled to her feet and ran into the cabin.

He grabbed the AK-47 and rolled across the deck to the stern. He slid upright against the back of the boat. He clicked off the safety and his mind told him to rise up, but nothing happened. He knew why. Death would claim him in if he stood up. It would bring him into the embrace of rotting flesh and pain.

With all his determination, he got on his knees and stuck the barrel and his head above the rail. He found the boat and started to hammer off the entire clip. The bolt clapped open with the last shell. He slammed another clip in.

He could hear Hallie yell for him. She was so loud he thought she must be hit. His gut clamped all the way to his balls again.

"The gauge! The gauge is all the way in the red again." She reached up to pull the throttle back.

"No!" he screamed, but it was too late.

She pulled it back, and the diesel stalled. The sound of the laboring motor stopped and the bullets stopped. Za slid across the deck and spun the wheel so the *Pantene* turned sideways to the approaching boat.

"We have to cool it down again." He put his head up, judging the distance to the shore. "We have to get it started and get to shore before they board us."

They scrambled to the protected side and filled the buckets, then poured water on the steel. It sang in angry reply. "Dear God, don't break," Za said, and Hallie joined him. She left to fill the bucket, then returned carrying the bucket.

"Go read the gauge," he ordered.

She scooted toward the wheel. She looked at the gauge and then at the boat. It was close enough she could see people on it. She came back to Za.

"Fill the bucket," he said, pouring the other out. The steam burned him. "What did the gauge say?"

She left without an answer. Hallie dipped the bucket into

the water, plunging the handle deep and driving the water into it.

She pulled back to lift it out. The bucket stuck. Confused, she pulled again. A hand reached out of the water and grabbed her wrist. Hallie screamed bloodily. The hand pulled her hard against the rail.

Za dropped his bucket and in a single lunge was on deck. He ran to her, grabbed her shoulder, and pulled. A black muddy form rose from the water. Za took his right hand and felt for the AK-47 hanging from his back.

Pulling on Hallie, with his left arm wrapped around her shoulder, he got the gun in his hand and clicked off the safety.

He put a burst into the river and the form let go. Both he and Hallie fell back onto the deck.

Scared and dazed, he jumped up and looked into the water. They were in shallow waters, and the bullets agitated the mud. Nothing could be seen.

Za shot into the muck, emptying the clip. The gunfire echoed off the shore and back to them.

He ran back to the wheel and hit the starter. It lit, and the *Pantene* rolled toward shore. "Get Evenel! We're going to jump."

Hallie was running toward Za to get inside the cabin when she stopped and her voice was cold. "Pan?"

Za turned toward where she was staring and saw a muddy form stepping toward them, took the wheel and spun it. The *Pantene* turned and headed right toward the oncoming boat.

CHAPTER FORTY-FOUR

The Amazon

Cool water flowed across Jesse's mind. He woke with a start. Pain rolled over him. He closed his eyes again, then slowly opened them.

A hand applied water to Jesse's forehead. "Drink," a male voice said. He lifted Jesse's head and poured water over his lips.

Jesse sputtered and coughed. Jesse drank down a few gulps and rested.

"Who are you?" Jesse asked haltingly.

"I am Hada from the village, brother of Lesise, and the friend of Piper."

"Hada."

Hada pulled on Jesse's arms and brought him to a sitting position. Jesse cried out. Hada propped Jesse up against a tree. Jesse felt foggy. Everything hurt, including thinking.

Hada held out the water. Jesse slowly lifted his arm, took

the water from Hada, and sipped. His thirst came on, and he poured it down. Hada held out some kind of dried meat. Jesse put it in his mouth, and in seconds, his appetite awoke. He chewed on the meat slowly, his jaw aching. "Where am I?"

"Near falls."

"How?"

"You crawl partway. I bring you rest the way."

"No, how did you find me?"

"I am born here. I am the jungle."

Jesse nodded.

Hada gave him more water and another piece of dried meat. "Finish that, and then we can talk."

Jesse worked on the dried meat and drank the water. Then he fell into deep sleep.

When he awoke, the daylight was fading. "Is it morning or…is it late?" Jesse asked.

Hada sat tending a fire. "The sun setting."

"Are we safe?"

"Yes."

"Do you have more food?"

"Yes," Hada said, pointing to the pack. "You get food."

Jesse struggled to his feet, hugging a tree trunk the entire way. The world swung left and right wildly before it began to spin. He put his head against the tree, and the world slowed down. "There, I'm good."

"As long as you can fight Tohanna with a tree to hold onto."

Jesse grunted in agreement. He moved from tree to tree toward the pack and then fell to the ground next to it. He managed to retrieve some food and rolled painfully to a sitting position. The natural light faded, and the fire flickered.

"Tomorrow we get you to the river."

"Will that help me?"

"It will help the smell."

Jesse laughed, coughed. "It hurts to laugh. I have to find a way to kill Tohanna."

"It looks like that not work last time," Hada said.

"What is he afraid of?"

"How I know?"

Jesse hesitated. "What are you afraid of?"

"What you mean?"

"If I wanted to fight you, what could I do to make you scared?"

Hada thought for a minute. "I don't like the dark. Bad spirits watch you in dark. And bad spirits use lightning. Steal you away."

"Explain that."

"Bad spirits roam the night where they hide. They grab you and they call on their God to strike you. The thunder is when spirit ripped from his body."

Jesse pondered this information. "What else?"

"I use to afraid my mother."

Jesse smiled. "You're still afraid of your mother."

Hada laughed. "True, but she not know it."

"That's what you think," Jesse said. "What about a shaman? Would Tohanna be afraid of a shaman?"

"A shaman a healer. Before my father born, they have magic, but no more."

"Did your village have a shaman?"

"Yes. Tohanna kill him, take magic."

Jesse sighed, feeling his beaten body draining. "What happened at the village after I left?"

"We buried Deza. Piper insist boys, girls, we all go. I dug grave. I only one who know how, with you."

"What...?" Jesse groaned and held his ribs. "What happened to, I mean, what became of Evenel's arm?"

"Piper insisted bury with Deza." Hada's voice broke and he hesitated. He wiped his eyes with the inside of his forearm. "It bad, like Piper left her soul in that hole."

Jesse turned his back to Hada. "I'm falling asleep. We can talk in the morning, okay?"

"Okay, Jesse."

Jesse squeezed his eyes shut as hard as he could, curling his lips tight and suppressing tears. He thought about Xting, how each shovelful of dirt separated him from his family. Piper had to endure that with her little girl.

I was stupid and ignorant.

She told me not to cross the river. And now she had paid the price. Suffered the worst pain that could be endured.

And I brought it to her. I wish I had never come here and hurt her. I will do this. I will kill him. And if I survive, I will leave, that is what she wants. She wants me to get as far from her as possible.

The next morning, Jesse hobbled to the river behind Hada. He felt 100 percent better, even if he did not look it. They both waded into the cool water. The sensation rolled up his torso, wonderful and biting. He dropped his head under the surface and let the current sweep away his soreness. It seemed everything hurt, including his pride. *I must be getting better,* he thought. His mind was berating him now, so his brain apparently didn't need all of its power to heal.

Hada popped out of the water, walked through the wake, and sat on a sandbar in the river. Jesse floated over and settled next to him. He lay with just his head out of the water and let the sun warm him while the water cooled him. He adjusted to get the right combination. "I've been thinking about what you said last night."

Hada looked toward him. Sat up on his elbows. "I can help—"

"No!" Jesse snapped. "This has to stop with me. If you get involved, you know they will try to kill you and the whole cycle will continue."

"Then I leave with you."

"Your village needs you here. You are the oldest male in your village now, and they are depending on you. They will starve if you leave. You have to be a breadwinner."

"What bednner?"

"The man who feeds and protects the family."

Hada lay back in the water. "If we kill all, they no know I helped."

"Well, that's where your problem is," Jesse said. "Right now, it looks like we're the ones who get killed. Then they will continue the killing."

"They kill someone else anyway," Hada murmured.

"So you see, I do this alone and leave this country."

"I no like it."

"Well I don't either, but promise me you won't interfere."

Hada said nothing.

"Hada?"

"Yes," Hada replied dejectedly. "What will you do?"

"In a few minutes I am going to go and do my job." Jesse plunged under the water and let it course over him until his bones were chilled. He stood and moved slowly toward the shore and his date with Tohanna. Hada sat waiting for him.

Hada gave him his pack. "You have food. Two days. And coca leaf to chew."

Jesse stared into his eyes and he could see an emerging man. "We each have a role to play." He put his hand on Hada's shoulder. "Let's do it well."

For a long minute, they stood together, and then Jesse turned and they each went in separate directions.

Jesse crawled in the grass above Tohanna's village. Never moving faster than the wind moved the grass. Sweat stung the new insect bites he had endured while lying in the brush. He lay on a small rise that allowed him to see the comings and goings of the village. The sun beat upon his back, and he desperately wanted to drink from his water. He would have to wait. Right now, people were milling around in the village. Over the three hours he lay hidden, small groups of men left the village and came back. Some women had left in a group. He could hear them singing as they worked a field a hundred yards from the village on his right.

He was not sure what he was waiting for, only that for the past two days he had hoped that a storm would come and a plan would come to him. He put his chin on the ground, resting his neck. *This just sucks*, he thought, *waiting for something but not knowing what it is*. He lifted his head and stared at the village.

Tohanna and two other men came out of the village and disappeared down a trail. They each carried a spear and a machete.

Jesse's heart thumped and fear coursed through him. That surprised him. He had pumped himself full of bravado, but that fled in a single sighting. "Well, move your ass," he said. Jesse moved slowly out of the grass and fell in behind them, keeping a good distance.

He watched the trail for any sign they had moved off it. *Like I can tell*, he thought. "Get a grip on yourself," he whispered, trying to calm his trembling. But images of the beating kept flashing in his mind. He realized he was running. His breathing was elevated and sweat dripped from him. He stopped, looked behind him, then turned to look down the trail ahead of him. *Concentrate, concentrate on your breathing*, he told himself. His mind snapped back to panic. *Behind the trees! Run, go go go!* Jesse shook his head violently as his adrenaline levels spiked. He focused, closed his eyes, and counted his breaths. *Breathe in, breathe out*, he repeated as he calmed himself. Slowly, he started down the trail behind his adversary.

314

The trail was well used, easy to follow, and he prayed Tohanna and the two men would keep moving. He held his machete in his left hand. "This cat-and-mouse game will be the death of me," he whispered.

He followed the path for another hour before it fell alongside a river. Then the trail began to climb upward, leaving the river but running parallel to it. The trail climbed until the river was a hundred feet lower than the trail. A steep earthen bank separated the trail from the river. The sky darkened, and Jesse stopped. He inspected his surroundings. This was it. His long-awaited plan came together. He dug a shallow hole with his machete just opposite the steep embankment and covered it with leaves. He tied his machete tight to his body inside its sheath. Then he sat down in the hole and covered himself with grasses.

Hours passed. He listened carefully, sometimes allowing himself to slowly stretch and then settle back down to wait. Sweat dripped from him, and things scurried in the jungle, sounding big as bears. Anxiety crept up on him and he forced himself to count his breaths. *Just rats, birds, lizards...calm down*, he thought. *They have to come back this way, they have to come back some time.*

Late in the day, the sky opened up and the rains poured. Soon, the rumble began and light flashed across the sky. The trail turned to mud, and the rains felt good in the heat. The day became dusk.

Jesse heard the tromping of feet splashing in the mud. His adrenaline spiked again, freezing him in place. His teeth rattled, he clinched them. *Come on, get control*, he whispered. He crouched, wound up like a spring. Every muscle ached to explode. The sounds moved toward him, and the crack of thunder was all around.

Jesse could see them now. His mind was bursting.

Tohanna was in front of the other two men, who both

looked agitated. Lightning struck so close the two of them jumped and yelled out. Jesse nearly screamed out. He bit down on his tongue and closed his eyes, blinking the rain from them.

They stopped and argued. They began down the trail again.

Jesse held still; they came closer. Tohanna moved in front of Jesse, and a lightning bolt struck, illuminating Tohanna in splendid white light.

Jesse lunged forward and tackled Tohanna off his feet, knocking him down the steep bank and toward the river.

CHAPTER
FORTY-FIVE

Amazon River

Shoot at them! Both of you!" Pan commanded.

Hallie picked up one of the loaded rifles and aimed. Za put in a fresh clip and let loose with a burst.

Hallie shook with the rupture spewing from the gun.

The other boat turned, froth from its twin screws rolling behind it. They were running and quickly outran the *Pantene*.

Pan loaded the grenade launcher and aimed. He hesitated. "They're out of range," he said. "No sense letting them know the range of our firepower."

He pulled the launcher back down, opened the breech, let the round fall into his hand, and turned to put it back in the crate.

Za stared at Hallie and at Pan, then back at Hallie. Hallie shrugged, wide-eyed and stunned. Smoke curled past her face from the AK-47 she held tight.

Pan throttled down. "You have the backpacks?"

"But—" Hallie said, her mouth hanging open.

"The backpacks," he repeated.

"Yes," she said. "But…Jesse said you got shot to pieces and fell in the river that night."

Pan picked up a flashlight and shined it on his chest. A heli-shaped scar blistered his chest with another on his shoulder.

"Jesus," Za said, wincing.

"My God," Hallie said reaching out to touch one of the scars. "How come you're, I mean, I would say you were dead."

"I am the river." He poked a thumb at his chest. "The bullets went right through me. So I got to shore and lay in the mud for a couple days, maybe more. 'Cept for an anaconda who wanted me, nothing was interested in a skinny boy. I waited till he thought he had me and I cut his head off." Pan held up a knife, scraped it across his neck. "Raw snake and mud, that's how I got through, at least till he started to stink. The crocs like 'em good and spoiled, so I crawled out of there."

"Without any medicine? No infection? I don't believe it," she said.

"I found a copaiba tree and later a chuchuasco tree. With this knife, I tapped them and cooked the sap down to oil. Native medicine. Lived on bugs and roots until I was strong enough to carve a bow and some arrows."

"Pan!" Evenel scrambled from the cabin and ran to Pan.

He scooped her up and twirled her around. "Evenel!"

He stopped, and the smile dropped from his face like it was hinged to a door. Hard lines framed his eyes as they pierced the twilight. He pulled her from him, sorely aware of the stump pressing his back.

He sought out the memory, the image of this precious child running toward him. Was she whole? Did he imagine it?

His mind snapped back to the present, shearing off his internal vision. He held her out…her vestiges, her remains, swung around before him. He pulled her back to him, a great, horrid sound rolled up from his guts. Rocking back and forth, he held her.

Evenel held him, wrapping her stump around his back and caressing him with her remaining hand, running it through his muddy hair.

"Pan," Za said. "The boat, where do we go?" The *Pantene* leaned to starboard and began to circle in the last remaining light.

Pan gasped, then he said, "Turn back to the river where you came from. They won't expect that." He picked up Evenel, carried her to the stern, and sat down with her on his lap.

Za turned the *Pantene* back upriver. He did not throttle up, but kept her at cruising speed. The other boat was lost to the dark now.

Hallie picked up a loaded clip. She loaded it into the rifle slung over Za's shoulder and released the bolt. It snapped across the night, somehow reassuring them both. She loaded her own. She kissed Za and left him at the wheel.

She went to the stern and sat down across from Pan. Evenel reached out for her, and Pan let go. Evenel crawled onto Hallie's lap and gave her a kiss on the bottom of her chin.

"What happened?" Pan asked.

"An asshole called Tohanna did this," Hallie said, waving her hand over Evenel's stump. "Chicken butt, go and help Za steer the boat." She wiped mud from Evenel's cheek.

Evenel slid down and went toward Za. She stopped and turned back to Pan. She gave a little wave with a cupped hand and broke into a grin before turning back to Za.

"Walk!" Hallie said automatically, then she turned back toward Pan. "He did it to piss off Piper, and then he killed Evenel's mother."

"Chicken butt? I like that." Pan grinned.

"You said the backpacks were fakes. You lied."

He shrugged. "Where's Piper?"

Hallie skipped a beat and her voice squeaked. "I don't know. We left them behind, her and Jesse, with some guns and ammo."

Pan grimaced. "You left him in charge? Well, that was stupid. They're dead by now."

"We left Piper in charge. And you don't know that. Now listen."

Hallie poured out the story to Pan right up to the point where Pan grabbed her arm in the river and scared the living crap out of her.

"Pan," Za called out. "How far we going? It's dark out here, man."

Pan and Hallie came forward to the wheel. "Where's Evenel?"

"I put her to bed. I carried her inside the cabin and covered her up."

Pan said, "We'll run upriver six, eight miles and put in for the night. They run too deep of a draft to get up this river, and they can't travel that far by foot in a single night. By now they know we ran up here to get safe harbor for the night. They'll wait for us at the mouth."

"And then?" Za asked.

"We make a plan. Until then, we can sleep, and I need a wash." He scrunched his nose. "So does one of you."

"Why did they run from us?" Hallie said.

"Because I know this guy. His name is Miguel, at least that's what they call him in Manaus. He's a Pogsas. Dirty dogs, every one of them. The boat we blew up last time, that was his brother Anton. And Miguel is the one who sent him to look for us. Anton, he was the muscle, but he wasn't smart like Miguel is.

"Miguel won't attack until he holds all the cards. That's why I knew he would run when we turned toward him. He didn't know who or what he was facing. He will wait until he can't lose. He has the advantage of firepower, and he does not have to answer to anyone. He will get us."

"Shit, not again," Hallie moaned.

Pan laughed. "I don't lose very easy. I am the river." He put his thumb in his chest again and said, "I am a Desanos warrior, where we use to eat Pogsas whenever the dirty dogs dared to cross our land.

"I was born out here, and I never saw a gringo until I was a grown man. Men like Miguel, he's in my backyard. Don't forget that. And I am ready to die. Nothing is more dangerous than something cornered with nothing left but the deathblow. Get that in your mind and you may live, or not."

Za said, "We did alright so far."

"You call that doing alright? You were two breaths from a bullet."

"So you waited for the backpacks?"

"And my boat." He gestured around him. "I knew I just had to wait until you brought back my boat. In the meantime, Miguel came looking for his brother, or rather for the backpacks. He found the leftovers from his brother's boat. He knew you either went up this branch or stayed in the main river. So all he had to do was wait.

"That's when I knew I had to get on board the *Pantene* before they did. I let them see me over there where you found me, a place that is as far from this branch as possible. I wanted to keep them working that shore. Then I would swim back here to wait. But every day or two, I had to show myself over there. It was just bad luck you came along when I was on the wrong side."

Hallie stood up. "I'm going to check on Evenel."

"We should sleep," Pan said. "Za, you stay watch first, give me a few hours and wake me."

Pan went over to the crate with the ammo inside. He opened it and rummaged inside with the flashlight. "Gringo! Come here."

Za moved over to the crate and looked inside.

"Hallie said you left ammo behind for Jesse."

"Yeah, two AK-47 rifles and two canisters of ammunition."

"Well, I had three cases of 30 mm ammo and two of them are gone."

"So where are they?" Za said.

"Dickhead!" Pan said. "The 30 mm cases are bright red. What color cases did you leave him?"

Za drew his asshole so tight it hurt.

CHAPTER FORTY-SIX

Za stumbled into the cabin, looking like a ghost.

Hallie turned to him. "What happened?"

"I left the wrong ammunition."

"What ammunition?"

"Jesse. I left him the wrong ammunition."

She swallowed hard. "We have to go back." She pushed past Za and out to the deck where Pan was standing.

Pan poured a bucket of water over his head, washing the mud away.

"We have to go back," she said.

"They're dead."

Za came forward. "We have to go get them."

"You're a bit late, gringo."

Hallie picked up a rifle. "I'm not asking you, I'm telling you."

"Listen, gringos, we don't have the fuel to go back and pick up scraps."

Za and Hallie stared at each other. "Well, what do we have?"

"We have enough to get back to Manaus. We don't have enough to go upriver, get killed, and get back to Manaus."

"Then we go back to the village and get Jesse and Piper and then we take the fuel from your friends who are waiting for us." She pointed downriver.

Pan let out a laugh. "You got balls, girl." Pan dried himself off and held out his hand.

Hallie dropped her shoulders, swore, and gave him the rifle.

Pan leaned the gun against the doorway of the cabin and went inside. Evenel lay asleep on the bed. He stroked her hair. She made him smile. He reached into the cupboard next to the bed and pulled out a pack of Marlboros and a book of matches. He walked out to the deck opening the pack and tapped a stick out, lit it up, and inhaled deeply.

"Alright, we go back to the village and look for them," he said. "By some miracle they didn't get killed, we gather them up and bring them back out. But Evenel comes back to Manaus with us. She won't last out here in the jungle missing an arm. That's the deal."

"That's a deal," Hallie answered. "I never liked having to leave them behind. But how are you going to get Piper to leave? She wouldn't come with us no matter how much we begged."

"I plan on using rope. For her own good." He inhaled, shaking two fingers and a smoke at her. "I'll tie her up and carry her ass out. By the time we get back here, Miguel will be bored senseless. Maybe he'll just give us some diesel."

"Seriously?"

Pan laughed, smoke blowing from his nostrils. "Gullible! You're an easy mark. Maybe you won't get out alive."

"What are we waiting for?" Za said.

"Not now, gringo. We got no lights. You in a hurry to get us dead? Then who is going to go look for scraps?"

"We start in the morning, Za," Hallie said. "With or without him."

"Well, I can't sleep now," Za complained.

Hallie turned her attention back to Pan. "And I want to get something else straight. I want to know what is in the backpacks." Hallie crossed her arms and thrust out a hip.

"Like you never looked," Pan said.

"How do you know we didn't just take it?"

"Because, missy, what would you do with some bones and a few stones?"

"Well, why don't you tell me?"

"How much you know about the history of this place?" Pan asked, sweeping his arms in a circle. "The big bad jungle?"

Hallie looked to Za.

"I got nothing," he said.

Hallie turned back to Pan. "I was sick that day."

Pan sat down. "We need some of them canned beans from the cupboard. Go get them."

She hesitated. "Why me, why not him? Because I'm a gullible girl?"

"Because I'm the captain. And you're the galley wag. And you're the galley wag because your mouth is writing bad checks."

She gritted her teeth, balled up her fists.

"Go." Pan cocked his head.

She went slowly, disappearing into the cabin. She returned a minute later with three cans, spoons, and an opener. She opened them, handed a can to Za, and threw one to Pan. She sat down.

"First off," Pan said, "you asked to know. Remember that."

"We know. Tell us," Za said.

Evenel appeared from the dark. She put her arms up for Pan, so he picked her up and cradled her on her lap. In seconds, she was fast asleep.

"The guy they credit with discovering the river was Vicente Pinzon, who was with Columbus on his first voyage and captain of the *Nina*..."

325

Hallie interrupted, "We have to write this down? And what has this got to do with your little bones and rocks?"

"How does a guy like you know this stuff?" Za said.

"When I worked on her uncle's ship," he pointed at Hallie, "I spent a lot of time as a sailor and Captain Vic made sure I read a lot of books." Pan slurped some beans.

"After that, a butcher named Francisco Pizarro came through what is now Peru along with his brother Gonzalo and slaughtered thousands of Incas. All justified because they weren't Christians. Had letters from the church saying to send them to hell. It was just good luck the Incas couldn't take their gold with them. After that Pizarro set up shop in Peru. That's where he heard it."

"Heard what?" Hallie asked.

Pan shuffled Evenel to her other side. "The legend. An empire in La Canella, the land of Cinnamon. And El Dorado, the man of gold. According to what the locals were saying, the gold had no end. That even the telephone poles were made of gold."

Za laughed. Hallie looked at him. "What's so funny...Oh, you asses. Stop it. I know they didn't have telephone poles."

"Maybe that's enough," Pan said.

"You're not stopping now unless you want me to hurt you with this spoon." Hallie squinted at him.

Pan grinned, lit a smoke and let it waft away into the stars, enjoying his own story.

"They go after the gold, and somewhere in the jungle, they realize they should be worrying more about their supplies than all that gold they cannot find.

"They find a river that flows east. Now remember that a river is a road in 1541. East won't take them home, but they still believe that all the riches are just ahead. They elect one of their captains to sail ahead and get some riches and the glory of the first killings, then bring it back to the main group so they can continue.

"That captain happens to be Francisco de Orellana.

"Orellana shoved off and I hope he got his boots wet because that was the turning point in his life. The day when he went from a highly regarded conquistador to piss boy."

"Why?" Hallie and Za asked in unison.

"You'll see," Pan said. He slipped a match along the floor and the scent rose to them. The light glowed at his face in the moonlight, flaring when he sucked hard on the cigarette. He waved the match to its death. "A lot of things have been said about El Dorado. But I heard them out here, where I was born, before I found it in some book. And tonight I tell you the truth. El indio dorado, or the golden Indian, was a story from somewhere in the western mountains."

Hallie and Za sat transfixed.

Pan repeated the match and cigarette as it had went out and began again.

"Orellana had bit off more than he could chew. The river got stronger, and the jungle became thick and evil. And neither food nor riches fell into their possession.

"After months they reached a sizeable village where, outside the walled city, a large wooden relief had been cut into an immense tree. The relief showed two great jaguars aside a beautiful mistress.

"The villagers told Orellana and his men that this was their ruler, Conori. And they paid homage to her and her subjects with gifts of the finest macaw and parrot feathers, which the women used to line the roofs of their temples. The villagers said the women were great warriors. The women would travel inland from the river, capture men in battle, and bring them back to their village. They would lay with them before killing them, or sometimes they were released into the wild. And if a son were born, it would be killed, but if a daughter were born, she would be raised as a warrior.

"Orellana and his men stayed in the village that night and received their hospitality from the villagers. In the morning, he killed them all with his swords, took their supplies, and burnt the village. The Spaniards got back on the river rafts and continued downstream. A mistake he would regret, as he found out later.

"That night, the Spanish landed on the shore and set up camp on the edge of the river, on a large sandbar swept clean by the current. They slept under a brilliant indigo sky that sparkled with life. The morning sun, still low on the horizon, sent hues of green through the forest filter. Long shadows returned to the trees that cast them. A guard shouted.

"Every one of the conquistadors rolled to his feet. At the forest edge, a form emerged, and then another. They were adorned with macaw feathers at their waists and nothing else, save the bright green stones hanging around their throats that gleamed like they housed fire.

"The women held long spears, pointed forward. And to the man, the Spanish said, a more beautiful woman they had never laid eyes upon. Light-skinned and tall, with long blonde hair that swept across their breasts. Each held a spear in one hand and a war club in the other.

"They walked forward, and in one motion a hundred men stepped from the forest. Orellana called for his pistols and shouted to the men 'Gentleman! Present swords!'

"The men scrambled to their weapons as the women cried out. The Indians attacked, led by the tall women moving like great cats across the sand. The lines met, and Orellana watched as one of the women met the sword and easily swept it aside. She landed her club and the Spaniard's face split as a tomato would, spitting flesh across the sand. His men were falling back and falling dead from the attack. Orellana raised his pistol and stepped forward, leveled the pistol at her breasts, and the hammer snapped down. For a long instant, the gun held silent and then roared its death into the woman. She fell as a stone crashes the earth.

"The smoke billowed. He turned to the other woman as she slaughtered a conquistador, his blood splattering Orellana. He pointed the other pistol, and the gun blew fire from the barrel and into the woman. She fell forward into the sand. At the second report, the Indians turned and ran for the forest.

"'To the boats, gentleman, to the boats,' he commanded. The Spanish loaded their wounded and their dead into the boats and shoved off. The current pulled them downstream still close to the shore.

"Suddenly an attack came from the jungle. Several dozen warriors leaped into the shallow water. The Spanish fought them back, but many boarded the boats. Blood began to slosh in the corners of the raft. Arms and guts spilled onto the deck.

"Orellana skewered a man and turned to face another woman. She swung her war club, and the blow glanced off his sword. A metallic clang rang across the river. He recovered and brought his sword down hard. She ducked aside and crashed a shoulder into his, knocking him down. In the same motion, she stood on Orellana's hand, clamping his sword to the deck. She raised her war club to strike when a sword plunged through her from the back and she buckled to the deck on top of him.

"One of his men pulled her from him and rolled her aside. Orellana got to his feet and engaged another warrior. But the tide was turned and all the Indians were slaughtered. 'Throw them overboard!' he shouted. 'The rest of you paddle to the center of the river.' He turned back to the dead woman. Blood pooled across her belly. The smell of freshly butchered effluents and raw guts rose over the boat. He reached down and seized the green stone around her throat. He slid his sword under the leather strap and cut it from her. He stooped and raised her from the deck and dumped her into the water.

'Sir! look!' Ahead the river turned 180 degrees, and along the shore hundreds of men stood waiting. A dozen tall women spread out in front of the army. They were shouting orders to the men. Orellana put the green stone into his pocket. 'Shoot the women. Move the guns to the front and kill them all. Open fire with the cannon.' As the men loaded their guns, a sizzle cut through the air and every man knew the sound well. Arrows rained down on them, cutting into wood and flesh alike.

"'Take aim! Fire!' The guns exploded, sending ripples across the river. Fire slashed out from the boats, and the women dropped dead from the invisible balls.

"An instant later, a cannon fired and bright flashes roiled out from the boats. Fifty men burst into gore that rained down on the others. The warriors raced into the trees, stunned from the carnage. The Spanish paddled around the bend and down the river.

"Orellana kept going and burnt more people, but the further he got, the more natives were waiting for him. He was forced to stay in the middle of the river, far from shore. He found the Atlantic Ocean eight months after he had left his boss, who had already made a criminal of him for deserting the brothers and making off with all the gold in El Dorado."

"So why did he call it the Amazon?" Hallie asked.

"Back in antiquity, the Greeks wrote about a tribe of women that killed any man who came near the place. They were the Amazons. Orellana thought he had run into them." Pan sat back and enjoyed the stars.

Hallie tapped his knee. "Is that it?"

Za said, "How does that fit with the backpacks?"

"A year ago, there were stories about bones and green stones. Graves. I found them." He smiled as the devil would.

"That's what's in the backpacks," Hallie said.

"Yes and no. I split it up and gave half to the boys in the river the first night you were on board. The rest are still in the backpacks we have.

"Why do you want this stuff?" Hallie asked.

"Sell it to the highest bidder," Za said.

"I am not a fool. I am selling it, but only to one buyer," Pan said.

"And who is that?"

"The University in Manaus. They will use DNA to prove our place in history. And if the stones match the one that Orellana took, then I am right. Orellana said they were white women. I say he lied. This is the history of my people."

"And a big profit," Za said.

Pan nodded his head. "A good profit. And I am the one risking my tail."

"You're risking our asses too," Za said.

Pan shrugged. "Along for the ride."

"And the pirates out there? They want them too?" Za said.

Pan stood up and pointed at Za. "That is where I differ from Miguel. They can get twice as much from a private buyer. Split it up, and it is worth millions. I won't do that. It belongs to the people."

"So how did they know you have it?"

"We kind of found it at the same time. Maybe they were there a little before me."

"You stole it from them?" Za said.

"It was more like rescued from them."

"Wait," Hallie said. "Piper had a green stone that she wore. She said the villagers gave it to her. You don't suppose...?"

Pan's eyes lit up. "A green stone?"

CHAPTER FORTY-SEVEN

The Amazon

Jesse hung onto Tohanna as they cart-wheeled down the steep embankment. Trees and brush streaked by, spinning in a circle. They crashed into a tree and bounced off, throwing them apart.

Jesse somersaulted into another tree that whipped over as he rolled across it. He landed on his gut, head first, sliding in the mud. Ooze filling his mouth.

He turned and spun his feet downward. Wet leaves slapped him, and he grabbed at anything, trying to stop. The wirey brush cut into his hand and broke away.

A lightning strike lit the dark in front of him, exposing a tree in his path. He braced for the impact, struggling to avoid it.

He rolled just as his feet hit, and his legs jammed as he bounced off the tree, throwing him back on his gut. He felt nothing, and he was falling.

Another burst of white light flashed and he saw the earth pulling away as he flew into the air. The light disappeared as he fell into the river.

He shot to the surface, disorientated. He swam toward what he hoped was the shore. Water poured into his mouth from the rain that was coming down in a deluge. Another crack of light confirmed he had been right. He let the current pull him past the steep embankment that he had fallen from and onto a sandbank.

He scrambled ashore and grabbed for his machete strapped to his back. Loud thunder boomed and the lightning flashed. There stood Tohanna, his machete drawn, crouched, ready, his back toward Jesse.

Jesse hesitated, fought his panic, sucked in hard, and screamed in the darkness as wild and as convincing of an evil spirit as he could.

He sprinted in the darkness, rain striking him and the sand mashing under his feet. A hundred feet, eighty, sixty-five, Jesse counted off his charge toward Tohanna.

He gripped his machete with all his might, and the fear fell away. The animal rose and he was beyond pain and life. He was the will to kill, to hack and bite and destroy. Another lightning crack flashed.

Tohanna stood ready to receive him.

Jesse leaped in the air and saw Tohanna react. *He believes he's fighting a God*, Jesse thought. He landed and cut to the right in the dark. He sprinted wide of Tohanna and ran past him. Jesse dove into the river.

The rain beat down, muffling all sound except the torrent beating the water and sand. Under the surface, the night lit again and the thunder rippled through the water. Jesse had disappeared. Tohanna would think he flew away.

He swam with the knife as far as he could before surfacing. He looked toward the shore but could see nothing, the

333

rain preventing him from seeing anything let alone the dark.

Jesse swam upstream, angling back toward the shore. He waded ashore near where the sandbar began to rise toward the embankment. He guessed Tohanna would come this way if he were going to return to his village. Jesse pulled himself ashore and rolled into the grass.

Mud flowed past him and into the river. The embankment was giving way. The thunder cracked and more lightning spidered the sky.

Explosions of sound and wind roared across the land. His enemy moved cautiously toward him. The great knife hovered in Tohanna's hand.

A dozen strides and he would be on top of Jesse. Jesse knelt in the grass, which bent with the wind and mud. He realized he was being buried by the eroding embankment. Jesse stood up, struggling to escape the mud and get to the sandbar.

The rain fell from his forehead and into his eyes. He felt the sandbar under him. He raked his arm over his brow.

Jesse raised his machete, ready to strike. And the Gods spoke, and from their lips came the thunder and the white-hot light. Tohanna stood before him, his eyes wide in surprise.

Jesse pulled his machete down, stepping forward and calling on all his power to deliver. He pulled down, and the knife struck steel, clanging and spitting Jesse's blow sideways, twisting Jesse's grip.

Tohanna's machete flipped away into the abyss.

Jesse turned and bowled into Tohanna. Jesse rolled his shoulder and brought the great knife down hard on Tohanna again. But the spine of the machete struck Tohanna's shoulder, and Jesse heard it break.

Tohanna caught Jesse's wrist and twisted Jesse over backward.

They fell hard onto the sand, and Jesse's machete slipped from him. Jesse bounced, rolled, and turned over, getting on top of Tohanna. He smashed his forehead into Tohanna's face again and again.

Jesse punched at Tohanna until a mighty kick lifted him off and onto the sand. He landed like a cat, and again the lightning flashed, bang bang bang.

Tohanna stood before him with one arm swinging useless. But his eyes…his eyes burned with hatred and vile evil.

Rage poured through Jesse. *The arrogant bastard has to die*, he thought. *I'll break him limb from limb.*

He leaped forward to remove the life from the bloodletting bastard. Jesse bowled into Tohanna, and they grappled, biting ears and gouging eyes. Jesse used his fists and his elbows and his knees. Pressure pushed across his body. It must have been blows, but no pain came with them.

Blind rage tore through Jesse, and he did nothing to defend himself. He only acted to hurt and bloody the monster. They stood and fell and rolled and stood again, each smashing into the other.

Jesse felt the heat coming off Tohanna, and he beat at Tohanna's chest, face, and neck. He bit chunks from all parts of the little bastard.

Tohanna bounced Jesse onto Jesse's ass.

Jesse stood up. This time Tohanna hesitated. Jesse roared his power from deep in his gut and out his throat. Blood and spit flew from him.

Tohanna was down on one knee, glaring his hatred.

Jesse knew Tohanna's mind still fired with malice and death, but his body couldn't follow.

He attacked, smacking Tohanna full force. Jesse landed on him and beat Tohanna about the face.

Tohanna pushed Jesse off but did not come after him.

Jesse stood up and realized the clouds had separated and allowed the moon to pour through.

Tohanna got to his knees. He struggled, but he could not stand up. Great gulps of air sucked at his lips. Blood poured down his face.

Jesse could taste his own warm blood. The slowing rain washed it through his mouth. Jesse could see past Tohanna, who waited for his attack. There, in the mud, a rock had slid onto the beach from somewhere deep in the earth. Jesse walked over to it and tried to lift it. He moved his hand for a better grip and felt something solid. A handle. A handle attached to his machete.

Jesse pulled the machete from the mud and turned to Tohanna. Tohanna's shoulder still hung at his side.

Jesse shook the knife, dislodging the mud from the blade. He took his left hand and slid the remaining mud from the razor edge. He threw the mud at Tohanna, and Tohanna shouted in defiance. Jesse flicked the machete, each time exposing more of the blade, defining it in the diminutive light. Stillness hung in the air after the rain, the heaviness of the atmosphere adding to the eerie color of the pale moon.

Jesse thought of the rock behind him. He turned the blade in his hand and struck Tohanna across the face, slapping him backward like a rag doll.

CHAPTER FORTY-EIGHT

The falls slapped the pool below, the water trading colors with the rays of the sun, sliding its orange glow along the rock.

Tohanna awoke.

Jesse stood over him. Tohanna spun to his feet and lashed out at Jesse, only to be stopped. His wrists were bound. He lunged again and was again repulsed. He trailed his eyes back along the rope that led from his wrists to the stone cliff face. There the rope ended, staked into the stone. He turned back to Jesse.

Jesse held a shovel on his shoulder, staring at him blank and cold. He turned and walked away from the stone cliff and the falls and into the jungle.

The women from the village moved toward the falls as they did every morning to bathe and wash their garments against the rocks. They moved as a group.

Piper had issued strict orders to stay together in groups. She slowly walked just behind the group. She hadn't slept, and she felt the weight of the people upon her shoulders. But it was Jesse she suffered for the most. She never imagined how hard it would be to wait for someone to return, knowing they may never. And if he survived, how could she send him away? After what she asked him to do. She bit at her lip. But of course, he could not stay here with her. Revenge killings would continue, and he and everyone here would never be safe.

Outwardly, she appeared strong, but inside, despair cut a slice from her every day, and anguish tortured her every night.

Lesise and Hada, thank God for them, she thought. After Deza's funeral, they had kept the village going while she lay emotionally paralyzed upon the ground. It was stress, she told herself, and loss too, but that would heal over time if she didn't suffer a total breakdown.

Voices cried out in alarm above the roar of the falls and snapped her back to the outside world.

She rushed forward, pushing to the front. Several voices blended in alarm. Tohanna stood across the river, alone and bound, next to the rock face of the cliff.

The women stood next to the river, staring at him across the water. An old woman stepped forward. Another stepped forward. Then Lesise stepped forward. Each walked toward the falls and the shallow place where they could cross to the other side, until Piper stood alone.

A steady line waded through the shallows, following the old woman who had not set foot on this side of the river for a long time. Her jaw was set tight, and she never wavered and she did not hurry. She moved across the rocky flats, stepping over stones the falls had split and battered over a hundred thousand years, stones that lay here until today.

The old woman came to a stop a few yards from Tohanna. The rest of the women lined up alongside her. All were silent.

Tohanna shouted at them, cursed their wombs. He searched the cliff face for a sharp stone. He slid the rope back and forth, cutting the ropes.

The old woman could remember when there was peace. When her husband had courted her here at the base of the thundering falls, here along the river. She would run along the bank and never did she fear for him. She could remember when this was the way it was. Her heart ached for him and for the peace that was taken from them.

The group milled around her. Uncertainty washed through the air. Piper crossed the river and stood behind Nokai, the old woman. Nokai reached down and picked up a stone. She held it in her palm. She closed her fingers around it and opened them again. She gripped the stone in her hands. All fell silent and motionless.

Tohanna bit at the frayed ropes, desperately biting and pulling at the fibers. Nokai brought her hand over head and she cast the stone.

Tohanna blocked it. He pulled on the rope, and it broke. Nokai reached down and gripped another stone. She cast it, at the same time as Lesise threw hers.

Tohanna blocked the stones. A torrent fell upon him, beating upon his arms and legs. He tried to climb, but a rock crashed into his head, and another smashed his hand against the stone face. He turned to run, but the hail of rocks beat him back. Blood dripped from his mouth and his ears.

Piper reached down. She did not act consciously, but she

picked up a stone and gripped it until the sharp edges bit into her hand. She watched the stones arc toward him and then fall on him. Another and another.

She stood with the stone in her hand until she snapped, hurling the stone, her anger boiling so hard it hurt. She crushed her teeth together, curling her lip, and she threw another stone. She screamed with the others, hoping to hurt and to maim, each stone not satisfying her bloodlust. She hurled again and again.

Tohanna fell to his knees and tried to crawl.

Piper lifted a large rock with both hands, hoisting it as high as she could. She stood over him and brought it down on him, crushing him to the earth. He struggled back to his knees as more rocks fell on him. She picked up the rock and dropped it again. The rage boiled long and hot inside her. Her despair and anguish broke from the cage inside her and hatred burst from her hands until she staggered backward and collapsed with the rock.

Lesise picked up the rock. She lifted it high above her head and crushed it down upon Tohanna.

Jesse waited until the stones no longer clanked. He sat until the noises stopped altogether. He returned to where Tohanna's body lay among the stones. It was a killing field of red. Jesse slipped a rope around Tohanna's ankle and dragged his body away, bouncing Tohanna over the stones and into the jungle.

Jesse stopped at the freshly dug hole. He pulled out his machete and put it to work. When he finished, he rolled the body into the hole and then carried stones from the falls and layered them over the body a foot thick. Then he filled in the hole with dirt. Sweaty and tired, he set out to finish the job. He followed the paths that led inland, away from the river, through the swamp and muck.

The dirt path that led into Tohanna's village was empty as he entered the village. He held his machete in one hand, strolling deliberately along the path. People gathered at the center of the village. The two men who had been with Tohanna when Jesse tackled him over the embankment stood still among them. Fear rifled through them.

Jesse stopped a few feet in front of them and the crowd cowered. He held up his machete, and in his other hand, he held Tohanna's head by the hair. He dropped it in the dirt. It thumped and dust rose. Jesse turned and disappeared into the jungle.

First light cut through the jungle when Jesse reached the river. As he got to the place he had last seen Piper, his heart began to ache. The birds were quiet and the river gurgled.

Hada sat alone with the canoes. He stood when Jesse arrived. For a time, they stared at each other. Jesse was bruised and blood-stained, Hada the image of budding manhood.

"Welcome, Jesse."

"Hada, you, um, waiting for me."

"Yes, since yesterday." He kicked at the sand. "It is done?

Jesse nodded.

"We are thankful—"

"No, don't," Jesse said. "I'm not able to be, I can't accept, um, I just can't right now."

Hada hung his head.

"How is she?"

"Piper, has…she has been sad."

"You tell her…" Jesse struggled for his breath, putting his hand on his exploding chest. "You tell her I…I hope she will

341

always be happy, and that when I feel the sun warm me, no matter where I am, I will think of her."

Hada fell quiet, and they stood facing each other. He nodded, then said quietly, "I loaded a canoe for you with food and supplies." Hada looked up. "Jesse, I will be a good breadwinner."

Jesse nodded, breathing deeply. He looked past Hada, to the village. He stepped toward Hada.

"You cannot, Jesse," Hada said, gripping Jesse's arm.

Jesse jerked free.

Hada turned and pulled the canoe into the river. "If you go to her now, then all is lost. Do you think you can ever leave her again?"

Jesse opened his mouth, but nothing came out.

"The killing is over. As it must be."

Jesse quivered, struggling with his craving, his desire.

Hada held the paddle out to Jesse. "Good-bye."

Jesse gripped the paddle, and they both held it for a time. Hada released the paddle while Jesse stepped inside the canoe. He put the paddle to the water and pulled. His entire being cried out softly.

He let the current carry him. Tears, salty and wet, slid down his cheeks, slipping into his mouth. He stroked again. He couldn't believe how much it hurt, how badly he wanted to be with her. He paddled with the current until he saw the rock where he first saw her, where his heart had beat so hard he thought it would break. Now he wondered how it could hurt so badly and yet he did not die. He hoped she would be here. That hope had kept him going through all this, the chance that she would be here, for him. That they could somehow, someway, be together.

But she was not. In spite of all his want and hope, the relentless water pushed him past.

Piper sat behind the rock. She had waited the entire day and night for him. To see him again. Back and forth, her mind had jumbled over and over as she waited for him, waited to hold him again. To see those blue eyes and the fire behind them. Could she still let him go if she felt his arms around her again? Could she bear it?

Her angst tore at her sides as she hid from sight while he passed by. Now it was over and she hurt inside so bad; she was drowning under her own grief. The canoe slid past, and she watched Jesse fade from her life.

CHAPTER FORTY-NINE

Amazon River

You don't suppose Piper's stone was from the tribe of women?" Hallie said. "It was like you said, brilliant green, like it was on fire."

"I'm sure of it." Pan yawned. "But I have to sleep, story time is over. Za, you still got the first watch."

Hallie went inside and lay down on the bed with Evenel. She was warm and beautiful in the moonlight coming through the window.

Hallie woke the next morning when the diesel started. The starter cranked, and the initial firing shook through the boat. The transmission clunked and the propellers splashed. The morning had yet to dawn as the first light expanded its glory.

Evenel stirred and sat up beside her. Hallie messed Evenel's hair. "Hungry?" Hallie asked.

Evenel nodded.

"Come on then." Hallie and Evenel went out onto the deck. Pan was steering the *Pantene* upriver. He smiled, cigarette smoke rolling in the wind behind him. Za sat in the stern behind Pan, looking like he needed another night's sleep. Evenel went over and sat in his lap, looking just as sleepy.

"What you got to eat on this tub?" Pan said.

"The same thing that was on this tub when you went on vacation in the tropics."

"Well, get it going, girl. I am about to rot away here. I could eat the ratty end of a snake."

"So glad you're back, Captain." Hallie yawned and wandered toward the cabin. Minutes later, smoke from the stovepipe trailed behind the *Pantene*.

"Pull that canoe on board!" Pan yelled out. Three days had passed since Pan had turned the *Pantene* upstream toward the village.

Za grabbed one end, and Hallie the other, bringing the canoe onto the rear deck.

"What's in it?" Pan said.

"Looks like some supplies, and the paddle's here too."

Pan put the rope on the wheel spoke and went to the canoe. "Dried meat." He reached down and unwrapped some leaves. "Manioc cakes, fried and wrapped. And a monkey bladder full of toasted termites. A native, and he planned on being on the river a long time."

"Then where is he?" Hallie asked.

"Not like a native to lose his canoe, that takes a gringo. But a gringo couldn't pack this light, or eat this good food. Want some?" He held out the monkey bladder.

They both held up their hands.

"Just me and Evenel then. Evenel! Wake up in there. Uncle Pan has treats."

The *Pantene* pulled up to the riverbank, at the same spot they had docked when Hallie, Za, and Jesse had first arrived.

Za jumped to shore, ran over to where he had left the guns and ammunition. He returned with the two rifles and canisters. "Everything is still here, but a couple boxes of shells are scattered on the ground."

Pan took one of the rifles. "The bolt is broken off this one, Jesus Christ."

"I hope to God they're alright." Za hung his head. "It doesn't look good. Fucking stupid."

"We were trying to get Evenel out of here," Hallie said, putting her hand on his chin, pulled it upward. "Anybody could have done it."

"Only a gringo would do it," Pan said. "Tie her off to the shore." He threw a rope to Za. "Not that one, over there." He pointed. "Hurry up and then get back on board. Recheck the weapons. If anything comes near you, shoot it," Pan gestured with his hand, "dead."

Pan got in the canoe with a rifle. "Stay here and stay on the boat. You too, Evenel," he said. "And don't start any more wars."

Evenel put her arms behind her back, gave him bug eyes.

He shoved off with the experience of a river rat. Pan prized the small rivers with just a paddle and a bow. That was a distant life ago, and he felt sentimental—not that he could return to this life, he was too soft now. Besides, it was just his past now.

Before long, he pulled up to the village, beached the canoe, and walked up the path.

Several of the women were in the main courtyard. In front of them stood a tall white woman looking shocked.

"Pan?"

Piper gave him a big hug and beamed that wonderful smile of hers. "Oh my God, they said you died."

"Piper!" Pan caught her up in his arms, then set her down. "Just bullets. I'm too mean to die."

She laughed and hugged him again.

"I came to bring you home. Hallie, Za, and Evenel are waiting back at the *Pantene*."

"What...how did...?"

"Za and them were going downstream, and I found them. And your first question is, 'How's Evenel?' Well, she's fine. Full of the devil."

"Really? They are all here? Evenel is...she's alright?"

Pan nodded.

"Where are they?"

"They're waiting for us on the *Pantene*."

Piper covered her mouth and nodded with tears in her eyes. "Did you see," her voice cracked, "Jesse?"

"No. That gringo must be dead if you sent him up against a tribesman."

"No, he's not. He's a hero." She thrust her chin out. "He saved all our lives."

"Then where is he? I would have put some money on the local talent."

"You know the answer to that."

He shrugged. "You sent him downriver to prevent revenge killings. Smart girl."

"You didn't find him? He wasn't with the others?"

Pan studied her. "We found an abandoned canoe. But that was a native's canoe. Had native supplies in it."

"That's because Hada packed it." She pointed at Hada. "Jesse wasn't with the canoe?"

"No," Pan said, shrugging.

She sat down on a log.

Pan looked up, then back at Piper. "Look, I'll find him on the way back to Manaus. When we go back to Manaus."

"I can't leave. Not now, when I'm needed the most."

Several of the children had gathered around, and Pan gave them each a cigarette. He pulled one out for himself and sniffed it. "See how good it smells?" Great smiles broke out.

"I got news for you," Pan said.

Just then Nokai and Lesise approached; they handed Piper and Pan each a bowl.

"Monkey." Pan nodded in pleasure, then said in English, "Ain't no west coast fish taco, is it?" He slurped from the bowl and smiled convincingly. Pan slurped again and said, "You have any friends here? Or do they all hate the stone wearer?"

"Pan, I need you to find him."

Pan took another slurp. "Don't worry. This is me you're talking to."

"Promise me." She held her bowl, but didn't drink from it.

"Tell me about the stone."

"What?"

"Stop worrying about that gringo. Tell me about the stone."

Piper fingered the cord around her neck, sliding her fingers along the soft leather and onto the glistening stone. "The clan gave it to me. Said I was sent to them. That the stone called out to me to save them."

"That's bullshit."

"Excuse me?"

"They have any more of them?"

"No! You don't believe me, do you?"

"Right up to the part where you saved them. Did it ever occur to you that they don't need you?"

"You don't know what has happened here, so don't judge. These people are the best people I have ever known. But they need leadership."

"And you are the only one who can provide that?"

"I'm the one who has done just that."

"Piper, Hallie told me what you have done here. It's over. I came from the jungle." He pointed at his chest with his thumb. "I see the good things you bring, but also the bad too. This culture," he waved his hand in a circle, "you judge it with your values. It should be judged with the values they have. The tribe survives because of the culture they developed over a long time and countless generations. You were here at the right moment, but now you're the weak link. It's time to go."

Piper sat quietly, fidgeting with the stone. "I never thought of it that way."

"It's a new day. Come with me. And besides Evenel cannot survive out here now. She needs you to become a modern woman."

Piper stared off to nowhere, holding her bowl. "It's hard to stop—"

"You could have real food again."

"Who would do…do the things…the decisions I make. We should plant the manioc soon—"

"That's not up to you." Pan said.

She nodded. "They're my family, or they feel like family. Lesise and Nokai especially. I don't know if I can leave. I…" She took a deep breath and finished, saying, "I don't want to lose that."

"Think about it. I can wait until tomorrow. Give them time to decide on a headman. And give me enough time to braid some rope."

Piper felt for the knot behind her neck, under her hair. She untied it and held the stone in her hand. She really wanted to keep the stone, but it never belonged to her. She held it out to Lesise. Lesise took the stone.

"Put it on," Piper said, her voice cracking. "You need to wear it. Otherwise, Hada will think he's in charge."

Lesise hesitated, looking to Nokai.

Nokai nodded. "Deza and your mother would be proud. The tribe has chosen you. Wear the stone, and be who you are. The old ones are watching, and the time of women is here."

"The old ones brought me here," Piper said. "Until you were ready to wear the stone."

Lesise hesitated, looking to Hada. "You will help me?"

He nodded.

Lesise put the ancient leather behind her neck and tied it. She hugged Piper. "I will always remember you."

Piper pulled back and held Lesise by the shoulders. "I will be back," she said. "And Evenel too. This is still her home."

"It does shine as if it's afire," Piper said, admiring the stone. She thought of the night before, when she had said her good-byes and packed the gifts they gave her. The decision to leave somehow felt right now.

"This is your home too," Lesise said. "Always."

Pan waited at the canoe while Piper said her good-byes again. "She's gonna be dehydrated," he said, pulling a drag on a cigarette.

She hugged the entire village, one by one. The time had come, and Piper got in the canoe. They paddled slowly, letting the current carry them. She wiped away her tears with the back of her hand. "You promised to find Jesse. I'm not leaving without him." She looked back at Pan over her shoulder.

"Lost gringos are extra."

Her heart beat wildly when the *Pantene* came into view. Evenel jumped up and down on the bow. All three scrambled to the edge of the *Pantene*. She waved wildly, and shouted, "Hello!"

"Piper!" they whooped. Pan slid the canoe up to the boat, and she put her hand out to Za. He pulled her out of the canoe and into his arms. He whirled her around. When he let her go, Piper held out her arms. Evenel ran into her embrace. Piper held her and kissed her as tears crawled down her cheeks.

"You're gonna be dehydrated," Pan said.

CHAPTER FIFTY

Jesse!" Piper called out.

The jungle returned only silence, and the *Pantene* gurgled in the river.

"Jesse!" Evenel called out.

A branch snapped along the shore. Piper whipped her head in that direction to see Za and Pan appear out of the jungle. They waded in and then swam to the *Pantene* as it drifted downriver. They pulled themselves aboard, with Evenel pulling on Za's T-shirt. He was breathing heavily.

"Any sign?" Hallie asked.

He shook his head. "Really thick in there."

"Keep an eye peeled," Pan ordered. "Watch the shoreline. If he's smart, he'll be watching the river for a ride."

"What if we missed him?" Piper said, her mouth quivering.

"We didn't miss him," Pan said, looking upriver. "Unless something ate him."

"He's a survivor, man. He's still alive," Za said.

"A survivor," Pan said, pointing at the jungle, "doesn't lose a canoe full of the things that keep you alive. No, I didn't miss him. Tonight we'll be near the mouth of the river. Close to where Miguel is waiting for us."

"Then we go back upstream and look again," Piper demanded.

"We don't have the gas." Pan lit a smoke, inhaled. "We got enough fuel for maybe an hour running upstream. We float down, tie up for the night, and find a way to steal some diesel from Miguel. Which was your idea in the first place." He pointed at Hallie.

"Drop me off here then," Piper said. "I'm not giving up."

"Us too," said Za, gesturing toward Hallie. "And we need some of the guns."

"You gringos," Pan said, putting the cigarette between his fingers. "You American gringos watch too much John Wayne. In the Amazon, you don't do your own shit. That's what got Jesse lost. We stay together, we get some diesel, and then we look for him. Are Evenel and I the only intelligent ones on this boat? I think you and I are going to have to steal some diesel ourselves." He held out his arms and she jumped into his embrace.

Pan signaled the *Pantene* from the shore.

"Yeah?" Za called back.

Pan came out of the dark and boarded the *Pantene*.

"What you got?" Za asked.

The group gathered around Pan, dripping with sweat and river water. Evenel brought him his smokes, which he had entrusted to her. He pulled a stick out and she flipped the lighter open and turned the wheel twice. She held it up. Pan bent over and lit the cigarette. Evenel swept the lighter across her hip closing the cover.

Pan winked at her and sat down on the deck. "I swam around Miguel's boat. Got at least twenty hands on board, and they all are keeping a gun on their person. They look real bored and pissed about it. Like they are dying to shoot something. We can use that to our advantage."

"And how?" huffed Hallie, putting a hand on her hip.

"We have to get on board and beach the boat."

"And how?" she repeated, throwing up her arms.

"We get on board, run it aground, and jump in the water before they get us. We can't hold the boat, they got too much firepower."

"And then?" Hallie got in his face and poked him in the chest. "We may have been ignorant on the way upriver, but you ain't going to drag us into another fight without our input this time, buddy."

"Za, put your mare away or I'm going to tie her ass up."

"She's right," Za said, pulling Hallie onto his lap.

Piper nodded, and Evenel did too.

Evenel moved from Piper's lap to Pan's and put her arm around his neck. "Listen to us."

Pan inhaled, the rosebud glowing orange. "We spray them with rounds from the shore. That will occupy most of them. I get on board and run it aground. That will clear the middle of the river so we can sail the *Pantene* past them. But we have a problem. They keep the bridge door locked. They keep a guy inside, and you can't get in unless he opens the door. We got maybe a minute to get the boat started and another minute to beach it before they shoot our asses."

"So how do we get in?" Za asked.

Pan shrugged. "There's a porthole."

"Could I fit through it?" Piper asked.

Pan shook his head. "It's about this big," he said, holding up his hands in a circle.

Evenel got off Pan's lap and stuck her head through his

hands. Piper jumped up and grabbed Evenel. "No! You are not putting her in danger."

"I'm not scared," Evenel protested. "I can do it."

"No, this entire trip is about keeping her safe, and we are going to do just that. She has already paid the price for our recklessness." Piper sat back down with a thump, pulling Evenel onto her lap.

Pan said, "Miguel is no fool. He won't do anything stupid. He'll wait us out. We can't outrun or outgun him. He has us right where he wants us, and he will get us. Unless you gringos with all your new jungle savvy got another way."

"You said we had enough fuel to run upriver for another hour," Piper said. "If something goes wrong, we may not have a chance to look for Jesse again. I want to give him that chance, and I say we use that chance. We need him for the plan."

Pan shook his head and opened his mouth to speak.

"Shut it," she said. "We go back upstream at the first light."

Early morning the next day, the *Pantene* sputtered and shuddered to a stop. Pan pulled the throttle down. "There goes the last drop." He tossed the anchor overboard, it splashed, and he let the rope slide through his hands before tying it off.

Piper and Hallie stood in the bow. Hallie hugged Piper, consoling her.

"We go ashore again, see what we can find," Pan said, staring at the river far ahead of them. He squinted, using his hand to shade his eyes. "I'll be a monkey's uncle."

"What's a monkey's unkall?" Evenel asked, her hand on her hips. Pan picked her up and carried her sideways under his arm, toward the bow. Za came from the stern, following them.

Pan swung Evenel onto his shoulders.

"Jesse!" she cried out.

The trio looked at her.

She pointed upriver. "It's him!"

A black dot with a lump on it sat in the river upstream. They all stared silently. The lump waved. A voice carried to them, "Evenel!"

The black dot grew into a floating log with Jesse astride it. He slid off and swam in earnest toward the *Pantene*.

Za and Pan pulled Jesse aboard. His eyes were big as marbles. "Pan?"

Piper leaped upon him, knocking him to the deck. Her body throbbed from her sobs as she squeezed him.

"Awe, fer Christ's sake," Pan said. "She's gonna be dehydrated again."

They spent the day preparing the *Pantene* and other equipment. The plan had been gone over a dozen times, and Pan had set it in stone.

"Tell me how again?" Za said, turning the rifle over.

"I heard some monkeys in the jungle," Jesse said. "And I pulled the canoe ashore and went to hunt them. I figured I needed the food. It started raining, which made the monkeys impossible to find. I tried for a couple hours and got lost. I finally got back to the river and to the canoe, but it was gone. The river had swelled from the rain, and where I had left the canoe was now part of the river. It just floated away, I guess."

"You didn't tie it to something?"

"No," he said sheepishly. "Days later, I heard a boat heading upstream, but I missed it. That must have been you. I saw you guys the second time, heading downstream. I had been hunting away from the river and I ran back, jumped in, and swam, but I lost sight of you. Thought I was going to lose it then, kind of gave up hope, until I found the floating log…"

Pan appeared. "Jesse, get the kite," he ordered.

"Got to go," Jesse said. "I'll finish later," he called back as he made his way to the stern. Jesse dropped the nylon case that stored Za's hang glider onto the rear deck. "Babe!" he called out. "Come help me with this."

Piper went to the rear deck. Jesse unzipped the large bag and removed the aluminum poles, handing them to Piper.

"Jesse, I have to say something while we're alone. When I asked you to...it was wrong to send you...away..."

Jesse sat on the deck and pulled her into his lap, putting the poles down. "I thought I had lost you, and I never want to feel that way again. I had to survive so I could...I had to finish it so you were safe."

"It was a mistake to separate. We have to stick together from now on. Wherever you go, whatever the danger...we go together."

Jesse looked into her eyes and kissed her hard. "Together, never lose each other again. I promise."

"I promise you too."

"And we're parents now," he said. "We have a beautiful little girl to raise together."

Piper's lip quivered. "I don't...both of us need to take care of her."

"We'll be alright, we have to trust Pan," Jesse said.

Za and Hallie came around the cabin and onto the rear deck. "He's being a macho ass," Hallie said, pointing to Za.

"I have the most experience," Za said, flailing his arms at her.

"What, you think I can't do it?"

"No, it's not that."

"Then what is it? You won't let me do it? Like you get any say in what I will or won't do."

"I do this, not you," Za said.

Jesse said, "We decided this."

"Bullshit," Hallie snapped. "I should do it."

357

"I can't stand for that," Za said. "I won't sit here and send you into danger. I just can't."

Hallie turned to Za, tears welling in her eyes, and she crunched her face trying to hold it all back. Za took her in his arms and held her.

Evenel appeared. Piper picked her up, and Jesse wrapped his long arms around them both. "Together, all of us, together we can do this."

As the light faded away, Pan untied the *Pantene* from the shore and they poled her to the center of the river, letting her drift silently downstream. The songs of the jungle changed from the day hunters to the voices of the night. Songs of fascination and songs of allure, the evolution of the hunt. On the deck, everyone was silent with his or her thoughts and fears.

Half an hour later, they poled the *Pantene* to shore and tied up. They could see the lights aboard the pirate ship as they slipped ashore. Jesse and his group were loaded down with gun belts and assault rifles. Pan carried a pistol in his waistband. They moved slowly through the jungle until they got to the shore of the mighty Amazon itself.

Just a couple hundred yards away, the pirate boat glowed, anchored at the junction of the two rivers.

"Remember," Pan said. "When the boat starts up, you smother it with ammo. Keep shooting until it runs aground. Then get to the next position. You all know where you're going, right?"

They nodded in the moonlight. "Don't shoot at the bridge," Piper reminded, her voice vibrating.

"I'll give you fifteen minutes to get in position," Pan said. "Then we go in. Now get going and find good cover, because they will shoot back."

The Americans disappeared into the dark.

"Jesus, they're noisy. Don't gringos know how to be quiet?" he asked Evenel.

She let out a little laugh and nodded in agreement.

Pan waited the allotted time. Then he swung Evenel onto his back and waded in to the river. "Come on, girly, we need to save our own asses again."

CHAPTER
FIFTY-ONE

Pan moved slowly. The little noise he made was drowned out by the water gurgling around the ship. With Evenel clinging to his back, Pan muscled up the anchor chain. At the top, Evenel crawled over Pan and onto the deck, silent as a burglar. Pan peered above the gunwale and then leapt over and came down gently beside her. The water dripped off them and puddled on the deck. Pan took her hand and led her along the deck, stepping over coiled rope and ammo boxes for the deck gun.

The dark night splattered no light upon them. Pan slid along the bridge until he came to the lone porthole. It was open in the night heat, and Pan slowly rose and looked inside.

A fat man with a too-small T-shirt and a battered hat covering greasy hair slumped in the captain's chair, snoring intermittently.

He kneeled back down and whispered to Evenel, "Okay, kid,

you know what to do." He lifted her up and showed her inside the porthole, then brought her back down.

"You see the fat man?"

"Yes," she whispered.

"Good, don't wake him up." He lifted her back up and she wiggled inside and slipped over the table that sat under the porthole and let herself down to the floor. The fat man woke with a snort.

Jesse sat behind a tree twenty yards from Piper. He was the furthest down the line; Za was at the beginning and Hallie was in the middle with Piper. Tall grass and brush enveloped the trees, giving good cover.

Nothing had happened in what seemed like forever. Pan and Evenel had to have reached the boat by now, he thought. He swatted at the bugs chewing on him, and sweat slipped down his back; he felt like he was on fire. With everyone in danger, it didn't set well with him. *I have to move*, he thought.

He decided to see if Piper was safe behind the tree where he had left her. She said she knew how to shoot, and her treatment of the weapons confirmed that.

He slipped over to her. "Piper," he whispered as he drew near.

"Shut up," she replied.

Jesse got behind her. "You remember to keep behind the tree and just put the rifle out around the tree. Right?"

"Yes, of course I do, you told me like a hundred times."

Yelling came through the dark. Men stood up on the deck, started moving toward the front. Guns cocking snapped through the air.

"Wait—" Jesse said.

"The shit is going down," Piper said. She sidestepped the

tree and flipped the safety. She shouldered the rifle and let it bark. Sparks streaked across the bulkhead as the bullets ricocheted down the walkway. The men dropped from sight below the railings. Gunfire erupted from the boat and sizzled through the grass, cutting it down in swaths.

Jesse pulled her down on top of him behind the tree. "Jesus, you're going to get killed."

"Let go of me and use that thing," she snapped, her eyes wide and sure. The lioness had returned. She moved to another spot just as they had planned and set out another burst.

Jesse got up and moved too, bullets flying all around him. He could hear Hallie and Za open up. He fired at the muzzle blasts on the ship, hoping to pin down the crew. He heard Za yell out, and Hallie screamed.

Pan watched through the porthole as the fat man jumped to his feet, reaching for Evenel as she scrambled to the door. She grabbed the handle, but he scooped her up at the same time.

Pan pulled out his pistol and stuck it through the porthole.

Evenel twisted in the man's grasp and begin to flail at him with her feet. The fat man swore and grabbed at her. He looked like a man fighting a wasp.

Pan struggled to get a clear shot at the fat man.

Evenel chomped down on the man's nose, and he screamed like a little girl. He tossed her into the wall.

Evenel bounced back on top of the man and continued to attack. He reeled forward as she slid down and grabbed his ankle, planting her feet and wrapping her arm tight. He wavered and then plowed over like a willow tree caught in the wind. He crashed onto a table and let out another scream.

Pan could hear men yelling and feet pounding on the metal deck toward him.

Evenel leapt up and in two steps was at the door. The door flew open, and Pan jumped inside and locked it.

He gave her the pistol. "Shoot anything that gets in front of that porthole, like I taught you," he said. He kicked the fat man, who let out another whoop. Pan pulled a plastic wire tie out of his pocket and bound the man to the metal table leg. Shots rang out and shells banged against the walls.

He started the diesel motors and began to reel in the anchor. A deafening blast rang out, and his head went numb. The pistol spun across the floor, smoke rolling from the barrel. Evenel chased it across the floor and picked it up again.

Gunfire clapped across the water in both directions. Pan started the other diesel and put both throttles full ahead. "Come on, baby, rip that anchor out."

The boat vibrated against its restraints. Gunfire rang out over everything, and he could not hear the diesels but the tachometer showed they were at full power.

Suddenly the boat lurched forward, and he spun the wheel. Pan switched on all the lights as the boat leaned into the curve. He ran her straight at the intersection of the two rivers, aiming for the submersed sandbar.

He heard the pistol roar again. The pistol bounced across the floor again. "It jumps out of my hand!" Evenel said.

He grabbed her, and they hunkered on the floor behind the console. Shots sprayed through the porthole and against the opposite side of the steel console.

Then shells burst against the bulkhead around the porthole, denting the steel inward. The shots that were coming through the porthole sprayed the ceiling and stopped.

"Love those gringos!" he shouted to Evenel. He stuffed her tight under the console and stood up, pistol drawn. He adjusted the wheel and yelled to Evenel: "Hold on, crazy girl." The entire boat shook as it plowed forward and then stopped, throwing him against the wheel.

Pan grabbed Evenel's hand and swung her to his back. As they passed, the fat man stood up. She kicked at him so hard that she slipped off Pan's back and landed with a thump. She got up and kicked him again.

Pan grabbed her and tossed her out the door and over the side into the water, then he jumped after her.

He surfaced and searched for Evenel. She found him first and got on his back. "You did real good," he said, and he began swimming with strong strokes toward the shore.

The other four were in place when Pan and Evenel got to the meeting point. Jesse and Piper were attending to Za and Hallie.

"What's wrong?" Evenel asked.

Piper replied, "Za got shot in the shoulder so Hallie dragged him to safety and got shot in the ass."

Pan pulled Piper's hand away from the wound and pulled the skin apart around the wound. He felt across Hallie's butt cheek.

"Ouch! You bastard—"

"Bad news, girl, they shot you a new asshole, an' you got no friends now. I didn't like you when you were just one asshole." He slapped her ass.

"Ouch, fuck you!"

"Relax, the bullet went right through both cheeks. She's gonna live."

He went over to Za. He lifted Za's arm and dropped it. Za yelled out, but Pan had covered his mouth at the same time. "You're not so good. The bullet hit a bone in there somewhere."

Jesse nodded.

Pan scooped up some river mud and covered Za's shoulder. "Use some river mud, like this," he said to Piper, "that'll stop her bleeding. You cripples get back to the *Pantene*. Finish patching your holes. You go with them, Evenel."

Pan grabbed the nets that were waiting for them. "Piper and Jesse get in the river and follow me." The three of them swam slowly near the bank. They could hear splashes from the boat as things were thrown overboard. A voice boomed across the water.

"Everything! You bastards throw everything until this tub floats again!"

They swam wide of the pirate boat.

"There," Pan whispered. He pointed at the boat. Four barrels splashed down on the water and bobbed toward them in the current. Pan slipped the nets over them and then attached them with ropes to the harnesses he had made. They slipped away toward the *Pantene* with the diesel fuel in tow.

When they got back to the *Pantene*, Hallie, Evenel, and Za were onboard. Pan, Jesse, and Piper rolled the barrels ashore and then rolled them up a plank onto the *Pantene*.

Jesse went over to Za. "Guess you can't fly too well."

"You got to do it, Jesse. You know Hallie will try to go."

"I promised Piper I would stay with her."

"I know, man, but it's too dangerous for Hallie."

Jesse heard a sob, and he turned to see Piper beside him. "I have to—"

"I know."

"Jesse, get in the harness," Pan said.

Hallie protested.

Pan pointed at her. "You got lead hanging out your ass, and I'm not above shooting you myself. I need someone at full capacity for this."

Jesse hugged Piper.

"You come back to me. You promised I would not be without you ever again. You remember that," Piper said. "Don't be a hero. You come back to us."

"I will."

Pan interrupted. "They'll carry the ammo to shore and

guard it. Then, when the boat is free from the sandbar, they'll carry it back on board and pile it on the back deck. Then they'll relay it back below deck. You got to hit it with the grenade launcher when it's piled on deck. That will blow the whole damn thing up. Give us room to get past them and downriver." Pan took a breath. "Don't miss, gringo."

"I won't."

"Good. I'm going to swim down and watch. When the time is right, I will be back and then we go." Pan looked at all the faces. They all nodded. Pan slipped into the water and disappeared.

Jesse stood on the deck, fidgeting with the hang glider. He looked at Piper. Her blue eyes and blonde locks burned into his memory. His thoughts of her seemed to distract him from what he had to do. She trembled, holding her arms against her. Grief doubled her over, but she righted herself again and attended to Za.

When Pan slipped back on board the *Pantene*, Jesse was still struggling with his fear.

"It's time to go," Pan said.

Jesse got in the harness. Piper helped him buckle in. She looked as cold as a person condemned.

Jesse kissed her hard. "I will be back."

She shook her head.

"I will."

Pan handed him the grenade launcher. "You got one round in the chamber and one taped to the stock."

"I can't cut the tape in the harness. Put it in my pocket."

Pan cut it loose and handed it to Jesse. "You have the pistol?"

"In the holster." Jesse tapped it with his hand.

Hallie and Za gave him a hug, along with Evenel. Jesse avoided their eyes.

"When I start the motor," Pan said, "they'll know we're coming. No turning back.

366

Za's got a bad arm, so he's on the wheel. The rest of us will put down firepower if Jesse misses. Remember, gringo, you got to be close before you release."

Za said, "Pan will slap the rope twice when you're at five hundred feet."

Pan looked at them, one after the other. "We live or we die tonight. It's up to us." He hit the starter, and the *Pantene* shuddered when he shifted into gear. He throttled up, and the *Pantene* came on plane.

Jesse held the glider to the wind and popped up instantly. Pan released the brake on the wench, and Jesse began to fall behind the boat.

Jesse pushed out on the bar, and the entire frame bucked and twisted. He swung back and forth, fighting for control. It settled down when he found the sweet spot. Jesse pushed the bar forward, careful to keep straight to the towrope. The glider began climbing again.

The air cooled as he lifted. The lights on the pirate boat dotted the night, the only thing he could make out in the dark.

Pan slapped the rope twice, signaling Jesse that the rope was all the way out.

Jesse waited. He felt he had to be closer, but at the same time, the *Pantene* had to stay out of range. If he waited too long, the pirates could spray the *Pantene* with rounds.

He struggled with the decision. The dot of light split into focus, outlining the boat. He could see men working. He put his hand on the release. He pulled, then stopped. Not yet.

His mind debated back and forth, oscillating a hundred times. He slapped at the release, his hand shaking and his mind on his friends below. His mind steeled. He had to go now.

Jesse unclipped, and the glider fell sharply.

The *Pantene* shut down immediately. Silence blanketed him. He got the grenade launcher in place and ready. The boat seemed damn small.

He knew they could not see him, but the thought of being a sitting duck sent chills through him. He flipped off the safety and took aim, the glider falling rapidly.

Jesse pulled the trigger and a streak of light blinded him as it targeted the boat.

The shell went over the top, splashed into the water, and went off harmlessly.

"No, no no," Jesse said.

The men working on the boat filled the night with streams of light.

He fumbled for the other round; the glider was falling rapidly. He pulled the control bar back and aimed straight toward the boat.

He flew over the back of the deck and unlatched the harness. He fell several feet, hitting the deck hard.

He rolled forward and tumbled right into the boxes of ammo stacked on the deck of the boat. His sudden appearance out of the dark sky startled the crew. All hell was on its way.

Stunned from the landing, Jesse tried to stand, but nothing worked. He could hear boots clapping on the steel and gunfire. He willed himself to his feet, still not able to feel them. Groping for the grenade shell in his pocket, a man shouted. Jesse sat the shell on top of the stacked pile of ammunition. He turned, and a man pointed his assault rifle at Jesse.

Jesse ducked, and the shells raked the air above him. He went around the pile of ammunition and came out the other side; Jesse pointed his pistol and let off several rounds.

The guard fell, and Jesse ran to the starboard side. A man running toward Jesse collided with him. Jesse lost the pistol; he threw the man down as they fought for control of the man's rifle. Jesse smashed the man in the throat with his elbow. The man gurgled and went limp.

More men were running toward him. Jesse got control of the rifle and let out a burst. The first man fell dead. He sprayed the men behind him and they dove for cover. He charged toward them, heading for a ladder attached to the bulkhead, and climbed up and over pulling the trigger. As soon as he reached the top, bullets raked all around him. He dived behind some crating, pinned down. Breathing hard, he crouched behind the crates as wood splinters raked him from the left side, stabbing into his ribs. Trapped and with the crates coming apart under a hail of fire, he crouched with his back against the crates and held the gun overhead pointing backward, then let several rounds bark. *Now!* he thought, and he sprinted to the back of the deck, overlooking the ammunition pile. He shouldered the rifle and took aim as bullets cut into the steel railing around him. His gun burst, and Jesse recoiled from the shock.

The grenade shell vanished and the ship exploded.

The blast flung Jesse into the air and over the rail, flipping him into the water. Stunned, he surfaced. Flames burned him, and he sank under the water's surface.

He struggled, trying to keep from sinking. His entire body felt collapsed as he fought for the surface and gulped for air. His lungs would not inflate, and he sank again. He steeled his mind and kicked, blackness filling his consciousness. He surfaced and gasped, air sucked in. Pieces of steel began to rain down around him. Jesse floated, sank, and kicked for the surface again.

Suddenly a spotlight caught him. He waited for the bullets to rake him.

"Jesse! It's him!" a voice called out. Piper's voice. The *Pantene* pulled next to him. Pan pulled him aboard, and he collapsed to the deck.

"Way to go, gringo," Pan said. "You blew up the whole tub."

Piper fell on top of him, along with Evenel. "You came back, you came back to us."

ॐ

The *Pantene* steamed downriver. Manaus and all its civilization loomed over the river, backlit by the eastern sun. Piper brought fresh coffee to Pan at the wheel. "You look a little lost," Piper said.

"It's the river, or rather the end of it. I call Manaus home, but every time I get here, I feel a little lost."

"Thank you," Piper said. "I'm feeling like I lost something too. It's the river, isn't it?"

"The people who live with the river have always survived, prospered. It's the river you miss, that gets inside you."

Evenel appeared. "Morning," she sang.

"Where's the rest of your crew?" Pan asked.

"They're coming," she said.

The trio came around the cabin.

"What are you going to do with the backpacks?" Piper asked. "The museum?"

Pan nodded. "I want to get the truth. They can do that. Besides, the wad of cash I get from them will do me good. What about you gringos? Where you going?"

"We decided Utah is a good place to start," Jesse said. "The four of us want to be with Evenel while she grows up. So we're going to get a place in the mountains, where we can fly—"

"It has to have a great school system," Piper added.

"Home schooling," Za said. "Then she can come with us when we see the world."

"Yeah, how about that?" Jesse asked.

The three of them looked at Piper. "We'll see."

Jesse scooped Piper up and kissed her. "Try to see it our way."

Hallie leaned back in Za's arm. "Kiss me now!"

Evenel ran over to Pan and jumped in his arms. "Kiss me too!"

❧

The road that ends at the top of the Door Peninsula winds back and forth as if it had been pressed back by the hand of the Maker to make it fit upon the land. And where it ran out at the water's edge, an old cottage sat upon the beach a few hundred strides away.

They parked their motorcycles, and the mist hung thin as the sun cut it away.

They walked across the sand, Hallie, Za, Jesse, and Piper, with Evenel holding her hand. They hurried across the beach and up the steps, their boots clicking against the wood, gritty from the sand. Jesse took Emma's outstretched hands in his and bent at the waist to kiss her cheek. She smelled of rosewood perfume, sweet and tangy. She was clad in an oversized and crisp white shirt with the shirttail worn free, just as her lover had worn it. And blue jeans rolled up to her knees.

"I want all of you to meet one of my favorite people in all the world," Jesse said.

"Emma?" Evenel asked.